The Xenos' bodies started to stack up. Shawna's faceplate dripped with red rain. She had no time to feel fear. Her mind was too preoccupied with exterminating the zombies who were doing their damnedest to tear her to pieces and dine on her guts. She turned in a circle, slashing the air with the saw, sweat running into her eyes, when she realized there were no more Xenos to kill and Bak-Irp was barking at her. When she lifted her finger, the piercing whine of the blades cut off immediately, deafening in its silence, only to be replaced by her own rapid breathing.

"There's more of them," Bak-Irp said. "Out there. And they're coming quick."

She looked in the direction where he pointed the smoking barrel of his gun.

Dozens. No, not dozens. Hundreds. Too many to count…

DEATH SYSTEM

S A Sidor

ACONYTE

First published by Aconyte Books in 2024

ISBN 978 1 83908 282 5

Ebook ISBN 978 1 83908 283 2

Cover art by Rafael Teruel

Distributed in North America by Simon & Schuster Inc, New York, USA

Printed in the United States of America

9 8 7 6 5 4 3 2 1

ACONYTE BOOKS

An imprint of Asmodee Entertainment Ltd

Mercury House, Shipstones Business Centre

North Gate, Nottingham NG7 7FN, UK

aconytebooks.com // twitter.com/aconytebooks

CHAPTER ONE
Bubblegum and Gunpowder

HIGH TERROR RISK Cellblock
Extreme Security Penitentiary (XSecPen)
Galactic Coalition Territory: Location Unspecified

Bad things start small, the sergeant thought as he inserted the contraband vial into the middle of a stale dinner roll. The vial was the size of his fat pinkie tip. The nugget it contained resembled a shriveled black raisin wearing a wiry purple vest. He pinched the top of the roll, sealing the hole he'd made, then slid the dinner tray back into the service trolley.

He warmed his hands on the cart.

None of my business is what that thing is, he added to his inner monologue.

The sergeant got paid not to think about situations like this. He let things slide. Ignored whatever he saw or heard. Turned a blind eye. Clammed up quiet as a bubble if his superiors asked him questions. Playing dumb for profit was the name of the game. The dark morsel was likely the latest variety of black-market space dope, an anodyne to soothe the pain and misery of being locked away and forgotten; it filled the hole of boredom.

Nope. It's none of my DAMN business, he reminded himself. Who cared if these prisoners fried what was left of their slithery brains? XSecPen's pop was exclusively hyperviolent outlaws.

Most of the time the sergeant's off-the-books side hustle paid him *not* to do things that were the key responsibilities of his main gig. That main gig being his position as a supervising correctional officer at the toughest, most secret, and inescapable penal institution in Coalition-controlled Terran space.

Rarely, as a part of his shady arrangement, he'd be asked to carry out a special favor and take a highly risky, illegal action, the kind that made his butt cheeks clench up and broke him out in nervous cold sweats from head to toe. There was no doubt about what he was doing here. Shit that not only would get him fired – if anybody legit discovered his dirty deeds – but would end with him locked away in a cage of his own. And a prison guard who ends up in prison is dead meat walking. That much was understood. So special favors were a big deal.

Usually, the inmates asked you to sneak in prohibited items, which might be anything, since their lives inside XSecPen were spartan, the result of punitive deprivation. For procuring ordinary goods, outside food or a communications device, he received handsome compensation. Other times, like today, he acted as a courier. For these missions the price tag was higher. This case of hide-the-vial-in-the-roll was going to earn him a pair of first-class shuttle tickets and a nice, long vacation to the swankiest, beachiest, rum-and-coconut-creamiest, luxury resort of his choosing. All he had to do was deliver the right tray to the right cell. Then he'd be home free.

He almost felt the rays of an alien sun beating down on

his thick, bullish neck. Virtually digging his toes into warm sand, he tasted the spray of ocean waves – big, pink, foamy ones, the smell of which reminded him of bubblegum and gunpowder. His brain flicked through the vivid screen images he'd searched up last night. Bartender droids wearing funny black bowties carrying platters of cocktails. Rich tourists laid out on loungers, sipping frozen drinks, without a care in the galaxy. If everything went smoothly today, soon he'd be joining their ranks…

An angry buzz tore him from his daydream. The cellblock gate was sliding up. It took a while. The gate slab was as thick as his massive chest, and it weighed enough to pancake a cell extraction bot. He'd seen that happen once, when the emergency gate-drop malfunctioned during a riot drill. The sergeant's biggest problem walked under the gate, beelining straight for him.

The new guard.

As part of a correctional department interplanetary exchange program, this Fushnallan gal was visiting to observe how things were done at XSecPen. She'd been assigned to shadow the sergeant for tonight's shift. The paranoid part of his brain wondered if she was a spy. He didn't really know her or want to. What he did know made him uneasy. As a descendant from the Trappist-C planet Fushnal, she was an ocean-breather who wore a recycling tank on her back to keep from suffocating. Her rough, orange skin and bugged-out eyes gave him the creeps. The worst part was the remnant dorsal fin running along the top of her head. It twitched whenever she got excited. Right now, it was jiggling like fresh bait.

When I go on my vacation, I'm going to charter a fishing skimmer to hook your relatives, he thought, chuckling. From all reports, the Fushnallan was a squeaky-clean, by-the-book operator, or at least that was how she acted. Some people could fool you. For example, nobody would've suspected that the sergeant was utterly corrupt. Publicly he made a point of being tough on the inmates, cracking skulls and kicking ass. It provided the cover he needed. In private, he was another – much worse – person. That secret sent a thrill up his spine.

"Sergeant Randle," the new guard's voice gurgled a greeting through her recycler mic.

"Good evening, Officer Fishstick."

"The name is Ishnik, sergeant. Ishnik Tal," she corrected him.

"My mistake."

Her chilly expression told him she knew it hadn't been.

He offered his hand, squeezing her fingers in a vice grip, feeling the clammy coolness of her flesh through her tactical duty gloves. "Call me Shark," he said. The corners of his eyes crinkled in amusement, thinking how ironic it was that here he was talking to seafood, yet he was the one that people called Shark. He held on until he felt her squirm. *A floppy fish!* He let her go.

"Ready to get started?" he asked.

Ishnik took a step back, looking less confident than when she first entered.

"Yes, sir." The recycler distorted her voice, as if she were inside an aquarium.

Sounds like somebody drowning, he thought.

Shark smiled, showing off his titanium claim to fame. Once upon a time, when he was just a newjack, one week into working his first lockup, an inmate shattered Randle's jaw, kicking out his front choppers after the gung-ho rookie made the mistake of trying to break up a fight alone. Concussed and bloodied, lying in the infirmary spitting out tooth fragments, the greenhorn guard decided that his repaired mouth would send a message. He asked the doc for a cyborg jaw and told him not to bother matching his teeth. "Leave the steel raw," he said. His face would be a sign every con could read: *Mess with me, and I'll take a big, shiny bite out of your ass.*

His plan worked. All the inmates soon knew about the guard with the metal grin.

The Shark was born.

He made a point of showing how powerful his new dental implants were to the dirtbag who'd jumped him that day. That was an ugly business, the first of many violent encounters.

"This your first time in High Terror?" Shark asked, already knowing the answer.

"Yes. I'm looking forward to seeing how the cellblock runs."

He watched her doing her best to appear calm. But nobody ever felt calm inside HT. If you did, you didn't last long. The place was a kill zone. If you lost your edge, you lost your life.

"Shall we begin the tour?" Shark pushed the trolley. Ishnik followed. The HT unit was quiet – the effect of solitary, soundproofed cells. Today, it was so hushed that the squeaking of the trolley's front wheel sounded like a cranky alarm going off. The unit had wide hallways and low ceilings. All of it was sterile white – the better to spot anything, or anyone, moving around that didn't belong. It felt like a cold storage warehouse, which in a way it was. Bodies were stored here. Inside XSecPen's walls lived the worst of the worst criminals in Terran space.

Shark lifted a thick, translucent badge he wore on a chain around his neck, waved it at a panel embedded to their right.

"How are the inmates classified on the unit?" Ishnik asked as they passed a body scanner.

"Equality reigns in HT. Everybody's a lifer. Locked up day and night except for exercise, meals, or scheduled appointments. We're in lockdown tonight. Warden's orders. No explanation. That's typical. Anyway, during lockdown everybody eats in their cells. One body per cell. Cells are always lit. The facility's white lights caused mood swings and headaches, so the cell lights were switched to yellow. Higher-ups aim to keep the inmates docile. It doesn't work. You never open a cell alone. Pass all objects through the delivery ports. Isolation is the point. Whenever convicts get together, the danger rises. But the do-gooders won't let us keep them in solitary indefinitely. Every contact is a lethal hazard. We do not rehabilitate here. Our job is to punish."

Ishnik didn't offer an opinion. Shark watched as her head fin twitched.

Squeak, squeak, squeak went the trolley wheel. Despite the constantly circulating ventilation system, the air remained musky and pungent. Shark wondered if Ishnik could detect it through her nose-hose. He'd heard Fushnallans had a superior sense of smell. At the end of a shift, the brilliant arctic whiteness of the walls made Shark's eyes hurt and gave him a headache. At least he could blink. Fushnallans had no eyelids, only a transparent nictitating membrane. He caught Ishnik focusing up ahead at the row of sealed, glassy doorways to their right: the cells.

"Showtime," he said.

CHAPTER TWO
Crimson Jumpsuits

"They can't hear us. Or see us." Shark thumbed his nose at the first prisoner to demonstrate. The inmate on the other side of the thick, transparent barrier showed no reaction. "Think of the door as an unbreakable screen. We can see them. From their side, the screen is opaque until we tap." Shark indicated an exterior control panel. On the display were a series of illuminated icons labeled Visual, Sound, Cell Open, Wash, Choke-Gas, and Stun. "This guy's a Thassian, as you can see."

The prisoner was performing handstand push-ups in the middle of his cell. Stocky, powerfully built, he pumped himself up and down mechanically. His thick tail curved forward for balance while his pale face remained expressionless. He might've been reading a book or meditating. Through the speaker, his exhalations sounded like jets of pressurized steam escaping.

"Do they all wear dark red jumpsuits?" Ishnik seemed intrigued by the choice of color.

"Crimson uniforms for High Terror inmates. Helps people remember why they're here."

"I don't understand."

"Spilling blood? They're all killers of one stripe or another," he said.

"Ahh." Ishnik raised her chin. "A human bias. You see, Fushnallan blood isn't red."

Shark shook his head. *The kind of shit that aliens noticed.* It bothered him not knowing what other observations she might be making while they worked together. He had to be careful. Shark cursed his luck that today of all days he had to be teamed with a wide-eyed alien outsider.

Shark used two fingers to hit the Visual and Sound icons.

The Thassian's gaze shot toward the door, instantly alert; he continued his push-ups.

"Feeding time, Bak-Irp," Shark said. "Come to the door."

The Thassian finished his set of exercises, then flipped to his feet, wiping his face with a dingy, threadbare towel before he approached them. His skin was bone white, like a skeleton morphed into a bodybuilder. Rows of subdermal nubs formed a "V" over his hairless skull.

Shark popped the Audio icon to OFF.

"Ugly bastard, isn't he?" he said to Ishnik. "I don't know which is worse, those Thassian face wrinkles, or the way they glare at you with their deadeye peepers."

Ishnik kept silent. Maybe she was pondering what his opinion was concerning Fushnallan physical characteristics. Shark opened the trolley, withdrawing a tray, not the one he'd doctored.

"What is this prisoner's crime?" Ishnik asked, studying the Thassian.

"Yaalo Bak-Irp? Guy was a bounty hunter until the day he decided he didn't need to bring in fugitives anymore. Appointing himself judge, jury, and executioner. Bagged a dozen wanted criminals before they caught him. You ask me? He was doing a public service. The courts discourage vigilantism. Bak's quiet, but he's smart. Never underestimate the quiet ones."

"I'll remember that." Ishnik assessed Shark coldly with her flat jellied eyes.

It sounded like she might be mocking him, but he wasn't certain. Shark knew he sometimes ran his mouth when he felt stressed. He didn't ask to be saddled with an observer. What was the point of these exchanges anyway? She wasn't about to tell him how to do his job.

Shark decided he didn't care if she was pissed. She was a nuisance and liability, not to mention a pain in his ass. He preferred working solo. He keyed open the port with his badge. After removing the lid, he served the tray.

Bak-Irp lifted the food to his face; his nostrils pinched open and closed. His lips curled in disgust. He poked at a slice of Thassian nutrient loaf, nudging the lump of congealed blue gravy.

Shark popped the Audio ON.

"Eat up, Bak. I had a look at this week's menu. It doesn't get any better."

Before the inmate could answer, Shark cut the Audio and Visual off from Bak-Irp's side.

The Thassian sneered in their general direction.

Shark walked up to the barrier, his face inches away from the Thassian's. "Sometimes I swear he can see us through the screenblocker." The guard raised a middle finger, rubbing it on the glass. Oblivious, Bak-Irp set his dinner aside and resumed his exercise. The guards moved on. Shark resumed talking to Ishnik, describing the unit's population.

"HT's headcount is twenty-one," he said. "That's max for us. We've even got a waiting list. That's how popular this hellhole is. Rumor has it the Coalition Council is talking about opening an XSecPen 2. The whole place would be an HT unit. Until then, top-shelf desperadoes have got to wait in line to visit our house. Although no con is eager to hear they're coming here."

"Hmm…?" Ishnik sounded like she was blowing bubbles underwater.

Shark screwed up his face. He didn't like her funny noises. "What's your problem?"

Ishnik shrugged. "It's curious, that's all. Conditions here are strict, but I've visited far worse prisons. The accommodations are clean; the systems appear orderly. I've witnessed no evidence of rampant abuse on the part of staff…"

Witness… evidence… abuse… Shark didn't like the words coming out of her mouth. Despite her glowing review of XSecPen, his worries about her role here only increased.

He said, "It's not the facility that gives this place its bad reputation. It's the company the inmates keep. Only badasses end up at XSecPen HT. Once they arrive, the cons find that out quickly. They all want to bust out. Most of them *have* busted out of other prisons. So, they get frustrated realizing there's no way out of here. Oh, they'll settle for butchering a guard now and then. Only we play hard to get. Their consolation prize is slaying each other. Shit happens."

"Interesting." Ishnik gave him an enigmatic look. He found her tone smug. "Surely not everyone here is a cutthroat. This next prisoner, for example. He doesn't seem threatening."

Shark stopped the cart and hooted. Leaning forward, he banged the side of the trolley like a steel drum. "You know who that is, don't you?" he asked, smirking. "This non-threat?"

Bristling, Ishnik shook her head. "I don't recognize him," she admitted. "Is he famous?"

Shark had to admit that the man inside the cell seemed ordinary. Average height and weight. About forty years old. He had a buzzcut and a widow's peak, a trimmed blond goatee. For the moment he was lying back in his bunk with his arms folded under his head, whistling. Stuck to the ceiling above his bunk was a poster-sized map of Terran space.

"Legendary," Shark said. "That is Nero Lupaster IV."

Ishnik gasped. A rush of bubbles and static erupted from her mic. "This is the Butcher of the Quadrants? I thought he was dead." She whispered, though the cell's audio was switched off.

Shark shook his head.

"You're thinking of Nero III. This is his only son, Nero Number Four. Nero Four is the person responsible for his father's untimely demise. His father was a cyborg, and our little Nero planted a bomb in his fake leg. Blew up his own daddy. Four is, or was, the richest man alive, ever, like in the history of the cosmos. An octillionaire who ran the Arms Guild and built his own private army, he had an appetite for conquest. Treasure does him no good now. It's sad."

The Fushnallan stiffened and puffed out her chest. "I know about this man, Nero IV. Assassinations. Terrorist bombings. His mercenaries' guerrilla attacks caused massive casualties among civilians and military personnel. A bloodthirsty killer. A third of the Galactic Defense Forces died at the hands of his army." Ishnik's voice was icy, as if her breather were freezing.

What did she care who Nero slaughtered in his conquest to take over known space?

Shark felt like arguing. "Seriously, you've got to give Nero credit. He dreamed big and went for it. He was damned close to running the whole show. Dictator of the universe." Shark couldn't hide his admiration. "It's hard to believe one man could cause so much mayhem."

"I didn't know he'd been captured." Ishnik clenched her fists. "This *monster*..."

"The Coalition kept it hush-hush. What's left of Nero's empire is still out there wreaking havoc. The Arms Guild is up for grabs. Supposedly he still controls it from here. But I don't see how. That's Coalition propaganda. Their intelligence services are busy running down Nero's lieutenants. This guy owns enough weaponry to take down a thousand XSecPens. But I can vouch for him – Nero's never caused me any trouble." *He pays me quadruple my salary to do him favors,* Shark wanted to tell her. But he didn't. "On the unit, Nero Junior is as gentle as a lamb. It doesn't profit him to cause problems. He's an executive-level gangster, a real businessman."

"His jumpsuit is as red as the others," Ishnik said.

Shark shrugged. Ishnik didn't get it, and probably never would. But it was straightlaced suckers like her that created a market for guards like Shark who knew when to bend the rules and when to break them, too. Like Nero, Shark was a businessman.

He popped the port open and delivered the prisoner's dinner.

Nero never acknowledged their intrusion. He just kept whistling – it was an ancient marching tune – while he stared at his map. His index finger kept time like a conductor's baton.

Shark shrouded the view from the prisoner's side of the cell door.

"Mind if I push the trolley?" Ishnik asked, as they proceeded along the cellblock.

Here was a quandary. If Shark said "no" she might get perturbed, perhaps even suspicious, but if he said "yes" there was a chance she'd foul up his drop-off. He made a quick risk calculation. "Sure!" he said. "Be my guest. Start here, on the right side." He pointed to a full column of trays lined up inside the trolley. If she delivered from that half, he was golden. The tray with the vial was the next one down on the left side. He'd tell her when to switch back.

Shark felt superior as he watched the Fushnallan pushing dinners into slots. He stood behind her with his arms folded, making certain that she didn't deviate from his orders. She was going to do the dirty deed for him without ever knowing it. He liked that. Better still, if shit went south, he'd blame the outsider. She was a perfect patsy. Shark didn't expect things to go badly.

And for a while they didn't.

Everything changed when they arrived at the war hero's cell.

CHAPTER THREE
Hotshot

Shawna Bright felt trouble brewing before she saw it. More times than she could recount, her tingly sixth sense of impending peril had tipped her off in time to pull her bacon out of the fire. Chalk it up to a fighter pilot's instincts, or the Appalachian Mountain wisdom that ran deep in her veins, but when her cell door changed from its usual gray static fog to a crystal-clear view of that asshole Shark, and a new guard she didn't know pushing the dinner cart, Shawna was ready for events to turn sour and unexpected. She wasn't sure when they'd turn, only that they would.

"Hey there, Hotshot." Shark winked at her. "Win any medals lately?"

"I ought to get a purple heart just for having to look at your face," she said.

Shark grinned his awful silver smile at her and wagged his finger. He turned to his partner. "Didn't I tell you she was a pistol?"

Shark gawked at her the way he always did, accompanied by his menacing style of flattery, a stream of unwanted, cringeworthy comments about her blonde curls or her slim, swimmer's build. She hadn't dipped her toes in a pool in ages, and likely, she never would again.

"You were in the Defense Forces?" The new guard's voice burbled, but Shawna made out the words clearly. The question raised her hackles. It was a tender subject – her service years.

"That's right," Shawna said, watching both guards from her bunk. "What's it to you?"

The guard pointed a thumb toward herself. "Galactic Marines Raiders. My last tour ended during the Kepler Insurgency. That bug hunt was it for me. I was happy to get out in one piece."

"I was there at KI." Shawna tried not to think of her squad mates' faces. The litany of names played in her ear: *Smirnov, Ral Eck, Cerotti, Patel…* She said, "My squadron flew air superiority fighters ahead of the last bombing raids. That was no picnic in the park, I'll tell you."

"Especially after we found out the bugs could fly." The Fushnallan was shaking her head.

"Yeah, how 'bout that?" Shawna smiled grimly. The insectoids had been full of surprises.

"Well, ain't this sweet?" Shark said. "A veterans' reunion party." His face turned hard. "We don't have time for a parade today. I've got swill to shovel. Pass the tray, Ishnik. Move!" He shifted impatiently behind Ishnik. Nastier than normal, he was heading for the next cell.

Ishnik stared at Shawna. Strangely, Shawna didn't detect any hostility. On the contrary, the Fushnallan seemed to be avoiding looking at Shark. She reached into the cart and withdrew a meal tray, passing it into the port. Shark stopped. Reversing direction, he peered into the trolley. In a blink, he exploded with white-hot rage, not aimed at Shawna but at Ishnik. He lunged, shoving his partner into the door screen, which flickered grayly, shouting, "What did you DO?"

He kicked the cart, sending it up on two wheels until it bounced down hard again. Then he was diving for the open port slot, groping inside, hunting after the meal tray.

Baffled by his reaction, Ishnik said, "I served her dinner. That's what you said to do–"

"Idiot!" Shark glowered at her. "You gave her the wrong one!"

"B- but they're all the same," the bewildered guard said. "The label said 'human' meal–"

"Shut up!" Shark buried his arm shoulder-deep into the open port.

But Shawna was faster. She leaped from her perch on the bunk and snatched up the tray. The port flap closed with a hard snap. Shark's fingers scraped inside the empty delivery chute.

"Give it back! NOW!" he growled. Veins bulged in his neck. His face flushed magenta.

The corner of Shawna's mouth hooked down in amusement as she inspected the food.

"What's for dinner, Sharkey Boy? Something special you're not telling me…?"

The livid guard raised his hand to the control panel. "Damnit, I'll choke-gas you."

"Over what?" She tipped her head aside, taunting him, as she licked gravy off her finger.

"This prisoner has done nothing wrong," said Ishnik. "I'm calling an officer." She reached for the communicator on her shoulder, ready to alert the command control center.

"Don't do it." Shark unclipped his shock baton. Sweat glistened on his face. "I got this."

Ishnik hesitated, her thumb feathering the button. But she hadn't pressed it yet.

"You're not calling anybody," he said, pointing the baton at her. "Be cool. I'll handle it."

The visiting guard slowly lowered her hand away from her comms.

She's waiting to see what his next move will be, Shawna thought. That was a mistake. Shark was unhinged. Ruthless, too. He'd juice Ishnik's skull full of electricity before she had a chance to get off a call. Whenever Shark got himself wound up, the situation ended bloody.

Seeing Ishnik backing down, Shark switched his focus to Shawna. He raised his free hand to the control panel, baring his metallic teeth at her. This was going to get gnarly, fast.

Shawna had to think. There was something going on in the background here between Shark and Ishnik. Ishnik didn't seem to be aware of it until now. Shawna wasn't sure what she was up to, but she had the distinct feeling that she wasn't going to be the only one feeling his wrath. He thought he had people fooled, and maybe the other guards, officers, and the warden were unaware. But the cons knew that Shark was dirty and for sale. Maybe Ishnik was interfering with his game. She was too clean, an unknown factor, and therefore a potential threat. His hurricane of fury would engulf her, too. The other guard might bear the brunt of it. Shark wasn't above that – he eliminated threats to his illicit income and well-being. With extreme prejudice.

Over what? Shawna asked herself again. *Why was he cranked up over a tray of tasteless grub?* His response didn't make sense, even for an excitable bully like Shark. The food looked as inedible as it normally did. He hadn't snuck in a 'special dinner' as a favor.

Unless something was hidden in the grub. It had to be small, whatever it was.

"Hold it, Shark." Shawna idled up to the door, loose and friendly, flashing him a smile.

He paused. His chest was pumping. White spittle flecked his lips. He was losing it.

Shark's fist was so tight around his shock baton that his knuckles looked bloodless. Tendons in his forearm flexed like live cables. He was a beast, plain and simple. His might, his right. People got their brains beat out in XSecPen over trivial matters daily. They died over nothing. Petty garbage like this. As a rule, Shawna didn't mix herself up in other people's business unless it couldn't be avoided. She tried to live in peace despite her environment.

Tyrannical Shark lorded over his tiny kingdom. Crazy with anger, balanced on the precipice of violence, his need for total domination would cause him to lose self-control, and he'd smash everything within reach. Shawna and Ishnik would pay the price. It wouldn't matter who started it or whose fault it was. He'd be their punishment. It wasn't worth it. Whatever was in the food had nothing to do with Shawna. It was someone else's trouble. Avoiding trouble was one way she kept hope alive. *Make it through today and see what tomorrow brings* was her mantra.

"I was only teasing you, dude," she said. "Lighten up. You can have your shitty food back." She popped the port, returned the tray, oozing charm as she gazed into his predatory eyes.

Shark retrieved the tray and slid it back into the trolley. He leveled his baton at Ishnik. "We have procedures for a reason. You follow my orders. I said to take the meals from the right side. Not the left." He snapped his baton against the edge of the trolley.

Shawna and Ishnik both jumped at the sound.

"I don't understand why you're so angry," Ishnik said. "The matter is trivial."

Shark took a deep breath. He talked to her like she was a child, and not a smart one either.

"You want to know how we survive in here with these animals?" He jerked his thumb toward Shawna. "We maintain order. No exceptions. A breakdown in discipline is an invitation for trouble. Your hotshot pilot friend here murdered all the other pilots in her squadron. Seventeen of them. Lieutenant Colonel Shawna Bright is not your comrade in arms. If you fail to follow orders, trust me, she'll notice. She'll take advantage. Next thing you know, we're toast."

Shawna stared blankly, letting his words flow past her, refusing to acknowledge them.

Ishnik's mic fizzed as if she were about to speak, but thinking better of it, she nodded.

"Got it?" he asked. "This is my turf. I live this every day. You're only visiting dry land."

"Yes, sir," she said. "It won't happen again."

"Good. Now deliver the prisoner a meal from the right side. As you were ordered."

Crisis averted for now, Shawna thought, though the blood rush was still thumping in her ears. She took the new tray Ishnik offered to her, and after she knew they'd gone, dumped it in the toilet. What was bothering her wasn't the missed meal. It was that her sense of impending doom hadn't gone away. It was worse. There was no way to figure out why. Not yet. So, instead, she leaned back against the chilly wall of her little gray cell and closed her eyes.

And she waited.

CHAPTER FOUR
Doctor Boom

To an outside observer it might've appeared that Dr Lemora Pick was asleep at the small table built into the wall of her cell at XSecPen HT. All the cells had these tables, but most were covered with personal items, reminders of life outside. Lemora used hers for her research and mental exercises. Her eyes were closed, her shoulders relaxed, her hands lay in her lap, feet flat on the floor. In fact, her mind was not at all disengaged from thinking. Quite the opposite, she was doing her best to maintain an extreme level of concentration, summoning up from her photographic memory every sensation – from the white-hot flash to the boneshaking roar that followed, to the sulfurous, charred smell of things burned up in the aftermath of a successful detonation. A violent shudder rippled through her body, a wave of ecstasy that tingled her skin.

How wonderful it was to watch the world explode.

To see objects blown apart at high speed. Never to go back to the way they'd been before. To wield that power, to own the hand controlling and releasing energetic forces. To be a destroyer. An agent of change, a leveler of obsolete structures, an eraser of the rotten, old world.

She lived for it. Those moments of maximum tension right before the event were the most exquisite. When the shockwave hit you, then passed through you, it was like communing with a divine spirit – she had to wear goggles to look at her creations, to keep them from blinding her. Foam plugs saved her eardrums from rupturing. The great fireball expanded, the column of flame and smoke rising like a dragon, higher and higher, boiling against the backdrop of a soon-to-be annihilated landscape – there was nothing else like it. How she missed those moments of raw intensity, witnessing a chain reaction that she had delivered into this slow, dull, gray world.

Everyone else was marking time, ticking days off a calendar. She was burning it down... whenever she had the chance.

Because of circumstances beyond her control, recently Lemora had been marking time like the others, confined to this space dungeon for longer than she cared to remember. She was by nature a restless being. Her mind leaped from idea to idea like a jaguar hopping from tree to tree in her ancestral homeland of Brazil. She'd seen a tropical forest cat once, and thought, *That is me! I am wild like you, my jaguar sister.* Lemora had descended from a long line of scientists on the maternal side, women like she was, huntresses, whether they were stalking viruses in laboratory microscopes and test tubes or wandering deep in the bush gathering up rare plants and insects to study. Her mother was a geologist who searched for signs of water on dried-up planets. That was far too tame for Lemora. She needed light, noise, and action on a grand scale.

What she discovered were bombs.

It began with rocketry as a girl, sending up missiles into the sky, lighting the fuse and running away, then later, not running, but standing in place under a shower of sparks. One day a random misfire singed her shoes, etching a snaky black spiral as it spun itself out in the dirt.

Lemora was intrigued. She took notes. She altered plans, maximizing incendiary effects.

Friends had long ago abandoned her. They called her crazy. Said she had a death wish.

A death wish?

No. It was quite the opposite. She had a life wish. She wanted every day to start with a bang, every night to culminate in a fireworks display. So, she built homemade explosives. Cute little ones, at first. They would sizzle and go off with a pop or a whistling crack, and the heads of passersby would turn sharply at the sound to stare into the fields where she tested her devices. What did they see? A twist of smoke riding on the wind like a phantom, a crater in the dry grass.

They would also see a strong, tall girl, much taller than the boys in her class, a young lady with shiny raven hair and a mischievous grin who'd found her passion early and indulged in it obsessively. Her field was soon pocked with holes, the stubbly weeds scorched as dark as her mane. She took to cutting her hair short after it caught ablaze and scarred her neck. She carried that puckered coin of flesh proudly, a badge of courage, because Lemora was not without fear. She mastered her fear, loved the taste of it in the back of her throat. Without fear, where was the rush? How could you truly live unless you knew you might die spectacularly at any moment?

Boys were afraid of her. She let them be. She was smarter, quicker, more resilient. With her short cut and wide, athletic build, at a distance she was often mistaken for a man. Never up close. Behind her back the boys called her "Dr Boom." While they were bumbling around like colts who'd grown extra limbs, she skipped through school and started doing serious research. The Galactic Defense Forces contractors noticed her work and hired her. She was always the youngest scientist in the lab, always the best, too. She made breakthrough discoveries and brought in barrels of cash. Her career took off like one of her rockets. To the stars she was headed. Who knew the heights she'd attain? The sky had no limit, because she denied it existed.

Like all heroes, Lemora had her weaknesses. She'd never said she was perfect.

Impatience. Irreverence. Some called her work rushed, cautioning that her methods were reckless, even sloppy. They were all jealous, she knew. While they fretted, she dared to act.

And rules. God, she hated following their arbitrary rules designed for those plebeians who were less gifted, her inferiors unwilling to push the boundaries of science to their extremes.

Of course, people died. Isn't that part of the story of life? The weak ones fall away.

She'd read the reports. Combing through her post-testing sites, she'd found a limb or two.

They weren't exactly accidents, rather she viewed them as learning experiences. The experimentation phase was never without certain unfortunate but acceptable, unavoidable risks.

Bombs by their nature were dangerous! Unpredictability was not necessarily a negative, she reminded her bosses, even once saying to them, "We're creating weapons, my friends, are we not? And what is more intimidating than a bomb whose capability is unknown? Look how frightened you all are!"

The nervous nellies at the Galactic Defense Forces insisted

upon her dismissal. Lemora was informed that she should consider herself lucky not to be facing serious criminal charges.

Funny. She didn't feel lucky.

She felt cheated. Enraged. Misunderstood. And vastly underappreciated.

A simple bump, or two, in the road wasn't going to stop her. She set up her own lab, using her savings, living like a hermit in a cave, but the cave was her lab. She never doubted herself. Never worried that she would fail to fashion revolutionary weapons that someone smarter than those bureaucratic fools from the Coalition would admire. Again, Lemora was right.

She *did* find that she had a buyer out there. A *very* wealthy one. A fellow visionary whose mind had the capacity to appreciate her aggressive style. Someone with zeal equal to her own. Her favorite fictional sleuth once said, "Mediocrity knows nothing higher than itself, but talent instantly recognizes genius." Lemora had found a home for her work with the Arms Guild.

With Nero Lupaster IV, who had talent, and who saw her for what she was.

A star.

The night they sealed their partnership on the sleek deck of Nero's latest state-of-the-art battle cruiser was but the beginning. They drank Reizitarian globular wine and toasted their alliance. "To the future," he said, making it sound as if their destiny were preordained.

She raised her glass and clinked it against his. "To *our* future. May we burn brightly."

How everything glittered in that moment! The wine, the stars, and the launch controls.

Ah, but those were better days...

Lemora sensed a change in the energy field of her cell. She was a delicate instrument, much more sensitive than her detractors accused her of being during her trial for mass genocide.

She opened her eyes, shifting her gaze to the cell door screen.

The dull artificial haze had disappeared; a clear view of two guards replaced it.

Her delivery had arrived. *How delightful!*

It took all the discipline she could muster not to dance to the port and accept her package.

Nero had promised her a gift. He was never one to renege on a promise. Lemora could hardly wait to unwrap her present. She would need to be cautious. If this goodie proved to be the real deal – she hoped it was! – an unplanned exposure might be catastrophic. Nero had made it clear to her that he'd paid an exorbitant price on the black market for this… fun-sized sample.

The guard who called himself "Shark" nodded to her as the other one, a Fushnallan with a breather tank, pushed the meal tray into the slot. *Don't be so obvious, you amateur,* she thought, avoiding Shark's gaze. *Why did other people find it so damned difficult to act cool?*

It was one of those things Lemora would never understand, having never been ordinary.

She placed the tray on her desk and sat down, as if she were bored. She suspected that there was a camera hidden somewhere in her cell, but she also supposed that no one monitored the live feed. The prison was understaffed, the guards poorly trained and underpaid. If there were a camera, it would be positioned high, likely in a corner, its lens certainly coated in thick dust. In any case, she hunched over the tray to obstruct any curious eyes. The door's screenblocker had gone fuzzy, but she was sure that Shark had moved on. He wouldn't want to linger with that Fushnallan hanging around. Her presence likely signified nothing, but an extra set of eyeballs made people like Shark nervous. The guards were down the cellblock by now, serving meals.

Now where would that ignoramus hide the sample?

The salad was too shallow, the gravied loaf too wet and flat. Her lime gelatin dessert jiggled translucently as she tapped the tray, so did her cup of water. Which left the dinner roll.

She prodded it ever so gently.

Yes, there was something hard in there. Something unforgiving.

Using her fingernail, she excavated, finding a cavity in the top of the baked bread. She pinched the end of the stoppered test tube, prying it loose, before freeing it from the bread.

Lemora held the sample up to her face for closer inspection. Even if she were to be exposed, she wouldn't be infected. She was human. And the "mold" from PK-L7 only affected alien species, turning them into homicidal monsters. Zombification. The contagion wasn't even a genuine mold; it was something else. Organic, but uniquely structured. It defied categorization. There was no cure. After all these years, they still didn't know why humans were immune. Still, she could do a lot of damage with a gift like this. Holding off made the pleasure all the greater.

She gave the test tube a shake. The dark nugget rattled around like a mutant gaming die.

She imagined it calling out to her. *Want to test your luck, Lem? Risk having a throw?*

Among Lemora's numerous vices was compulsive gambling. Other than laboratories, casinos were her favorite places. The hurly-burly, the gaudy, loud action, the vividness. The *life*. She'd place a bet on anything. You name it. Gambling salted the meat of daily existence.

Lemora pulled the plug and took a deep, lung-filling sniff.

The sample smelled vaguely sweet, but a bit off, like an overripe fruit verging on rot; a dankness lived there. She shoved the plug back in and slipped the test tube inside her jumpsuit for safekeeping. Then she ate her dinner. If Nero was right, they'd be leaving soon. Who knew the next time she'd have an opportunity to nourish her body? It took a lot of energy to break out of prison. After she finished, she found the end of a braided thread secured to the drain cover of her sink. Tied to the other end was a miniature comms device she'd secreted down the pipe.

Nero would want to know everything was on schedule, that their plans were a "Go."

Before she keyed the button and began tapping out the code on her device, she shot her tray back into the port for the garbage pick-up. Her mined-out dinner roll remained uneaten.

Even for a gambling addict like Lemora, some bets were better left on the table, unmade.

CHAPTER FIVE
Ghost Transfer

Nero spotted Lemora out in the exercise yard, taking a stroll around the enclosed track. Her tall, curvy figure was unmistakable despite the prison jumpsuit, as was her shiny wave of dark hair which appeared miraculously stylish notwithstanding the harsh circumstances. There were other women locked up in XSecPen but only one Dr Lemora Pick. Nero admired her swagger.

He sped up to catch her. Nothing too obvious to draw attention. They often walked together in the mornings. The guards wouldn't be too suspicious. The ones he paid would run interference for him if they were. He felt safe from authority, and he had business to conduct.

"You have the vial?" he asked under his breath.

"Good morning to you," she replied, haughty as ever. Her aloofness was armor.

Her strides were longer than his, and he found himself breathing hard to keep up.

"Well, do you … *have* it, Dr Pick?"

"I sent you a message last night. You acknowledged receiving my transmission."

"I mean, do you have it with you now? On your person?"

Lemora didn't look at him, but she was grinning. She picked up her pace.

"You do have it, you naughty scientist. Now, let me see it," he said in a husky whisper.

"I don't think that would be wise. We are being watched. The poor darlings can't help it."

"Just a peek," he pleaded. "Pretty please."

"No. You must wait for the big show like everyone else. It will be more exciting."

Nero stared up at her bronze cheek, considering what she'd said. She was correct; it was too risky for a glimpse at his purchase, and once again Nero was glad that he employed minds like hers on his team. To possess her was to own better judgment than he'd been born with.

"Right you are, Lemora. But you've seen it. It looks like the real thing?"

"How would I know, darling? I've never been to PK-L7. I'm no infectious diseases expert. I build bombs." She thrust her chin forward, as arrogant as she was brilliant.

"But does it feel real? You know what I mean. Don't pretend you don't. Is it… wicked?"

"Very." She turned her head to look at him. Excitement gleamed in her smoky eye.

Nero nodded, temporarily satisfied. "The rest of the materials you requested will be on board the transport. You can fashion the explosive device quickly?"

"If everything I requested is there, yes. The incendiary is simple, a glorified firework, only instead of pretty sparks, you get the mold." Leftward they circled around the oval track.

Guards armed with sniping rifles occupied the watchtowers

at either end of the loop. Fixed turret sentry guns covered the only exit. Choke-gas nozzles sprouted from the ceiling. They pumped in a bland drone of synthetic music to mollify the walkers. It reeked of pitiful despair. How he loathed this place. To be rid of it would be a pleasure.

The other prisoners gave Nero and Lemora plenty of space, keeping far enough ahead or behind to make eavesdropping impossible. No one else knew any specifics about the escape plan. Nero trusted Lemora to a greater degree than his other associates. He needed her skills to bust out of this infernal gulag in the sky. When the time came for the breakout, the rest of his team would follow his lead. They weren't planners. Most of the cons in XSecPen didn't even know that the prison had been built on an arid lonely moon in the PK-L system out in the Coalition space boonies. If they had any imagination, the inmates daydreamed they were within reach of a city, or at least an outpost. The Coalition was too clever for that. There was nobody out here in the harsh hinterlands; the entire PK system was verboten. Any blip showing up on a screen in this system would throw up red flags, triggering an immediate response.

Nero prided himself on being a student of history, Earth's long criminal history to be precise. XSecPen was the equivalent of the Château d'If, Alcatraz, or Devil's Island updated for the present age. When they brought you in, they stuffed a black bag over your head. Nero hadn't seen a window, porthole, or outside camera since his arrival. None of them had. A glimpse outside would've shown them a picture of desolation, an inhospitable pitted lump of rock, its color varying on a scale from pewter to slate, to chalky colorless moondust. He'd been putting this plan together for nearly a year, months of payoffs and gathering intel from both inside and outside XSecPen. Nero had been a busy con. To get away you needed more than a solid plan. You needed a ship. If everything worked with Lemora's mold bomb, they'd soon have one.

"Once we take control of the transport vessel, we're good as gold," he said. "There'll be no record of the flight, the transponder will be switched off, and a military-grade cloaking device installed in the navigation system ensures that our flight path can't be tracked. Even the warden doesn't know all the specifics about our upcoming 'ghost transfer' to the pristine XSecPen 2."

"It's almost a pity we'll never get to see the new penitentiary," she said.

"I'm sure I'll get over it. The place cost a fortune. I should know. One of my subsidiaries won the contract to build it. Coalition fools. They brag about intelligence networks. Mine puts theirs to shame." Nero noticed Shark perched in a tower. He waved. "I own this place, too."

He didn't mean it literally. If Nero owned XSecPen, he would've let himself out years ago. Instead, he'd suffered through three failed escape attempts and a half dozen bungled attempted assassinations. He wasn't sure who was trying to kill him. His list of enemies was incalculable. Whoever it was, they were relentless. Still, they failed. Nero checked over his shoulder for the Thassian, Bak-Irp. He was paying the former bounty hunter to watch his back.

"Are you certain the others will follow our lead?" Lemora asked.

"They'll have no other choice if they want to survive."

A loud whistling screeched overhead.

Exercise time was over.

They were herding them back to their cells. The lockdown would remain in effect until the transfer of the HT population was completed. Nero wasn't sure of the hour the top-secret airlift was scheduled to take off. But it would be tonight. His intel came straight from the top.

He knew he could count on a third of the HT inmates to help him once Dr Pick's "mold bomb" exploded. His escape team was mostly human. Bak-Irp was the odd alien out. If possible, he'd get a gas mask to him, but life was unpredictable. He wanted his people alive and uninfected. Roughly half the guards were aliens. The cloud of energized mold particles would infect them as soon as they inhaled. Then it would be seconds before they transformed. Half the prisoners on the flight would be human, the other half would find themselves zombified; their only life goal would be to slaughter anyone they encountered who wasn't a fellow zombie. For some the change wouldn't make a big difference. Nero had to laugh at his own joke. By all accounts, zombies had no memories that didn't involve killing in some way, no emotions, only an insatiable hunger for gory carnage. They would be more than enough for the remaining human guards to handle.

Or so he hoped. Taking advantage of the chaos, his team would seize control of the bridge, take the pilots hostage, and force them to fly to a prearranged destination.

That was the plan.

As Nero filed out of the exercise yard, he felt a hand grip his shoulder. He stiffened.

Was this another attempt on his life?

He had no weapon. Reduced to relying solely upon his training in a variety of martial arts, Nero felt confident he'd hold his own, unless his executioner was carrying a poisoned blade.

He swiveled around, gripping his adversary's wrist, preparing to flip them.

"Easy," said Bak-Irp. The Thassian grunted in amusement at his boss' reaction.

If there was one con in HT who could kill Nero without a shiv, it was Bak-Irp. Luckily, Nero had paid for his loyalty. But loyalties were always up for renegotiation, and a higher bidder couldn't have found a better fighter. Nero sighed with relief. If Bak had wanted him dead, he'd already be lying on the floor with his neck snapped. The Thassian had a quiet menace that never failed to unnerve him. It was what made him such a precious commodity in outlaw circles, and one reason why Nero would try to spare him from the mold bomb. He needed him in his corner.

"What do you want?" Nero said.

"Something bad is brewing. All of HT is on edge, but no one knows why. I feel it."

"Don't worry. That's good news for us." Nero fell into line before the guards noticed.

"How so?"

"I can't tell you now. Be alert. If I give any orders, obey me. Hesitation would be the worst mistake of your life. I'm your ticket out of here, Thassian. You best keep that in mind."

Bak-Irp grunted again, softly this time, as they passed Shark, whose sniper rifle hung casually off his shoulder, his metal grin shining as he stepped behind Bak and shoved him hard.

"Move along," Shark said. "No talking, Thassian scum."

"Sure thing, chief," Nero said after Bak ran into him, knocking him off balance.

"Shut up, rich boy," Shark said, jamming the butt of his rifle into Bak-Irp's spine.

Bak-Irp grimaced but said nothing. The cords in his pale neck bulged. He kept walking.

Nero gestured back at the guard, pulling an invisible zipper across his pink, smirking lips.

CHAPTER SIX
Blackout

Shawna had fallen asleep. She was drifting in a dream world, that surreal nightmare land where she relived the terrible day her squadron died. Once more, the details came back with all the clarity and horror. Her instruments failed to respond to her commands, they froze, rebelling against her will, moving under the will of some invisible pilot. She watched and could do nothing. Her radio spit static, jammed, unusable. She became a passenger and a helpless witness to the carnage and her own destruction as her fighter sliced through the sky, gunning down her comrades' ships with deadly precision. Her comrades had no time to make sense of what was happening. They could only react, fall back on their training, as one of their own made them into targets and dispatched them from the air. Fighter after fighter perished, trapped in balloons of fiery wreckage and gouts of poisonous black smoke, spinning, falling to the surface of Kepler 186-F and the ferocious bug armies. Asleep, Shawna called out from her bunk, twisting under her blanket, her cries echoing the screams she'd made that terrible day inside her cockpit.

When Shawna's cell door opened, it was a reprieve from

the bad dreams. A temporary reprieve, because they would be waiting for her every night, crouched to pounce in the dark.

She blinked in confusion, wiping the cobwebs of sleep from her eyes.

Helmeted guards in full body armor were flooding into her cell. She had no time to react. They grabbed her and bagged her before she managed to sit up. The hood plunged her back into darkness. Blackout. Rough hands stood her up. Jerking her arms in front of her, they locked her wrists together with bands. The magnetic boots they snapped over her slippers made every step a slog through perpetual sludge. What was going on? This was no simple cell transfer. A midnight raid in search of contraband? Was this connected to the weird encounter with Shark and Ishnik? Or was it something worse? Maybe the prison was under attack? A riot? No, they'd lock them down, not let them out. If there was a fire, she'd smell smoke. Whatever it was, this was no drill.

The sense of doom she'd felt earlier – the bad thing that was coming – this was part of it.

The guards shoved her into the corridor. A crosscurrent of recycled air flowed past her.

"Where are we going?" she asked, her voice muffled by the hood.

Nobody answered.

The guards responded by twisting her body around; facing her to her right, they pushed her farther down the cellblock. The hood prevented her from seeing what was happening. She fought disorientation. Without her eyesight, the world was a dark struggle. But her other senses came alive. This action was anything but routine. Her stomach dipped in panic. *Stay cool.*

"Where are you taking me?"

A rush of bubbly air, liquid sounds, then a soft, aquatic voice.

"You are being transported," it said.

The Fushnallan. Shawna recognized the ticking of her breather, the echoey transmission.

"Transported? Where?"

"Quiet, dirtbag! Move along before I start breaking fingers."

Shark – that was his guttural speech, his familiar stream of threats and abuse.

Other guards were struggling to propel her against the hobbling force of the heavy boots. She could only go so fast with them on. As she moved down the cellblock new voices blared out from the void, her fellow inmates, their angry shouts and curses as they were likewise hauled from their beds, prodded with shock batons to the ribcages, issued with head slaps from tactical-gloved fists.

They're taking all of us. The whole HT unit.

What is this?

Her leg muscles ached from the awkwardness of the boots. She felt like she'd walked a mile. Then she was halted. Waiting for something. She smelled sweat, her own stale breath trapped under the hood, and fear. Inside her jumpsuit was hot. Perspiration ran down her spine and the backs of her legs. The other prisoners had gone mostly silent. A few of the most unstable were shouting. They were afraid. Nothing like this had ever happened before at XSecPen. Crazy thoughts ran through her brain. Was it a natural disaster? A quake or a solar flare might compromise the cell electronics. Maybe all the doors were open.

Maybe Nero's terrorists were knocking at the gate. Maybe we're at war.

Then, a frightening thought flickered across her blacked-out vision …

The government has changed hands. Am I being marched in front of a firing squad?

Shawna pushed those fears away. She had to remain calm. React to the situation at hand.

Control her imagination. Don't race out too far ahead of what was actually happening.

What did she know?

Nothing.

What could she sense? *Analyze your data, Shawna. What do you know?*

Lacking visuals, she heard people breathing. Guards and inmates on all sides. In the distance a muffled slamming. What was that? She recognized it but hadn't heard it in a while.

Airlocks.

The guards were opening and closing the airlocks as they drove the group along.

What could she feel? *Pay attention to your sensors, pilot. What're your readings?*

Heat. Body heat. They were bunched up together in a passageway, too tight to still be in HT corridor. It felt small, airless. But the bag on her head made her feel claustrophobic. Then someone coughed. The sound bounced back quickly, hollow sounding. Underground. A tunnel. Where were there tunnels at XSecPen? Shawna only remembered one time she'd been inside a tunnel here. The day she arrived. She came in on a military prisoner transport flight; its jetway ran through exposed rock, the temperature inside dropped, no wind sounds outside, only silence.

She was back there again. A different scent filled the air.

The hot smell of machines. It was so familiar that she didn't acknowledge it at first. Familiar but nearly forgotten.

They're taking us outside, she thought, feeling at once both exhilarated and terrified.

On a ship. We're going on a ship.

"Keep moving."

The line of prisoners ascended a retractable ramp. She recognized the warped clatter of the steel as the steady stomp of magnetic boots progressed. She felt a gritty traction surface under her soles. Guard voices grunted, front and back. They sounded hyped. The scene carried a vibe of increasing pressure. They were in uncharted territory, guards and prisoners both. Anything might happen. A moment of vertigo threw her off balance; her hip grazed a railing.

"Slow down. Stop." This was Ishnik talking ahead of her on the ramp.

"Step up," she said to one of the prisoners right in front of Shawna. "Now duck."

When it was Shawna's turn, an unseen hand grasped her shoulder. A second guard whisked the hood away. She blinked, adjusting to the frosty nighttime glow from the interior of the ship, a vomitus pink haze emitted from overhead lighting; ice-blue tracks ran along the floor.

A Tri-Terrain troop transport.

Tri-Ts had the ability to fly, drive on the ground like a tank, or turn amphibious if the situation called for that. It served all three roles but did none of them well. The utility of these vehicles was that they could be called upon to do whatever was needed to propel an attack force around a combat zone. Their reputation was dismal. Grunts had good reasons for referring to the Tri-T as "try-not-to-die" and "The Deathcan."

Fat-bodied, stripped down to skin and bones, they were lightweight when empty but had an impressive hauling capacity. Tri-Ts were designed to carry densely packed personnel and support equipment into combat. Most of them came equipped with reactors and FTL drives, giving them the ability to make longer jumps, if necessary, but typically they launched from a mothership onto a battlefield. They were meat movers, plain and simple: multi-purpose assault/resupply/evac vehicles. It made sense that the Corrections Department would repurpose them for shuttling prisoners. The aura inside a Tri-T owed a lot to scrapyard chic and claustrophobic nightmares of being buried alive.

Shawna had flown them before, on training missions when she was a cadet in flight school. This one was ancient; it looked ready for decommissioning. The cabin appeared partly disassembled. Cracked, stained wall panels hung askew. Wiring bundles snaked in and out of the ceiling amid puffs of leaky insulation. The prints of countless boots that had banged their way along the aisles on missions throughout the galaxy lingered ghostly on the grated metal floor. To combat vets like Shawna, one whiff of that canned mix of sweat, musty gear, and overheated electronics raised memories like old battle scars that ached in bad weather.

"Stop," Ishnik said. She was decked out as if she were heading off to war again.

"Where are we going, Ishnik?" Shawna asked, hoping for any snippet of positive news.

Ishnik avoided making eye contact.

"Duck," the guard said.

Shawna bent her head and crossed the threshold. To her left was the locked cockpit. To the right an empty passenger compartment, quickly filling up with bodies. The configuration was a custom job. A central section of seven rows of seats crammed in three across. Twenty-one seats for twenty-one prisoners. On either side of the center section was an aisle, a row of inward-facing seats ran along each side of the fuselage, pointed toward the central section. The guards would sit there, on the periphery, where they could keep watch. The seatbacks displayed cracked and peeling upholstery; their stitching was busted along the seams; the armrests had all traces of their original color rubbed off. Thin, butt-worn cushions. Whether they ran into turbulence or not, they were in for one hell of a sore-ass ride. The seatbelts and buckles had been refitted; they were brand new. The first prisoners through the line were already buckled in. Dazed from being snatched from their bunks, disheveled, bleary-eyed, breath stinking, every single con was busy calculating the situation at hand. What chances might they take? What were their odds? You could hear the gears grinding in their brains as they absorbed their strange, new surroundings.

Two alien guards strapped Shawna in for the flight. Just her luck, she had a middle seat.

To her left was a cyborg everybody called Tingler, a serial arsonist who'd burned off a large percentage of his human skin setting fire to a methane mining pipeline on Uranus. He wore an aquamarine dermal suit and thick gel goggles. Tingler made bad jokes and had no friends.

The other seat remained empty.

For some unknown reason, the guards had skipped it, which was curious. She glanced around trying to figure out who was missing, who hadn't found their seat yet. They began filing in cons to fill up the remaining seats. The cons who were buckled in started whispering to each other, pointing with their chins to the exits, the cockpit, and the weakest of the guards.

Shark was arguing with someone out of sight behind a partition near the cockpit door.

"I'm sure as shit not sitting next to that thing. Put Nero with me up front."

"The warden said the Too-ahka sits alone. He was very specific," said the other guard.

"I don't see the warden on board. Do you? Listen, if the warden wants to accompany that thing, he can be my guest. We don't know the first thing about it, other than its feeding habits."

Too-ahka? Shawna wondered if she'd heard them right. *Who, or what, is a too-ahka?*

She couldn't see Shark, Nero, or this other variable. They must all be behind the barrier.

Shawna turned in her seat, looking around without being obvious.

There weren't any officers on board, which was troubling. If no one of rank was present, that made Shark the senior guard on duty. He was already used to getting his way.

"You sign off. I'm not taking responsibility."

"Give me the tablet," Shark said disgustedly. "Grow a spine while you're at it."

Shark emerged from the hidden area leading Nero. He put the arms dealer in a seat beside the cockpit, and he plopped down next to him and fastened his seatbelt. Shawna looked for Dr Lemora Pick. She was Nero's sidekick and never far from him. Shawna spotted the demolitionist slouched down in the front row of forward-facing seats. Bak-Irp was next to her.

So, who was going to be sitting next to Shawna?

Whoever this Too-ahka was, Nero must've had a good view of the new inmate. He was giggling, leaning into Shark to make a comment. Shark didn't respond with the customary sharp elbow to the ribs. He was too transfixed to react or speak. His mouth hung open like a steel trap.

In a second Shawna saw what he'd been looking at.

And then she understood.

CHAPTER SEVEN
T.O.O.A.K.A.

Nero leaned into Shark. "Get a load of the fuzzball freak. I don't know whether to laugh or cry."

Shark was speechless. He'd read the reports about their newest arrival at XSecPen, but he hadn't met the unidentified alien creature until they brought it aboard. A quick glimpse told him he didn't want to see any more. But he couldn't help himself now that they were buckled in, and the escorts were walking the thing past him. He skimmed his wrist recording of the summary.

The One-of-a-Kind Alien – AKA: T.O.O.A.K.A.; 2AKA; Too-ahka; The Vivisector.

Discovered inside a deep-space station by Galactic Special Ops (Royal Purple Unit). T.O.O.A.K.A. is the sole survivor, and likely perpetrator, of the mass slaughter of the science and engineering exploratory team (thirteen members) assigned to investigate space debris inhibiting long-haul freighters on the outer belts of the [REDACTED] and [REDACTED] zones. The alien may have entered the station after being picked up hitchhiking on a dead satellite or space junk recovered by the team. No record of the alien's arrival at the station exists. Evidence suggests that the team members were killed in rapid succession. Furthermore, it appears their deaths occurred from massive blood loss following bodily evisceration. Tissue samples, organs, etc. were not entirely ingested but seem to have been manipulated and "studied" while the scientists were still alive. The alien displays no verbal or telepathic communication skills but may have the ability to utilize cosmic sign language. Attempts at dialogue were inconclusive. The subject shows signs of intelligence and acute awareness of its environment. In lab tests, T.O.O.A.K.A. successfully hunted targets employing echolocation and is to be considered EXTREMELY dangerous. Recommended incarceration for unknown natural lifespan at XSecPen HT Unit…

What the hell…? Why didn't they kill that thing when they found it? Shark tucked his feet under his seat as the alien shuffled forward in its mag boots. It wasn't big, maybe half as tall as the average human. It had a smushed-in face and maroon fur the shade of drying blood. Its head was squat and fat as a jack-o'-lantern, no neck to speak of, humped-up shoulder muscles, a barrel-chested body and broomstick spindly legs covered with saggy, plum-colored skin like old stockings that had been through the wash too many times. The arms were sinewy. On the end of each finger, a thick claw sprouted, clipped down to the gray quick but already growing back, hornlike yellow, tough-looking, tapering into what would be hooks. The total package was so ugly it was almost cute. Until you looked into its eyes. They were monochromatically red, like small matching buttons of congealed blood nestled into furry sockets.

The dish head rotated smoothly, scanning, highly alert. Too-ahka's teeth – its fangs – were a mad jumble its stretchy lips failed to contain fully. They protruded at frightening angles, forcing a person to imagine how nasty its bite must feel. The creature – although it had never been housed at XSecPen – wore a crimson jumpsuit like the rest of the High Terror unit prisoners. The pair of escorts led it back to a spot beside the war hero pilot. They belted it in. Calm and observant, Too-ahka silently surveyed. It gave off a moist scent of freshly dug soil.

I do not know what you are, dirtbag. And I don't want to learn either, Shark thought. He wished they'd put it in a kennel somewhere else, preferably under a tarp. He was distracted from further contemplation of the new prisoner by Lemora Pick.

Her head was up, facing forward, and placid. But her hands were fidgeting in her lap.

What is she doing?

He'd seated her where Nero had asked him. Sat the octillionaire near the exit, too, as requested. The Thassian bodyguard was nearby as well. Shark had rewritten the seating chart.

"Psst, hey," Nero whispered to him. "Give me the lowdown. Where we headed?"

"You'll find out soon," Shark said. He couldn't be seen fraternizing with cons. Part of him was deeply concerned about his lost income once this batch of inmates moved out. Nero, especially. The guy was a gravy train. He'd inquired for himself about their destination. All he figured out was that this was a mass transfer to another XSecPen. So, the rumors had been true. Corrections higher-ups wanted the worst of the worst baddies housed alone in the same shithole.

"You want to earn a little going away money?" Nero asked, pressing his knee into Shark.

"Keep it down. Don't touch me."

"What? You getting shy now? After all we've done together?"

What was Nero's problem? They'd stuck that Fushnallan on the other side of Nero, and she could hear everything he was saying. What if she decided to talk to the bosses?

Nero's voice got louder. "Look at me when I'm speaking to you, Sharko. Hell-*ooo*..."

Heads swiveled in their direction.

"What do you want?" Shark asked. "A smack? Cuz I got a smack for you, rich boy."

Lemora was still squirming in her seat. A nervous flyer? Those brainiacs always had psychological problems, phobias and shit. They couldn't function in the real world like Shark.

"Sharko, look at me, OK? All I want is a little attention. All my life I've been seeking it."

The hatches were sealed. The ship shuddered. A loud clanking rang from outside as they separated from the jetway. Constant humming came up through the floor – rough vibrations.

"Shut it, shithead," Shark said, adding in a whisper, "We'll talk later."

Nero laid his head on Shark's shoulder. "Tell me a story so I won't be afraid, daddy."

"Get off me!"

"I'm scared," Nero said. "Don't you ever get scared, sergeant? I've got a *baaad* feeling."

"How's this for a bad feeling?" Shark rammed his index finger into Nero's ear.

Nero howled, "You hurt me!" He stomped his mag boots.

Everybody was looking at them now. Prisoners, guards, even Too-ahka.

Shark grabbed a handful of the front of Nero's jumpsuit. "Quit it, asshole! I mean it!"

"What'd you do that for? That's abuse! I'm going to file a complaint. I have rights."

Shark grimaced. Part of him knew that messing with Nero was a dumb idea. Another part of him didn't care. He was seeing red. How was this chump going to get back at him if he was locked up in a tougher pen? Nero Lupaster was on his way down. Hell, soon he'd be a nobody.

The idea of giving him a proper beating on this flight was tempting.

The ship's thrusters lifted off. They left the moon's desolate rocky landscape, angling upward. The force of the maneuvers knocked everyone back in their seats. As they gained altitude, the fuselage rattled. Suddenly, the ship banked hard, rolled on its starboard side, then pitched up sharply. Prisoners and guards yakked on the floor.

Nero had shut up, finally. He sat there with a stupid grin pasted on his face.

Shark wanted to take a bite out of him if only to wipe away that smug look. A bite never failed to shock. It tapped into something deep down, primal, and ancient.

We're beasts, it said. *Me and you. Everybody is part of the food* chain. *I'm bigger and badder than you, and I can eat you if I want to. Forget civilization. The only law here is blood.*

The thought that he could tear Nero apart in his seat was enough to calm Shark down.

Now that Nero was settled, Shark turned his focus back to Lemora. She was finished with her fiddling around. Her hands were empty, laying on her thighs. She was looking over his way.

Mouthing words.

Not at Shark.

But at Nero.

Shark tried to read her lips. What was she saying? His mouth's movements mimicked hers as he attempted to solve the meaning. Voicing her words aloud he said, "Shall we, darling?"

Shall we what?

He snapped his head to stare at Nero sitting there beside him. The earlier outburst had been a distraction to take Shark's eyes off the scientist. Nero must've paid someone else to plant the workings of a bomb in Lemora's seat. It was foolish to think he'd been Nero's only servant.

"Let's do it," Nero said to Dr Pick across the seats. "Give it here. I want to be the one."

She threw something. *A ball?* That's what it looked like to Shark. A hand-sized ball – she'd had it tucked down between her legs. But it was flying now. What kind of game was this?

Nero caught the ball with his locked-together hands. The sphere fizzed, spitting smoke.

"Hot potato!" Nero laughed right into Shark's astonished face. The guard had no time to react before Nero chucked the unknown device. "Eat this, suckers!" Nero cackled maniacally as he threw the improvised grenade. Airborne it sailed, sparking over the heads of the prisoners.

Lemora was yelling at Bak-Irp to hold his breath and feel under his seat.

What the hell?

The ball popped with a soft bang like a bursting party balloon. No big flash; no frags blew out. The sphere disappeared, and a black powdery cloud emerged, filling the cabin.

A smoke bomb? Shark thought, relieved to be alive.

His relief didn't last long.

CHAPTER EIGHT
Hot Potato Party Balloon Mold Bomb Boogie

Lemora loved it when an experiment went according to plan. It was the kind of thing that made a person have faith in science. The spores of mold from PK-L7 floated invisibly in the air; clinging to tiny silicate dust particles, they only needed a moist place in which to grow, surfaces like nasal passages, mouths, throats, and lungs bathed in saliva and mucus.

XSecPen had access to an extensive digital library. Its contents were available to prisoners for educational purposes. Dr Pick was nothing if not a lifelong learner. Having had all her other creative outlets stymied, she resorted to old habits. Reading was her earliest form of escape. It meant freedom. Exploration. The opportunity to dream. In the sterile solitude of the HT unit, she'd found the perfect environment for tuning out distractions to study the vast scientific files and soak up details. Sipping contraband yerba mate, she'd gotten down to reading.

Years ago, at the start of her employment at the Arms Guild and her partnership with Nero, the topic of biological weaponry came up in a meeting. Was it viable? The Guild members had no qualms about adding nature's deadliest, most virulent infective agents to their arsenal.

"Find something gruesome to sprinkle on my enemies, Dr Pick," Nero had said.

Lemora set out to do just that. The idea of a biological bomb sounded fun and … *different*.

She didn't get far into her research and development. Other tasks came up that demanded immediate attention. The Guild council ultimately favored tried and true methods of mass destruction to keep the war machine churning. In short, Nero needed bigger, better bombs. He needed them delivered on a predictable schedule. Production was key. So, R&D was paused.

Lemora reluctantly set aside her biological investigations, bookmarking them for later. The unfortunate business on BAZ-9 put a damper on all her projects. After you've destroyed an entire planet, decimating the population and leaving the environment lethally contaminated for the next ten million years, the Coalition gets testy. They hunt you down and cage you like a sad little lab monkey. She never gave them the satisfaction of testifying in her own defense. What was the point? Anything she said would've been twisted and taken out of context. No, thanks. She wouldn't do that. Sitting there in the docket, watching a silver-tongued prosecutor pepper her with inane questions, putting on a show trial for the masses. It was beneath her dignity.

Her lawyer wanted her to cooperate. He recommended she start with acting remorsefully. "Tell them you're sorry for what happened to the population living on BAZ-9," he said.

"I don't talk about BAZ-9, darling. It's over and done with, as far as I'm concerned."

She meant it, too. Looking backward was a waste of time. Shit happens. You deal with it.

And you go forward.

In her case, forward meant the slammer. So be it. She'd adapt like she always did.

When Nero arrived at XSecPen, less than a year into her incarceration, Lemora was elated. Finally, someone to talk to, an intellectual equal. It went without saying that she felt terrible about his arrest. But that had nothing to do with her. It was a mystery, even to Nero himself, how the Coalition had found him. He'd put a great deal of pride in his personal security.

Nonetheless, now they could talk again. She'd always loved their conversations, and in prison they grew even closer.

"Talking to you is a thrill ride. I forgot how out of breath you make me feel," she said.

"We need to go back to basics," he'd said. "Fear is what works. Find me something to scare the Coalition, a weapon so jaw-droppingly horrific that they sit up and beg for mercy."

Lemora took him seriously and hit the books. Remembering her biological false start, she returned to the task of sifting through the greatest plagues in galactic history, like the Fushnallan flu and Kolbanian encephalitic fever, keeping a special eye out for those outbreak incidents that the Coalition swept under the rug as quickly as possible. The near misses that never caught like a wildfire. Infectious disasters averted in the nick of time. The ones they snuffed out, or said they did, before calamity had a chance to take root and spread widely throughout Terran space.

That's how she found PK-L7. What a weird little rock, hardly a blip on the screen, originally a mining outpost, where alien Xenos dug up the precious energy commodity xenium until things in the mines went sideways. An unknown infection entered the Xeno miners through their exposure to a strange mold, and they went from being diligent, tireless workers to ravening "zombies" who attacked the humans. A few lucky survivors made it out. The Coalition put up a virtual fence around PK-L7. Quarantine enforced by legal penalties and missiles. The planet was still off limits, trespassers shot on sight, a no-go zone. Lemora loved the idea of forbidden places.

What secrets must be buried there? What knowledge was the Coalition trying to hide?

What if? Lemora allowed herself to ask the question and its many permutations. She let her imagination wander. The more she read, the more her heart rate increased.

The digital record became quite scant after that initial event among the mining community. The problem seemed to be confined to the Xeno population. One conspiracy theory held that there had been no "real" infection; the disease outbreak story was a coverup for a violent workers' rebellion. Xeno trouble, in other words. She pulled on additional threads...

A new discovery of xenium on PK-L10 in the same system led to another outbreak. Alien infections and human casualties. That's where the files abruptly ended. Outlandish rumors persisted on the fringes, involving everything from Caridians to wormholes. But there was no evidence to back any of it up, at least not in the scientific literature. Lemora was stumped.

Xenium was far too valuable to give up on because of a few dead scientists and engineers, even if their poor families did die with them. No one in their right mind walked away from such profits. The job the miners signed up for was dangerous. They knew there'd be risks. Honestly, they were well compensated for their exposure. True, a few early operational mistakes were made. It simply boiled down to this: the miners were unlucky. Wrong place, wrong time. So, why were no further mining attempts made? Using upgraded safety procedures? More robust security? Why did the extraction of xenium come to a halt? Lemora suspected there was a lot more to the story.

Maybe xenium wasn't the real treasure. Maybe the revolutionary discovery hadn't been a powerful new fuel but the mysterious mold that turned Xenos into berserk killers.

Inside the troop transport, the infectious dust was slowly settling. People were coughing and rubbing their eyes. The tin can of a ship was still climbing at a precipitous angle. Lemora figured any behavioral changes among the passengers, if they were going to show up, would take place rapidly. She took a quick look around. Half of the prisoners were non-human and susceptible to the mold agent. Coincidentally, the same alien-to-human ratio existed among the guards.

A fifty/fifty split.

Adding up everyone on the flight, Lemora estimated about fifty living souls in total, including the pilots. Approximately one zombified alien for every human. She liked those odds when it came to killing the guards. But what were the survival chances for Nero's escape team?

Well… she was glad she had a blade in her mag boot for starters. She slipped it out and began sawing through her wrist restraints. Nero was doing the same. Bak-Irp was still not breathing. Lemora knew that Thassians had the capacity to hold their breath for ten times longer than the average human. That feature was an evolutionary benefit of their ancestral ambush predator days. He executed an exploratory finger sweep under his seat and came up with a baggie containing a blade and a gas mask. Nero had paid his crooked guards to stash the supplies. She motioned for Bak to put the mask on. He nodded. Soon he, too, was cutting his way free.

Shark had unbuckled himself and tried to get up. But the pitch of the ship was too vertical for him to stand. Instead, he twisted around, digging his mitts into Nero's midsection, trying to pry the cutting tool out of Nero's hands. Nero pressed his face against Shark's ear, barking at him. Both men were red-faced, their systems pumped full of adrenaline and rage.

In the meantime, Lemora scanned for the other members of the escape team. One row behind her sat a German master smuggler of Arab descent named Hans Yasir Krait. He'd helped Nero obtain the PK-L7 sample. She called out, "Hans, you've got a blade in your boot. Use it."

The smuggler registered an initial surprise but was known not to let advantages slip by him. Hans had a calculating, slippery mind born of survival; as a former street peddler who'd adapted his skill set to securing lucrative black-market profits, his Machiavellian instincts had served him well. While his personal fortune fell short of Nero's, he was a self-made man, the son of a butcher, and no stranger to carving implements. He found his hidden shank and got to work.

Since Nero was temporarily preoccupied, Lemora, as his number two, acted in his stead, issuing orders to the final three escapees – a pair of South American hitman clones and a Belgian whose computer hacking thievery led to the deaths of hundreds of medical patients after he remotely switched off their life support systems when the Coalition refused to pay his request for ransom. The Belgian could've used a doctor right now; he'd accidentally slashed his wrist while severing his cuffs. Judging by the amount of red on his hands, he'd hit an artery. This was no time for carelessness, and she hoped Krait knew enough about computers, because the Belgian was going to bleed out and die on them. She sighed. It was always something, wasn't it?

The Tri-T leveled out. The sound of coughing grew louder, competing with the rattling fuselage. Non-human passengers began to claw at their own throats as they sputtered out a chorus of croaks and dry wheezes. The mold bomb was working. Lemora detached her mag boots. Too early to make her next move. The chaos had yet to reach the top of the crescendo.

Shark jumped up and pummeled Nero with hammer punches.

The Fushnallan guard leaped from her seat. She was doing her best to pull Shark off and halt the beating. "You'll kill him!" She managed to crank Shark's right arm behind his back. During the temporary lull in his assault, Nero concentrated on separating the final stubborn strands of his synthetic, zero-flex restraints. At last, they snapped. His hands were free.

He swiped his blade across Shark's chest. But the guard's tactical vest prevented cuts.

Nero switched to stabbing, aiming for the fleshy underside of Shark's jaw.

Shark tucked his chin, taking the blows on his helmet.

The shiv skidded on his visor, leaving deep gouges with no penetration. Nero grunted, slamming the blade sidearm into the earhole of Shark's helmet. Red droplets spray-painted the inside of Shark's facial shield.

The Fushnallan couldn't see the weapon concealed in Nero's hand. She was getting sandwiched between Shark and the front row of prisoner seats with her view blocked.

"Let me go, you fish witch!" Shark screamed, elbowing her ribs. He headbutted Nero who dropped back into his seat, stunned. A trickle of blood flowed from under Shark's visor. He grabbed his shock baton. Whipping it front and center, he laid it against Nero's breastbone and hit the button. With an electric crackle blue bolts of plasma danced on Nero's jumpsuit. The arms dealer clenched his teeth. His eyes rolled up into his head. Shark held the baton there, administering an extralong, but nonlethal, jolt. "You like that, Richie Rich?" he said. The baton chattered. Nero's body stiffened, speechless, as rigid as a girder.

"I'll fry your oysters next," Shark said.

The Fushnallan slipped the tip of her own baton into the crook of Shark's neck and zapped him. He twitched. Quickly, she interrupted the flow of juice. The baton dropped from Shark's hand. He struck her visor with his fist, then, grabbing hold of the edge of her helmet, he cranked up, snapping her head back in a painful stress position. "I'll pop your damned head off!"

"Aarrrghh…" She struggled free of his grip, but there was no room for her to retreat.

Leaving aside the stunned Nero, Shark bumped up chest to chest with the guard.

Hooking his fingers into the front top of her tactical vest, he yanked her down, while at the same time driving his knee into her helmet. The visor cracked. The Fushnallan grunted amid a harsh rush of bubbles. Fluid spilled from her mouth.

He threw her aside.

She crabbed along the aisle, putting space between them. As she staggered to her feet, stunned, he rushed forward, ripping out her breather.

A jet of Fushnallan atmospheric liquid splashed onto Nero, still recovering in his seat. The alien guard gasped. A line of white blood drained from her nose. She reached for the compact combat pistol on her belt, and Shark hit her again, this time connecting with a heart punch that aggravated her breathing issues. He swept her legs out and kicked her viciously in the head. Once. Twice. Bending, he jammed his thumb into her earhole and wrenched her helmet off. She collapsed on her side, curling into a defensive ball.

"Newbie's gonna jam me up, is she? Not today, Fishstick."

He stomped her again.

Desperately, she patted under the row of seats, searching for her mouthpiece.

Shark found the end of the hose spewing its vital solution into a puddle between his boots. Snatching up the hose, he bit down with his steel teeth, severing it. He chucked the mouthpiece to the rear of the ship, out of sight. Then, with a look of disgust, he spit out the fluid that had flooded into his mouth.

The Fushnallan moaned, attempting to rise. Gulping, her eyes glazed, she rested her forehead on the edge of her empty seat. Black powder from the bomb smeared her cheeks.

She was barely moving, teetering on the verge of unconsciousness.

Shark returned to Nero who lay blinking, yet to come back fully from his baton-shock.

Lemora had faith in Nero. But after watching what Shark had done, she wondered if they'd underestimated the sergeant's ferocity. It was too late now. They all had jobs to do. Shark was Nero's responsibility. He'd picked him, and he'd have to deal with him one way or another.

Removing her mag boots, Lemora slid herself out of the row. Bak-Irp followed her. In the commotion, some prisoners were unbuckling from their seats, but they were still shackled at the wrists. The humans looked lucid; the aliens suffered under extreme duress. Guards shouted at everyone to keep in their seats. An alarm blared. Hand-to-hand skirmishes had broken out between the human guards and their convict counterparts. No one was firing shots. Not yet.

"To the cockpit," Lemora said. "We need to breach the doors before they auto-seal."

"I can't leave him," Bak-Irp said. He jerked a thumb in the direction of their mutual boss.

"He'll be fine."

"Shark is going to kill him."

"No, he isn't," Lemora said. "Look."

Certainly, Shark did have the intention of using deadly force on their employer. He'd pulled out his combat pistol and seemed ready to put a slug into Nero before his better judgment stepped in – shooting high-powered firearms inside an airship was generally a bad idea.

Put a big enough hole in a tin can like a Tri-T and you'd risk the whole ship depressurizing. The hulls were thick but not indestructible. Add to that the real possibility the entire fuselage might start shredding apart, bolts popping, its outer skin peeling, failing under the huge structural strain they'd face in space. This ship could take a beating on planetary terrain but not when it was flying high in zero atmosphere. Even an oaf as dumb as Shark had to know that.

Shark probably saved them when he decided not to pump holes in the Deathcan.

But he didn't do himself any favors by re-holstering his weapon.

The Fushnallan had risen off the floor. She didn't need her breather now. Because she was dead. Dead but not out of commission. The PK-L7 mold invading her system had won.

A new lifeform sat in the driver's seat, controlling her brain, pulling the strings.

Lemora had to admit it was an amazing sight, the power of nature and glory of science.

The Fushanallan took hold of Shark's hand – the one that recently held his pistol – and she put it in her mouth. All of it. The whole damned thing. Shark's face went through a range of emotions that would've made a vids actor proud. Surprise, repulsion, dismay, and stupefaction each took turns. You'd think he'd have pulled his hand back instantly. But he didn't. Not at first. He seemed to be too shocked to act. By the time he realized what was happening, it was too late.

She had him now. A combination of suction and sharp teeth gave her possession of his hand, and she wasn't giving it back. He grimaced, displaying his steely grin. She bit him, hard.

Shark screamed. There was a crunch, followed by a grinding, squishy noise.

Then she let him go.

"Oh, hallelujah," he said. The Fushnallan had shown him

mercy. His relief turned to terror as he gaped at the blood-spurting stump where his hand used to be.

The Fushnallan chewed. It sounded like her breather – bubbly with periodic wet gurgles.

Shark raised his stump high over his head, showering the nearby passengers with his blood as they hollered their displeasure, voicing insults concerning his injury and wellbeing.

The Fushnallan swallowed and gazed around the cabin, sorting the food from the feeders.

She wasn't the only one changing.

Lemora poked Bak-Irp.

The Thassian, who was normally not one for conversation, appeared to have fallen into a profound silence as he attempted to absorb what he was witnessing.

"You feel normal?" she asked him.

"Normal?" His voice was muffled by the gas mask.

"Yeah. Are you choking? Any trouble breathing? Headache?"

He shook his head. "No. I'm fine. But none of this is normal."

"Here comes Nero," she said, smiling. "All is well. Forward. We go forward."

Their leader climbed over the top of the blood-spattered inmates blocking his path.

From the rear of the ship, the South American hitmen were making their way to the front. Lemora searched for signs of the Belgian. His head jerked up, a piece of torn material clamped between his teeth as he tried in vain to staunch the blood squirting from his wrist, his face growing increasingly ashen. The Fushnallan sniffed the air, her jaw chewing involuntarily on nothing in anticipation of her next kill. Adroitly, hungrily, she advanced toward him.

"He's not going to make it," Lemora said. The Belgian always seemed like a weak link to her. This whole experiment was an exercise in high-speed evolution – survival of the deadliest.

"What's the plan?" Bak-Irp asked, the mask making him sound even gruffer than usual.

"The Silva brothers are with us. So's Krait. We don't have much time to reach the pilot."

"We need weapons," Bak-Irp said.

"Half this ship is turning into weapons," Lemora said. "Living weapons."

"Guns. We need *guns*."

"First the cockpit," she said. "They'll have a gun locker. We can bolt the door."

Nero joined them. He had Shark's combat pistol, which he'd scavenged from the dying guard as he bled out. He handed the gun to Bak-Irp. "Don't shoot the pilots. We need them."

Behind them, the cabin erupted with violent frenzy. Cries of attack and human carnage.

The slaughter had begun.

CHAPTER NINE
Tug-of-war

The incendiary device detonated right above Shawna's head. When the smoke cleared, the alien belted in beside her – Too-ahka, according to the guard who had introduced them with a bemused snicker – sat staring inquisitively at the fine black powder covering its fur.

Nero had tossed the smoke grenade. This was no doubt part of an escape plan. What role the dust bomb played was a mystery, but it caused a major distraction, that was for sure. Shawna tried to make out what was happening in the hazy commotion near the front of the ship. It was hard to determine. One glance into the eyes of the guards seated on either side of the prisoner section told Shawna that the corrections staff were outmatched, terrified, and unable to handle whatever was coming.

Her sense of impending doom had vanished. The doom had arrived.

There were a lot of guards on this flight, at least as many as there were prisoners. Shawna counted about two dozen. The guards hadn't all come from HT. Shawna knew the ones who did, mostly longtime jailhouse veterans, bulked-up muscleheads with granite dispositions and low brain power. The other XSecPen personnel were of lesser quality. The alien guards shared a temperament with their human cohorts. They were worker types. Able-bodied, resilient, and dependable. Day in, day out, they showed up to do the dirty jobs their bosses were either too corporate or too chickenshit to carry out. Cogs in the Galactic Coalition wheel, they knew the score and accepted their roles. But if a situation became unpredictable, and no one was giving direct orders, they froze as if their batteries had died, reverting to standby mode. Given the chaos erupting around the ship, things were going to degenerate until somebody stepped up to lead. Judging by the vacant looks, it wouldn't be a guard.

Shawna resisted her instinct to take charge. Nobody was going to listen to what she had to say anyway. To them she was another con, or worse, a traitor. *Traitor.* That label burned worse than the others: coward, psycho, murderer. She knew they were all wrong. But her life had turned into a surreal odyssey that final day in the cockpit, and she'd been unable to find her way home, to get back to her life, career, and family. Everything good had vanished that one afternoon because of events she could not explain. How had she lost control of her airship? Who was really flying that day? Who killed her squadron and made her the patsy? Even mentioning these questions made her sound like a paranoid headcase. Most people in her position would've given up. Yet Shawna still looked for signs of hope, any reason to go on.

So, instead of jumping up and taking charge of the group, she acted to save herself. Her upbringing and training drove out selfish tendencies, so embracing them made her feel sick. She wasn't made that way. Team-first was her style. But her team was dead. For now, self-preservation remained her only option. There weren't many team players jailed in HT, let alone those who would ask her to join forces. She was forced to think selfishly. If she died on this flight, she'd die as a convicted traitor. That wasn't going to happen, not if she could help it.

Shawna read the state of play.

Too-ahka was busy licking the dust off its arms. When it caught her staring, it tilted its fuzzy round head at her and pointed one of its freshly licked, spindly fingers at the cockpit door.

Shawna followed the finger.

Yes, she thought, *the pilots. They could turn this junker around. Get us back to XSecPen before the shit that already hit the fan had a chance to hit it again.*

Maybe the beady-eyed furball had something going on beyond what its appearance first suggested. She was going to say words to that effect, but the alien had removed its boots, and was currently jackknifing itself like a contortionist to suck the bomb residue off its gargoyle toes.

"I'll catch up with you later," she said.

Shawna unbuckled. She wondered if the cockpit had a live screen showing them what was going down in the passenger compartment. Probably not. She scanned the walls for a comms panel she might use to talk to them. *There.* A gap yawned in one of the rear corner panels, where a medusa of multicolored wire was spilling out – that was where the comms *should've* been. *Great.* The pilots must've heard the boom when the device exploded. Now they had a ship full of distressed and coughing passengers. Whatever rules had been in place were gone now. Nero and Shark were whaling on each other. Some pilots acted as if cargo was none of their business. They flew, and nothing else mattered. Shawna knew that was a copout you paid for ultimately.

The ship leveled off.

The aliens on board began acting sick. The dust affected them more than as an irritant. They were experiencing serious respiratory symptoms. Their faces revealed mental confusion as well as pain. *Poisoning*, Shawna figured. Something in the bomb must've been a toxic chemical or biological agent that worked on non-humans. Shawna had no idea what it could be. Military grade? Knowing Nero, it probably violated every treaty in the books. The aliens were in trouble.

Not Too-ahka. Too-ahka had switched from licking its feet to grooming its fur. A disturbingly long and nimble tongue shot out of its mouth to lap up every trace of the black dust. Snack time, apparently. It appeared no worse for eating the substance. In fact, the thing purred.

"If that's the only food we're getting on this flight, I'll wait until we land," Tingler said. He sat back, grinning at his own joke and rubbing his blue hands together as if they were chilled.

Shawna ignored him. She reached down and disengaged her mag boots. Ready to go, she climbed out of her seat and cautiously squeezed past the alien who continued its self-cleaning.

"Excuse me," she said.

"Now *is* probably a good time to use the bathroom," Tingler said to Too-ahka. Fluids pulsed beneath the surface layer of his artificial dermis. His goggles were smudged. "No lines."

Too-ahka stared blankly at Shawna before turning its focus on Tingler.

The alien flicked its noodle tongue, making a whiplike sound, a tiny *crack-cracking*.

Shawna moved away, proceeding up the aisle in a low crouch. Tingler was saying something about lollipops and ice cream cones, then his voice cut out, falling suddenly quiet.

Shawna was halfway to the first row of prisoner seats when she paused.

Ahead, Shark was giving Nero an old-fashioned tune-up. His shock baton sizzled. That sound set every con's teeth on edge. The energy in the room amped up to the max. If Nero had an escape plan in the process of hatching, he wasn't exactly seizing the moment. But Shawna wasn't above taking advantage of the opportunity to skip out. Hell, she was innocent of the crimes that sent her to XSecPen, and freeing herself might be the only way to clear her name. This was going to be her first genuine prison breakout. So, how was Nero planning to do it?

A midflight intercept?

But that meant he had to have another ship ready to dock with the Tri-T. It would be far easier to hijack the ship and bring the Deathcan down safely. Then he could switch to a better, faster ship. He owned a fleet of them. Nero was a schemer. Everything he did had a purpose. But a hijacking was stupid. The Galactic Coalition had to be tracking them. An apprehension team would catch or kill them the second after they landed. If they couldn't pinpoint the rendezvous location, the Coalition would order them shot out of the sky. Once Nero took control of the transport, the guards were as good as dead. He had to have a better strategy. The guy was smart.

Think, Shawna. Think…

When she looked back at her seat, Tingler was gone. Too-ahka had its hands free. It was stuffing its mouth with a blue membrane that reminded her of a wetsuit. It must've bitten its way out of its restraints. A tremor of anxiety rippled through her. But Too-ahka also gave her an idea. There were two guards sitting on her right side. One human, one alien. The alien lay keeled over on its side, its head resting in the human's lap. The human was waving his hands frantically in the air, his eyes bulging in horror. Shawna's fingers explored around the edge of the alien guard's seat. Thin padding but nothing that might help her. She probed the armrest. Worn away cushioning and… yes… a small tear. She spread the tear apart, splitting it farther. The exposed frame inside the rip had a sharp contoured edge. Shawna stood in the aisle, sawing her bonds back and forth across the edge as chaos erupted around her. Too-ahka watched her curiously, its folded hands perched on the headrest in front of it.

Was Too-ahka wearing Tingler's goggles? Where was Tingler? The blue wetsuit… oh my God… The realization sank in, and she felt sick to her stomach. Too-ahka had peeled and eaten Tingler. But this was no time to dwell on things if she wanted to live. Tingler was no great loss.

Shawna was nearly finished hacking through her bonds when the alien guard lifted its head and tore out the human guard's throat. The human didn't have time to scream. Shawna fell on her butt and scrambled backward in retreat. What the hell was happening to the aliens?

The bloody-faced alien lurched against its seatbelt. Enraged, it fumbled with the buckle.

One seat away an older guard was having problems disengaging from the seat; his ample stomach and several layers of tactical gear impeded his efforts. The alien strained to reach him. Frustrated, it roared. A clarity spread across its face; looking down, concentrating, it unlatched.

"Oh shit," the older guard said.

The alien leaped at him.

The man got his chance to scream. Not that it helped. He tried stiff-arming the alien, planting his left hand on the alien's chest and pushing away his attacker. His right hand dug for a weapon. Silvery lines of drool cascaded off the alien's lower lip onto the man's face. It growled.

"No, no, *nooooo* ..." the guard cried out. He'd found his holster and unsnapped it. His elbow banged into the armrest as he tried to bring the gun up. "C'mon ... Roy, you got this ..."

The alien backed up a half-step. And nipped the guard's fingers neatly off his left hand.

Roy finally drew his combat pistol and fired it twice into the eye of his assailant. Bits of alien skull and brain blew out the exit hole. The dead alien fell across Roy's ample lap.

"Got you! I got you, you son of a–"

It was a short-lived victory.

Two more alien guards, who must've smelled the blood, or sensed wounded prey, swooped down on the still-buckled guard. This time his shots did nothing to stop them. He fired into their bodies. They each grabbed an arm and played a short but gory game of tug-of-war.

Holy crap. What was in that bomb? Shawna thought. It made the aliens go crazy. The situation was too surreal, as if she were stuck in a blood-soaked horror vid game. Her brain shifted into pure reaction mode. Fight or flee. Or do both, whatever worked in the moment.

She remembered how much black dust Too-ahka had

eaten, how it had been watching her so intently. She threw off the broken restraints and jumped up, spinning around. If Too-ahka came at her with those pointy teeth...

She peered down the row in question.

Too-ahka's seat was empty.

The alien was gone. Just like Tingler. Well, not exactly like Tingler. The cushions were damp with freshly squeezed dermal suit. *I've got to get into the cockpit.* She retrieved a pistol from the floor. The torn-apart guard wouldn't need it. The two aliens were busy fighting over the scraps. Shark and Ishnik blocked the aisle ahead of her. Shark was kicking Ishnik's head. A dazed Nero shook himself, trying to regain his bearings. Shawna glided down her empty row. She turned up the other aisle, needing to find a way into that cockpit. Her life depended on it.

CHAPTER TEN
Fun & Games

The thing most people didn't realize about being the richest man who had ever lived was that it wasn't all fun and games. Nero had responsibilities. Problems to solve. So many problems. What he didn't have was patience. He hired the best people, paid them higher than they'd make working for anybody else, therefore he expected excellence. In fact, he demanded it.

"Get that door open," Nero said to Bak-Irp. He'd given him Shark's combat pistol.

The Thassian tried the handle. It didn't budge.

"Locked," Bak-Irp said.

"I need to talk to the pilots before they do something stupid. Blast the lock."

Lemora put her hand on Bak's upper arm. "Be careful. We can't penetrate the hull."

"He's not shooting at the hull," Nero said.

"If the bullet goes through the door, it might hit the nose of the ship or pierce a monitor." Lemora was one of the few people whose council Nero heeded. "It's a matter of picking angles."

Nero nodded. Then to the Thassian he said, "Choose a good angle. Now punch the lock."

The former bounty hunter turned bodyguard pressed the gun barrel against the edge of the door beside the handle and pressed the trigger. The blast was loud. There was little reaction from the crowd behind them. The humans were too engrossed in fighting for their lives. But Nero was certain that Bak's bang had captured the pilots' attention. He wasn't worried about them communicating with XSecPen or any Galactic Coalition forces in the area. The director of the Coalition Corrections Office had ordered the flight to follow a strict comms blackout. No channel was considered safe enough, and any intercepted calls would not only let potential eavesdroppers know the status of the transport, but they were also traceable and could give away the ship's position. A precautionary pre-flight scan of the moon's airspace revealed the presence of signal feelers. These feelers combed frequencies, sifting noise for pieces of information. Nero knew about the feelers because he'd ordered them. He needed this flight to maintain silence, and he paid to keep it that way.

Bak-Irp turned the handle, but it only moved a little. He slammed his shoulder into the door, and the hatchway burst open. On the bridge of the ship, two pilots were flying. A third crew member, the navigator, partly dressed in body armor, stood at the open gun locker, pointing a short-barrel shotgun at them. He was trembling. A box of tactical shells lay open and spilled out on a shelf. Several of the purple-colored cartridges rolled around on the floor.

Bak-Irp shot him at the top of his unfastened vest.

The navigator fell into the locker, scattering more ammo,

leaving a bloody streak on the locker's door before slumping against the wall, dead.

The Thassian turned his pistol on the pilots.

"Whoa!" yelled the taller of the two aviators, a cowboy with gray hair at his temples and a Stetson hanging on a wall hook above his suede fringed coat. "Don't kill me. I got kids."

Nero's team crammed onto the Tri-T's flight deck, minus the Belgian who'd never made it to the front of the passenger compartment. The South American clones, Matias and Mateo, closed the door and put their hulking backs up against it to prevent anyone from coming in. The pair thought of each other as brothers. They were both huge, a pair of identical bodybuilders whose only outward difference was that Mateo shaved his head and Matias sported a mohawk dyed tropical red, yellow, and blue, like a macaw.

The glow of the instruments stained the pilots' faces a ghoulish green. Like the rest of the Deathcan, the cockpit was outdated. Nero hadn't been inside such a vintage vehicle since his boyhood. He was accustomed to the latest cutting-edge technology, the cleanest and most intuitive controls. Before him was an array of archaic dials, switches, and buttons cluttering every surface of the instrument panel. Low-res monitors mimicked a windshield. He felt like a space battle reenactor, cosplaying the final gasp of the Corporate Rebellion at Titan.

Bak-Irp put his gun to the second pilot's skull, flipping aside her curly, red ponytail, and nudging her head forward. "How 'bout her? Does she have kids?" he asked the cowboy.

"No, sir," the cowboy said.

"Yes, I do! The captain's lying. And he doesn't give a damn about his kids," she said. In profile, her face looked like an advertisement for vacationing on a West Coast of Ireland simulation module. Even in the bad light, her angular cheekbones and creamy, sea-kissed skin were undeniable, as was the hard crystal green of her eyes. "All he does is complain about how lazy they are and how much they cost. They're adults, too! I'm a mom. My kids are still in school. If you're going to shoot one of us, shoot Buck. He's a gobshite from start to finish." Having a gun to her head was like truth serum. Fear focused the mind and loosened the tongue. Nero thought the world would be more real if everyone had a gun pointed at them.

"Oh, Dierdre, you're so full of it," Captain Buck said. "Your kids are robots!"

"But they're still mine!"

Nero stepped up. "Captain Buck. Dierdre. Believe me when I say that I hate all children, and whether you have them isn't going to stop us from hurting you."

The two pilots swallowed and watched him in their rearview cameras.

Captain Buck spoke first, "They're parasites, sir. My whelps never utter a kind word."

"You're the parasite, Buck," Dierdre said. "I do all the flying. His controls are set on auto. Check 'em." The co-pilot scoffed, turning up her chin. Her freckles were like pepper flakes.

"Is that true, Captain Buck?" Nero asked. "Don't lie to me. If you do, I'll know it."

Bak-Irp shifted the pistol toward the cowboy.

Sweat soaked the back of Buck's shirt. The tip of his tongue appeared under the awning of his walrus mustache to lick his lips. "I cannot lie, sir. Being a good pilot is knowing when to fly and when to sit back and let the AI hivepilot take over. I've ridden in a lot of rodeos. As my time soaring the heavens nears its end, I'd rather mosey into the sunset than gallop."

Dierdre rolled her eyes.

"Listen, you two." Nero grasped the pilots. He was running out of patience, and their bickering felt petty. "Nobody has to die… if you obey my orders."

The flyers were quick to commit themselves to doing whatever Nero asked of them. They weren't military but freelance contractors that Coalitions Corrections hired out to bus prisoners. The dead navigator showed them what would happen if they resisted.

"Great." Nero removed a slip of paper from his jumpsuit. "Take us to these coordinates."

Captain Buck snatched the paper and read the numbers.

"Here, Dierdre." He passed the coordinates to his co-pilot. "You heard the man. Git to it."

"You're a genuine arsehole," she said, fuming.

"Now, be polite. We have guests." Captain Buck bristled. Dierdre's manicured nails punched in the numbers. Her mapping screens started blinking red.

"Sir…?"

"What is it?" Buck asked.

"Not you." Dierdre looked over her shoulder at Nero. "That area is prohibited. Looks like the Coalition hung a Shoot-on-Sight restriction over PK-L7. That means they've got the planet ringed with robot sentries and remote-controlled drone patrols. They might even have an active surveillance protocol in place. Ships with actual living operators. We can't fly in there without drawing the kind of attention nobody wants. Worse than a no-go, it's suicidal."

"Don't worry about that, Captain Dierdre," Nero said. "I've got it covered."

"She's not a captain," Buck said.

"Shut the hell up, Buck," Nero said. "Or Dierdre will be flying solo. Got it, pardner?"

Buck's Adam's apple bobbed inside his collar, and his suntan turned a jaundiced yellow.

"Yessir. Will do."

Nero saw Dierdre was smiling. He allowed her to enjoy the moment. It was essential that he had one capable pilot, preferably as cool as cucumber. He planned on keeping them both alive for now, though he found himself preferring Dierdre's style. Buck was too folksy for his tastes, and she seemed more capable and less fussy. Nero cherished competence. After they touched down on PK-L7, Nero would reassess and do whatever was necessary to stay alive.

The Tri-T shuddered and dipped into a momentary freefall. Warning lights winked; buzzers and bells rang out. Everyone on the flight deck grabbed on to something for balance.

"What is it?" Lemora asked.

Dierdre consulted her screens, flipping switches and taking readings. "Part of our avionics is just banjaxed. We've got a depressurization alert in the main cabin. I'll silence the alarms and do a manual override, but this old bucket is in bad shape unless we stabilize, pronto."

"Tell it to me like I'm dumb." Nero could make no sense of the archaic displays.

Dierdre sighed and said, "They're shooting back there. And they're hitting vital stuff. It's brutal. This ship flies on luck and prayers as it is. We might go down if it doesn't stop."

Nero pointed at the hitmen.

"Matias and Mateo, arm yourselves from the gun locker. Take out whoever's putting holes in my ship. Be precise. Bullets are for soft bodies. Understand me?"

The clones nodded. They picked up shorty shotguns, loading them with tactical shells from the half-empty box on the shelf and the spillage strewn on the floor.

Nero turned back to the pilots. "Are there any more weapons on board?"

Deadpan, Buck said nothing. Dierdre hesitated but looked less sure, until Bak-Irp nudged her shoulder with his weapon, successfully convincing her to cooperate.

"See that security hatch in the floor?" Dierdre said. "It leads to the avionics bay. In there, you'll see batteries, a mini toolbox, and computers. Pass through the bay to the next hatchway. Through the hatch is the cargo hold, underneath the passengers. You'll find a small on-board armory and a stowage bin for larger tools. The keypad code is COFFIN8TED. I don't know if it's been restocked. If there are more weapons on this ship, that's where you'll find them. I don't check on guns preflight. That's the prison's job."

"Thank you, Dierdre," Nero said. "You keep us on course. We'll handle the rest."

"Can do, boss," she said.

You see, Nero thought, *if you act like you're in charge of things, pretty soon you are.*

CHAPTER ELEVEN
Mind Parasite

Screw it, Shawna said to herself, *I've got to take charge here or we're all going to die.* She'd made it up to the front of the cabin. Nero's crew had forced its way into the cockpit. His game plan *was* to commit a hijacking. She watched Bak-Irp use a pistol to blow apart the door bolt. Shawna was afraid that if she knocked on the door now, Bak-Irp would shoot her before she had a chance to talk. For the time being, she found herself stuck in the "death" part of the Deathcan.

The human guards were out of their seats now, shaken from their paralysis by the aliens who were intent upon either eating them or ripping them to shreds for giggles. The problem was that the guards were disorganized, and in their current state of full-blown panic, several of them had responded by shooting at anything that moved.

One particularly trigger-happy sergeant unslung a light machine gun from around his neck and gleefully used it to mow down a row of prisoners, only one of whom was a zombified alien. The machine gunner then emptied the rest of his magazine above a second group of tangled bodies,

Swiss cheesing a third of the ship's hull. It didn't matter that the group consisted mostly of humans.

Shawna knew that all those bullets hadn't penetrated the outer layer of the hull. If they had, then the passengers would've been exposed to the vacuum of space, and their bodies now would be in various stages of boiling, expanding, and vaporizing. No bueno. Tri-Ts were outfitted with a standard self-healing semi-liquid "skin" between the hull layers which plugged holes – but only minor punctures. The skin wasn't designed to deal with catastrophic mass penetrations. It was a stopgap measure designed to help a battered ship get home. It didn't perform resurrections. She had to put a halt to the reckless firing. *Good luck with that.* When someone's about to be eaten, they don't listen to reason. "Don't shoot at the hull!" Shawna yelled. "Choose your targets. Not the damned walls!" Giving orders helped to calm her. It mimicked being in control, which she knew she wasn't. She felt like an island with a boiling sea of chaos surrounding her.

It was impossible to tell if any of the shooters were going to follow her suggestion. The aliens were proving hard to kill and impervious to pain. They'd gone berserk after the bomb, and their only purpose was a powerful, unstoppable drive to attack, attack, attack.

The machine-gunning sergeant was reloading.

Shawna knew that XSecPen didn't issue knives to their guards. But she also knew that many guards carried knives they bought on their own, tactical blades that could also be used for self-defense in a jam. Most guards secreted the knives in their boots. Shawna went on a search for a blade tucked into the boot of a dead guard. The first two came up empty; the second guard didn't even have feet. But the third dead guard was the charm. "Bingo," Shawna said, springing open the blade. Its grip fit well into her hand.

Time to go to work.

As a fighter pilot, Shawna didn't have extensive hand-to-hand combat experience. She'd pick a dogfight over face-to-face warfare any day. Fortunately, she liked to mix it up for fun. To keep in shape when she wasn't in a cockpit, she filled her idle hours with various martial arts and close quarters self-defense training classes from Muay Thai kickboxing and Judo to Thassian Ubak-Ko grappling. Her skills might be rusty, but they were there. Admittedly, her reflexes weren't what they were ten years ago, but the scars of thirty years proved her toughness. Getting punched in the mouth wasn't about to knock her off her game. She had another advantage: Shawna had nothing to lose.

Nothing to lose but her life, that is. Without honor, living wasn't worth much, not to her. That made Shawna a dangerous force to reckon with, as the aliens were soon to find out.

Shawna took a reverse grip on the knife, holding the edge out to slash her alien attackers.

Killing *all* the zombies seemed overly optimistic. What she wanted to do was decrease their numbers enough so that the remaining humans might have a fighting chance. They'd deal with Nero and his gang later.

First objective: don't die.

Second objective: kill the infected.

Third objective: don't die.

They might be able to corral the bomb-crazed aliens into the rear of the ship and build a barricade. Or they could dump them down in the cargo hold. Shawna found a shotgun lying on the floor. She stuck the pistol in her pocket. The aliens didn't seem interested in using weapons, meaning that they weren't a risk to the hull of the ship. They were content with thrashing, biting, and ripping their way through the human population. It was working, too.

They were winning. Nero's dirty trick had done its job. The surprise brute force assault took the guards completely out of the equation. He and his gang were free to move about the cabin and commandeer the ship. No one was going to do anything to stop them. So what if he sacrificed his fellow HT comrades to achieve his goal? It was the price he'd pay for freedom. He had no loyalty except to himself. The arms mogul had a well-known reputation for forming highly negotiable relationships and making sure that he came out on top of every deal. He bragged about what a snake he was. Shawna wouldn't have trusted his conniving ass as far as she could throw–

An alien leaped at her from between two rows of seats.

She gripped its outstretched arm, and using the creature's momentum, tossed it into the aisle. Before the alien could fully recover, she slashed the back of its neck, exposing its spine. The zombie displayed no signs of feeling any pain. It spun around, crouched on all fours, preparing to launch itself again. She didn't know where this species came from. The galaxy held more types of creatures than could be catalogued, not to mention all the hybrids, cyborgs, and genetic experiments that the Guilds used as laborers in their factories and resource extraction operations.

This one had a head shaped like an earth alligator, and a grinning snout full of conical, yellow teeth. Unlike an alligator, purple tendrils sprouted from the back of its skull. A pair of vertically slit pupils encased in crystal-clear green eyes stared at Shawna with cold, mechanical ferocity. Primarily bipedal, the thing's front limbs were truncated, and it wore a sleeveless guard uniform; each arm ended in a scaly, three-fingered hand and a trio of nasty-looking, hooked talons. It wore no Coalition-issued standard helmet, which told her that its skull bones were too thick to pierce with her short knife. She lunged forward and took a swipe at its nose. Her blade came back wet.

Snorting blood, the alien pawed at its injury. Not out of pain, but to wipe away the blood.

To breathe.

They may be transformed into murderous automatons, devoid of feelings and thoughts, but they aren't dead, Shawna thought. Whatever was in that bomb altered their minds. But their bodies still worked like machines or robots. Like zombies out of a cheap splatter vid. If you inflicted enough damage or took out the brain – the main control system – they'd fail to function.

If it has no eyes, it can't see me.

On her second dive inside she removed the right eye. The alien opened its jaws to crush her torso, but, instead, it got a mouthful of headrest that Shawna pulled loose from the closest seat and stuffed into its maw, wedging it deep. Talons tore at the headrest, finally dislodging it.

"GRAAAVVVVPTHHH..." the thing growled at her, spitting blood and snot.

Here it comes. It's going to bull rush me.

The zombie alien launched.

Shawna hopped up on the armrests of the aisle seats, her legs split wide.

The surprised alien hit her around the ankles and went

sprawling, clutching at, and missing her legs, with its short arms. She dropped onto its back, twisting around to plunge her knife into the first cut she'd made. Inserting the blade, wiggling it side-to-side, she heard a juicy squelching and then a pop. She'd severed its spinal column.

The alien continued to growl, but it couldn't get up. It lay there drooling.

"One zombie alien gator down," Shawna said, stepping on its head and walking over it.

A flourish and a cry off to her right side, in her peripheral vision, drew her attention.

"Aidez-moi! S'il vous plaît! Hey, you there, help me!" a voice said.

Valmont. The Belgian hacker, and cyber extortionist, was doing his best to hold off Ishnik, using her breather tank as a shield. He looked paler, feebler than normal. An unraveling makeshift bandage trailed from his wrist; his wounded left arm dangled uselessly at his side, dripping crimson from the fingertips. His jumpsuit bore a similar stain. That explained a lot. Massive blood loss was a bummer. Shawna was surprised Ishnik hadn't been able to dispatch him. On his best day, Valmont needed an alias and keyboard to hide behind. He was no real-world warrior. But then she saw that Ishnik was struggling, too, beating at the tank with lethargic, poorly aimed overhand chops. Although the zombified Fushnallan no longer needed her supply of atmospheric fluid to function, the loss of it depleted her severely. She moved in syrupy slow motion, as if she'd been heavily drugged. Shawna figured that if Ishnik went for long enough without her tank, her body would become immobilized, a raging lump of zombified meat unable to muster the energy necessary to pose a threat. *Good to know.* She tucked the knowledge away.

"Get this screw off me," Valmont cried.

"Why should I?" Shawna said.

"For the sake of humanity!"

"You look like you're doing fine there, buddy."

"I am not fine!"

"Sure, you are. You've got the makings of a nice little draw. Uh-oh, get your shield up."

Ishnik reached over the breather and grabbed a fistful of the hacker's oily combover.

"Ahh!" Valmont shrieked. "She ensnares me in her clutches... stealing my dignity!"

Shawna winced, watching as Ishnik latched on, curling strands of Valmont's limp hair between her fingers. With a twist, the zombified guard uprooted patches of the hacker's scalp. He cried, shoving the hollow tank against her chest. Pushing her away only caused her to yank harder. "Vicious, insufferable bitches..." he muttered under his breath. "I am besieged..."

Shawna wasn't predisposed to rescuing Valmont. His insults didn't change her mind.

Ishnik's mouth hung open, gulping. A sour milky cloudiness had crept into her eyes. Part dead, part alive. That was how she looked. It made Shawna feel bad, seeing a fellow vet reduced to this low state, and acting savagely against her own will, a tool in the hand of a mind parasite.

Shawna didn't want to kill her, but she'd put her down if it came to that. No question.

It was a tough situation. Prison turned people hard and cynical. Everything, everyone became a threat. In a world full of villains, who could you trust? Who's going to watch your back? Even the most independent con needed friends to survive in this place. Who would be a friend now?

Not Valmont. He wasn't friend material. He was a gross, treacherous dog who followed the pack. Shawna decided she had no dog in this race. Higher priorities needed addressing first.

"You got her right where you want her. I'll check back later," she said.

"Nooo!" Valmont moaned.

She left him to fend for himself, uncertain who she was rooting for, or if she cared.

CHAPTER TWELVE
Pitstop

Above them in the passenger compartment havoc was breaking loose. Lemora wondered how long it would take for the zombified aliens to kill all the humans. She estimated a quarter of an hour. Tops. Then the zombies would come looking for them. They would attack the cockpit.

"We need to think about how we're going to keep the zombies out," she said.

Nero, who had joined her in the excursion to the armory, was unconcerned.

"Soon enough we'll be setting down on PK-L7," he said. "This ship won't matter."

They passed through the avionics bay accompanied by the hum of the Tri-T's brain center. The air below the main deck imparted an unpleasant flavor of artificiality. The illumination was poor; drab, blue-gray tones more befitting a sepulcher. Feathery dust smothered the bulkhead-mounted lights, a third of which had gone dark as a result of the shooting.

Stepping through the hatchway, the passage opened to reveal the cargo hold: a wider, murkier space that offered no relief. Finding the armory was easy. It was a caged-off freestanding vault at the midpoint of the hold. The word ARMORY was stenciled in red across its doors. A myriad of soldiers, who had utilized the walk-in unit over the years, scratched into the gunmetal paint their initials and other cryptic graffiti. *GRABBA GUN 'N GRAB ME SUM FUN!* read a large, blocky message. Further examples followed: AMMO = MI AMOR. UNLOAD, RELOAD, REPEAT... and so on. An author self-named "Sniperpsychoranger" had drawn a realistic doodle of their rifle. Below the image they wrote, "But to die once is not enough. – Virgil." Lemora figured it must be a misquote. Either way, it troubled her.

"What's waiting for us on PK-L7?" she asked. "Please tell me you've got it worked out."

Nero punched COFFIN8TED into the keypad, and the cage door swung open.

"I've got it worked out," he said absently. "It's a cinch. Stone-cold lock. Guaranteed."

Nero never shared his whole plans with anyone. It was a power trip thing that annoyed Lemora, but she'd learned to live with it. Her boss was high maintenance. His tough exterior was a put-on; his ego was easily injured, and he could be petty and spiteful over the most trivial matters. But he was a proven winner who she trusted to play as hard as she did. So, she handled him like a bomb: a thing powerful and glorious to behold but only if he didn't go off by accident.

He ventured inside the armory, picking up weapons, unzipping his jumpsuit to stuff handguns into the waistband of his underwear, hanging two machine guns and a heavy shotgun over his shoulders. Belts of ammunition crisscrossed his chest. "Not the best cache I've ever seen, but it'll do. After we get back to the cockpit, I'll send Bak-Irp to haul out as much as he can carry. I should've had Mateo and Matias pay a visit. They can gear up with him, later."

"If there is a later," Lemora said.

"Since when are you a pessimist?" Nero cocked a quizzical eyebrow at her.

"I'm not. I calculate the odds. Odds are we don't all make it to our final destination."

"So, Mateo and Matias are the goners of our group?" He pressed his eye to the scope of a laser sniper rifle; laying it aside for a moment, he searched the armory for energy cells. Without a charged cell the energy weapons were useless, unless you employed them as clubs. After discovering that the cells on hand were drained, he returned the long-range gun. "Just like that, huh? The M&M killer clone crew get written out of the program?"

"Well, I won't be dying," Lemora said firmly. "Or you. But somebody's going to."

"Love you, Lem, but everybody dies," Nero said, smiling. "That's life."

"Who knows?" Lemora shrugged. "With enough money and tech, one might live forever. Your father gave it a shot."

"Yeah," he said softly, rummaging through a trunk filled with body armor. Never big on playing defense, he tossed the equipment aside, which didn't surprise her. He clapped the dust from his hands and opened another cabinet. "Remind me, how far did my old man get?"

She let the topic drop. They never discussed the hit on Baron Nero Lupaster III. More machine than man by the time he checked out of this world, the head of the Lupaster clan had steadily upgraded his human parts with robotic improvements, becoming a full-blown cyborg by the time that a bomb, cleverly hidden in his recent hip replacement, exploded – sending pieces of the baron flying, and shattering all the glass panes throughout his vast greenhouse (where he'd been tending his collection of rare Malaysian Gold of Kinabalu orchids). Lemora wasn't involved in his death. Nero IV promptly executed the surgeon who'd performed the hip operation, although rumors swirled that she'd been paid to implant the device per his personal instructions. Anyway, she wasn't around to take questions.

Along the far wall of the armory, Lemora spied a line of motionless humanoid forms lurking in the dimness. She startled – only after cautiously drawing closer did she relax, chuckling at her own paranoia. What at first glance appeared to be a line of rotting, decapitated corpses hanging on meat hooks, upon closer inspection were a dozen Galactic Defense Forces surplus spacesuits. A row of helmets rested on shelves above the suits. Lemora picked one up, wiping off the accumulated grit of long-term storage. The headgear appeared shiny and new beneath the locker grime, not a scratch on it. She inspected the matching suits and boots, discovering they were the same, never worn; fashioned out of institutional navy-blue material, stiff and bulky off the rack, the uniforms earned no style points, but they were functional. Each item bore the Coalition Corrections Department insignia – a rock and hammer-pick circumscribed in a bubble. A pyramid rode atop the bubble; floating above its peak was an all-seeing, radiant, magisterial eye. The Coalition is always watching you! Lemora laughed. *Fools.*

In the corner beside the suits, she spotted the tool bin Dierdre had mentioned. The lid swung upward, puffing out more dust. A curved shape lay tucked inside, under a canvas. She uncovered the curiosity, letting out an involuntary squeal:

a triple-bladed circular saw! *Yowza*. Kolbanian diamond-dust-coated blades. Lemora touched her finger to a glinting sawtooth and a drop of blood ballooned. She never felt the cut. Sticking her finger in her mouth, she tasted salty copper. This gadget would slice through anything. "You didn't answer my question, Nero. What's on PK-L7? If I'm right, it'll be more zombies – Xenos – who've been left to their own devices for a couple centuries."

"Maybe they're extinct. Did you consider that? I mean, who's been cooking dinner for the zombies? Maybe they starved, and the place is a cemetery full of Xeno skeletons."

"They eat rocks," she said.

"No shit." Nero paused, a look of genuine shock on his face. He didn't usually bother with boring granular details. He prided himself on being a visionary, a big picture thinker.

"No shit? Listen, it's a mystery what they've been up to. Evolutionary situations are remarkably fluid. Failures often lead to startling success. They might be thriving or… altered."

"Frankly, I don't care about stinking Xenos. PK-L7 is going to be a shuttle terminal for us. A dirty, out-of-the-way transfer station. We'll be in and out. We're not staying to build a colony. It's a layover. Worst thing that might happen is we'll get bored, and it'll smell bad." He used a heavy cutter machete to pry open a crate, giving a loud whistle after he revealed the contents. "Oolala… we've got grenades and choke-gas canisters." He dumped emergency med kits out of a duffle, refilling the bag with munitions.

"Layover?" Lemora said, incredulous. It sounded a lot more complicated than that.

"We'll barely have time to whiz and stretch our legs before we're off again."

"You have another ship waiting?"

"Not exactly."

Lemora lifted the giant saw. *They must use this sucker to crack open tanks and crashed ships.* It might come in handy. She wished it wasn't so heavy. She was going to need a back massage after lugging it around. The rest of the tools weren't going to be of any use. She shut the bin and set the saw on top of it. "Nero, stop for a sec. You haven't clued me in on anything past taking control of this transport. I need to know more. What *exactly* is the plan? Sketch it for me."

Nero frowned. Then he nodded. "I guess I owe you that. No problem. Here's the plan, all right? We land this hunk of junk rockhopper on PK-L7, then fire off a transmission to Neera."

Lemora's stomach sank at the mention of Nero's twin sister's name. Her nerves jangled.

"Please don't tell me you're depending on Neera to save us."

Nero bristled. "Why shouldn't I depend on her? She *is* my sister."

"I don't trust her. *You* don't trust her. You've told me so a million times. I happen to think you're right. She's got a real attitude problem. Her immaturity is always an issue. It's not outside the realm of possibility she likes you being locked up. No big bro around to bother her."

Nero pointed at Lemora. "I won't have you slander my blood. Take it back."

"You're the one who told me she wants to play the big boss. Her story's always been the same. Your father played favorites. He put her down because she wasn't a son, just a silly girl. Since you've been out of circulation, she's been running your operations at the Arms Guild. Maybe she likes the view from the mountaintop. And she doesn't want to share her toys."

"If what you're saying is true, then she doesn't have to lift a finger. Just let me rot in jail. She could've said no when I asked for help. Hell, if I were her, I'd let me die, that's for sure."

Lemora had no comeback. Nero possessed a gift for honesty without self-reflection.

"I'm not saying she's out to get you. But I'm worried that we're relying solely on her. Her record for follow-through isn't stellar. She can't be counted on when she's needed most."

Nero considered her point. "I won't argue with you there, doc. Neera's always been an unholy mess on wheels with flaming jetpacks attached. I think she can handle this. My gut tells me she's really grown up a lot. We must give people the chance to surprise us."

Lemora didn't doubt that surprises were coming. But *good* surprises? All she could think about was Neera's living cybernetic tattoos, the ornate bio-ink creatures that danced and writhed around on her skin. Some of them made noises – awful noises. Neera lived to provoke people.

Nero might've killed his father literally, but Neera had been slowly murdering him for years, eating his insides up with anxiety and disappointment. She was an embarrassment to the Butcher of the Quadrants. Nero III railed against his female offspring's public behavior, her getting thrown out of every private space academy he bought her way into. Her boyfriends were an odd assortment of eggheads and miscreants. On the sly, Nero III directed a fair number to be "vanished" into blackholes or encounter unexplained mishaps. The poor kid thought she was unlucky. When she got older, her antics quieted down, or she kept them better hidden. Nero III's death brought her back on the scene. She came looking for her inheritance.

But the Lupasters never did anything the easy way. In order to receive her slice of the pie, the baron's will stated that she must work for the Guild for five years, showing up every day and facing regular council oversight. Next month would be her last review. She'd done well. Her eye for detail surpassed Nero's, and she had daddy's instinct for the jugular. While Nero was a mad dreamer, Neera relished the mayhem of a bloody fight. Soon she'd be free to claim her share and leave to pursue her heart's desires, no strings attached. That was, if she chose to leave.

Neera was something Lemora abhorred – she was unpredictable. A wildcard. Lemora didn't want to see that wildcard deciding to abandon them on a zombified planet.

"Whoa! You've got to see this!" Nero hefted a thick-nozzled weapon covered with metal tubes and piping; it had a lift handle on the top and a grip mounted on the back with a trigger.

"Is that what I think it is?" she asked.

"Flamethrower, hell yeah!" Nero pretended to torch the armory.

Rich men and their childish playthings. But there was no denying the tickle Lemora felt in her belly, wanting to see a geyser of peach flames boiling out of the end of the flamethrower like an angry dragon's breath. Imagine wielding fiery destruction with the touch of a fingertip!

"Are there fuel canisters?" she said in a husky voice.

Nero stuck his head inside the cabinet where he'd found the weapon.

"A whole box, seals intact."

"Excellent." Lemora swore the temperature in the armory was rising. She was sweaty with excitement at the prospect of portable infernos, of flaming bodies fleeing in defeat.

"We can use this," she said. "In the passenger cabin, I mean. Right now. Burning at these relatively low temperatures won't compromise the hull's integrity. It isn't hot enough. But flesh and bone? *Puhh-leez.* Zombies can't withstand fire. We might be able to control them with it. Every creature is afraid of fire."

"I love it," Nero said. "Let's have a barbecue. Zombie burgers or hot wings?"

"We mustn't be reckless, darling. There are parts of this ship that are flammable, too."

"Who cares? We'll put the fires out after we fry them all. Hell, we can roast the human guards that are still alive. It's too damn perfect. Help me with this box of canisters. We'll lug it back to the cockpit." Nero passed the flamethrower to Lemora. It was surprisingly lighter than it looked, and far easier to carry than the triple-bladed saw. But they might need both items.

"Hold on," she said. "I want to check something."

Lemora left the armory cage. Walking to the rear of the cargo hold, she brought out an emergency glowstick she'd taken from the avionics toolbox. She cracked it, aiming the green light at the ceiling. "Just as I suspected." Then she called out to Nero, "Come here, bring the flamethrower and a fuel canister. I have an idea I think you're going to like."

She'd found a hatchway like the one in the cockpit. It was a service access to the passenger cabin directly above. She climbed a utility ladder attached to the wall. Reaching overhead, she tested the hatch's handle, trying to lever it open. But the handle didn't budge.

Damn it!

Then she spotted a small slider under the handle. She

thumbed it to the opposite side. This time when she pulled on the lever it squeaked, but it moved. The hatch popped up.

PRESTO! She opened it for a quick peek, her pulse racing before she got a glimpse.

CHAPTER THIRTEEN
The Snap of Crackling Fires

Shawna's attention turned from the hitman clones, who had emerged from the cockpit firing a pair of pistol-grip shotguns, to the trigger-happy human guard – now screaming – engulfed in a cape of flames. At least he'd stopped shooting. But where had the fire suddenly come from?

The guard flapped his arms like a phoenix trying to fly. Instead of rising from the ashes, he melted seats and banged into walls. Still, the zombie aliens rushed him, only backing off after they registered the extreme heat he was giving off. They snarled as he bubbled and cooked. Mercifully, he toppled over, crispy but unconscious, while they huddled around as if he were a cozy bonfire. The only thing missing was marshmallows. Shawna thought she might barf.

Smoke filled the cabin. She was coughing. All the humans were. She looked for an extinguisher and found one mounted at the midpoint of the fuselage. Pocketing her gun, she unhooked the extinguisher and used it to foam the charred corpse on the floor, cutting down the flames, but the smoke persisted – a haze that tasted like melting plastic and burned meat.

The aliens, who'd been entranced by the conflagration, shifted their focus to her. She blasted them in the face with the dregs of the fire retardant, hoping the chemicals might blind them, but all it did was make them madder; exasperated, she threw the empty extinguisher at them. The closest alien batted it away. She was standing in the gap behind the prisoner seating section, alone with a half-dozen zombies. Everyone else had fled to the front. Mateo and Matias pumped shells into the crowd. They knew better than to shoot at the hull; they were marksmen, contract killers who'd learned efficiency in their craft, and this was just another job for them – two exterminators spraying for pests. *Squirt, squirt.*

Shawna pulled the pistol from her pocket, aimed at the alien standing in front of her and pulled the trigger. The gun clicked. No bullets. The advancing aliens formed a phalanx. It was too late to run around them. They had her trapped.

"Oh shit." Shawna tossed the weapon aside.

The only thing she had left was her knife, and that literally wasn't going to cut it.

WHOOOOOOSHHH...

A funnel of red-orange-yellow heat rushed from the floor behind the alien cluster. The fireball hit them, and they took off. The nearest one knocked her flat on her ass. But that wasn't necessarily bad. Because if she had remained upright, she would've been breathing flames.

The alien darted to the back, leaving a trail of teal blood droplets. Shawna glanced at her blade, saw bluish alien fluids smeared to the hilt. Alert to the threat of fire, the zombie searched for a place of safety. There was none. It turned to fight. That was when she noticed the deep gash across its throat. She'd gotten off a good swipe. The creature pawed at the wound, staring at its azure-stained fingers. Outraged, it roared, quickening the flow.

Shawna never got the chance to watch it bleed out.

A hatch in the floor popped, and Nero rose out of the hole, armed with a flamethrower.

He was laughing as he torched the throat-cut zombie.

She didn't know whether to thank him or to run away. That's not true. She knew.

She ran. Ducking under the top of the blistered and fusing seats, she hoped that the smoke, which had grown into a thick noxious cloud in the upper portion of the cabin, would provide cover. Maybe Nero would choose not to kill her. Maybe he was hunting zombies.

Fat chance.

A giant tongue of fire licked the headrests, adding to the toxic fumes.

"Die, assholes! Die!"

He cackled and pulled the trigger again, broiling the inside of the ship. Blackened panels dropped from the ceiling. Light fixtures burst, casting the cabin's interior into a bizarre nightmarish half-light of surreal, polychromatic flames. It was almost pretty.

Is Nero insane? She'd never considered that question before. Shawna had assumed he was simply a megalomaniacal jerk. The galaxy was full of sociopathic narcissists these days. But why else would he set fire to the only thing protecting him from the vacuum of space?

The flames stopped abruptly, and she heard the voice of someone unseen talking to Nero. Dr Lemora Pick. She must've been thinking along the same lines. Pitching a hot sizzle on a few of your enemies was a lively time, to be sure, but if the blaze spread out of control…

Shawna held her breath, lifting her head to peek between the smoldering cushions; she saw the doctor quickly dragging Nero back into what must be the belly cargo hold. *Of course!*

They'd found the armory below. The storage compartment ran underneath her feet, and it must have access to the cockpit. Nero retreated reluctantly, with Lemora tugging him by the arm.

"Buddy, we gotta go," she told her boss over the snap of crackling fires.

The hatch slammed shut.

Shawna raced to the trapdoor. As much as her brain shouted for her to stop, she had to follow them. She had no illusions of joining their gang or persuading them to let her tag along. But the chances of living were a lot worse in the cabin than they would be in the cockpit. The truth was she had no plan. But staying in the cabin meant dying by fire, by shotgun, or by tooth and claw. Maybe her chances were no better at the nose of the ship in the company of a crazed, egomaniacal tyrant and his band of hired killers. But she had to find out.

She opened the hatch – *screech* – and climbed into the dark hole.

CHAPTER FOURTEEN
Minor Talent

"Did you hear that?" Lemora asked.

"Hear what?" Nero cocked his head, listening for a sec. "I don't hear anything."

"I think someone, or something, crawled down the hatch after us. Did you lock it?"

Nero stepped over the threshold, entering the avionics bay. She was right behind him. Both hijackers were loaded down with weaponry. Still, she was sticking close to her comrade.

He said, "I didn't even know the hatch had a lock. You rushed me out of there. And I was having some fun." The hum of the electronics and cooling fans buzzing softly surrounded them.

"As a rule, you shouldn't set fire to any space vehicle you're traveling in." She tried not to sound too sarcastic as she kept looking backward, hunting for the source of the disturbance she was certain she'd detected. A stealthy zombie? Did such creatures exist? Or were they clumsy oafs bent on destruction? They didn't look particularly hampered by their zombification.

Nero was still complaining. "You're the one who told me to do it. You said flames were better than bullets. Then you're shutting me down before I get my mojo working properly."

"All things in moderation, Nero. You know that nobody loves a conflagration more than I do. But we must be prudent." She patted him on the back. "You did a fine job. In this case, less is more. The ship isn't entirely fireproof. Take these computers, we wouldn't want them to burn."

"You're a hypocrite, Lemmy. Moderation? Give me a break. You going soft on me?"

"Never, darling."

"Lock that door if you're so worried about what's behind you," he said, irritated. Nero never was one to look back. Not in business, or in life. His determined forward focus could be an asset, but occasionally an unresolved issue he'd forgotten about snuck up and bit him in the ass. Lemora knew this, as well as she knew what he would say if she brought up his habit of ignoring the past. *"Tidying up loose ends is below my pay grade. I hire people like you to do it for me."* He had no pay grade. How do you calculate a salary for someone who owns everything?

Lemora kept silent. That was something else Nero paid for: the acquiescence of his subordinates. He wasn't immune from taking counsel, but his advisors had to be wise and pick their spots. Too many disagreements with the boss meant a ticket out of the Guild, or worse. Lemora discovered that the hatch between the bay and the cargo hold had no lock. She informed him.

"Block it then," he said. "But be quick about it. I told you I didn't hear anything."

Lemora looked around the bay for something heavy but movable. The computers and batteries were all in use, and the mini toolbox was too small to prevent someone from pushing through. What if it was a zombie on their trail, one of the big ones? What if it brought friends?

She was carrying the cumbersome triple saw. Although she regretted leaving it behind, Lemora wedged the saw against the bottom of the closed hatchway door. If any zombies tried to barge their way inside the avionics bay, the saw would slide a few centimeters until it butted up against the batteries, which were bolted to the floor. It might not stop them, but it would certainly slow them down. She'd come back later for the saw. Better yet, she'd send one of the muscle boys to retrieve it, Bak-Irp, or Mateo and Matias... if they were alive. They'd need to make another run to the armory for additional weapons and to retrieve the spacesuits. PK-L7 was a hostile environment in more ways than zombifying molds. If they got lucky, the xenium mining outpost would still be standing... and they'd land the Tri-T and drive it up to the station modules.

"Let's go, Lemmy," Nero said. Guns and ammo weighed him down. He was out of breath, sweat-soaked. He'd heaved the flamethrower across his shoulders like a yoke, and his jumpsuit bore scorch marks from where the hot tubing scorched the fabric. But he was so pumped with adrenaline that he wasn't feeling a thing. He walked under the trapdoor and banged on the cockpit hatch with his fist. "Hey, Bak, open sesame. We're back, and we brought treats."

The Thassian jerked the hatchway door free and poked the barrel of his gun in Nero's grinning face. When he recognized his boss, he took it away. "Sorry, I'm checking IDs."

"Is that an example of Thassian humor?" Nero asked.

"Sort of."

"Well, is this ID acceptable?" Nero turned around, modeling his new arsenal.

Bak-Irp offered a helping hand, boosting the former Arms Guild leader off his feet into the cramped nose section of the ailing ship.

Next came Lemora.

"Lock the trapdoor. We may have a stalker following us," she said.

Nero passed a light machine gun to the Thassian. Bak-Irp kneeled and stuck his pale nubby head into the void for a look-see. "An infected?" He swept the barrel around, scanning.

"I didn't have a visual of who it was. I only heard them," Lemora said.

"She's imagining things," Nero said. "Paranoia isn't a bad thing. But it can be annoying."

Bak-Irp dropped the hatch lid, twisting the recessed handle, which sealed off the access.

"With all that racket in the cabin, how'd you hear anything?" Bak-Irp asked Lemora.

"Exactly," Nero said.

Their comments bugged Lemora more than she wanted to admit. She *had* heard the hatch squeaking. Maybe even footsteps. Pissed that she'd reined him in, Nero became oblivious to everything except the next thing he wanted, as usual. His attention zeroed in on one thing at a time, and he gave it one hundred percent plus. But she was used to cleaning up all his messes and couldn't afford to be a single-minded force of nature. Such was the luxury of his being Nero IV.

"What the hell did you two do?" Bak-Irp asked. "I smell smoke."

"A little shake 'n' bake," Nero said, smirking, as he showed off the flamethrower.

"Nice." Bak-Irp admired the weapon. Like all of them, he had a passion for violent tools.

"There's more back there," Nero said. "Once things settle down, we can load up for real."

"Uh, excuse me, gentlemen, but I don't think things are going to settle down," Dierdre said. "These cameras are garbage, and there's a shit-ton of smoke back in the cabin, but it looks like your guys are in trouble." She tapped her monitor. Nero, Bak-Irp, and Lemora leaned in. The image was grainy. Mateo was hammering the butt of his shotgun into the chest of a smoldering zombie. His brother was struggling to reload. Matias shook his head as if he was trying to clear out the cobwebs. He steadied himself against a bulkhead. Infected aliens raged around them.

"Why is Matias's face grayed out?" Nero asked the pilot.

"I believe the effect you see is the result of our limited optics capability and low-res color imaging." If Captain Buck had hopes of regaining a portion of his lost status, he failed miserably.

"It's blood," Dierdre said. "Your guy's got a face full of blood."

"Get them back in here," Nero said to Bak-Irp. "Watch you don't let anyone else inside."

"If they're bit or scratched, don't they get infected?" Bak-Irp asked.

"Humans can't be infected by any transmission route. Aliens are vulnerable to them all."

"Terrific."

"Might I offer an alternative solution regarding the Silvas?" said a velvety voice.

Everyone was startled, surprised to hear from Hans Krait.

He'd managed to make himself invisible; blending into the background was one of his talents. As he tilted in the navigator's chair, putting his feet up on a console, he looked almost serene.

"Hans, what the hell, buddy, I forgot you were present," Nero said.

"Yet here I am."

"What alternative solution are you suggesting concerning the clones?" Lemora asked.

"Leave them out there," Krait said.

"What–?" Bak-Irp objected.

Nero laid a restraining hand on his bodyguard's massive chest.

"Why?" Nero asked, showing a curious expression.

"They are expendable. Good foot soldiers, yes. But foot soldiers, nonetheless. Minor talent." He wiggled the fingers of one elegant hand, as if he were flicking away crumbs.

"They're better fighters than you are," Bak-Irp said. "We need them."

Krait shrugged. "Depends on the kind of fight you're in. Can they reprogram a dormant comms control system? If what I heard you telling the pilot is correct, then we're going to be arriving shortly on a dangerous planet. What resources will you have? A derelict mining station that's been sitting there for a couple hundred years? With *very old* tech and code. How will the shotgun boys help you get things up and running? Are they going to blast apart the computers to reboot them?" Krait steepled his fingers and gazed over the top of the church directly at Nero.

"What does that have to do with fetching Mateo and Matias?" Bak-Irp said.

"He's talking about a risk assessment." Lemora coolly considered his argument.

"Precisely," answered the German smuggler. "I saw Valmont trying to join us. He was your keyboard warrior, wasn't he? Well, he's not here. I am. And I'll do it better. One of the clones out there has had his head split open by a zombie. He's a negative asset. His doppelganger won't be very useful either if he's grieving about his vat-brother's demise."

"What's your final assessment?" Nero pushed Krait to make his point. "Spit it out."

"They're not worth it. You were lucky to get that door closed the first time. They'll provide more value out there dying than they will in here. Allow them to meet their fate."

The cockpit was silent. Swallowing ice-cold facts often left people speechless.

"He's not necessarily wrong," Lemora said. She'd seen the logic of where Krait was going from the start. The clones' importance declined sharply if they couldn't fight well.

"Bullshit." Bak-Irp didn't wait for Nero to make a decision. He unlocked the door and flung it open. "MATEO! MATIAS! GET IN HERE!" He peppered the zombies with a barrage of bullets from the light machine gun, firing it from high over his head, so that any over-penetrating bullets would go down into the belly of the ship. "MOVE YOUR ASSES, MUCHACHOS!"

CHAPTER FIFTEEN
The Black Forever

Despite the stale gloom inside the cargo hold, Shawna could make out enough details to keep from tripping as she navigated her way steadily forward. Hearing distant voices, she slowed her pace, not wanting to surprise Nero and Lemora. Spotting the armory, she made a quick stop-off. They'd left the doors unlocked. Based on the gaps, a few choice weapons were missing – she'd expected as much – but they'd left plenty behind. She picked up a replacement pistol and a light shotgun, loading them quickly, stuffing her pockets with extra shells and ammo boxes. Neither of these guns were ideal for the situation. But the shotgun was the best of the bad options. Shawna stifled a cough. The tangy smell of smoke was strong. After what she'd witnessed upstairs, she had to assume multiple fires were burning.

The Tri-T shuddered, listing hard to port. Shawna braced herself against an armory wall and rode out the turbulence. The ship had suffered damage, but the pilots were in control for now. How long that would last was unpredictable. Punch a new hole in her hull, who knew if the Deathcan would absorb it? It was just as possible she'd go into a tailspin or fold up like an empty MRE packet. The self-healing layer of the Tri-T could handle stray tactical pellets, if not a point-blank blast. The same shell fired into the face of a zombie obliterated its head.

She'd take the tradeoff despite the risks.

Investigating the armory meant that Nero and Lemora had a bigger head start on her. Shawna didn't mind; she preferred it. The last thing she wanted was to eat a hot cone from the end of Nero's flamethrower. Besides, she knew where the two hijackers were going. And it felt good to be out of the passenger cabin melee, even if the relief was short-lived. Not that she had time for a picnic in the cargo pit of darkness. It was scary as hell down here. She wished there was decent light to see whatever might be lurking around the next corner. A smart warrior craved intel. Because intel allowed you to plan. Planning, more often than not, made the difference between killing your enemy and being killed. Nothing was worse than walking into a hostile situation full of unknowns. Shawna liked to know all the facts up front. *Especially* if the news was bad. The only bad news she didn't want to know beforehand involved her own death – she wanted her final chapter to come as a surprise. No warning. Somebody flips your switch, and you dive headlong into the black forever. Worrying didn't make dying easier. It made you stupid.

Rummaging around the armory, Shawna discovered a pair of night vision goggles. When she slipped on the NVGs, her view of the surroundings brightened. The cargo hold took on an eerie, swamp-green tint, but now she could see where she was going and whatever might be coming to get her. Shawna realized she was riding an adrenaline high. Despite the extreme shittiness of her circumstances, she felt fantastic.

There was no rush like combat. After years of confinement, she was out doing something instead of being locked in a grayed-out cell with time and her bad memories for company. A taste of freedom meant a lot. She let herself enjoy it.

That's when somebody started pumping bullets down through the ceiling with a machine gun. Glowing trails slashed her vision. Booms reverberated in the empty hold. Her heart thundered as she dodged around, trying to avoid getting shot. She watched the direction of the gunfire and ran from the armory, heading the other way. Above her, a cacophony of screams mixed with the machine gun chatter. Somebody up there was spraying the floor with lead. Either they had a terrible aim or a reason for the angle that she couldn't fathom. A bullet whizzed past her ear, clipping a blonde curl, nearly ventilating her skull.

"Damn!"

Shawna somersaulted into a corner, making herself as small a target as possible. Too close for comfort. She pressed her spine against the cold skin of the inner hull. Crunched up into a tight ball, staring out into the green-black void, she spotted something: a big, round, fuzzy blur, zooming behind the armory, darting through the heavy barrage raining from above.

Shawna wasn't sure the shape was an alien. But it didn't look human.

Her finger found a toggle on the side of her NVGs. She switched to thermal imaging.

The adrenaline dump made her sweat; her muscles felt like hard rubber balls. She reined in her speeding thoughts. High-stress scenarios played havoc with your senses. If you peered into the shadows long enough, you'd start seeing things –

globular demons bubbling up out of the tarry mire. The dark came alive, and it was always hungry. She concentrated on keeping still.

Shawna stuffed down her jitters and stayed quiet. Breathing through her mouth.

Watching and listening.

Then it happened again.

A yellow-orange-red thermal sphere rushed through the cargo area – like a fiery inflatable beach toy scooting across the hold in a hurricane. It gave off a heat signature – therefore it must be alive. So, human? But the moves were all wrong; they didn't read as human. More like a cloud of sentient gases, which sounded ridiculous as she considered it. The thing bopped behind the armory to… she wasn't sure where… lickety-split, it veered out of sight.

What the hell moved so quickly?

One thing was clear: she wasn't alone. But who – or what – was down here with her?

She quickly ruled out Nero and Lemora.

Humans weren't that compact. Or low to ground. And the motion… it wasn't running as much as skimming along like a greased ball bearing following a track. If the thing had legs, they were pumping too fast for her to detect. The heat signal was a smear of warm colors. Flashing for a sec and then disappearing. It passed so quickly that Shawna almost doubted she'd seen anything at all. Except she was a pilot and knew she saw something out there. She trusted both her eyes and her brain. The next question presented itself: were zombies that fast?

For a moment she wondered if the goggles might be malfunctioning. Equipment failed at the worst of times.

Her squadron had died because Shawna's fighter ship didn't respond to her commands. Instead, it took on a life of its own, gunning down every friendly target in the sky...

She reminded herself not to think about the past. Stick with the now.

How old were these NVGs?

She was about to shed them when the thing jumped up for a third time – hopping and tumbling like an acrobat showing off and having fun doing it – a real circus act.

This time it paused, allowing her to observe it more closely. It stuck to the wall, pinned in an upper corner on her side of the hold, diagonally across from her hiding place. Tucked in a joint where the bulkhead divided the cargo area from the avionics equipment bay on the other side, like a plump arachnoid it sat there, puffing away, its bristly, plump body expanding and contracting. It spread out four sinuous limbs – so, not an arachnoid – fixing itself in place, motionless except for respiration. Then its head began to swivel, panning from side to side like a parabolic antenna, then repeating its back-and-forth methodical sweep. Was it a robot or cyborg?

She'd never come across anything like it. Something about its vibe cried out "organic life form," the result of years of evolution. This entity wasn't concocted in a lab.

Goosebumps prickled Shawna's skin. Like a bucket of ice water dumped over her head, the shock of recognition suddenly hit her. She knew exactly what she was looking at...

Too-ahka.

Of course. She hadn't identified it when it was zooming around in the dark.

Now she recognized the odd, curved shape of its face. Too-ahka was all ears. The creature must use echolocation. That would explain its tiny eyes – it didn't rely on them to see. The alien was probably nocturnal – a night hunter. *Fantastic.* This bizarre species was possibly zombified AND it was stalking her in the dark. Shawna had to get the hell out of there, but she dared not move. Not yet. She didn't think Too-ahka had located her. Careful to move only her eyes, she scanned the room. There was a forward hatch right behind her, three meters to her right, toward the cockpit. That hatch led to the avionics bay. She didn't know if the hatch was open. But if she could get inside and slam the door behind her, she might have a chance–

SCREEEEECH!

Shawna snapped her head to face the far end of the hold. The sound came from the *aft* hatchway – the one she'd climbed down to enter the cargo area from the passenger cabin – it was being lifted and its hinges let out a squeal. Too-ahka's head swiveled, zeroing in on the noise.

A heavy thump – something jumped down into the hold, not bothering with the ladder.

Then a dragging. Followed by another thud. *Drag, thud. Drag, thud. Draaaggg, thud.*

Whoever had decided to join them was getting closer.

She tried to pick up a visual of the newcomer with the thermal scan. Nothing. Maybe zombies didn't generate enough body heat for the sensors to read. Maybe they were all-but-dead inside. Fluids pumping, parts moving, but no life force animating them: flesh dolls set to KILL.

Shawna looked back into the corner for Too-ahka.

The odd alien had fled its web. A chill rippled through her body.

Shit, shit, shit…

The idea of Too-ahka zipping around her faster than her eyes could follow... all she could think about was its teeth. What did it feel like when that freakish furball bit down on you?

A volley of bullets drilled down into the hold.

Move or stay put? The forward hatch loomed. She worked up the nerve to bolt. She didn't think Too-ahka could've gotten in there without her seeing. Plus, Too-ahka registered a heat signal. Did that mean it wasn't zombified? She didn't know what to think, or which rules were in play for this battle. *Drag, thud.* Loud noises were coming from the armory, at the midpoint of the hold. The dragging-thudding new arrival clanked clumsily through the armory doors. Maybe a wounded human had escaped from the cabin and was looking for a weapon. If that was true, then why couldn't she pick them up on the thermal? It had to be a zombie. A slow, cold one. Shawna sorted through her options. Nero and Lemora were ahead of her. They'd reached the cockpit by now. From the armory came another door clanking, then a solid *thwack* – followed by wet, bubbly gurgling, close to the floor. A rasp. Choking. A bout of phlegmy coughing preceded a chest-rattling moan that filled the cargo area with its sense of pure outrage.

Drag, thud.

Here was the picture Shawna put together in her mind: the zombie was leaving the armory. It tripped and fell, then picked itself up and continued trudging forward. In her direction.

Her eyes strained to find it. She switched the NVGs back to night vision and spotted it: a green-cloaked, hunched form – staggering, heaving itself along.

A blur shot past Shawna on her right. She felt it go by, the rush of air tickling her arm.

She gasped. How long had Too-ahka had been right next to her?

Its blur disappeared around the armory vault. Shawna switched back to thermals and scanned the room looking for signs of Too-ahka's heat signature. Her heart banged in her chest.

Nothing.

Back on night vision, the heatless, green-faced zombie turned, lifting its head. It wore an apparatus that covered part of its face. Armor? It had heard her gasp. Now it hurried, increasing its slog, but still crawling along, having difficulty ambulating. Shawna raised the light shotgun, pointing right at the exposed part of the zombie's head. Sliding her sweaty hand along the stock of the shotgun for a better grip, she felt the bottom edge of a cylinder, and realized the gun had been modified with a side-mount tactical flashlight. Her thumb grazed the light's button, but she waited for the zombie's approach. *C'mon, a little closer.* She didn't want to miss. Her blast had to count. There were two things in this cargo hold with her, and she had to be prepared to shoot them both quickly. But Too-ahka could have killed her at its leisure. Was it playing a sick game?

Her hands shook. She shouldered her weapon. A drop of sweat trickled into her eye, stinging. She blinked. The zombie advanced. *That's it. Take another step, you son of a...*

Shawna slid her NVGs up and mashed the flashlight button.

A blaze of brightness issued from the tactical flashlight.

The zombie didn't react. Or the zombie's reaction was so delayed and sluggish that it seemed unfazed. It stared into the lamp and crept another step toward the outstretched barrel of Shawna's gun. Two cloudy disks for eyes. Shawna aimed her shotgun between them.

Ishnik.

She must've finished off Valmont. Or he'd gotten away. Or she grew bored. Anyway, she was down here now in the cargo hold, and she looked like absolute hell. The Fushnallan's orange skin sagged like a popped balloon. The crest on the ridge of her skull flopped off to one side, inert. Shawna's trigger finger tensed. Ishnik was less than a meter away. Oblivious to the danger.

Shawna hesitated.

Taking her finger off the trigger, she felt terrible about shooting the undead guard.

Ishnik drew closer. *Drag, thud.* Swollen and bruised, her left foot turned outward ninety degrees. Bones ground together sickeningly as she put her weight on it; her ankle was broken. Ishnik's jaw hung crookedly, dislocated inside her disconnected breather mask. She opened her mouth. "AGAAAAAAGHRHHH…"

I'm putting her out of her misery, Shawna told herself. She put her finger back on the trigger. *I'd want the same if our places were switched. Make it quick and clean. A mercy.*

Ishnik walked right into the end of the shotgun. Her forehead mashed against the barrel.

Shawna pulled the trigger.

The muzzle flash was blinding in the dark. Spots danced in front of her eyes. She didn't see where the body fell. She didn't hear Ishnik go down either. She pointed her light at the floor.

WTF? No Ishnik to be found. She'd literally been against

the end of the barrel when the gun went off. *Where in the hell is she? How could my shot have missed?*

Shawna swung the flashlight beam wildly around the barren, tomblike compartment.

There she is – Ishnik – oh god, what's Too-ahka doing to her?

Back in the upper corner of the hold, Too-ahka had returned to its previous position. But this time it had the Fushnallan hooked on the tips of its front claws. The alien's dish-like face was smeared with a pudding of white gore. Like a marionette with its strings cut, Ishnik hung slackly in the alien's grasp, her head tipped impossibly far back. Her throat was missing.

Too-ahka ignored the glare of Shawna's flashlight. It went back to licking and probing the stump of the guard's neck with its long, worming tongue. A knife-like flick of Too-ahka's finger cut the final string of orange skin, and Ishnik's head fell – *clonk!* – onto the floor.

Did zombies attack each other? Was that what happened? Shawna didn't have time to digest the scene. Instead, she seized the opportunity to get the hell out of there.

Reaching the hatch, she discovered the door to the avionics bay was shut. The handle turned. But something was jammed against the other side of the door, preventing her escape.

No, no, no... I can't stay in here with that, that... whatever Too-ahka was...

Shawna put her shoulder to the thick metal door, slamming into it over and over. She stepped back and gave it a couple of angry kicks. To her left, in that dreadful upper corner, Too-ahka kept slurping. The alien made a soft purring sound that unmistakably indicated pleasure.

"You're not going to eat me!" Shawna shouted.

She refused to gaze upon the horrific display again. If she did, she was afraid she wouldn't be able to stop looking. And then it would be the last thing she ever saw. Her heel pummeled the hatch door. She succeeded in creating an opening along the edge wide enough to fit her hand. Forcing her arm inside, she tried to squeeze through, but the gap was too narrow, and the door refused to budge. She pulled out, backed up three steps, and crashed into the door.

Shit, that hurt!

She tried to slip inside again. The door had shifted but not by much. She managed to get her shoulder and her head past. Pushing, she groped around for the blockage.

GAH!

She jerked her hand back. Something cut her! A gash crossed her right palm, seeping blood. It stung but didn't look deep. She could move her fingers. Poking the shotgun inside, using the flashlight beam, she spotted the circular saw. Sliding the barrel of the gun inside the saw's handle, she lifted it – only a few centimeters. She shoved her weight against the door again, using her whole body, pumping her legs, feet skidding on the floor. Any second she expected Too-ahka to latch on to her back, sinking its needle teeth into her, shredding her flesh to ribbons. She cranked up on the saw handle again, grunting with maximum exertion, until it cleared the top of the obstruction. The door opened! Shawna rushed inside.

Tossing down the shotgun, careful not to repeat cutting herself, she hoisted the saw with both hands, hauling it farther into the avionics bay. She closed the hatch door. When she went to lock it, she understood why Nero or Lemora had put the saw there. The door didn't have a lock.

Shit! Are you kidding me?

Gritting her teeth against the pain from her stinging hand, she put the saw back. After a struggle that felt like it took ages – but was likely a handful of seconds at most – she managed to block the hatch. Shawna slumped to the floor, wrapping her arms around her knees, her lungs heaving with exhaustion. The shotgun lay on the floor beside her. Its light cast devious rays in the avionic bay. Distorted shadows loomed hugely on the walls. *I'm safe*, she thought. *I did it.*

When Too-ahka tapped her lightly on the shoulder, she screamed.

CHAPTER SIXTEEN
Proximity Warning

Nero asked Lemora to check on Matias. She peeled back his eyelids to inspect two bloodshot orbs spinning in their sockets. The hitman sat slouched between the pilots' seats blowing spit bubbles. His hands fluttered nervously: a pair of injured birds struggling to take flight. When Matias noticed them, he tried to back away, as if they didn't belong attached to his arms. He uttered a shriek and lost consciousness, snoring up a storm. The guy resembled a boneless meat sack. He'd be worth about as much going up against the zombies. "What's the diagnosis, doc?" Nero asked.

"I'm not that kind of a doctor," Lemora said. Exasperated, she stood up and sighed.

Nero read doubt in her face. He made a wet raspberry sound with his lips. "Don't give me any bullshit. I want your honest opinion. Try to be positive. Is our boy going to live or what?"

The bluntness of the question elicited a whimper from Mateo who shrank into the gun locker and buried his face in his arms, sobbing. Nero's opinion of him dropped a few notches, seeing him act out his grief in front of strangers. He favored keeping weaknesses private. But the Silva brothers wore their emotions on their sleeves. It was a surprising feature to find in lab-grown warriors, even black-market ones.

Lemora said, "That's a serious head wound. He's concussed or severely brain damaged."

"Geez, that sounds awfully negative," Nero said. "Luckily, I don't need him to think." After uttering the second part, he observed Mateo for signs of his reaction. Nada. The guy kept his head down, sniffling. There were gobs of blood clinging to his clean-shaven skull. Maybe the worst had passed. Nero had to rally the troops before it was too late. If their spirits sank, he'd never win them back, and he needed them to function efficiently as a team in order to survive.

Krait made a halfhearted attempt to cover his smirk. Mateo couldn't see his expression, or Nero would've had another casualty on his hands. Unsurprisingly, the hitman struggled with anger issues and was quick to violence, particularly concerning the subject of Matias. The facility where they'd been born had been manufacturing soldiers, no one remembered for what cause, but an explosion destroyed the lab before the boys fully matured. They were the only survivors. Having escaped the forest fire, they grew up orphans living on the streets of an equatorial jungle town. They stuck together, becoming a family, closer than brothers, as they continued to develop into a deadly two-man kill squad. Top-notch fighters, they possessed tactical abilities that enabled them to climb the local criminal ladder, freelancing murder-for-hire jobs for the gang bosses. Without each other, they would've been long dead by now. Nero never felt any such bond with his twin sister, Neera. They were more like strangers competing for the same prizes.

The only time they worked together was to hassle the baron, getting on his nerves when they were younger, stealing shit from the mansion or outwitting his bodyguards just for the hell of it.

"Give him a chance," Bak-Irp said. "The man had his bell rung. He's got to regroup."

"I'm afraid we don't have the kind of medical expertise or equipment he needs." Lemora shook her head discreetly to let Nero know it was a hell of a lot worse than a rung bell: Matias was a goner, just as she'd predicted. Escapes were risky business, sometimes people died.

No plan was perfect. But Nero wished they could stow Matias out of sight. Having him there was a mood killer, and the cockpit already felt crowded. Maybe they could dump his body into the avionics bay. He wasn't sure Mateo would go along with that even if they did it respectfully.

As if he'd received a telepathic message regarding his brother's fate, Mateo erupted with anguish, slamming his fists repeatedly into the sides of his head. "No mueras, mi hermano!"

Krait could hardly contain his gloating. He'd been right, and now Nero had more problems to deal with than before. In retrospect, it would've been better to leave them outside. But he couldn't do anything about that. Bak-Irp had made the decision for him, a fact Nero wouldn't forget.

Nero turned to Dierdre. "Hey, Red, how long until we land this Deathcan?"

"PK-L7 is right under us. We're nearing the quarantine zone. If we encounter no problems getting through the defense system, we'll touch down in two shakes of a lamb's tail."

"Fabulous!" Nero pumped his fist in the air. The others appeared less enthusiastic.

Dierdre smiled at Nero. He'd known she had the guts of an outlaw. Lots of people did, but they never realized it until they got pushed outside the lines. Which was a damn shame. Crime was fun.

Landing would solve a few of his most pressing issues. If Matias wasn't up to abandoning the ship, they'd have no choice but to say goodbye. And if his brother didn't like that, he could stay and die. That was his choice. Nero needed his warriors fit for battle, guns a-blazing. Everyone who wasn't ready for gametime was disposable. He wanted off this junk ship, too. It felt less like a getaway ship and more like a funeral barge. Hopefully, the conditions on the ground were better than predicted. They'd hole up at the mining station and contact Neera for a pick-up. Easy-peasy. Why was he the only one who could see the future so clearly? Boldness of vision was one quality that elevated him from the pack, marking him as a leader. It might be his top attribute. Either that or his willpower. He couldn't decide which asset was his greatest.

Captain Buck cleared his throat. "Excuse me. Are you sure those sentries are going to allow us to pass peaceably? I may be an old stick jockey with more miles than good sense, but I don't like the idea of flying into a meat grinder." The cowboy stiffened his back, showing he'd retained his personal pride. He adjusted his bolo tie and tapped its turquoise slide three times.

Nero frowned. "What'd you do that for?"

"The stone brings me good luck," Buck explained.

Nero slugged him in the arm, saying in an exaggerated drawl, "Screw luck, hoss. Don't you fret yerself none. That ornery hardware may belong to the Coalition, but my people at the Guild wrote the code that runs them big guns."

"I assume you have access to a backdoor?" Krait chimed in. "You've applied a patch? Something that will allow us to appear invisible to their sensors. Quite ingenious... if it works."

"Correct on all counts, Hans," Nero said. The German smuggler was starting to annoy the shit out of him, questioning his every move. *Who organized this jailbreak anyway?* "We're going to boogie right on through," he said, wishing he felt as confident as he was trying to sound. He bribed people all the time. Sometimes they were incompetent, and other times they double-crossed him. In both cases, his ass got hung out to dry. He hoped this wasn't one of those times.

"Entering Q zone," Dierdre said. She sat forward, keeping an eye glued to her proximity warning lights. "If they see us and don't like what they see, we'll know right... about... now..."

The main display revealed a minefield of autonomous ordnance. There was an undersea quality to the image, as if they were deep-diving in a trench on the floor of a liquid world where life was scarce because of the extreme pressure. Nero didn't enjoy feeling like he was a wee bitty fish swimming in dangerous waters. He preferred to think of himself as the top predator in the food chain. Undisputed ruler of the realm. The prospect of being wrong gave him the willies.

Everyone held their breath. Even Mateo unfolded himself from the gun locker to watch the screen. Only Matias remained unperturbed, although he'd gone disturbingly silent. Nero glanced down at him wondering if he'd finally punched the clock; he stepped over the body to get a better look at the monitors. Matias's eyes were rolled up, all whites. He wore a dunce smile. Pink-tinged fluid leaked from the crack in his skull, puddling into a damp halo around his head.

The others stared at the screen. The Tri-T approached the array of floating weapons. Dierdre picked a gap, steering them between two orbiting sentry guns. Proximity alarms blared. Dierdre silenced them and licked her dry lips, hands steady at the controls. Nero knew she couldn't save them at this range. If the guns started shooting, the Deathcan would never outrun a barrage. They'd get chewed up and spit out. With disgust, Nero noted the sentries were obsolete models: black metal orbs capped by single turret cannons that fired armor-piercing shells; the orbs were vented on the sides with gill-like slots capable of launching anti-ship cluster bombs, basic and terribly outdated, but more than capable of decimating them. To die this way would be a humiliation. Nero obsessed about his reputation and legacy, yearning to live forever just as his father had. "One life is not enough," he'd told Nero. Both men experienced a horrid sense of dissatisfaction with what they had and an unquenchable desire for more, more, more…

The prison ship drifted among avatars of death. Nero hummed a military march. He knew he was whistling past the graveyard. *But I can't die today. I'll live through this. I'll go on…*

The guns were so close he could stare down into the bores of their long black barrels.

Nothing happened.

The Deathcan sailed on, undisturbed.

"Hell yeah!" Nero shouted. "What did I tell you? It's good to be king."

Dierdre weaved a path toward the planet's surface, descending through the rotund sentry guns and swarms of wasplike hunter-killer drones. None of the robotic sentinels twitched at their presence. The pilots exhaled in relief. They all relaxed a little. The musty odor of fear-induced sweat was redolent in the cockpit. Raucous cries continued behind them in the zombie mayhem of the passenger cabin, though the outbursts were fewer and more muffled now. A scream echoed; its sound carried up from below. But no one reacted to it. Nero figured the zombies must be winning. It might be callous of him, but as the leader of his team he had to direct his thoughts toward the future and PK-L7. Perhaps it had been foolish on his part not to research their destination more thoroughly. He knew the brief rundown Lemora had given him. Mysterious mold, frenzied alien zombies, an overrun mining station, etcetera ... if zombies on PK-L7 were anything like the transformed aliens on board the Deathcan ... if there were hordes of them running amuck ... swarming over the entire planet ... but surely not!

He couldn't imagine that would be the case. Things must've gotten somewhat better in the two hundred or so years since anyone had last visited. How long could a rampage go on with no one to rampage against? The moldy hubbub must've died off by now. Whatever the situation, they'd deal with it after they touched down. The pilots, of course, were doomed. Nero wouldn't need them once he was safely delivered. Dierdre seemed to be a good egg. He'd give the job of scrambling her to Mateo, something to distract him from his brother's condition.

Murder was hardly beneath Nero; he enjoyed getting his hands dirty. It simply set a bad precedent. He was the boss, not muscle. He'd discovered that people often misinterpreted the genius things he said or did. They proved incapable of seeing his side of things. That's why he loved robots. No bad attitude. No backtalk. They worked until they broke down, and then you replaced them with better versions of themselves. That was progress. It was people who made his life hell. They were really… draining.

"So far, so good," Dierdre said. "A bit of a sandstorm north of the mining station. That's the only structure on the planet so I assume that's where you want us to land. It's clear for now."

"Yes," Nero answered distractedly. He was observing the defense system in action.

Or better stated, the system's *inaction*. Machines were only as effective as their builders.

"The sentinels think we're one of them," Nero said. "A wolf in wolf's clothing. They greet one another. The computer comms broadcast simultaneous hellos. If the messages match the daily secret password, they simply ignore one another. It's totally synchronized. Efficient."

"But easily defeated by a higher intelligence," Krait added, kissing his ass now.

"Hooray for us," Nero said.

An alarm bleated. A red warning flashed on Buck's controls.

"We've got an incoming ship," the cowboy pilot said.

"What?" Nero ground his teeth and pounded his fist into the cockpit roof. "I paid those asshole programmers top dollar. They assured me there'd be no glitches. I'll have them killed when I get back. They're dead. *Dead.*" He took a deep, cleansing breath. "Is it a drone?"

"I'm not sure," Buck said. "There's only the one target approaching."

"Can't we shoot it down?"

"I'm afraid not," Buck said dryly.

"Why the hell *not*?" Nero pulled a pistol and pressed it into the captain's temple.

"Because we're no longer a warship," Dierdre said. "We're a prison transport – a bus."

"Explain. Do it quickly," Nero said. "Or Buck's brains are going bye-bye."

"We have no active weapon systems," she said.

"Then activate them." Was he the only person capable of solving problems?

"There are no weapons," Buck said, stressing each word. "They've been removed."

Nero lowered the gun. "That was a dumb idea. Any other way to stop a drone?"

"It's not a drone," Dierdre said. She tapped at her keyboard. A magnified image appeared on the big screen: a military vehicle, smaller than the Tri-T, and fully weaponized. A clawed crane curled up on the back of the ship like a scorpion's tail. Twin pincers tucked into the sides.

"What is it?" Nero asked. He felt like a boy again, paging through his father's volumes of archaic military histories. It was no wonder the Coalition lost to the Guild's armies. They were outfitted to take on their past enemies using equipment that provoked nostalgia rather than awe.

"Carrion class," Dierdre answered. "A garbage picker. They've been around for ages."

"More ancient shit?" Nero said disgustedly. *All this planning and money laid out and we're jerking around with a Carrion class garbage recycler...* it jogged something loose in his memory. "Hey, I remember these things. They collected debris from battle zones for sale in military scrapyard auctions. It's not going to cause us any problems, right? We can ignore it."

Lemora pointed to the monitor that occupied the upper third of the nosecone section. Although it was a computer simulation, the view looked real, like a recently scrubbed windshield of glass. "It's a manned patroller," she said. "That means someone's flying it. A living crew."

Nero said, "The last thing we need is a watchman calling home. How many on board?"

"Regulations stipulate a minimum four-person crew – the pilot, a comms officer, and two crane operators to snag material," Dierdre said. "You want me to try hailing them?"

"And tell them what?" Captain Buck asked. "We don't belong here."

"Say we're lost," Nero said. "Do it. Call. We're having propulsion issues. Play dumb."

"If they ask, how do I explain why the robot sentries are ignoring us?" Dierdre said.

"That's a positive. These guys aren't out here gunning for desperadoes. They're scooping up space junk that floats in by accident. Tell them we're a repair ship. Random debris hit us," Nero said. "We need to make an emergency landing. Once we're on the ground, I don't give a shit what they do. Or who they call."

Dierdre hailed the other ship. "Coalition Patrol, this is the *Andronicus*. Do you read us?"

"They'll never permit us to land," Buck said.

"I agree. You really think they use Tri-Ts as repair ships?" Krait said sneeringly.

"I don't know. Maybe they don't either," Nero said. "Who cares? It's only a bluff."

"I care," Krait answered. "If it's obvious we're lying, they're more likely to take us down. Or summon backup." He cocked his head, waiting for a reply, either from Nero or the patroller. "If they don't attack, maybe they'll call to verify our story. Then what?"

If Krait didn't shut up, he was going to have to put a bullet in the man's brainpan. For now, he held himself in check.

The Carrion patroller didn't respond to their call.

"They're increasing speed. Coming right for us," Buck said. "You want me to pull out?"

"No," Nero said. "Hell no! Stay on course."

Dierdre keyed her ship-to-ship comms channel. Sending out an SOS. She repeated it.

No reply.

"What should we do?" Dierdre asked. She was wobbling, appearing to side with ole Buck.

"Lose altitude. The chickenshits won't follow us down. Put us on PK-L7! Land!"

The comms channel crackled, making everyone jump. "Attention, *Andronicus*. This is the *Red Kite*. Sorry about the silence. We've had comms problems all day. Visuals are down, we've only got audio linkup working. Signals are never strong out in the Q Zone, but we're jammed with unusually high levels of interference. You've been our only contact. What's your emergency? We're here to help. *Red Kite* out."

Nero slapped his forehead. "Oh, I forgot. The interference. That's us. The Coalition launched a jammer flare ahead of us on our flight path to prevent any outside contact. Seems they were worried about a hijacking. An intercept ship might force a docking and seize control."

"Where did they get that idea, I wonder?" Lemora asked. She was the only one with a clue about how carefully he'd planned the escape, knowing the sacrifices he made, and the deals.

"From a confidential informant," Nero said. "With inside information and connections."

"Aha."

"We're far enough off course, the flare ripples must've weakened," Nero said. "I've got an idea. Request an emergency evac. Say we have a minimal crew and we're losing life support."

Both pilots turned to look at him.

"You want them to dock with us?" Buck said.

"The docking point connects at the main cabin, right?" Nero said. "Once they open their hatch, a few unwanted zombies will storm their way on board. Then it's adios for the *Red Kite*."

Buck took his hands off the controls. "That's murder. And I won't play a part–"

Pow! Nero shot him in the back of the head.

Unlike the rest of the ship, the nosecone of a Tri-T is hardened for battle. Nero wasn't aware of this fact. The bullet that passed through Captain Buck's skull hit a monitor and ricocheted off the fuselage. The round that killed him pinged around the cockpit. Stopping inside Dierdre's chest. She didn't die immediately. It took a minute before she slumped forward. Blood and brains slicked the control instruments. *Of all the shitty breaks*, Nero thought. *Buck, your lucky bolo tie was worthless.* He dragged the cowboy out of his seat, sliding him onto Matias.

"What the hell?" Bak-Irp said in disbelief. "You killed them both?"

The comms crackled. "*Andronicus*? Do you copy? This is *Red Kite* requesting info on your emergency. What's the problem? Over."

The image of the *Red Kite* grew larger on the display screen. Nero climbed into Buck's seat. It was warm and moist; the old buckaroo was not a cool cucumber after all. Nero scanned the controls. Most of the switches and knobs had their labels worn off. "Where's the comms?"

Lemora removed Dierdre from her seat and added her to the body pile in the middle of the cockpit. "I think Dierdre hit this." Lemora keyed a switch. "*Red Kite*, this is the *Andronicus*. Do you read us? Over."

"Copy, *Andronicus*. You're loud and clear. What's your emergency?"

"We suffered a debris impact. It's impacted our life supports. We have multiple dead, and the rest of us won't last long if we don't land or dock with you. Over." Lemora looked at Nero to see if he approved of her lies. He nodded; the cords of his neck tensed as they awaited a reply.

"Nobody lands on PK-L7," the other pilot said. "We can dock with you for an evac."

"Excellent," she said. "Hurry. We don't have much time."

"Copy," the *Red Kite* pilot said. "Is your vid comms out? We only have you on audio."

"Correct. Vid is out. Power draining." Lemora clicked the switch a few times and spoke in broken garbled nonsense, then she said. "It's getting hard to breathe."

"Aren't you in your atmosphere suits?" the pilot replied, puzzled.

Nero stopped her from answering, putting his hand on top of hers.

"*Andronicus? Andronicus?*"

"We should get those suits from the armory," Nero said. "We'll need them when we land."

"Who's going to land?" Krait asked. "Are either of you capable of piloting? I'm not."

"Shit," Nero said.

"Rotate fifteen degrees, *Andronicus*. Steady hold pattern. We'll sync-up and initiate a Type 4 mating interface..."

Nero and Lemora sat there without answering the *Red Kite*. Alarms started going off. They had no idea how to turn them off. The image of the *Red Kite* overtook the entire screen.

"Is there any way we can grab their pilot and get him to fly this ship?" Nero said. If Buck hadn't been so damned obstinate, none of this shit would've happened.

"I don't see how," Lemora said. "We'd have to go through the cabin with the zombies, grab him, and force him back in here, then undock. All before the rest of his crew catches on."

"Can we steal his ship?" Krait asked.

Nero shook his head. "All they have to do is undock. We'll be sucked out into space. If we shoot our way inside, we risk killing their pilot which makes the whole enterprise pointless."

On the screen, the *Red Kite* drew closer. One of her pincer arms deployed and reached for the *Andronicus* like a crab about to grab its dinner. The claw opened and closed, missing them.

Lemora said, "We're still in a descending pattern. If they can't grab hold of us, we'll crash. PK-L7's gravity is pulling us down already."

The panels were lighting up like a Xabryrian discotheque dance floor. Nero's stomach clenched, and he felt like he had a block of ice melting in his lap, droplets running down his legs.

Bak-Irp said, "Where are we going to get a pilot, Nero? We've got to have a pilot."

The floor knocked three times. Hard. They all jumped.

It wasn't the floor. But somebody under the floor hatch. They pointed their guns at the trapdoor, but no one fired. Nero held up his hand, then put a finger to his lips for everyone to keep silent. He aimed for the front edge where the trapdoor would pop open the widest, then he remembered that it was locked. Three more knocks, softer this time, because whoever was underneath them knew they had their attention. Zombies didn't knock. Guards were all bastards.

"I can fly your ship," a female voice said. "But you all had better hurry and let us in."

CHAPTER SEVENTEEN
Final Warning

Bak-Irp cracked open the hatch and stuck a machine gun into Shawna's face. He'd fired it recently. She could smell the tang of gunpowder. His sharp Thassian eyes darted around, spying into the darkness surrounding her. Shawna knew him, but they'd never spoken back at XSecPen. The HT cellblock wasn't conducive to striking up conversations or making new friends.

"You said 'us.' Who you got down there with you?" the bodyguard asked.

"It's that new prisoner they brought aboard. Its name is Too-ahka," she said.

"Where's he at? I don't see him."

Too-ahka leaned in out of the shadows. A furry keg of a body and fearsome features didn't do much to inspire calm. Giant ears dominated its face like two woofers. The eyes were red pips. Where there was no fur, soft petals of wrinkly, pinkish brown skin mushroomed into a pair of lips, their flamboyance curled upward into an underdeveloped, piggish nose, giving the creature a smashed-in appearance. Mostly it was its teeth that made the alien a fright – a horrid array of translucent spikes, prickles, and thorns. Shawna was glad Bak-Irp didn't immediately start shooting. But the Thassian must've seen his share of nightmarish oddities when he was a bounty hunter, because he hardly blinked. That didn't mean he was welcoming.

"I'm not letting that thing up in here," he said, shaking his head. "No way."

"Look, I understand what you're saying. And I don't know Too-ahka well. But we've become sort of acquainted in the last few minutes, and I think you'll want to reconsider."

"Oh, why is that?"

"Because this red fuzzball is a stealthy killer who frankly scares the livin' shit out of me. The way I've seen it offing zombies down here – well, that's got to be worth something to you."

Bak-Irp considered what she'd said. "Hold up. Let me check with Nero."

The hatch slammed shut. He threw the bolt.

Shawna waited. She'd left her shotgun lying on the floor because she didn't want to draw fire the second the hatch lifted. The flashlight aimed at the wall, burning a bright circle there, but it made the murk feel gloomier. After it had first frightened her, the alien stepped back and calmly attempted to soothe her nervousness. Too-ahka's hands formed shapes in the semi-dark. Hand signals. The creature was using sign language that Shawna had learned in a linguistics course at the flight academy. In some regions of Terran space the languages were so numerous that the aliens who lived there developed non-verbal forms of communication for trade and storytelling. Not everyone could afford handheld translators, and the plethora of dialects made interpretation especially difficult. Shawna liked learning languages, but her sign-talk skills were rusty. Too-ahka was patient and went slowly, moving its hands into different shapes and positions, repeating patterns until Shawna understood. The message boiled down to this: *I am no threat to you.* After Shawna's initial fear subsided, she wondered where the alien had come from.

"What do you call home? Where're you from?"

"*I have no home. I go from place to place. Always.*"

"You're a nomad? That's cool. I've traveled a lot myself. Never met anyone like you."

"*I looked for others of my kind. But wherever I go, I am the only one.*"

"Why did you kill the guard?"

The alien cocked its head and turned up its hands. "*I do not understand.*"

"The zombie in the cargo hold? The Fushnallan. She was a guard before she… changed."

"*She was sick from the bomb. You were going to shoot her. I killed her first.*"

"But you drank her blood," Shawna said. "Why did you do that?"

"*I was hungry. She filled me up. Now I am not hungry.*"

Shawna gulped. "Don't you worry about getting sick from eating an infected… meal?"

"*I eat what I want to eat. I never get sick. Inside my belly is tough like [unknown sign].*"

Too-ahka petted its stomach, rubbing it in little circles.

Shawna didn't recognize the last sign, but she got the gist of it. The alien wasn't a picky eater. Fair enough, if not entirely reassuring. The tummy rub creeped her out, but she let it go.

"What do you want from me?" Shawna asked, unsure if she wanted to know the answer.

"*I want out of here. You help me. I help you. Together we will go away.*"

She couldn't argue with any of that and told the alien so. If Too-ahka had wanted to kill her and suck her juices, she'd be dead already. Despite her fear, she had to trust the alien. It wasn't easy. The image she had in her mind of Too-ahka slurping on Ishnik's neck stump was impossible to unsee. The creature sensed her doubt. It laid a cool finger gently on her arm and blinked slowly. Despite the unease that came with being touched, Shawna felt herself being flooded inside with a warming sense of peace and relaxation. Maybe the alien was influencing her mind. That was a troubling thought, but she couldn't muster the energy to reject the attempt at camaraderie.

Now they waited together to see if Nero would let them into the cockpit or tell Bak-Irp to lift the hatch and mow them down. To distract herself, she resumed talking with Too-ahka.

"It's better not to be alone when you're in deep shit like this," she said. "Too few friends and too many ways to die. I'm glad we've agreed to help each other." She smiled weakly.

Too-ahka fixed its beady eyes on her and nodded. Shawna caught her breath when the alien's lips spread, revealing a jumble of needle teeth. She realized it was smiling back at her.

The mind-merge, or whatever, must've still been affecting her because she wasn't freaking out. Her thoughts were crystalline. "The prisoners up in that cockpit are dangerous. They're bad guys. Like, we can't trust them *at all*. But they're our only way out of this mess. We've got to find a way to deal with them if we want to live. It'll be tricky. Follow my lead."

Too-ahka nodded. *"We are stronger together than apart. Tell them that."*

"I'll try," she said. "But I don't know if they're in the mood to listen."

Too-ahka made two finger guns and pantomimed a person shooting in every direction, its skinny arms crisscrossed, as it popped its lips in a staccato mimicry of shots – *puh-puh-puh…*

"Exactly."

Side by side, Shawna and Too-ahka stood waiting, and listening. They'd already overheard the transmissions with the *Red Kite* and the shot that killed the pilots. Conditions upstairs were deteriorating. The cons' desperation was growing. The plan to nab the *Red Kite* pilot would never work. She whispered, "I need to stop them before they do something stupid."

Too-ahka pointed its forefinger at the hatch. Then it signed a message.

"Be careful."

This time it was Shawna's turn to nod.

Bak-Irp jerked the hatch open. No machine gun barked in their faces. He extended a hand to Shawna and hauled her up out of the bay. As he lifted her, he spoke quietly into her ear.

"Any funny shit and I'll end you both. Got it?"

"Got it," she said.

Shawna took in the chaos of the cockpit. She counted five able bodies. Bak-Irp, Nero, Lemora, Krait, and Mateo, although she didn't see his clone brother. There was a hole in one of the monitors, a splat of lumpy brain matter and blood dripping down a flickering screen. Three corpses sprawled between the pilots' seats. Nero sat in the captain's chair, swiveling around to aim a pistol at her. Lemora was next to him, her eyes glued to another screen, which showed the Carrion ship nipping at them like a hungry Yyargarien craboid. The Tri-T maintained a steep descent pattern through a minefield of autonomous armed sentries and drones. In other words, it was a total shitstorm. Shawna had about ninety seconds to do something before they cracked up in one way or another.

"I've got to take the controls," she said to Nero. "Right now."

The megalomaniacal entrepreneur eyed her suspiciously. Then he snapped out an order.

"Lemora, give the war hero your seat."

Even if the cons didn't talk much in XSecPen, they gossiped. In order to survive, prisoners needed to keep mental notes of who they could use and who they had to avoid at all costs. The demolitions-crazed doctor slipped away, but not before throwing a chilly glance Shawna's way. Shawna climbed over the triple stack of bodies as if that was a normal thing. She tried not to look too closely. Her hand went to the comms, ready to tell the *Red Kite* to back off. Nero grabbed her wrist, giving it a tight squeeze. "They think we're out cold. Life supports cut."

"I have to get them to give us room," she said. "If we collide, that's it. We're dead."

Nero loosened his grip. "Be careful."

It was the same advice Too-ahka had offered a few moments ago.

Shawna opened the channel to the other ship. "*Red Kite, Red Kite*. Abort docking. I repeat. Abort docking. We've regained control of our ship. Over." Shawn didn't wait for a reply. She banked the *Andronicus* away from the garbage recycler and applied maximum thrust in the opposite direction, tilting the

Tri-T hard to starboard to avoid the reaching claw that kept coming at them, growing larger and more menacing on the screen. In layman's terms, she was shrugging off the *Red Kite*. She dropped the nose of the *Andronicus* and pulsed the rear jets, hoping that the turbulence would destabilize the other ship, thwarting her advance. It worked.

The comms hissed like an angry snake. In the background, the crew were agitated.

"What the hell!" the *Red Kite* pilot shouted. "*Andronicus*, are you crazy? We're trying to HELP you. You're blowing waves in our faces. Desist, and we'll bring you in, safe and sound."

"Sorry about that," Shawna said. "We have severe damage. Controls are rough. But we are steady. Continuing our descent to land on PK-L7. Disengage. We've got to put her down."

Shawna winced, knowing what was coming next.

"That's a negative, *Andronicus*. You do not have permission to land. NEGATIVE TO LAND. PK-L7 is off limits. Extremely hostile environmental hazards are present. Discontinue landing maneuvers. Steady and rotate. We'll snag your tail, tow you out." The comms crackled.

Shawna put the *Andronicus* into an even steeper dive. The ship shuddered and rocked. Everyone who wasn't strapped in place flew backward. Forced into his seat, Nero grimaced, fighting to keep his pistol pointed at her head.

"Are you trying to die, aviator?" he said.

"Nope."

Lemora and Bak-Irp were picking themselves up from the cockpit floor, when suddenly the hatch filled with reddish fur and Too-ahka sprang into the compartment, deftly tapping the ceiling to adjust its rebound angle, and landing on top of Krait, who cried out with a high-pitched squeal. Bak-Irp raised his machine gun but was too slow to stop the one-of-a-kind alien from reaching across and engaging the gun's safety. Too-ahka's moves were fast and fluid, graceful.

"Dammit," Bak-Irp said, pulling at a locked trigger. He thumbed the safety off. By that time, Too-ahka had lurched back onto Krait's lap, holding up two empty hands, waving them.

"*No threat. No threat.*"

The smuggler shrieked in terror again. Bak-Irp shouldered his weapon. Shawna twisted around. "Everyone, just stop!" she yelled. Her icy-hot gaze froze them in place, chests heaving.

From under the body pile someone said, "What the hell? Where am I?"

Mateo immediately began to unbury his brother, shoving aside the deceased pilots. The Silva brothers hugged as the others watched, amazed at Matias's recovery. Milky faced, he swayed as if he were drunk and about to puke, but he was smiling as his clone tied a bandana and a first-aid gauze pad around his wounded head.

"We thought you were dead!" Mateo said.

"I'm dizzy as hell, mano." The hitman adjusted the bandage, looking at his reflection in the gun locker door. "I need a pistola. Something loud. My head already hurts, so who cares?"

Mateo giggled as he hustled a loaded shotgun into his brother's shaky hands.

"Shoot the zombies. Not us," he joked.

"Are these pendejos the zombies?" Matias asked, raising the weapon, racking it.

"Don't kid around," Mateo said. "You're scaring them, bro." He cackled.

Matias looked unsure of whether to open fire or laugh. He chewed on his chapped lips. No one else was laughing. Mateo reached out, lowering the barrel of his brother's shotgun.

"Stay cool," Shawna said to the room. "We're all on the same team here. I'm going to land this ship. We need those spacesuits from the armory. Bak-Irp, you take Krait and the twins with you. Put your gear on. Bring us ours. I can't do much to level the ship and still avoid the *Red Kite*'s claws. You'll have to make the best of a bad situation. It'll be hilly. Go! Now!"

The escapees looked for Nero's approval to obey her commands.

"Do what she says. For now."

Bak-Irp and the others, including a dazed Matias, descended the ladder into the avionics bay. Too-ahka closed the hatch then gestured for Lemora to take his spot in the navigator's chair.

"Thank you," she said. "It seems the only gentleman on this ship is no man at all."

Too-ahka displayed his needle grin and Lemora cringed.

"Quite a smile, isn't it?" Shawna said. "He can't talk. But he listens great. Too-ahka's got special abilities that might come in handy. He's as stealthy as shit and can see in the dark. Which reminds me, why the hell are we going to what sounds like the worst place in the galaxy?"

"I don't know that it's the *worst*," Nero said. "There are some pretty bad places I've been to. Have you ever visited Kassobiria during the late winter phase? The ice roaches are as big as grapple-dozers, and the temps drop so low that any exposure to the air flash-freezes your tissue."

Shawna didn't have time to debate Nero. The *Red Kite* was gaining on them, pincers out, and if she was seeing things correctly in the rear cams, their plasma guns were prepping to fire.

"They're going to shoot at us," she said.

"Jerks! Can't they let us go?" Lemora said. "What I wouldn't give for a missile, honey."

Alarms kept going off as fast as Shawna could silence them. The *Red Kite* wasn't giving up. "*Andronicus*, you are in violation of Coalition Order 9344511XO. If you do not alter your present course, we will be forced to open fire. THIS IS YOUR FINAL WARNING!" The Carrion class pilot's voice wavered. He was no fighter pilot. He'd probably never shot at a live target before, and the idea that he might be gunning for a damaged spacecraft and taking out a crew of repair workers who were struggling on limited life support systems was crippling his decision-making. Shawna had to take advantage of his inexperience. She keyed her mic.

"Losing oxygen... need to land and send power from flight systems to life support..."

She wagged the Tri-T's tail end to evade the outstretched mechanical claws. To the *Red Kite* it might look as if they were fighting for control of their ship, which in a way they were.

"They're in trouble, man. I'm not murdering Coalition citizens because their ship is malfunctioning." The pilot's words came to them over the staticky open channel. He was too jacked-up to turn off his comms. Shawna hoped that meant he was also too jittery to fire at them.

The *Red Kite* backed off and withdrew her pincers. But she remained in pursuit.

PK-L7 came into sharp focus on Shawna's front camera

display: a barren, scoured surface of red-orange rock. No signs of life. Scattered ruins came into view. A complex of modular units spread out from a central hub. All the surviving structures were low and hugged the ground. It was a typical build-as-you-go shake 'n' bake operation, by appearances centuries old and probably intended as a short-term workstation and habitation for laborers and scientists who were posted in the boonies to extract resources. Once upon a time they might've been protected by a small security detail to keep them safe from potential hostiles. But all that was gone. The facility looked mostly intact but abandoned. Ghostly. Seeing it gave her the creeps. The chances they'd be able to resuscitate its basic systems were minimal. If nothing else, they'd have temporary shelter. Shawna sure hoped Nero's escape plan had more meat to it than that, because all their air supply was attached to the spacesuits and whatever spare tanks they might be able to scrounge from the station's storerooms. From this altitude, prospects were looking bleak.

"Why are we heading to PK-L7?" she asked again. "What's there?"

"Nothing," Nero said. "It's a dead planet. The old mining station is our target. Put her down as close as possible. We're going to have to outrun whatever zombies decide to chase us."

Shawna wondered how many zombies were in the cabin now. On the plus side, it would be easier to evade them on the ground. "Why did the Coalition construct a fortress around a dead planet? What's the big secret?"

"Xenium deposits. Rich, deep, and worth a fortune once they're dug out," Lemora said.

"What's the catch?" Shawna asked.

"They're contaminated."

"Contaminated?" Shawna said. "With what?"

"Mold," Lemora said.

Tumblers were clicking into place in Shawna's brain. She'd studied this place in her history books back at the academy. It didn't have a name. Or more accurately, the name and location were kept under government wraps. The planet was a test case for a total quarantine scenario. There'd been an outbreak. Infected alien miners went berserk. Procedures ran amuck.

"This mold. It wouldn't happen to turn aliens into crazed killer zombies, would it?"

"Maybe…?" Lemora answered, with the slightest smidge of chagrin.

"Terrific." So, they were jumping from the frying pan into the fire, a wildfire that maybe engulfed a whole planet. "And what, we're going to live here forever? Form a commune where we hold hands and sing Kumbaya? What about the air? Water? Not to mention food–"

"We're using it as a rendezvous point," Nero said. "A quick stopover."

There came a knocking on the hatch, and Too-ahka opened it. The rest of the team returned wearing their spacesuits and carrying four extras. They filed into the cockpit, strangely silent. It was like the reality of things had finally hit home. The drama of the hijacking was wearing off and the idea of leaving the ship – however messed up and chaotic it was – attained a new level of terror, fear of the unknown. Shawna was willing to bet that except for Nero and Lemora, they probably didn't know much more than she did. Time to change that.

"After we land someone's coming to pick you up." Shawna was putting the pieces together as she flew a series of flat-out evasive maneuvers that must've baffled the *Red Kite* crew. It felt awesome to be at the controls of a ship again, even if she was likely about to die. "What about the rest of us? How do we survive? Because I think we have a right to know."

She could tell that Nero wasn't used to being questioned, especially in front of others. He didn't like it. His skin flushed deep red, and she could feel the anger coming off him like heat.

"What? You want a travel itinerary?" Nero clutched his armrests as the Tri-T dipped and waggled, hurtling into systems of dry ravines. The cliffs were so close you could've taken rock samples. After dumping the dead pilots into the bay, Bak-Irp helped Lemora into her spacesuit. Once they were dressed, the team members leaned on each other for support, bracing themselves while they watched Nero and Shawna.

"I'm not going to land just so you can kill me or leave me behind," she said. "What's my motivation?" Shawna checked her cams. The *Red Kite* had dropped farther behind. The pilot was unable or unwilling to follow her into the narrow canyons. He followed high above.

"How about a bullet to the head?" Nero said.

"If you're going to kill me, do it now," Shawna said. "It makes no difference. Dead is dead. But if I die up here, you die, too." She flew as close to the plateaus as possible. With the land formations in view, the sense of their speed increased. It didn't bother Shawna, but she was sure it was puckering the backsides of everybody else, except for Too-ahka, who had dozed off.

"What do you want?" Nero asked her. But he wasn't only talking to Shawna now, he was talking to the whole crew.

She'd put him in a corner, and he knew it, and she knew he knew. The best time to negotiate with an adversary is when you had their life in your hands, flying hundreds of kilometers per hour, meters above the terrain, while a gang of zombies pounded on the door.

"Make me an offer. How do I – how do we all – get off this infected, dead planet?"

Nero thought about her question. He surveyed the attitudes of the team behind their dusty faceplates. "Anybody who helps keep me alive earns a ride off PK-L7. How does that sound?"

"That goes for all of us?" Bak-Irp said.

"Yeah, sure."

"What if he's lying?" Krait asked.

Nero rolled his eyes. "I'm not lying. This is business."

"I'm only asking the question we're all thinking," Krait said. "No offense intended."

"None taken." It was clear from Nero's tone that he was deeply offended and pissed off. "The deal stands. Protect my life until my ride arrives, and you get a free ticket off the planet."

"Well, that's hardly free," Krait said.

"You know what I mean!" Nero said. "It's an expression. Free ticket… ride… whatever."

"I take him at his word," Shawna said. "That's about the best we can do right now."

"Wow! Look at that fireball! It's so colorful," Matias said, pointing to the rear display.

Shawna switched the view to show in split screen on a larger monitor.

The *Red Kite* had nicked the cap on a tall column of rock,

and it opened her belly like a fish knife. "They scraped one of those hoodoos. Shit. Those guys should've let us go," she said.

Enveloped in flames, the fatally mangled ship tumbled into the ravine – where their pilot had been too scared to fly. It exploded on impact, the rumble sending a vibration into the *Andronicus* and an echo of painful memories rippling through Shawna's mind. *I didn't kill them. And I didn't kill my squadron either. I'm only responsible for what I can control, and I'm not in control of any of this.* She had no time for self-reflection and even less for self-pity. She popped the Deathcan up out of the narrow canyon and made straight for the flat desert pan where the mining station sat half-buried in drifts of sand like the remnant of a lost civilization.

"Brace for landing," she said. "I'm putting her down."

CHAPTER EIGHTEEN
A Chorus of Growls

If nothing else could be said of her, Shawna Bright was a damn fine pilot. The *Andronicus* on its best day was a clunky bird without an ounce of gracefulness, and all the shooting in the passenger cabin had inflicted major damage. One of the losses turned out to be the power supply to her landing struts; gunfire had ripped through the circuits, leaving her as stiff-legged as an arthritic hound dog. When Shawna brought her down, she landed hard, shearing the front two struts completely and dragging her back legs like a double plough blade, busting into rocky terra firma. After the ship stopped, its tail stuck up in the air and the nose was buried in a pile of gray rubble and ochre-tinged sand. They stirred up a dust cloud that hung around the ship like fog.

Zero visibility on the external cameras. They'd be exiting blind, walking into who knew what. At least the station was right there, about a hundred meters from their port side.

"Get your suit on," Shawna said to Nero, who was checking himself for injuries.

"Say what now?"

"Time to abandon ship. If we cracked the generator with

that hard landing, she might blow." She stepped into her suit and boots and zipped up. Bak-Irp helped to secure her helmet. Then he joined Lemora in preparing Nero to venture outside. Too-ahka, waiting patiently, was the only one still undressed. "Put this on if you're planning to go outside," Shawna said, holding out an empty suit. Too-ahka shook its head.

"I do not need it."

"So, what? You're going to hold your breath until we skedaddle off this rock?" She pushed the suit at the alien, but it refused to take it. Shawna lost her temper. "Don't be stubborn! I need you to cooperate. We've got enough members in this crew who can't follow the rules."

Too-ahka was adamant. Its tranquil demeanor only served to tick her off more.

"Are you stupid or ignorant?" she said.

"Neither. I can hold my breath for six Earth days. And I do not need oxygen to breathe."

The alien peeled apart the front V of its red jumpsuit and lifted a tuft of fur, revealing a pair of ridged plates on its abdomen. They resembled book lungs common to several species of arachno-insectoids. This space critter was packed full of surprises.

"Well, ain't that handy?" she said.

"It is."

"Sorry I tried to bite your head off," Shawna said, quickly regretting her choice of words.

Unfazed, Too-ahka pointed to the flamethrower propped in the corner, tilting its head inquisitively. It reached out to grab the weapon but then paused and asked for permission first.

"Please, may I use this?"

"Does anybody care if Too-ahka takes the flamethrower?" Shawna asked.

"I'll agree to it on two conditions," Nero said. "One, no roasting me accidentally–"

Too-ahka nodded in agreement.

"And the second condition?" Shawna said.

"Fuzzy goes first when we open the door."

Shawna looked at Too-ahka for its answer. The creature was already standing at the door with its fingers curled around the handle. The flamethrower tanks were strapped on its back. The silent alien clicked the ignition button; a bud of sapphire flame appeared underneath the nozzle.

"Looks like Too-ahka's ready," Shawna said.

"We're ready, too," Nero said. "I'll keep to the middle. The Silvas will go behind Fuzzy. Krait, you're next, along with Lemora. Bak-Irp, watch my six. The war hero can turn off the lights behind her while we scram out of Dodge." Nero had a magnum revolver in each hand. He spun pistols like an old-fashioned gunslinger; the glint in his eye was equally ancient and deadly. "My merry band of deviant killers! Are we locked and loaded and good to go?"

The twins grunted in the affirmative.

"Yes, sir!" the Thassian said, stone-faced. Shawna couldn't tell if he was being sarcastic. "Has everybody got their weapon of choice and extra ammo?" he asked, tapping the pouches hanging off his belt. "Cuz we're not coming back here, and who knows what we're going to find inside that station." The team members rechecked their guns and bullets. The spacesuits were armored but lightweight; they looked like they'd never been used, probably spending years sitting in a Coalition-owned warehouse until Corrections purchased them and dumped them in the Tri-T's armory. That was the good news. The bad news was that they were going to need all this protection, and more, to survive. PK-L7 was a harsh planet even if there were no zombies. Who were they kidding? There would be zombies, even if it was the gang in the Tri-T's cabin.

Nero whooped. "Damn! Will you look at us? We're one badass squad of death dealers. Let's hear some noise!" He was doing what he could to pump up the team before the battle.

"Yeah, boy!" Mateo called out, punching a wall. "Let's bake some zombie brownies!"

Matias closed his glazed eyes, leaned his head back, and howled like a wolf.

Krait kept silent but narrowed his eyes, concentrating on the door as if he were trying to dissolve it with his mind. Lemora, ever the gambler, showed no emotion, but surrendered a sly, appreciative smile to Nero, who nodded back at her. Shawna knew the look they exchanged, because she'd seen it before; it was always the same between soldiers who'd been through hell together and back. *We've got this*, it said. *No matter who's on the other side, we're tougher.*

"Too-ahka, scorch us a path to the exit," Nero ordered. "Mateo, Matias, get that door open to the outside. We'll haul ass for the station. Bak, keep any biters off our butts. NOW LET'S GO!"

Too-ahka opened the cockpit door. The zombies were waiting for them. Not crowding too closely, but in a show of intelligence, they crouched behind the first row of seats. However, as soon as they caught sight of the escapees, they rushed forward. The rotund, hairy alien gave them a taste of flames, and they backed up fast, arms burning like torches. It was loud out there. Pent-up fury and pure rage – whatever the mold had done to the aliens who sucked it into their lungs, it made them go apeshit crazy, berserk. The sounds that came out of them vibrated your bones and turned your guts to cold jelly. It spoke of violence beyond all reason, past all hope.

The team moved toward them, guns barking. There were no humans left alive out there, so it was unnecessary to take aim. They shot at anything that moved or made a loud noise.

Shawna heard banging on the cockpit. But it wasn't coming from the cabin. It was behind her. Coming from outside. Heavy thumps repeated like a colossal jet hammer, getting louder and faster. She looked one last time at the flickering monitors. Nothing to see but a veil of unsettled dust.

The banging intensified. First, she was curious, then she felt frightened. Could a few zombies have left the *Andronicus*? It might've been her imagination, but she thought she saw the hull deforming. That was impossible. Even a direct high-speed impact wouldn't put a dent in a hardened nosecone. It might detach, but it couldn't be crushed.

The team filed out steadily. Too-ahka's flamethrower whooshed as the alien painted the oncoming zombies with a fiery brush. Screams, roars, and a chorus of growls. The Silvas ripped off shots. Shawna couldn't see anything past Bak-Irp's shoulders. She ducked in time to observe Krait slinking sideways, heading toward the exit. Lemora followed him. Nero was hot on her heels, reaching back to pump lead into the writhing mass of zombie guards and prisoners.

CRUUUNNCHCH!!!

Despite the bulky suit, Shawna spun around. Something... some huge thing was trying to smash through the hull above the monitors, making deep impressions bigger than her helmet. It couldn't be the zombies from the cabin. This thing outside was too big as well as astonishingly powerful. Not knowing what it could be only made her fear grow. *What was out there?* No more time to look back. When she saw it, she'd deal with it. That's what she told herself. Bak-Irp was on the move. When he finally stepped aside, she got her first full view of the cabin after the landing. Burning zombies flailed, smoking hunks of corpses lay under and between the seats. Through the smoke she detected movement, but she didn't want to waste any bullets, so she held her fire. Somebody from the team shoved the exit door open but not all the way. She glimpsed the top of a sand pile that was blocking it. They had to shimmy through the opening one at a time. Too-ahka was out and gone. The same with Krait, Lemora, and Nero. The clones stayed back after they sprang the door, sliding against the inner fuselage and providing covering fire; Matias was dumping one load of buckshot after another into the smoky haze. Mateo hooked him around the neck, attempting to drag him out of there. Bak-Irp was squeezing through the gap to the outside, banging it with his shoulder as he muttered expletives.

He turned to shout at the Silvas, "We've got to go! C'mon, man."

"I'm trying," Mateo said.

Matias had run out of ammo and was reloading. Mateo used the opportunity to slap the sides of his helmet, knocking sense into him, bringing him back to reality. They were bumping faceplates, shouting at each other. But it was all good, Shawna realized, just brotherly enthusiasm and bloodlust. Arm in arm, the clones stumbled for the exit.

She got there before them.

"You go," Mateo said. "We'll hold them off."

She didn't have time to thank them. Bak-Irp had forced the door farther open, so it was easier for her to fit. Stepping outside, her boot landed on something soft. She lost her balance, falling back on her butt, slipping down a dune of windblown sand the color of bruised apricots with chunks of cracked pavement poking out. She looked for the sky but only saw dust smeared with golden light. At the bottom, Bak-Irp was waiting for her. He yanked her up onto her feet.

"This way," he said.

She didn't know how he could see anything. The cloud was impenetrable, disorienting.

"Where did they go?" she shouted.

The Thassian didn't answer. He was hunched forward, running. From somewhere up ahead came the *rat-a-tat-tat* of a machine gun, followed by the boom of a shotgun and pistol fire.

Had they met up with some kind of resistance?

Shawna looked over her shoulder, waving to the Silva twins to follow. Mateo waved back. In the doorway at the top of the sand slide, a zombie crawled out of the Deathcan and scrabbled down the dune, somersaulting, bouncing up on its feet and running right at the brothers. Mateo turned and blew a line of meaty holes in it from its belt to its chin.

The zombie fell, still moving, kicking sand. Roaring, spitting. Angry at being shot.

More zombies poured out of the *Andronicus*. The dust swirled.

The gooey sensation of running from monsters in a nightmare seized Shawna. No matter how hard she tried to pump her legs, they felt like they were stuck in a mucky bog. *Slooow.* She was so slow. They were going to catch her. Dismember her. Mateo was firing. His clone brother's shotgun boomed. *How many more zombies were left? What did it take to bring one down?* She'd heard them behind all that smoke, tearing up the seats, throwing tantrums. *They're not indestructible. We can stop them.* But she didn't turn around again to look.

The particulate cloud thinned. She could make out the shapes of the station's buildings. Ahead of her, the white shell of Bak's armor suit plunged forward, like a wedge of sea ice bobbing against the drab mounds. Farther on, three more white-suited figures emerged. In the distance, a blaze of fire bloomed: Too-ahka, signaling them from the station entrance. She didn't see zombies anywhere ahead. The whole team had made it out alive. If the zombies from the ship didn't catch them, they'd reach their target. They needed shelter… only a few meters farther…

As Shawna was running, she spotted craters in the station's former runway. Glancing down into one, she recognized that they weren't made by objects that had fallen from above. Ejected pieces of pavement and rocks surrounded the pits. Whatever made these holes burst up from below. Explosions in the mines? Gas eruptions? Nothing she came up with made any sense.

And that made her worry even more.

The team regrouped in an archway. Mateo and Matias were the last to arrive.

"What happened to the zombies that were chasing us?" Shawna asked.

"We got all of them," Matias said. "Blasted their asses."

Shawna looked at Mateo who was bent over, hands on his thighs, trying to slow his breathing. He shook his head. "I don't know. I couldn't see... but I think maybe they ran away."

"Ran away?" Shawna said.

"Naw, bro. We killed them to death," Matias insisted. "If we didn't, they'd be here."

Mateo shrugged. "He could be right. They're not behind us now."

Shawna had a hard time believing the zombies would turn tail and quit pursuing them for no reason. But Matias was right, the zombies should've been there by now, and they weren't. She decided to accept the positive and focus on what was in front of them. It was a loading zone, with ramps and turbolifts. Minecarts were parked on rails that led off into tunnels and farther underground to the xenium. Pieces of heavy equipment sat idle around the area. Every machine was smashed, totally wrecked beyond repair. If there'd been a cave-in or explosion, she might've expected to find such an extreme amount of destruction. *But, holy shit, did zombies do this?*

"What's it saying? Hey, Shawna? Interpret." Nero stood with Too-ahka, who was signing at him without any luck. The team members climbed halfway up a ramp; the station doors were rolled down and battered, but they appeared to have withstood the assault. Shawna stepped in.

"Too-ahka says we can't get inside," she said. "Not here, anyway. The doors are jammed in their tracks and the power system's down. We can't lift them manually. We need to look for another way in." The alien nodded along as Shawna relayed the message.

Nero was soaking up the intel when Lemora suddenly interjected a bit of welcome news.

"I saw another entrance." She turned and pointed. "Around the corner. Fifty meters."

"That's where we'll go then," Nero said.

Bak-Irp had his back to the team, his eyes combing the horizon for any signs of zombies.

"Where'd they go?" he said.

"Who cares?" Nero said. "As long as they're not in our way, I don't give a shit."

Shawna remembered the shots she'd heard. "What the hell were you guys shooting at?"

"I thought I saw movement around those minecarts," Krait answered. He put his machine gun scope up to his eye, scoping the carts and tunnels again. "There's nothing there now."

"I was only shooting because he was shooting," Nero said.

"Same here," Lemora admitted, as she reloaded her shotgun.

"But none of you actually saw any zombies?" Shawna asked. "Is that right?"

Krait shrugged and said, "I can't be sure."

"What are you so worried about?" Nero asked Shawna. "We made it. Be happy."

"I am happy. But something was trying to bash in the cockpit. It had to be… gigantic."

Everyone was quiet, thinking about what she'd told them. She read their faces. They were expecting zombies, not giants. Zombies, they thought they could handle. *Giant zombies…?*

"Bullshit," Nero said finally. "I didn't see anything. Bak? How's it looking out there?"

"All clear."

"Fantastic. That's what I like to hear. Let's find those doors and get inside. Lemora, you and Fuzzy lead the way." Nero holstered one of his magnums. Since they'd escaped the dust-up caused by their landing, the visibility was good. Things were quiet. It was like a ghost town from ancient times that Shawna read about when she was a little girl – cowboys and desperadoes, America's Old West frontier – a time and a place where the only law was the iron in your hand, the lead in the other guy, and the gold in your pocket. She always wished she'd lived back then.

Too-ahka and the doctor went to the front of the line. Single file, sticking close to the station wall, they marched from the loading zone to where she'd spied another set of doors.

Bak-Irp was hesitant to leave his lookout post.

Shawna tapped his arm. "What is it?"

"Thought I saw something."

She joined him, gazing at the *Andronicus* hunkered down in the bleak PK-L7 landscape. The debris cloud had dissipated; as far as the eye could see stretched a barren, lifeless landscape.

"Zombies from the ship?" she said.

"Nah… probably nothing. A dust devil, or something, whirling up out there looking dark and dangerous. I'm not sweating about it." He broke his stare and moved off to rejoin the team.

"Why not?" Shawna jogged to keep up with the Thassian's longer strides. His muscular tail whipped back and forth inside its expansion sleeve, so she didn't get too close. He swiveled his head to the side without making eye contact, though she detected the hint of a smile.

"Too damn big for a zombie," he said. "Looked like it was standing up behind the ship peeking over the top." Bak-Irp chuckled, picking up his pace. "That'd be one ginormous beast."

Shawna continued to watch the ship as they walked, but she didn't see anything.

But she knew she'd heard something taking out its frustration on the Tri-T's nose. Bak-Irp *had* seen something, even if he wasn't ready to believe it. She knew it was out there, too.

And it was massive.

CHAPTER NINETEEN
Team Meeting

"I *did* see another entrance. Here it is," Lemora said. "Look how the zombies breached these doors all those years ago." The doors had been torn off their hinges and lay twisted, crumpled into balls like gift wrap after a birthday party.

"What kind of bomb did they use?" Krait asked, surveying the damage.

"They didn't use any," Lemora said. "There are no signs of an explosion here. They managed to achieve this vandalism utilizing only their hands and claws." Deep gouges marred the outside of the module, as if a giant hungry child had run their fingers through cake frosting. The extreme degree of devastation pointed to a frenzied attack – sustained, vicious, and highly effective. Lemora wondered how long it had taken them to defeat the heavy-duty materials; these same building blocks were used throughout Terran space in the most rugged and unforgiving environments and had a reputation for being virtually indestructible. She guessed it was a matter of minutes, not hours. The miners would've been in a state of total panic, if they even had time to think. In this way, the Xenos acted like a natural disaster, striking without warning on an awe-inspiring scale, seizing hold of a place and shaking it to its foundations. She pictured them in her mind's eye: infected Xenos boiling over the structure like an army of Frantician zealot ants, a species known to eat across an entire planet, devouring all life before anything could be done.

She clambered over the debris stacked in the hallway. The miners must've tried to block the entrance, or at least slow down the Xenos, by putting as many obstacles in their path as possible. But the Xenos were relentless, invading the station like an infection entering a body covered with open wounds. Too-ahka quickly disappeared into the innards of the station's modular complex, finding small openings in the barricade and pushing into them without a moment's hesitancy. The alien showed no fear, stuffing itself into holes no wider than its forehead; watching him choked Lemora with claustrophobia. She couldn't decide if the creature's boldness was the result of a reckless disposition or a compulsion to explore mysteries of the unknown regardless of the cost; a driving, perhaps insatiable, curiosity powered its motor.

In Too-ahka's absence, she became the walker on point, scouting the trail while the rest of the members followed her in a "V" formation. Steps ahead of them, she investigated the barricade in more detail. Desks, tables, bed frames were fitted together in a jigsaw heap… the station's inhabitants would've grabbed what was nearest at hand in a desperate attempt to impede the invasion, therefore the living quarters had to be around here. They weren't ferrying furniture across the complex. Chances were slim, but they might find usable supplies in proximity to the habitation site.

She wasn't sure what hour it was on PK-L7. The planet

existed in a twilit limbo, suggestive of neither night nor day but lit in muted sepia tones, no suns or moons visible through a thick cloud layer congested in the sky – a monotone gruel that varied little in coloration from the land, giving one the sensation of being buried alive. Venturing a few steps inside, the darkness of the station enveloped her, as if she'd been swallowed whole. Lemora switched on the headlamp mounted to the front of her helmet. If this were an armed conflict, such an act would've been suicidal, but she hadn't read anything about zombies using guns. They employed no weapons other than what nature had bestowed: brute strength, teeth, and claws. Survival of the deadliest – aided by the virulence of the mold, which erased desire and motivation, replacing them with a single, homicidal directive: KILL EVERYONE WHO'S NOT A ZOMBIE.

Although the weather now was calm, an accumulation of past sandstorms had sifted its way deep inside the structure – a granular dust whipped up by the winds, blown into cracks and crevices over the decades with no one to sweep up the mess. Hard grit coated every surface, crunching underfoot with each step that she took. Something about the noise set her teeth on edge, and she yearned for a long, hot, relaxing soak in a bubble bath and to feel clean again.

There was more than grit blighting the station.

An ugly, sticky substance covered the walls. In some places it appeared dry and spongy, branching off and attaching itself to just about anything it touched, creeping along, growing, spreading, thriving – in other spots it resembled a glistening, jellylike slime. She touched a moist patch and observed how it adhered to her fingertips, stretching like an elastic band as she pulled her hand away, only breaking when she sliced it with the knife from her utility belt. She studied the severed strand, holding it up to the light near her faceplate. Ropey, viscous, and composed of a dark amalgam of colors – whorls and spiral shapes danced inside it like tiny galaxies.

Yes. This was the mold. Same as the nugget she'd inserted into her bomb. The smuggled sample must've been dehydrated so that it could be handled more easily, preserved, and transported. Here the Xeno contagion existed in its natural state – active, alive, and variable in presentation. *Fascinating.*

The scientist in Lemora wanted to gather more specimens, to catalog them, and bring them to a proper laboratory for further inquiry where she might magnify, dissect, and conduct tests. But this moment was not the time or place for purely intellectual pursuits. Although the potential for this substance as a biological weapon remained unprecedented, she had to resist the temptation to indulge in further analysis. The highest priority was to avoid the zombies – if there were any of them still populating PK-L7. Maybe Nero was correct, and they'd died off, turning on each other and murdering themselves into extinction. That would be an ironic fate. Tragic to a certain extent, but a great cause for celebration among the XSecPen escapees, if they entertained any possible hope of making it through their ordeal. On the other hand, if the Xenos had survived, she hoped they'd grown weak and enfeebled as they swirled the evolutionary drain – a dead end for a species born of death.

Otherwise, there'd be a lot of Xeno exterminating to do until Neera came to rescue them.

If Neera came at all …

"Wait up," Krait called to her. The lithe smuggler wormed his way past an overturned filing cabinet and a jungle gym of mangled shelving racks. Sweat beads covered his face like bugs.

"Is there a problem?"

"No problem," Krait said. "I wanted to talk to you, alone. Ask you something."

"So, ask."

Krait smiled a cool, closemouthed smile. He knew she didn't trust him; he didn't care.

"What is your confidence level in Nero's plan?" he said, in a carefully neutral tone.

Ah, here it was, Krait feeling her out to see if she might be up for a double-cross. Would she like to join him in forming a plan of their own, or a back-up plan, or any of a myriad of betrayals?

"One hundred percent." An outrageous lie. Fifty-fifty were the best odds she was giving.

"Glad to hear it. I concur, by the way. I was only checking to see if you agreed."

Bullshit, bullshit, bullshit.

Krait shifted his gaze, scanning past her. "What are the chances any part of this hellhole is still sealed? I mean, if we can't make it airtight, then turning on the oxygen will be pointless."

"One module up and running will be enough to sustain us," she said.

"If we can resurrect any of these mummified systems and direct them to that module..." Krait trailed his glove across a tabletop, curling his lip in distaste. She knew little about the mega-smuggler. He was allegedly a recluse, shunning the company of other people, living in a remote, cloaked ship floating in uncharted space, where he sat behind a suite of the world's most powerful computers, directing his minions, both humans and bots, to carry out his schemes. He'd made his fortune hijacking carriers, stealing their cargo and reselling the goods on the black market, often to the Guilds; he converted the ships to serve his operations: galactic piracy, basically. Krait flew the black flag, but did so virtually, without ever leaving his office chair.

Lemora decided to massage his ego. It sometimes helped to remind clever men how clever they were. Then you could wind them up and watch them go like little toy soldiers.

"I leave the systems revival up to you," she said. "You're a tech legend. I only make things go BOOM. A project of such complexity is well beyond the scope of my abilities, sadly."

"Each of us are gifted with special talents. I, for one, am no good at building bombs."

It was Lemora's turn to smile. He didn't mean it and no doubt thought demolitions research was beneath him. He was a procurer, a finder and provider of uncommon goods and skills, and he surely saw himself as above it all, tugging at the marionette strings, in control and hidden out of sight. As master manipulator, he lived on high, staring down in amusement. He saw himself as a god. Lemora might create thunder and lightning, but Krait bent them to his will.

Nero climbed toward her light. He was out of breath but excited about something.

"There you are. What are you two doing? Plotting to overthrow me?" He grinned, but Lemora knew he was only half-joking. He was also half-right; Krait *was* plotting. The smuggler had better watch his step. Lemora had known Nero for years, and the man had an uncanny knack for sniffing out the stratagems of his opponents. Rarely did they defeat him. *Just ask the baron.*

"I was only saying it's too bad we don't have a map of the station," Krait said.

Nero turned on his headlamp, panning the cluttered passageway. "Where's Too-ahka?"

Lemora pointed at a notch in the barricade. "He went in there. Quick as you please."

"Crazy little guy. I don't know if I trust him. Do you trust him?" he asked Lemora.

She saw Krait stiffen almost imperceptibly – the slightest of flinches. *Did he think Nero was also asking about him?* Perhaps, in a sneaky way, he was. The gamesmanship never ended.

Lemora shrugged.

"Keep an eye on him. If you notice anything weird, I'll have Bak punch his ticket. One to the back of the head. POW!"

Lemora watched as the muscle along Krait's jaw twitched. He was clenching his teeth. Nero was getting to him, wriggling his way under his skin and into his head, seeding fears.

"Everything about Too-ahka is weird," she said.

"You know what I mean." Nero shone his lamp at a slot near the curved ceiling. "We can push in there. We need to find the comms center and see if we can wake up the computers. If the station's power generator exploded, we'd have noticed a big hole in the ground from the air. So there's power. And if there's power, then there's a way to send out a signal to Neera. I don't care if it's a simple distress beacon. She needs to know we made it here, then she'll come."

"And so will the Galactic Defense Forces," Krait said. "They'll figure out it's us."

"We lit a short fuse no matter what. When the *Andronicus* doesn't arrive at XSecPen 2, they'll know something's up.

That Carrion ship isn't going to be reporting to base either. It's a question of timing. If we contact Neera before GDF drops a black ops team on us, we're golden."

The other escapees materialized like ghosts out of the gloom behind them.

"Team meeting?" Bak-Irp said. "I didn't get the notification."

Matias snickered.

"We were discussing our ride," Krait said. "Nero wants to bring the station's comms online and call his sister. I have concerns about alerting the Coalition to our whereabouts."

Nero glared at him. "Krait's panicky. He thinks a signal will draw GDF like flies to shit."

"We're the shit," Matias said, laughing, slapping his brother's back in gut-busting glee.

Mateo frowned, gazing at him with a look of uncertainty.

"They'll lock in on our position and scramble a kill team," Bak-Irp said.

"And … ?" Nero said.

"What are we going to do about it?"

"We'll wait for Neera!" Nero's patience was spent; Lemora was familiar with his volatile reactions. A dictator at heart, he asked for input but liked to think every good idea sprang from his own head. She'd learned to live with his quirks. Egotism wasn't the worst sin. But managing Nero's fragile ego was a tedious task that could be exhausting at times.

"What makes you think that your sister can beat them here–" Krait was saying.

"Because she's using a wormhole," Nero said, eying him smugly. "And they're not."

"Your sister's got a butthole?" Matias said, sounding perplexed. "I don't get it, bro."

"WORMhole," Nero said. "It'll open above us. We fly into it, and POOF! We're gone."

"How did Neera gain access to that technology?" Lemora asked with a mixture of awe and skepticism. Neera wasn't interested in cutting edge innovations. She didn't have the attention for them, flitting from one enthusiasm to another like a now extinct honeybee drinking nectar; in this way she was exactly like her brother. Nothing was ever fast, bright, or new enough to satisfy them for very long. If Neera did have a way of harnessing a wormhole, that would change everything. But wormholes, like Lupasters, were notoriously unstable and dangerous.

"She didn't develop it on her own, if that's what you're asking. There's this Caridian scientist. He knows how to work that wacky wormhole magic. And we've got him on our side."

"Nice, if it's true," Krait admitted. "The Caridians are the experts in that area."

"Look, pal," Nero said, "I'm getting tired of you. If you want to go your own way, be my guest. I've got a plan and it's going to work whether you agree with me or not. Capeesh?"

"I believe in transparency," Krait said. "The more we share, the better we'll function as a team. We need to learn to trust one another if we're going to accomplish big things together."

"Screw you!" Nero rocked on his heels. "Was that transparent enough?"

All their headlamps were lit now, except for Matias who bobbed his head up and down to the beat of a tune only he could hear. His brother switched his light on for him.

"Now I can see where I'm going," Matias said. "Is this place haunted? I feel creeeeepy."

A noise stopped their conversation. It wasn't loud, but it

was clear. Headlamps swung bright illumination over to the barricade wall. Bak-Irp had his gun up, searching for a target. The Silvas did the same thing. Shawna crouched low, making herself a smaller target, ready to shoot. Bak held a finger to his faceplate, requesting silence. The noise came again – a wiggly squeaking of metal on metal coming from behind the barricade. Suddenly, something snapped, and the jumble of furniture started collapsing, shifting against itself as it fell.

When the heap finally settled, Too-ahka was standing in the middle of things, smiling, holding the flamethrower on its hip. He motioned for them to come forward, but no one moved. With his free hand, he talked to Shawna. Lemora marveled at the bond these two had formed.

"He says to follow him," Shawna said. "He's found something we'll want to see."

"Let's go," Nero said, heading to the front of the pack. "Fuzzy, lead the way."

CHAPTER TWENTY
Clowning

Nobody gives me enough credit, Nero thought. It must be nice to be a follower, doing whatever you're told and taking no responsibility beyond the tip of your nose. *Try leading.* Everybody wants to be the boss until they get the job. He'd conquered worlds. *Worlds!* Sure, getting locked up was a setback. But that wasn't his fault. The Coalition overlords hounded him, outnumbering and outgunning him for years, yet he'd still evaded them, making a game out of it, and drinking their tears. An informer was his undoing, and no matter how hard you vetted your underlings, the weakest among them would fail eventually, and like a cornered sewer rat, they'd do whatever it took to save their skins. He didn't know the identity of the traitor who stuck the knife in his back, although he had a list of suspects. The problem was there were too many. Despite what his critics said, Nero had ample patience; in time he'd find the informer and make them pay, painfully. Revenge was his xenium. It gave him limitless energy. For now, the issue was contacting Neera, and staying upright until the wormhole blossomed over PK-L7.

They broke through the congested end of the modular

hallway, and the remainder of the passage was surprisingly clear. Apart from the bones. Mounds and mounds of them. A real charnel house. Nero was aghast at the level of catastrophic failure. Too-ahka squatted to pick through them, studying the shards, inspecting toothmarks scored into the surfaces. The alien put one of the bones in its mouth and gnawed at it.

That's got to be unsanitary, Nero thought. "Taste anything interesting?" he asked.

Too-ahka didn't respond. Nero couldn't blame the creature. He hadn't been able to read the alien's sign language before, and there wasn't much of a chance he'd figure out the meaning now. The alien took the bone out of its mouth, comparing grooves. Then it went back to digging in the pile for more, tossing broken femurs and humeri over its shoulder. Nero saw a whole human ribcage fly by. No skulls, though. Maybe the Xenos saved the heads for… reasons.

Shawna went up to Too-ahka, and the alien showed her the skeletonized remains.

"There were at least three varieties of Xenos who killed these humans," she said, translating for the group.

"Too hard, too soft, and juuust right?" Nero asked.

Shawna ignored his attempt at humor. "Three different bite patterns appear with regularity. All of them are bigger than Too-ahka's mouth. A few of the bones are completely shattered, indicating at least one of the species has a bite strength that's off the charts." Shawna examined the fragments for herself. She passed them to Lemora, who scrutinized the evidence.

Lemora said, "I read that the infected Xenos were comprised of multiple subtypes. Workers, Hunters, and Tanks. Their sizes varied. The bite patterns may reflect these differences."

"These bones are old relics," Nero said. "Don't get me wrong, it's interesting. And irrelevant."

"Not if there are still zombies around," Shawna said.

"Yeah, well, we can cross that bridge…" Nero didn't finish. He walked away. He wasn't about to show the others that he was worried. If they didn't find any zombies on PK-L7 except those they'd flown in with on the *Andronicus*, they'd be fine. So far, so good.

Lemora wandered past the bone pile. "Look at this." She motioned Nero forward. There was a junction; a modular hallway bisecting theirs. To the left was another occluded passage full of junk from the station, old bones, and wavy drapes of mold, but to the right she'd discovered an emergency drop barrier made of titanium with a mining company logo. "They must've triggered these walls to come down when they realized the station had been breached. Like a ship, the failsafe system is designed to seal off the unaffected areas. It's intact."

Nero went to the screen pad next to the barrier and tapped it. "Dead, as expected."

Krait smoothed his hand over the barrier, then he approached the blank screen. "May I?"

"By all means," Nero said. "Play us a tune, maestro. Prove to me you're a team player."

Using the tips of his nimble fingers, Krait pried the panel loose, gently letting the display dangle from a colorful braid of wires. "Does anyone have a knife?"

"Here." Lemora passed him her blade.

The smuggler separated the wires, picking out a variety of colored lines, which he quickly stripped. "Matias, will you lend me a hand?"

Matias strode up to the smuggler. "What'd you need? Somebody to hold it for you?"

"Turn around," Krait said. "If you don't mind."

The hitman faced away from the smuggler, staring at the others with bugged-out eyes, mockingly sticking out his tongue and trying to lick the inside of his faceplate. Krait removed the cover from the back of Matias's spacesuit, exposing the life support nerve center. He started splicing wires, twisting ends together. He poked inside it with the knife. Matias's headlamp flashed, dimmed, and went out.

"Whoa! What the hell?" Mateo said, raising his gun barrel, pointing it at Krait.

The smuggler paused. "I'm jacking into his power supply. It won't harm him, I can assure you of that. I only need a tiny spark…"

"Bro?" Mateo asked.

Matias shrugged. "Let him spark me. I've been through worse. You can't kill me, see?"

Mateo nodded at Krait to continue.

Krait fiddled with the suit's circuitry, joining Matias to the control panel via a tether of cables. After several failed attempts, Krait's expression grew sour. He stripped more wires, plugging and unplugging connections.

"*Mano*, you good?" Mateo asked.

"All good," Matias answered. "You smell burned meat? I smell burned meat."

"What?" Mateo raised his gun, sticking it against Krait's torso.

"He's screwing with you," Krait said.

"It's true, bro," Matias said, grinning. "I'm only clowning."

"Stop it," Mateo said.

"The day I can't clown no more is the day you can blow my ass out the airlock."

Krait lifted the dangling panel close to his faceplate, shining his light at it. He touched the screen, and the emergency barrier's gears began to whine. Slowly, the emergency security wall lifted. It retracted into a pocket in the ceiling. Matias turned to watch it go. Krait blinked smugly.

"Hold still," Krait said. "You're on a short leash, my friend."

Nero pointed his headlamp into the newly revealed module. No remains on the floor. No mold on the walls. It didn't look pristine, but he was feeling delighted. "No sand. The seal held."

The barrier stopped moving, and the whining ceased. But a different sound replaced it.

A grinding: low and mechanical, a cranking of gears that meant business. It was the kind of sound that if you'd heard it once, you never forgot. For many, it was the last noise they heard.

Bak-Irp cast his headlamp beam over the heads of Nero, Krait, and Matias. "Oh shit! GET DOWN!" He dove at Nero, wrapping him around the waist and taking him to the ground. Mateo tackled his brother, snapping the cables hooking him up to the panel. The clones covered their heads.

Krait just stood there, speechless.

As the Falchion sentry gun bore down on him and started firing…

CHAPTER TWENTY-ONE
Joy

Krait had never encountered a Falchion sentry gun before, so the sound of it taking aim had no impact on him. The bullets were another story, if there had been any left. Luckily for him, the gun was empty, having spent its ammo centuries ago. The Falchion whirred, cycling through empty chambers, its trigger clicking until he disconnected it. Krait felt only curiosity at his brush with death. If he were going to die, he'd be dead. It was that simple. Part of him thought he'd live forever; another part of him was ready to see what might be next, waiting beyond the veil.

"It must've been wired to the door," he said, examining the control panel and the cables ripped from the back of Matias's spacesuit. "When I jolted the barrier, it reactivated the sentry."

"Almost deactivated you," Nero said, tapping the smuggler's faceplate.

"I didn't see any dead Xenos on the floor anywhere in that opposite module," Bak-Irp said. "Did the sentry miss them? The only bones inside looked human. Maybe it malfunctioned."

"Or the Xenos might collect their dead." Shawna joined them. Too-ahka stood beside her.

"What if they bury them?" Bak-Irp said.

"Or eat them," Krait added dryly. "That would be an efficient use of resources."

The bodyguard looked at him strangely, but Krait was used to it. People had always viewed him as an odd fellow, more comfortable around computers than living, breathing beings. His mother had told him he was missing something inside – a heart, perhaps. It was true that he didn't feel things the way others seemed to; he had strong interests, but no passions, rarely did he ever experience a sense of excitement or the worst-sounding of all emotions – joy. What he did sense acutely was stimulation, arousal, a bristling of his inner antennae, and he knew satisfaction, satiation, and rest. To be perfectly honest, he wished he were the only thing alive in the universe, but if he could not have that, then he preferred to interact with the world at one remove, detached if not physically, then emotionally. He pictured himself as an infinitely deep, frosty cold cylinder that occasionally needed filling. If the sentry gun had killed him, that wouldn't have been so bad.

"I think I can re-drop the barrier," Krait said. "I won't need Matias either. If I can trigger it, the barrier should have a freefall option." As he said this, he found the tab inside the control panel compartment he'd been looking for and depressed it; the heavy barrier slammed down with a thunderous racket. Everyone was on the right side, fortunately, though they ran for cover at the loud crash of it falling into place. "Sorry," he said, not meaning it. Seeing them jump was fun.

"If there's anything with ears on this station, they heard that," Bak-Irp said angrily.

Krait ignored him.

"It held once," he said, "it will hold again. The seal looked tight. Now we need to locate the life systems and turn the air back on. If we're lucky, the scrubbers are still working, and we won't asphyxiate ourselves." He glanced around, taking in their new surroundings. "These rooms appear to be the workers' living quarters. It's almost homey." Honestly, he found it filthy.

The group fanned out cautiously to search inside the module.

They entered the dorm rooms, clearing them, one by one. Nero didn't help with this security measure; he paced ahead seeking out the comms center. Krait could've told him that it was nearby, he spied the thick comms cable coiling inside the wall, a telltale sign. But their dear leader's arrogance pricked at him. If Nero's scheme to call his sister for a ticket to ride through a wormhole off this planet didn't pan out, Krait figured that he could trap the others in a module and suffocate them, then whatever else he might find at the station would only need to support one life: his. The Coalition would come for him. There'd be no avoiding that. He'd tell them Nero forced him to join in the escape. He'd show them the bodies of the dead escapees and see if they might consider commuting his sentence to repay him for his act of bravery. They'd never let him go, though. He was serving one hundred consecutive life terms for trafficking in sentient cargo and remotely sabotaging his own pirated ship, murdering fifty GDF soldiers who'd tried to confiscate it. Maybe he could finagle them into giving him better accommodations. He didn't mind solitary confinement, but he'd like a nice view and some new vid games to play.

Nero cried out, "HUZZAH!"

He'd discovered the comms center. That meant he'd be putting Krait to work. Krait hadn't made up his mind if he would make the call to Neera or only pretend to try. He'd decide after he saw what he had to work with. He'd never traveled through a wormhole. It might be invigorating. Then he could add it to the list of things he'd done, one of the few examples that he hadn't done alone. He'd heard that Neera was just as nasty as her brother. If he played his cards right, he might find the chance to murder them both and send himself through the wormhole.

Now that would be fun!

"Krait! Where are you?" Nero tromped down the corridor. "Oh, you're right here."

"I was distracted," Krait said. "By my own thoughts. Sorry. I'm spacey sometimes."

"I found the comms center. It's time for you to earn your keep," Nero said.

"My pleasure," Krait said, and he almost meant it, but not how Nero thought he did.

The comms room hadn't been wrecked. It looked like an exhibition at a museum, a slice of the past frozen in time, where you could visit and imagine your ancestors trying to talk to one another. It was quaint. The control panel curved smoothly around the room. Krait rolled up a chair. It was like sitting inside a seashell, listening for the ocean, a hiss of waves, the hollow, cupped sounding that was like your ears filling up with warm seawater as you drowned.

"Can you make it talk?" Nero asked.

"I just sat down," Krait said. "Give me a sec."

Nero unfolded a scrap of paper from a pocket of his spacesuit. He handed it to Krait.

"What's this?" Krait asked.

"That's our contact. Neera? My sister? Message her at that number. It's untraceable."

Krait pushed the paper aside. He tipped a keyboard and soft gray crud floated out of it onto the control desk. "You know this isn't going to be easy, right? I have to locate an emergency power source. There should be one in this room somewhere. But it's probably kaput."

"Kaput?"

"Maybe there's no juice to squeeze out of it. What's the phrase, 'Water from a stone'?"

"Make it work. No excuses," Nero said. "You've got one hour. If you don't send the signal by then, Bak-Irp will execute you. I don't like you, Krait. I don't need any more reasons."

Krait believed him.

So, he went to work, dreaming of ways of killing the team while he tried to save them.

CHAPTER TWENTY-TWO
Small Holes

"What are they arguing about?" Shawna said.

Bak-Irp put his ear to the door of the comms room. He had his shoulder braced against it in case they suddenly tried to burst out. If Nero accused him of eavesdropping, he'd say he was just doing his job, guarding the boss like he was paid to do. But the two of them, Nero and Krait, weren't going anywhere anytime soon. They were too busy tearing each other new assholes.

"Nero's losing his shit. Says he thinks Krait's lying," Bak-Irp said.

"Lying about what?"

"Not being able to bring the comms system back to life. Krait says that there's no local backup power source, which should be inside the comms room. But it isn't." Bak-Irp took his ear away and leaned his back against the door, letting out a long sigh of exhaustion. "I'm tired."

"When's the last time you slept?"

"I catch a couple hours every night. But truth be told, I haven't had a good night's sleep since they locked my ass up.

My brain is always on high alert, listening, waiting for trouble to arrive on my doorstep."

"You can relax," Shawna said. "I think it's here."

The Thassian smiled.

Nero was screaming at Krait now. You couldn't help but hear him.

He said, "Bak's going to kill you, you bastard! Time's up. He's going to come in here and break your fingers, bend your elbows backward, and kick out your kneecaps. Then I'm going to have him choke you to death. Slowly. Wring your neck until you pass out, then shake you awake and do it again. I'm going to sit here and watch you suffer. And I'm going to enjoy it."

Shawna raised her eyebrows at Bak-Irp. "You wouldn't do that, would you?"

"I might," he said. The whole situation was turning into crap while they waited to sort out the comms. Those zombies outside weren't playing beach smackyball. They'd be coming soon.

"How can you work for a guy like Nero?" she asked him. "You seem better than that."

Bak-Irp thought about it. "I need the money. I got kids. Four of them, all still in school. They live with my wife on a floating medical island. She's a doctor who works with refugees."

"How did she get mixed up with an outlaw like you?"

"I charmed her," Bak-Irp said wistfully. "She fixed me up after a scrape with a fugitive I brought in. This Russian dude who was wanted on a triple murder beef. He'd joined up with a mercenary crew fighting a border skirmish between Safeholders and Upholders. The Interplanetaries refused to

send their cops to capture him. The area was too hot. I found
the guy eating MREs in an Upholder mess tent. He attacked
me with a fork. Put about forty holes in me."

"Oh shit," Shawna said. "That must've hurt."

Bak-Irp shrugged. "They were small holes."

"Did you end up getting him?"

"Oh, yeah." Bak-Irp remembered the Russian's reaction
when he took the fork away and put it somewhere the Russian
couldn't reach it. He chuckled. "My wife had to treat him, too.
But I was the better patient. I talked her ear off, convinced her
to let me make her dinner afterward." His wife was beautiful
even in a war zone. She had kind eyes that crinkled in the
corners when she laughed. He liked to make her laugh more
than anything else in the world. He pushed his memories
down before they started flooding into his head like water
from a busted dam.

"How'd you get yourself outside the law? If you don't mind
me asking," Shawna said.

"I do mind. It was personal business. I'll tell you this much.
I lost my cool and then things spun out of control. There was
a gang who thought they could spook me by threatening
to hurt my family. They learned a lesson. I did, too, and if I
could take it back I would. But I can't." Bak-Irp saw a vision
of himself, the rage he'd felt, the way it changed him, how it
made him feel crazy and like a stranger inhabiting his skin.
He pictured what he'd done to the members of that gang, but
it was like he was watching another person doing it. After he
was finished with them, he wandered, his head full of staticky
fuzz, and a bad taste lingered in his mouth that he couldn't
rinse away no matter how much liquor he poured in it. He
couldn't go back to being the person he'd been before –

that was how it felt – so he stayed out, an empty husk who hounded evil men.

Until the Interplanetaries hunted him down. He didn't even put up a fight when they came for him. He gave up. Just like that. The next thing he knew he was a prisoner in the HT unit, like waking up from one nightmare to find yourself trapped inside another bad dream.

The door opened behind him, and Bak-Irp caught himself before he fell back. Nero came rushing out. He ducked past them.

"What's up?" Bak asked.

But Nero wasn't talking. He marched straight for Lemora, hauling her into a dorm room where they started whispering to each other. *It sounds like a Thassian viper pit*, Bak-Irp thought. He turned and looked in on Krait. The tech genius was still alive; he looked bored, aloof.

"What's the deal? Are you two fighting?" Bak-Irp said.

"Did he order you to kill me?" Krait asked, his voice dull, as if it were AI-generated.

"Not yet."

"Hooray for me," Krait said. "Your boss is a lunatic by the way. Watch out for him."

"Tell me something I don't know."

It was a figure of speech, but Krait seemed to take it seriously. He got down on his hands and knees and rapped his knuckles against a thick, hard plate welded to the wall under the control panel desk. "This sucker is the problem. I expected to find a backup battery down here, but what we've got is reinforced steel, and there's no way to remove it that I can find. Nero thought he discovered the comms center, but it looks to me like this is a suboffice." Krait sat on the floor, slumping to his right side and playing with a screwdriver he'd found, digging the tip of it into the floor, carving a row of cemetery crosses on a hilltop. Seven of them.

"Suboffice?"

Krait quit his carving and balanced the screwdriver upright on the back of his hand. "The real comms hub is somewhere else in the station." He flipped the tool and caught it in midair.

"How do we find it?"

"One sure way is to cut through that steel plate. I'm guessing there's an airduct back there. The cables run through it. Follow the cables to the hub, and BINGO, you're a winner."

"Bak!" Nero called out.

He met his boss in the module's hallway. "I'm here. Krait was catching me up."

"You're not staying here for long," Nero said. "I want you to return to the *Andronicus* and retrieve something. There's a triple-bladed titanium saw that we found in the armory. Lemora left it in the avionics bay. She can show you where it is. We're going to use it to cut into that steel plate and enter the airduct." Nero chewed on his mustached lip. "I'm so thirsty."

"I can go with him," Shawna said. "I know where the saw is. I moved it when it was blocking the hatch." She'd acted restless since they sealed themselves in the module. Bak-Irp was fine going with her. She was smart and capable. Unlike the others, she might be trustworthy.

Nero considered her offer. "How do I know you won't try to fly off in the Deathcan?"

"That bird's hurting. I don't know if she can take off," Shawna said. "And Bak-Irp will be with me. You think I'm going to take him down? Get real. The guy's colossal. I'm tiny."

Nero nodded as he calculated. "I need Lemora. That's why

I'm going to say yes." He jabbed his thumb at Krait. "Open that drop wall again and let them out. Saddle up. We're burning daylight, and Neera's going to be wondering what happened to her precious brother."

Bak-Irp wasn't looking forward to going back outside. That thing he saw hanging around the *Andronicus* – he guessed it might've been a mirage, his eyes playing tricks, but it had looked right at him, a pale mammoth with laser beam eyes and a forest of tentacles sprouting from the humps of muscles packed on either side of its neck.

"I want a bonus," Bak-Irp said.

"What?" Nero asked, pissed-off.

"This saw delivery is beyond the scope of our arrangement. I'm not guarding you if you're staying here and sending me out there. So, if you want your tool brought to you by me, then I want extra compensation to collect it. Simple as that. Otherwise send somebody else."

"Name your price," Nero said.

"Fifty percent on top of what we agreed." He didn't think Nero would really go that high.

"Done," Nero said.

Bak-Irp was surprised the boss agreed so quickly. Maybe he should've asked for more.

Nero said, "Now take the lady pilot and bring me my saw."

CHAPTER TWENTY-THREE
Clever Bastards

Too-ahka wanted to go with Shawna and Bak-Irp back to the *Andronicus*, but Nero insisted that the alien stay to defend the module in case any Xenos showed up. Too-ahka reluctantly agreed. Krait managed to get himself halfway out of Nero's doghouse when he found a method for manually cranking up the viewport's steel shutters. Now the team inside the module could see outside, a 360-degree panorama spied through intact slabs of transparent "glass"; the view was grimy but surprisingly unobstructed on three sides. The module's connection to the larger base structure blocked the fourth side, except for a sliver of curved rooftop. The daylight remained unchanged: casting a yellow stain over PK-L7's desert landscape.

"There's the Deathcan," Lemora said. "We can observe your progress, darlings."

"These suit comms won't function that far out," Bak-Irp said. "I know you'll come running to save us if the Xenos show up. You wouldn't sit here and watch us die just for kicks."

Shawna liked the way Bak-Irp reminded Lemora and Nero that despite the fact they were in charge, he didn't have to act like he believed their bullshit. He only had to follow their orders. She was warming up to him, and except for possibly Too-ahka, he was the only one on the team that she would've volunteered to go with back to the *Andronicus*. They needed that triple saw.

Krait used Matias's power pack to raise the wall. He brought it up high enough for Bak-Irp and Shawna to crawl underneath. When it clanged back down, it wasn't as loud as the first time, but if any Xenos were in the vicinity, they'd have no problem figuring out their location.

"Is this a suicide mission?" Shawna asked Bak-Irp semi-seriously as they left the station.

"Not if I have anything to say about it. I plan on living *and* cashing my paycheck."

"You think Nero will make good on his promises?"

"If he doesn't, I'll force him to bite on this." Bak-Irp lifted the barrel of his machine gun.

They crossed the stretch of sand to the ship without incident. As they approached the *Andronicus*, Shawna veered off on a path toward the nosecone. "See? Look at the dents." She pointed out the damage. There were at least twenty deep indentations visible on the side of the ship facing them. "It's dimpled like a golf ball. Something was trying to bash its way in." Seeing the vandalism close up sent renewed shivers along her spine. The force it took was unreal.

"Whatever did that, I don't want to meet them," he said.

Shawna agreed that they needed to get inside, fast.

They picked up their pace, scrambled up the small dune leading to the exit door, and squeezed inside the cabin. Shawna swept the interior with her headlamp. No sign of zombies.

"I wonder where the bone munchers went," she said.

"Probably running around like fools." Bak-Irp cleared the cockpit, waving her in.

Shawna holstered her pistol and dropped down into the floor hatch. She found the heavy-duty cutting tool right where she'd left it. The circular saw came equipped with dual padded straps that fit over her shoulders. She slid them on and tested the ergonomic grips. Not too bad. She could walk with it, if not exactly sprint, and she only needed to lug it a few hundred paces. They'd agreed it was smarter for her to transport the saw and for Bak-Irp to provide protection as they retraced their steps to the mining station. Although he was physically larger, she was backwoods country strong, coming from a bloodline of rangy, tough-as-nails Kentuckians. She could more than carry her own weight and didn't know the meaning of the word "quit." The Thassian was a better shot and an expert in ground combat. Shawna had never killed anyone other than when she was strapped to a flying nuclear reactor, soaring through the ether high above. It was a different game down here with her face in the dirt. Both contests were deadly, but that didn't mean they were the same thing. Shawna trusted Bak-Irp to get the job done right.

"You about packed up?" Bak-Irp asked.

"Almost ready. Give me two secs."

Shawna tested the straps. The saw was heavy, but manageable with the weight distributed. She took it off and passed the tool to Bak in the cockpit. Then she climbed up and put the harness on again. It felt risky, almost naked, to be walking around without a gun in her hand. She touched her holster. If any Xenos got in too close, she'd see how they liked three high-speed diamond blades slicing into their business.

This cutter was made for chopping apart steel; flesh and bone would be no match for it. Her biggest problem would be ducking the splash back.

"Good to go?" he asked, walking through the cabin into the wedge of yellow light spilling through the open door. "I don't like it here. Feels like a mousetrap, and we're the mice."

"I'm as good as I'm going to get. Let's do this," she said, hoisting the cutter.

A sinewy gray arm studded with armored nodules reached inside the crack of the doorway. A scaly, tri-clawed Xeno hand clamped onto Bak-Irp's ankle like a leg iron.

Shawna leaped back, shocked that the zombie had gotten so near without their hearing it.

"What the hell?" Bak-Irp said. He kicked the arm with his other foot. It wouldn't let go.

The Xeno growled and twisted his leg.

Standing on one foot, Bak-Irp found himself yanked off balance. The Xeno tripped him, and the Thassian crashed hard to the floor. "*Mother–*" He struck out with his boot, driving his heel into the Xeno's face, which now filled the gap. The face was oblong and a lighter gray than the charcoal body skin. Between the dull, murderous eyes, a red vertical nasal cleft quivered. The mouth was a primitive slit trailing two pairs of swollen, scarlet barbels – the thinner top set dangled from the corners of its lips, and the lower, tapered pair drooped from its jowls, twitching like fat whiskers. "You are one ugly bastard," Bak-Irp said. "Now, let go of my foot!"

He shot the Xeno in the forehead.

Its grip slackened instantly, and the Xeno's lifeless body slithered out of the doorway, rolling down the sandpile, minus a forebrain.

"You hurt?" Shawna asked. Her heart was pounding like it wanted to leave.

"Nah. I'm good. Damn thing surprised me, though."

"Yeah, and it didn't come from the Deathcan. That thing lives here," she said.

The realization was sinking in for them. Bak-Irp looked even paler than normal. Shawna's legs felt rubbery. How many more of them were out there? How many different zombie types? Lemora said she'd read about three. But couldn't there be more after all these years? The mutations alone staggered the mind. Her stomach flipped over just thinking about it.

"You think they all look like that?" Bak-Irp asked.

"Beats me," she said.

"Sucker had a mug only a mother could love. But I doubt these things know what love is."

Shawna helped him to his feet. They crept up to the exit door and peeked outside. "Seems like he was by himself. A lone wolf," she said, wishing it were true but not really believing it.

"Or a scout." Bak-Irp slapped in a full magazine and unsnapped his ammo pouch. He stepped past her. His bulk filled the doorway. His eyes were moving, taking everything in, looking out, and up and down. He wasn't about to get grabbed again. "You ready to run for it?"

"What choice do I have?"

During the fight with Bak-Irp, the Xeno had ripped the exit open wide. The Tri-T's door swung freely now, unimpeded. Bak-Irp pushed it out slowly, holding his machine gun with one hand, eyes wide, on the lookout, finger poised on the trigger. "We go on three," he said. "One. Two…"

Shawna never heard him say *three*. He shouted as he leaped

for the middle of the sandpile, tobogganing down on his shiny backside, the smooth armor of the spacesuit offering little resistance. His words were lost, drowned out by the roar of a dozen Xenos identical to the one he'd killed. They'd been hiding around the back of the ship, using the tail to conceal themselves.

Clever bastards, Shawna thought.

Shawna didn't hesitate. She bounced out after Bak-Irp, holding the saw in front of her and starting it as she slid down. When she reached the bottom, the Xenos were on her. But they never expected to run into a buzzsaw. They'd probably never seen any weapon like it before. And she was quick to give them a demonstration.

Arms flew, spinning off like pinwheels, throwing banners of blood on the sand. She decapitated the first Xeno who tried to dart under the whirring blades to take a bite out of her. Its teeth scraped her armor, and one of them got stuck. She shook the head loose and booted it like a football. Bak-Irp was kept as busy as she was; he emptied his first magazine and reloaded without losing a beat. "Die! Die! Die!" he yelled as he picked his targets skillfully. Head. Chest. Head. Chest. He didn't waste any bullets.

The Xenos' bodies started to stack up. They showered Shawna with their blood. Her faceplate dripped with red rain. She had no time to feel fear. Her mind was too preoccupied with exterminating the zombies who were doing their damnedest to tear her to pieces and dine on her guts. She turned in a circle, slashing the air with the saw, sweat running into her eyes, when she realized there were no more Xenos to kill and Bak-Irp was barking at her to release the saw trigger and follow him. When she lifted her finger, the piercing whine of the blades cut off immediately, deafening in its silence, only to be replaced by her own rapid breathing.

"There's more of them," Bak-Irp said. "Out there. And they're coming quick."

She looked in the direction where he pointed the smoking barrel of his gun.

Dozens. No, not dozens. Hundreds. Too many to count... but hundreds of Xenos were moving *en masse* like a single amoebic organism, coordinated, advancing at a clip, pumping their muscular legs and kicking up a mini dust storm, arms flailing wildly over their heads...

Worst of all was the noise they made – the sound started as a low, guttural moan that almost sounded like a cry of pain, rising and rising until it was ringing in your ears, a piercing elongated scream imbued with pure hatred and an insatiable, ravening hunger...

CHAPTER TWENTY-FOUR
A Miniature Sun

"They're so fast," Nero said. "Where'd they come from all of a sudden?"

"Underground," Lemora said. "See that fissure in the big rock in the distance? They're still crawling out of it." She'd watched in horror as the Xenos poured up from the bowels of the planet. She hadn't heard it approach, but Too-ahka stood inches from her side, staring out the viewport. Other than occasionally blinking its tiny red eyes, the alien remained motionless. She wondered how sharp the creature's eyesight was, but from the intensity of its gaze she figured it was keen enough to absorb the dire situation that Shawna and Bak-Irp currently faced.

The horde of Xenos arranged themselves in a pincer formation, preparing to surround the pair's position as they advanced toward the station. It was going to be close. The orchestrated movement of the Xenos was truly remarkable to watch. The literature about the outbreak on PK-L7 was spotty, but Lemora was certain she'd never read a word about the infected Xenos displaying any behaviors suggestive of sophistication, collective thinking, or forming group strategies. They were independent homicidal brutes, plain and simple. Perhaps they'd learned a thing or two in the intervening years, and contrary to her hopes of their devolution, the term of isolation bestowed upon them a newfound intelligence and discipline. If that proved to be true, the escapees were in bigger trouble than they possibly could've predicted. Fighting as individuals, berserk Xenos, even in great numbers, were easier to defend against than coordinated teams who planned, executed, and revised their attacks. But it was too soon to draw any solid conclusions. First came observation and data gathering; she needed more evidence.

Nero said, "I didn't realize those things were so smart. Did you tell me they were smart?"

"I summarized what I read in the case studies," she said. "Which in retrospect might've been incomplete. The record is highly redacted. The Coalition kept the details under wraps."

"Yeah, well, the case studies can kiss my ass." Nero turned angrily away from the window. "Where did Fuzzy go?"

"It was just here a second ago," Lemora said. The creature was crafty, with a feline ability to slink away noiselessly when one wasn't paying attention. "Couldn't have gotten far, I think."

The richest man in Terran space poked his head into the hallway, and came back, grumbling. "Too-ahka is hanging upside-down from a support beam, asleep. Matias, on the other hand, is awake and ordering his dinner into a dead intercom. He wants a double cheeseburger and curly fries with extra ketchup. What do you think about that?"

"I prefer curry sauce," she said. But Nero was in no mood for her jokes.

He clenched and unclenched his fists. She saw that humor wasn't going to defuse the tension or distract him from the reality of what they were witnessing: the Xenos were still here, they were acting as if they were quite intelligent and really, *really* pissed off. She refused to let her emotions drive her thinking. Above all else, she sought to rely on cool, logical reasoning.

Bak-Irp kept shooting on the run, picking off the Xenos at the front of the charge. But as soon as one Xeno fell, its replacement would fill in the gap, leaping over or trampling the fallen zombie without even breaking stride. Shawna did her best dash for the station doors but lugging the cumbersome saw slowed her. The Xenos were gaining. It looked like they'd reach the station around the same time, which meant that Shawna and Bak-Irp would be shredded to pieces.

"Isn't there anything we can do to help?" Nero asked.

People who didn't know Nero like Lemora did might've mistaken his question for sympathy. But he wasn't being sympathetic, merely practical. He needed that cutting tool, and every team member who died now would be one less gun to defend him should the Xenos come calling. Or maybe she was wrong, and he was going soft, turning all emotional since he'd tasted freedom again. Maybe he cared about his team but didn't like to show it. She wouldn't bet money on that.

"I can think of one thing. But it would mean us leaving the module," Lemora said, arching her eyebrow. "Are you game?"

She was surprised when Nero volunteered to go with her. Krait bumped up the emergency barrier, and they crawled under. Lemora worried that Krait might not let them back inside, but she didn't tell Nero that. Everything with Krait was transactional, and she was willing to wager that he still needed them no matter what schemes he was hatching inside his squirmy reptilian brain. If he double-crossed them, they'd deal with it. She couldn't imagine that Krait was feeling too comfortable barricaded inside a module with Too-ahka and the Silva brothers. He wouldn't be able to cut a deal with them, and at this point, he wasn't strong enough to go it alone.

Nero stopped just inside the station doorway. He dropped to one knee and shouldered his machine gun. Rivulets of sweat dripped from his close-cropped hair. "The Xenos look a lot closer from down here," he said. He glanced at Lemora as she unpacked one of the flamethrower fuel canisters. The canister was a fat, metal cylinder shaped like a ship's escape pod; she hefted it in her hand, testing the weight, making calculations of height and distance in her head.

"I'll throw the canister when they get closer. Try to hit it at its apex," she said.

"The explosion isn't going to kill Shawna and Bak?"

"I don't think so." She felt fairly confident in her assessment, but one never knew.

"Because that kind of defeats the purpose," he said.

"On impact it should give us a big, bright flash and a nice loud bang," she said. "Which should be all we need to freeze the Xenos for a few seconds. They'll be disoriented. Stunned."

"Won't our people be stunned, too?"

"We have to trust they'll realize what we're doing," she said. "I don't know Shawna, but Bak-Irp is experienced. With any luck, he'll drag her home if he has to. It's worth a try."

Nero checked his ammo. "After I pop the can, stick your head out and let them see you. Then I'll lay down fire to cover their retreat. Tell me when you're ready to throw." He braced his elbows, taking aim. Rarely had she witnessed him so focused and in the moment. Maybe a daily dose of life-or-death situations was what his life was lacking; he needed everything to be on the line all the time to keep his brain from wandering. He thrived on adrenaline rushes and pressure.

"Ready... set..." Lemora took three long steps and tossed the canister high into the sky above Shawna. Bak-Irp was a few meters behind her, twisting as he emptied the last of his magazine into the zombies trailing. "Go!"

The canister flipped end over end.

Nero hit it with a short burst. The canister exploded; flames ballooned overhead. The blinding flash grew into a miniature sun – a boiling cauldron of blistery lemony-orange.

Shawna and Bak-Irp both ducked.

The explosion sent a percussive thrust into Lemora's chest. She couldn't help but thrill at the jolt of it – a heavy thud hitting her body's center and spreading out as the vibration lingered. She felt the incalescence despite her suit – her cheeks warmed as if she'd opened a hot oven.

The Xenos stopped in their tracks, skidding, tripping over one another as they covered their eyes or stumbled, momentarily robbed of their sight, groping in the air, snarling and dazed.

Lemora ran out of the shadows and beckoned to Shawna and Bak-Irp.

Nero followed her, shooting from the hip, peppering the stunned Xenos as they spun and dropped to the ground, bleeding. Whatever discipline the monsters had achieved dissolved into chaos. Shawna dug into her last reserves, pushing to the finish line. Bak-Irp – taking longer strides and unencumbered by the triple-bladed saw or the thankless task of keeping the Xenos off their backs – drew up alongside her. Together they crashed through the station entrance.

"Nero! C'mon, time to go back!" Lemora swung the shotgun she'd been wearing across her back into her shaky hands, pumping several buckshot into the crush of Xenos.

The monsters recovered from the improvised flashbang explosion. Their faces changed as they snapped back to awareness, picking her out, spitting and roaring at the sight of a human within their reach – so close they could taste her, drooling as they licked their lips.

Nero took out their legs, sweeping his barrage at knee-level.

Lemora had to give her boss credit for ingenuity – it was a hell of a lot easier to disable the Xenos than to kill them. While pain incensed the zombies more than it impeded them, a hobbled Xeno didn't present the same challenges as one that had maximum mobility. Xenos from the back rows pushed aside their wounded peers, who rather than acting appalled, cheered them on, glaring crazy-eyed as they writhed in the bloody sand, their legs bent at wrong angles, bones shattered.

The four outlaws burrowed into the module, dodging obstacles and knocking objects loose in their wake. Anything to slow down their pursuers. Xeno roars echoed off the walls.

Bak-Irp reached the emergency shield wall first. He banged at it with his fists.

"Open up, man! Krait, get this wall up! They're right on our asses."

Silence.

"What's the holdup?" Nero asked.

"That snake Krait, that's what's up," Bak-Irp said. "He's not letting us in."

The Xenos flooded into the station. Their sheer numbers

and impatience clogged up the works. In their eagerness to tear into the fleeing convicts, they blocked one another, pressing into the confined space and slowly crushing the Xenos on the edges who became trapped against the piled furniture and pinned to the walls. A few of the more cunning zombies avoided the crowd, seeping into the module's shadows without a ruckus. Lemora had her back against the security wall. She saw eyes in the darkness. Wily and studious. These select Xenos weren't rushing forward, but taking cover, concealing themselves as they examined and learned about their prey.

"Stand back," Shawna said as she fired up the cutter.

The high-speed diamond blades whined. She stepped up to the barrier and was about to slice into it when the wall began to rise. Mateo stuck his arm underneath, then his head appeared.

"What took you so long?" he said.

"We went sightseeing," Bak-Irp said. He stood back to allow Nero, Lemora, and Shawna to slide into the expanding gap. The barrier stopped rising, and Mateo helped them get under. Lemora couldn't stay on the safe side of the wall; she felt compelled to dart her helmet back under the barrier, gazing into the hall to keep watch on the Xenos. Something about them transfixed her – an uncanny quality, their actions appeared artificially influenced. She couldn't put her finger on it, but they were just wrong. *They're like pets on a leash*, she thought. *Their behavior is unnatural, as if they've been trained like monkeys who ride on motorbikes* – and training implied the existence of a trainer.

"See anything you like?" the hitman said.

Lemora shook her head. She could feel the Xenos thinking, sizing them up, planning.

"No tourist attractions on your sightseeing tour?" Mateo asked Bak-Irp.

"Nah. It was boring."

The bodyguard didn't turn his back on the Xenos hiding in the shadows. He reverse-scooted under the barrier.

"Why aren't they coming at us?" Mateo asked.

"I don't know," Bak-Irp said.

"How about you, doc?" Mateo said. "You got an opinion?"

Lemora took a last long look into the glowing zombie eyes. Unblinking, cool... and mechanical... the feeling she couldn't shake was that the Xenos weren't the only ones watching them. It was crazy, she knew, but she had a weird suspicion that someone else was observing them *through* the eyes of the Xenos, as if they were cyborgs, or there were cameras planted in their optical organs, transmitting and recording things. The idea was pure paranoia, but she couldn't deny it. "I don't like the spooky way they're looking at us. Get the door down."

She crawled back, resting on her haunches, plagued by thoughts of surveillance. *It's probably nothing,* she thought. Stress and anxiety. *We're on the run, and I haven't slept.* But it was more real than that – a clammy sense of disembodied eyes spying and plotting against them.

The two burly killers retreated. No Xenos tried to slip into the gap as it got smaller.

The barrier fell into place with a resounding, echoey clang.

CHAPTER TWENTY-FIVE
Augments

"You fool, what are you waiting for? Now it's too late. They've dropped the barrier!" Neera Lupaster pushed away from her display screen. A fuzzy image revealed the security emergency barrier for the mining outpost module on PK-L7. The image blurred as the camera lens swung wildly upward toward the ceiling before pulling away and being swallowed by the darkness of the station's dingy, cluttered hallway. Angrily she punched a button, switching the display off.

"Your Imperial Highness, all is well and good," the engineer said, in his fawning voice that irritated her but not enough to dissuade him from addressing her using the title she sought but had not yet achieved. He was well-practiced in the art of flattery. "The augmented Xenos are learning just as they have been programmed to do. We mustn't rush things. Prudence is needed."

Neera had heard enough of his constant assurances. He preached caution and restraint. But what kingdom was ever built by restraint! She swept her arm across the conference table, scattering maps and digital notepads. Her personal assistants dove for the mess, sorting it back into order as she jumped from her seat at the head of the table to pace around the room.

"I am through with prudence," she said. "I want results!"

Other than her assistants, four others occupied the room, seated at the opposite end of the long table. The three members of the Cybernetics Guild sat together with the engineer in the middle, smiling his best toady smile. *And didn't he look like an amphibian?* Hairless and plump, a sheen of moisture glistened on his mottled skin, and his enormous double chin seemed to inflate as if he were about to croak at her, and then in his unctuous manner, he did just that.

"Buurrrup... excuse me, Your Imperial Highness, I have digestive issues, and I am not used to the rich cuisine you serve us here as guests of the Arms Guild. My constitution is as delicate as it is humble. I am a simple villager, born on a lonely colony on the outer rim of–"

"Your bio holds no interest for me," she cut him off. "But I am in a position to write the final sentence." She did not need to spell out her threat. It registered immediately; the engineer's eyes grew wide with terror, and he began to squirm gelatinously in his seat. His guild partners tried unsuccessfully to hide their amusement at his discomfort, yet if they believed they were protected, they were fatally mistaken. "I will author all three of your endings... if need be."

Gulps and trembling. *There now* – that was what she'd been shooting for. She caught sight of her reflection in the soundproof, snoop-proof Securityglass cube that enclosed their meeting. From outside, the cube played images of different people, all talking nonsense; sometimes the characters who appeared were young children sorting out puzzles, other times they were animated cartoons, fantastical dragons and pointy-hatted wizards sitting around a fireplace smoking pipes – the one thing no one ever saw was the actual meeting taking place within the cube. On the inside the reflections were as clear as polished mirrors. Neera liked how her hair looked today – cascading layers of scarlet, crow's-wing black, and aquamarine. It reminded her of a wildfire raging on a path toward the sea. Her cybernetic tattoos matched her mood: ancient Panduchan warriors, their longswords razor-sharp, dueling one another with audible clashes of blades and bloodcurdling screams as slices opened like mouths in their skins, or the tip of a weapon plunged deep inside an opponent, releasing jets of creamy, ice-white Pandu blood; each warrior wore gaudy face paint and dressed in vivid, elaborate robes, like walking dolls of death.

"Need I remind you that the Arms Guild has borne the brunt of funding the project on PK-L7? The reason we have done so is tied directly to my main objective – which is the untimely death of my infernal brother!" She struck the table with her fist. The Guild members were startled. The fourth participant at the table wasn't. He steepled his fingers and narrowed his eyes.

"Do we have a problem?" Neera asked him. She hadn't yet learned to read his expressions with any accuracy. She'd never met another member of his race. *Were they all such gloomy sad sacks?*

"None, Your Imperial Highness," he said. The wrinkles in his face bunched together, telling a different story, and his twin antennae jiggled in mild revolt to his reassuring words. He sat low in his seat, slumping back as if he were trying to disappear into the plush chairback.

No matter whether he agreed with her or not. The Caridian wasn't a war advisor; he was a scientist, and foremost, he was a thief who had come into possession of some very interesting research materials concerning the conversion of solid xenium into a liquid form, which made the energy source exponentially more powerful. His seat at the table came as a courtesy, and Neera hoped he would appreciate that fact. She needed the Caridian to be content, if not happy, at least for the time being. After she'd gotten what she wanted from him he could go off and sulk.

"Good," Neera said. "Now, gentlemen, who among you can give me what I yearn for?"

The stunned looks told her that they were as stupid as they were ineffectual.

"Wha- wha- what is that, pray tell?" the engineer asked. His tiny, oily utterance repelled her almost as much as his complete inability to grasp the thrust of her meaning. *The simpleton!*

"The head of my dearest Nero rolling across this table!" she shouted. "Will you deliver?"

A chorus of agreement. Only the Caridian was smart – or bored – enough to keep silent.

"Quiet!" she said. "When will the Xenos attack? Can you tell me that at least?"

The engineer cleared his throat. "I should think it will be soon…"

Neera groaned loudly.

"Very soon," he added. "Our experiment has been incredibly successful. The Augments are now established as leaders among the Xeno population. They have been able to assert a level of control over their lesser comrades in relatively short order, and we can say with a high degree of confidence that *we* are now in control of PK-L7. Regarding your brother, I should think we want to wipe out his team in one fell swoop. The Xenos are learning the best way to accomplish this objective. In no time, they will formulate their plan, with programmed external input, of course, and victory will be ours." The longer he talked the more pleased he became with himself, and this fact enraged Neera to the point that she contemplated gutting him simply to shut him up.

She sashayed toward him.

"When?" she asked, as she scraped her titanium fangnail teasingly over the top of his ear, enjoying the feeling of him shivering at her touch. *How she wanted to gouge him!*

"A matter of a few… days?" His chin twitched and his hands wobbled tremulously.

"No!"

The quaking engineer laughed mirthlessly. "Did I say 'days?' Pardon me. I meant *hours.*"

"Very well," Neera said. "I have your promise. We all heard it. If you do not fulfill your commitment, I'm sure you'll understand why I will feel compelled to execute you."

Let that settle in, she thought. Nothing created inspiration like a death threat. Neera turned to the assistant on her right. Unlike when Nero ran things at the Guild, her soldiers wore uniforms and were drilled daily. "Do we have any word from Nero the Hero? A blip or buzz?"

"No, Your Imperial Highness, we have yet to receive any signal from PK-L7."

"The man can't get anything right. Yet he thinks he should be heading the Arms Guild. It's astonishing what hereditary rights do to a man's perception of himself. They cloud his reason and muddy his view of the world, making him bewildered and blind, a thing of pity."

All the men at the table – even the Caridian who rarely spoke in public – agreed with her.

Which was wise of them, if they wanted to live long enough to enjoy the vast sums of wealth that were surely coming their way. Nothing compared to hers, which was as it should be.

Reflecting on the past, she understood that she'd been planning to overthrow her brother her whole life. Now that the moment was within her reach, she could hardly stand the tension, yet she savored it as well, knowing the sweet release from his influence would soon be upon her.

Neera smiled inwardly and adjourned the meeting.

CHAPTER TWENTY-SIX
Pitch Darkness

"You're dead!" Nero screamed in Krait's face.

"I said, 'I'm sorry.' I couldn't get a spark out of Matias's power pack. It must've been a bad connection." Krait cowered in the corner of the comms room. Nero had beaten him down to the floor and had the barrel of his machine gun pressing under Krait's chin. "Everything worked out in the end," Krait said. "You guys are safe. The barrier's down. We got the cutter. All that's left is to bust through that plate, and we're on our way to the comms hub. It's all good, Nero."

Nero wasn't buying any of it. He was finished with Krait's treacherous bullshit.

"Say goodbye, asshole," Nero said.

Krait's eyes darted around until they settled on Matias. "Ask him!" He pointed at the head-injured enforcer. "Tell the boss how I was trying to get the barrier up. I wasn't playing games with you, Nero. Tell him, man!" Nero enjoyed watching Krait plead for his life, squatting in the dust like a common beggar who lingered outside a warlord's castle hustling for table scraps. It brought back childhood memories of trailing after the baron as he exercised his most brutal and fickle manner, encouraging weak citizens to debase themselves for his entertainment.

Matias looked at Nero.

"Well?" Nero said, waiting.

Matias scratched his chin, which was actually the outside of his helmet.

"Tell him!" Krait said again.

"I think he was doing something, boss," the hitman said, finally, as he nodded. "Yeah."

Nero grunted in disgust and pulled the gun away from Krait's head. The smuggler whimpered in relief, drawing his knees against his chest, snot bubbling from his nose.

"Shawna, cut that plate," Nero said. Then to Krait he added, "If I didn't need you…"

He didn't finish the sentence.

Krait avoided making eye contact. He crawled under the control panel to show Shawna where to make the cut. It was grubby down there, and somebody had left behind a pair of pink, plastic shower shoes. His voice was soft and controlled. The whirr of the blades filled the room and then golden sparks sprayed out from under the workstation, and the steel cried as they sliced into it. The sound gave Nero an instant headache that started in his teeth and encircled his skull like a crown of concertina wire. The bright sparks flashed painfully even if he closed his eyes.

"Let's give them space to work," Lemora said. "Join me in the hallway, darling. Please."

He allowed her to walk him out. His jaw felt as hard as a billiard ball as he clenched it.

"My head is killing me," he said.

"I know," she said. "You've got a lot of responsibilities."

"I've got all the responsibilities! Me! This whole... game plan is mine. I dreamed it."

"Of course, you did. We all owe you a great debt," she said, leading him to a chair. "Now you just sit and try to relax. Let us carry the weight. That's what a team does. We pull together."

Was she seriously kidding? How was he supposed to relax? Didn't she see the Xenos watching them out there? It was worse than fighting them. Those cold dead eyes. He felt them on his skin like a ghost's icy hand, like the baron's fist that gripped him while he slept... a corpse's hand from out of the grave, from beyond this world... reaching back for him and not to provide comfort either but to drag him into a frigid hell where he would watch his entrails being ripped from his belly, flopping onto the floor like a basket of slimy fish; the Xenos' eyes were like his father's eyes... cursed, accusing... they came for revenge and would never ever stop...

"Nero? Nero, can you hear me?" It was Lemora. Her faceplate was almost touching his.

"Yes, I'm fine. You're coming in loud and clear, Lem."

He rested his arm on hers. But their armor kept them from making real contact. If anyone in this corrupt, dog-eat-dog world cared about him, it was her. Their relationship wasn't romantic. Nero had no time for romance. He trusted no one. He didn't want intimacy, wouldn't allow anyone in that close. But they were friends, Lemora and he, and if there was one person in the world that he relied on it was her. To a certain degree, of course. Everybody had their price. A number that their betrayal would cost. But hers was probably very high – she'd ask a lot to give him up. And that was special. It was. He valued her. He hoped she knew that, too. Just like he hoped she knew that he'd only stab her in the back if he, like, really, *really* had to…

"Neera showed you some proof about the wormhole?" Lemora asked, matter-of-factly.

"What…?"

It was so like her to pry into his psyche while he was down, feeling depleted and tired. But he could tell she was mulling something over with that big brain of hers, tumbling it inside her head, trying to make sense out of a chunk of evidence, a tidbit of data that didn't fit into her hypothesis. She wouldn't let it go, either. Tenacity was a quality he admired, but it bugged the shit out of him, too. People needed to learn to move on. Life didn't always conform to reason.

"How do you know she isn't… exaggerating?" Lemora said. "Overpromising."

"Say what you mean, Lem. You think she's lying. And I'm a chump for believing her."

Lemora said, "I'm not making any assumptions. I'm planning for contingencies, which is one of the things you love about me in case you forgot. You don't have time for sweating the little things… like details. I love details. Inconsistencies jump out at me like clues. They tell stories."

He was thirsty as hell; it was distracting him. Maybe he was coming down with something. He couldn't have caught the PK-L7 mold flu. But he felt rundown. And there was so much to do. Lemora was right. He needed to believe in the team, to count on them. They needed supplies: ammo, oxygen tanks, water (which wasn't likely), and anything else they might use against the Xenos. It was time to come together and stop the infighting. Cohesion.

"Sorry, Lem," he said. "I've got a lot on my mind." The

recycled air inside his suit smelled like dirty work boots. He knew it was blowing cool, but it didn't refresh him. It tasted like stale swamp breath, like rot. And he realized it was this place, this zombified planet; he was smelling PK-L7 despite his spacesuit. Death warmed over. Generations of Xeno madness permeated the atmosphere, and they were soaking in it up to their necks. He suddenly wanted to be clean, to take a shower and rub a thick, warm towel over his body and get a full-body massage.

"Neera's got this Caridian scientist. She vidscreened me on a stolen link I had on my vidpad in my cell. The call was quick, but I saw him. The bughead told me how the wormhole worked. I don't remember what he said, but it sounded right at the time. They use xenium, change it into liquid. That's what opens the wormhole."

Lemora nodded. She was biting her lower lip, working out a problem in her head. "The Xenos that chased Shawna and Bak-Irp, there's something off about them. They didn't act like the infected zombies from the Deathcan. A percentage of them – not a huge percentage but a select few – are behaving out of character for aliens who've had their brains hijacked by mold. It strikes me that an outside influence, a third party, may be at work here." She sat on the dorm bed beside him. He felt the cheap cot sag. "I know you have a complicated relationship with your sister. Do you think she might be trying to kill us? That sounds awful, right? But what if she lured us here and nobody's coming." Lemora was a tall, beautiful woman, who had this fantastic aura of energy and edgy excitement, and whenever she told Nero news that he didn't want to hear he tried to think of how much harder it would be to listen to it coming from a crusty old guy advisor like most of the Guild leaders had as their counselors. He was lucky she was on his team.

"Then we're screwed," he said.

The triple-bladed saw made quick work of the steel plate. Shawna had it out, and Krait was correct – there was an air vent back there, a big one; the comms cables ran right inside it.

"Who's going?" Krait asked.

"All of us," Nero said.

"Wait a sec," Bak-Irp said. "Shouldn't we leave a few people here? I don't want to be crawling around in a slaughterhouse chute unless I have to. That's a deathtrap scenario. No room to maneuver. We run into Xenos, and they'll eat us one by one like candy." The Thassian had a good point, but Nero didn't care. The module was a safe place for now, but having no comms made it worthless in the long run. They didn't need a bolthole to hide in. They needed a signal.

"We're all going," he said. "We stick together until Neera arrives. No more splitting the team up. We're a unit, and we need to start acting like one."

The Thassian's shoulders fell. He looked dejected, muttering to himself inside his helmet.

"What's wrong, tough guy? You afraid of tight spaces?" Krait sneered.

"How about I give you a hug, and you tell me if it's too tight for you?"

Krait held up his hand in mock surrender. "I'll go first into the vent. I don't mind."

Nero said, "No. We'll leave in the same order as when we left the cockpit. Fuzzy takes the point with the flamethrower. The Silvas go next, then Krait and Lemora. Then me in the middle. Bak-Irp and Shawna guard the rear. Anybody got a problem with that?"

Nobody did. Or if they did, they didn't say, which was just as good.

"All right," Nero said.

Too-ahka was already inside the hole, and he quickly and silently entered the vent, following the comms cable that ran along the bottom of the vent like a fat, juicy nerve.

"It shouldn't be too far," Krait said. "This whole station isn't much of a complex. I would imagine the comms hub is centrally located. We're starting out in the left wing of the base, if you're standing on the runway viewing the station. They probably added this comms room in the barracks so the poor, lonely miners could call home and speak to their loved ones." Krait seemed well-adapted to crawling inside tunnels, his slender frame oozing along.

They all climbed into the vent.

"See?" Krait said. "The first turn is up ahead. It goes to the right, toward the central part of the site, as I predicted."

Nero had trouble seeing anything. The vent was boxy in shape, a rectangle lying on one of its short sides. It was too low for standing fully upright; the convicts had to crouch, and it made their backs ache after a few steps. Slow going, to be sure, but doable. Nero heard Bak-Irp grunting and grumbling, complaining about the cramped environment and their vulnerability.

"What's all your whining about, Bak?"

"Nothing. Just that we can't shoot anything we come across in here. Not unless we want to light up the other members of the team. It's too cramped and bullets will ricochet. Too-ahka's got his fire, but I feel like I'm naked."

Nero shushed him. "Quiet down. Too-ahka's on to something. Switch your headlamps off. Lights out. Maybe we've got company. Too-ahka's going ahead to check things. We wait here."

Bak-Irp passed the message to Shawna. Soon the vent was as black as a vat of tar. They were all paused like a game of stunray-tag. But nobody could see how stupid they looked. Nero pressed an armor-gloved hand to the side of the vent. He didn't know what he was doing. Trying to pick up vibrations? *What was that going to tell him?* He wasn't like the fuzzball with his alien echolocation jazz. He stood there, hunched like a dumb ape man. He switched his light back on.

"What're you doing?" Bak-Irp said in a hoarse whisper. "You told us, 'Lights out.'"

"I know. I wanted to see if anything changed... Hey, Shawna, are those night goggles?"

"Yes."

"Where'd you get them?"

"The armory on the *Andronicus*."

"Let me have them," Nero said.

"No."

Here he was trying to encourage them to be a team like Lem said, and Shawna was hogging the night vision glasses. He was about to make a fuss, but he decided against it. She was a fighter pilot, and she probably had better eyesight than he did. He had to learn to give up a little control or he was going to drive himself crazy. This situation was crazy. It didn't need any more.

"Scoot by us," Nero said. "See if you can get a look where your furry buddy went."

"He's not my buddy," she said.

He switched his lamp off, so he didn't blind her. He couldn't see her, but he felt her.

She wasn't wasting any time getting moving though. Luckily, she was nimble and not bulky even decked out in her armor. Twisting and turning, she wriggled past Bak and Nero.

"Lem, tell Krait to let Shawna by. Get her up there. She's got night goggles, and she can talk to Too-ahka if it comes back. Make the Silvas aware. I want Shawna at the front," Nero said.

Without a word, Shawna squeezed ahead.

Nero was in the dark, in the silence, feeling impatient as hell but keeping his cool. He still had Bak-Irp behind him. No Xeno was going to make it through the Thassian without a struggle, and if one of them tore his bodyguard to pieces, Nero wasn't going to stand a chance either.

Suddenly the vent up ahead lit up orange and the wave of heat was so strong Nero felt it through his suit. They had light. Fuzzy was around the bend, and it must've crawled quite a distance because the roar of the flamethrower seemed not exactly quiet but not as loud as he expected – it was like a hot wind blowing, like somebody turned the station's heater on full-blast.

"He's cooking something," Bak-Irp said in his ear. "Got his barbecue roasting."

Nero saw Shawna holding her goggles away from her faceplate, so her vision didn't get washed out. The orange glow disappeared, and they plunged into the abyss again. Nero wanted to move. Forward. Backward. He didn't care. But this keeping still had him jumping out of his skin. He was impatient and he had goosebumps. Fuzzy must've met one of those things, which meant they were in the air vents. They were smart and they were hunting them, and Bak-Irp was right that there was no place to go in here.

Except forward.

Nero wasn't telling the team to retreat to the dorm module. That was a dead end.

"Shawna thinks we should advance," Lem said to him.

"Why? What can she see?"

Lemora didn't have an answer for him. She was taking off. He couldn't see her go, but he felt her stepping out. Felt a lot of boots hitting down on steel. STOMP STOMP STOMP. They were being so loud it was no surprise the Xenos were on to them and their plans. Nero couldn't see, but he started duckwalking. Bak-Irp put his big mitt on his back, and he wasn't pushing but he was physically encouraging Nero to keep going… into the darkness, the pitch darkness…

CHAPTER TWENTY-SEVEN
Blind Alley Massacre

Oh shit, Shawna thought. This was disturbing. It might've been a lot worse, considering. But it was unnerving. The spectacle of it. The intensity of the scene wasn't something she was prepared for, and there was no way she could ever look at Too-ahka the same way again. He wasn't her buddy. That was what she'd told Nero. But this incident took her opinion of Too-ahka to a whole new level. And she felt sick, like her stomach was doing scissor kicks with high heels.

She'd come around the corner, following the orange glow which had to be the flamethrower. And it was. But when the fire shut down, her goggles revealed that Too-ahka was farther down the vent than she'd figured. She didn't even make him out at first. There wasn't any mold in the air vent, but she could discern a blockage, like somebody had dumped a load of garbage inside the void. Her goggles picked up a solid mass, and she was worried that they'd reached a blind alley. But that didn't compute. Too-ahka had gone somewhere. She flipped on her thermals and saw that the walls were red hot and so was the lump of material radiating heat at a point about forty steps ahead – the blockage, whatever it was, looked like cooling lava. She raced to it. Because she saw something moving in there: an arm, Too-ahka's arm, rising and falling, and she thought, *oh my god, they got him. The Xenos made a real mess in here, and Too-ahka's beckoning for me.* Turns out, she was both right and wrong about the situation.

There was a real mess, but Too-ahka hadn't been calling for her. The alien was too preoccupied with the Xenos it had found. Two of them. No – check that – three. A trio of the smart ones – they had a larger underslung lower jaw and an appendage that sprang out of their mouths like a snaky, sinuous tongue with a nasty stinger on the end. She'd seen a few examples of them before, when they were being chased outside, and then later these Xeno geniuses were hiding in the corridor outside the module barrier. She hardly recognized them here. For one, they were dead. Too-ahka had burned them. Crispy critters – their skins were black and blistered, hides peeling off in sheets like hull paint on a rusty junkyard airship. But that wasn't what made them unrecognizable. It was what Too-ahka had done to them afterward. The one-of-a-kind alien carried out a speed dissection. Except dissection was too delicate a word. Too-ahka had butchered them. It was worse than what the zombies were doing to the humans on board the *Andronicus*. Because you detected the pure glee Too-ahka had taken in killing them and turning their insides out. The alien was going at them with busy fingers and teeth as if Shawna wasn't there watching. This was worse than what she'd seen it doing to Ishnik in the cargo bay. The Xenos looked like ripped bags of steaming strawberry preserves, and Too-ahka was smeared with gooey red stuff. Gobs of Xeno guts caked up its fur, and the alien was busy gnawing on their bones, chewing meat, licking up the sauces, as its eyes rolled back into its head in ecstasy. It made a sweet purring sound. Shawna felt hot, queasy, and dizzy all at once.

She swallowed a jet of stomach acid erupting into her mouth. It made her cough.

"THE HELL IS THIS?" Matias said, coming upon the scene. He started giggling nervously. "HO-LEE MOE-LEE on a mountain of WHAAAT? I can't even...! Bro, check it out."

Mateo stayed glued to his clone brother's back, so close they were like one dude. "Whoa," he added to Matias's appraisal. "I've seen some intense shit, but this here is gratuitous."

The thing was... it seemed so private, like a ceremony they were interrupting: Too-ahka at worship. What the creature was doing to the bodies differed from what the Xenos did to their victims. This wasn't a frenzied attack. It was methodical. Too-ahka was spiritually transported.

Shawna couldn't talk to the alien. She didn't think it wanted to talk to her either. Past the massacre site, she saw where the Xenos had entered the air vent. A violent rupture in the steel, the metal torn open and curled back, like when you shot a can in the desert and looked inside at the bullet holes. Punched in – but big enough to fit a human, or one of these plus-sized Xeno hunters.

Holding her breath and trying not to look at Too-ahka who was eating and drinking up the Xeno carnage, she craned to investigate the room from where the Xenos had come. Banks of computers coated in ochre dust. A wall of display monitors, everything blacked out, screens webbed with cracks. Microphones, headphones, VR rigs hung from a wall of storage hooks. There was a viewing window like the one they'd found in the comms room, and the shields were drawn up to let the piss-yellow light in. Beyond it was a view of PK-L7's flat, cruel landscape. A ruffling of loose items in the hub. *Wind.* This room must be open to the outside. She couldn't see the doors. But it didn't have to be a door. A wall could be missing, given the scale of destruction. She didn't spot any Xenos. That was a positive.

"We found the comms hub," she said. "It's been breached."

But the Silvas weren't listening. They were transfixed by Too-ahka's bloodbath. The rest of the team caught up with them. There were gasps. Krait retched in his helmet. Matias cackled. She had to tune them out before she lost it completely. Madness heaped on madness.

"Shawna, hey Shawna?" It was Nero. "Can you talk to Too-ahka? I want to get into that room, but I'm afraid of what your buddy might do. The little weirdo is scaring folks."

"Like I told you, Too-ahka isn't my buddy." She didn't want to look at anybody.

Finally, she forced herself to meet the alien's gaze – beady red pips staring back like two drops of coagulating blood, and a mouth like a cactus patch after you emptied a slop bucket into it. *Was he signing something?* It held out its sticky hands. It had something it was showing her.

"He's made a discovery," Lemora said. "I think he wants to give it to you."

"Whatever it is, I don't want it." She was more repulsed than afraid.

Too-ahka tilted its head slowly, first rotating one way, then the other. It seemed confused by her reaction, acting like she was hurting its feelings. *Screw that.* She'd made a bad mistake thinking Too-ahka saw the world like she did. But this incident proved they were not the same.

"Look what I found. Isn't it curious? Unusual to find it where I did. Deep inside."

"I don't want it," Shawna said. "Give it to her. Lemora is a scientist. I'm only a pilot."

Too-ahka offered the object to her once more – it looked like a tiara, but instead of jeweled ornaments it had an assortment of electrodes and braided silver wires. When Shawna refused to accept it, Too-ahka handed the thing to Lemora, who took it, inspecting the drippy instrument, turning it over in her hands to study it, wiping off pieces of soft, gray tissue.

"Is it a headband of some kind?" Nero asked. "Ask Fuzzy where it came from, Shawna."

"It came from inside one of those damned Xenos," she said.

"Yeah, but where exactly? Is it a shock collar? Who'd put it on these violent suckers?"

Shawna looked at Too-ahka again. A numbness washed over her like cool, minty waves. The alien answered Nero's question and waited for her to translate, as if nothing had changed.

"Too-ahka says it came from one of the Xeno's brains."

"Not a headband," Lemora said, as if she were talking to herself. "But a brainband."

"What's it for?" Nero said.

"This device must control the Xenos," Lemora concluded. "I was right. They are not entirely themselves. Someone's been fiddling with them. Altering them. I'm willing to bet that the electrodes tap into the Xenos' sensory receptors. It turns the Xenos into cameras and listening bugs. Anything the Xenos perceive is converted to data that's transmitted and played back in real time. The ultimate spying device." She sounded like she admired the invasive gadget. "But also, it might work two ways, to implant thoughts, ideas, motivations into the Xeno's brain."

To Shawna it was an example of people churning out weapons for the sake of making space even more dangerous. The Silva brothers and Bak-Irp agreed that the discovery made no difference in their dealing with the Xenos – they still had to kill them before they got killed.

"Mind control," Nero said. "I absolutely love it. Not used against us, obviously. But the concept… that's what I love. Don't look at me like that, War Hero, I'm only saying what we're thinking. The tech part of it is gorgeous. Wouldn't you want to own a Xeno attack dog?"

"It never would've occurred to me," Shawna said.

"*Pshht.*" Nero waved her off. "This is Cybernetics Guild shit if I ever saw it. Their fingerprints are all over it. Krait, you ever work with those Cyberassholes?"

Krait was still recovering from his upset stomach, and the expression on his face said that the inside of his suit didn't smell too good. "I worked for a lot of interests. Whoever paid me. So, the short answer is *yes*. But I don't know about this. The Coalition would never allow experimentation on sentient beings, even zombified ones. It's off-the-books. Something they cooked up on their own, and they'll decide later whether to keep it or sell to the highest bidder."

Too-ahka pushed the Xeno carcasses into the side of the vent, allowing the team to pass.

"Much obliged," Nero said, jumping through the steel hole into the comms hub.

Shawna went straight for the opening to the outside. It was a door, and it didn't look damaged. She closed it. The dry atmosphere of PK-L7 turned remains into leathery husks. The comms hub had a dozen or so mummified corpses inside it. They weren't wearing armor, and Shawna spotted only a smattering of small arms. "These engineers got overrun. It was over fast. The Xenos opened the door and that was all she wrote." The hub was connected to no less than six hallways. Shawna checked the doors. "Seals are solid, intact. We might've gotten lucky here. The Xenos killed and did a bit of vandalism, but structurally things look sound. Krait, see if you can revive the IT systems."

"I'm on it." The smuggler located a tool kit and began unscrewing access panels.

"Silvas, we've got to patch that air vent. We don't want any guests dropping in. There's a supply closet over there. Inventory it." She laid down the triple saw on a work counter. "I can cut some sheets from the cubicles, but we're going to need to attach them. Maybe a sonic drill gun?"

"I'll see what we can find," Mateo said. He and Matias disappeared beyond the door marked SUPPLIES. The shelves looked full based on what she could see. That was promising. They could make a base of operations here and hold off an attack if it wasn't too overwhelming.

"Home sweet home," Nero said. "I'm feeling good about this. How about you?"

Shawna said, "It'll do. Bak and I can move the corpses into the closet when the boys are done with their salvaging. Our location is good, and the doors lock." She didn't want to get Nero's hopes too high. But the hub offered the best position they'd had since the bomb exploded on the *Andronicus*. Then she remembered who set off the bomb. "It's better than we deserve."

"Now that's the spirit!" He slapped her on the back. "You gotta believe to win, player!"

CHAPTER TWENTY-EIGHT
Winning the Galactic Lottery

Dr Kix sat alone in his suite at Neera's. The Arms Guild's headquarters was the most secure undisclosed location in Terran space, but he didn't feel particularly safe. When you were locked up with monsters you always had to be on guard. *Make no mistake,* he told himself, *you are dealing with creatures as heartless and dangerous as those modified Xenos the Cybernetics engineers brag about.*

Dr Kix moved from his desk to the bed and pulled off his slippers before lying back, interlacing his fingers behind his head. He entertained no illusions about sleep, he hadn't been able to log a good night's rest since contacting Neera Lupaster more than a year ago. He suspected he'd never sleep well again. Ah, but there would be other benefits once she paid him the fortune that he was due. *Kix* wasn't his name, it was an alias, yet knowing his real name wouldn't make a difference, he was a nobody. Although he'd spent years in school, he never qualified to be called a doctor. No, he was a thief, and an embarrassment to his people.

The Caridians took pride in their intelligence, their scientific achievements were well-known throughout the cosmos, particularly in matters of energy production and interstellar travel. Wormholes. The mightiest tool of exploration, folding a sheet of the spacetime continuum... creating galactic bridges... tunnels... he didn't really understand the physics of it. But he didn't need to. He had the research he'd "inherited" from his ancestors, and he was willing to trade it for hard currency. That was his breakthrough innovation – he would sell out the legacy of his species, and he'd found the perfect buyers, Neera and the Cybernetics eggheads, who had their own plans as far as traditions and inheritances went. Neera was following in the bloody footprints of her father, the dread baron, and her ambitious brother.

She'd made no mystery of her designs. She was going to pick up where her family had left off. Domination. Ultimate power wielded by a single hand – hers. And she would obtain and exercise that power using the cybernetically altered Xenos as her own private shock troops, transporting them instantly and in great numbers using the xenium conversion formula to control the wormholes, which Dr Kix would happily provide. Liquid xenium was an amazing discovery. PK-L7 had more than enough solid xenium, which, once it was converted, delivered the capacity to fuel the engine of wormhole travel almost indefinitely. After Dr Kix approached her with his stash of documents – page after page of number columns and tables, charts and diagrams – she responded with skepticism. No, he wouldn't simply hand them over for her scientists to peruse. But he would offer to supervise a demonstration... for a fee, call it a downpayment on their future deal. She agreed. Her scientists were top drawer. They quickly assessed that Dr Kix's goods were the real deal, even if he himself might be a bit vague and sketchy. The final proof came in the form of a quick excursion to PK-L7 for Dr Kix, Neera, the Cyberidiots and a heavily armed unit of bodyguards. They popped into the skies over PK-L7 and rode down in a cloaked dropship. Put down on the mining station's runway and took a short walk to the station, although they never went inside. Xenos charged their position at the station doors.

That's when the first Cybernetics' traps went off; the cages had been robotically dropped and buried in the sand while the Xenos slept. The rampaging Xenos found themselves scooped up in titanium boxes, airlifted to the pulsating wormhole, and whisked off to the Cybernetics lab.

"We are excellent bait," the lead engineer said, massaging his chubby hands.

Neera didn't say much.

Dr Kix understood. It reminded him of his own reaction when he first downloaded the files that he'd stolen from the Caridian archive warehouse. He was hoping for a cache of blackmail material. But this was so much better. It was like winning the Galactic Lottery. Too good to be true. That's what Neera was experiencing that day they visited PK-L7. Her mind was rushing through a kaleidoscope of possibilities, dreams and aspirations – her new potential futures. Neither Neera nor he had returned to the desert planet. But the Cybernetics Guild's robots had been going back for months, snatching Xenos, experimenting on them, altering their bodies using various brain implants… Dr Kix didn't want to know the details. He was squeamish, but he watched the vids of their progress at meetings. The Xenos were speed-evolving, a telepathic leader class had been created and deposited on the planet to "teach" the zombies how to organize, to strategize and improve their tactics of warfare.

The Cybernetics engineers insisted that they were the ones really in control, but Dr Kix had his doubts. Evolution had a way of surprising you when you least expected it, but that was none of his concern, really.

He was close now to reaching his goal. They needed to kill Nero and his team, then they'd gather up the altered Xenos and give the Galactic Coalition a demonstration of just what they were up against – an unimaginably mobile, hyper-aggressive army of perfect soldiers, unafraid, relentless, and filled with a bottomless appetite to lay waste to any place at any time.

Dr Kix surprised himself. He was feeling relaxed, and as he visualized the day when Neera transferred the funds to his account, seeing the gigantic number appear on the screen, he slept without remembering his nightmares, although he was sure he'd had them. He always did.

A sharp knock on the door woke him.

"Yes," he said. His mouth was gritty, and he felt overly warm. "What is it?"

"Her Imperial Highness wishes to see you at once." It was one of Neera's assistants. They all looked and sounded the same. He might've suspected them of being robots if he hadn't witnessed them bleed whenever she struck them in her fits of anger. Maybe they were clones.

"What is the nature of my summons?" Dr Kix felt his anxiety rising quickly, as if the luxurious chamber were flooding. These attacks weren't new but lately they'd gotten worse.

"It's Nero," the assistant said, sounding pert and cheerful, as if all the news was good.

Dr Kix forced himself not to rush to the door and fling it wide open. He put on his slippers and opened it but a crack. Furrowing a brow, bending an antenna, he asked, "What about him?"

"He called for his pickup. Nero's ready to come home."

CHAPTER TWENTY-NINE
Laughing Somebodies

"What did she say? When is the wormhole going to open?" Nero asked Krait, who was parked at the comms display wearing headphones angled over one ear. His helmet sat on the work counter, airing out. They all had their helmets off. Despite the module air tasting stale, it was an improvement over the suit's claustrophobic aura. Krait was in a great mood. He'd been scoring touchdown after touchdown the whole day. He had the life support systems up and running in the hub, and a third of the computers were showing signs of life, blinking and whirring. His biggest miss wasn't his fault, the antennas were down, probably chopped by the Coalition before they pulled everyone off this godforsaken rock. It didn't mean a signal couldn't go out. But it meant that transmissions were broken and fizzy, the words coming through as garbled bits of audio fuzz.

"Sounds like they're experiencing a temporary delay," Krait said.

"Get Neera on vid for me. I want to talk to her face-to-face," Nero said.

Krait shook his head. It was hard to believe this guy ran the

Arms Guild, since he didn't seem to grasp how basic comms tech worked. A Big Picture chief. Maybe he only knew guns and bombs. Or maybe he was a lucky bastard who'd stepped into his daddy's boots and still couldn't figure out how to run the show. He'd gotten locked up after all. Krait had to remind himself that incarceration didn't mean you'd made a dumb mistake. He was a prisoner, too, and he hadn't screwed up, just found himself hanging out in the wrong place at the wrong time – and like that! – he was surrounded by Galactic police agents, a sting operation launched on the same frigging day he decided to pay a personal visit to oversee renovations on a refitted carrier he'd picked up in a Trappist system boost. The baron had built up a lot of reserves. It would take time to drive that money machine off a cliff and kill it. Krait knew Nero IV's reputation, but it didn't square with the person he was dealing with. Nero was a shadow running on vapors, a total fraud.

"No can do. We don't have vid capability. It's a miracle I got audio up," Krait said.

"Then let me talk to her."

"There's a significant lag between transmissions. She knows we're here. The problem's on her end. I acknowledged that we heard her. Now we wait for a cleaner sat link."

"She has to open that wormhole and get us out of here!" Nero pounded his fist into his hand over and over, as if he were trying to break in boxing gloves. He was such a petulant child.

Given that they'd established a home base, Krait wasn't too eager to leave it. Here, he had some measure of power, but once Neera arrived, the hierarchy was bound to re-sort itself, and Krait's place in it would certainly drop. That said, he wasn't sabotaging their enterprise, only creating a more equitable balance. There was no urgency to rush from his point of view.

"Look! Out there!" Bak-Irp interrupted. He'd been glassing the horizon, keeping watch with a long-range spotting scope mounted on a tripod. The mining engineers must've used them for surveying their operations, keeping track of the Xeno workforce before they went haywire.

The Silvas had turned out a treasure trove of supplies from the closet. They discovered unopened boxes of bullets and shotgun shells, spare air tanks, and even a water filtration pump that still worked when they switched it on. The original station builders must've drilled down and tapped into a cavernous lake for their well. At the back of the closet was a spigot next to an assortment of empty plexijugs and canteens. The filters were humming. Nero surprised him by taking the first sip. The water tasted sulfurous but was drinkable. The clones raided the station security team's weapons locker and found the military-grade optics along with more guns. The scopes were outdated, but they still worked. After testing them, Bak-Irp was impressed. "We've got movement at our one o'clock," he said, peering into a viewfinder.

Lemora squinted through the blurry window, shielding her eyes from the lemonade-sky glare. "The Xenos must've sensed the power-up in the hub. Like ringing the dinner bell and shouting, 'Chow time!' It isn't a matter of *if* but *when* they'll be coming."

"You bet your ass they're coming," Bak-Irp said. "Acting real sneaky, too, using the rocky outcrops and the old busted machines as cover. But I see you. I see you, loud and clear."

Nero rested his hand on Krait's shoulder. "Keep doing what

you're doing. Get my sister on the horn. Tell her, 'No delays.' Say I want her ass down here now, or there'll be hell to pay."

"Will do." Krait tapped keys on his keyboard and twirled knobs for maximum effect.

"Matias and Mateo!" Nero called to the brothers who were finishing up the repairs to the rupture in the air vent, screwing in the last corner on the patch. Matias was up on a ladder and Mateo was holding it steady and passing him the sonic drill – a couple of hardheaded warriors.

"What do you need?" Mateo said.

"You two get your helmets back on."

"What for?" Matias asked. They'd found a first-aid kit and put a clean dressing on his head wound. Mateo shot painkillers into his scalp and bandaged him up; his mohawk peeked through the white gauze wrappings.

"You're going outside," Nero said.

"Why are we the ones who gotta go?" Mateo said, sounding attitudinal.

"Because I said so. Listen, I'm not talking about anything fancy. Just a little surprise ambush for our zombie friends. Something to shake 'em up. They won't be expecting it."

"I didn't expect it," Matias said. "Because it's stupid… if you don't mind me saying."

"I do mind," Nero said. "Because it's not stupid, Matias. It's unorthodox." He turned to Lemora. "Lem, can you whip up a few homemade boom-booms for the brothers Silva to toss? I saw det cord in the closet. We've got shotgun shells. Gunpowder. Use screws for shrapnel."

Lemora slid off her stool at the viewport, prying her gaze from the smudgy glass. "I'll cook up something," she said. "I don't know if it will be lethal to those Xenos. But it'll smart."

"Do it fast," Nero said. Then to the twins he said, "You'll crawl out in front here. See?" Krait quietly watched him point out a modular arm of the base that led away from the hub at forty-five degrees. "Set up under the anchor poles that keep the station from tipping and blowing away in a sandstorm. It's twenty meters from the door to the poles. Boom, bang-bang, and you're back inside in a jiffy."

The Silvas were securing their helmets. They weren't the type to resist orders. It went against their genetic programming. Krait felt nothing but contempt for them. Although he saw the benefits of obedience and loyalty in others, he never had the slightest urge to replicate those qualities himself. He was a solo act.

"How far out are the Xenos?" Nero asked.

"Two hundred meters," Bak-Irp replied. "Two groups. I count about a dozen in each."

"That's a picnic at the beach for you guys," Nero said to the Silvas, grabbing them in a playful double headlock and jostling them like this was pre-game for sportsball. "Am I right?"

"I don't like picnics," Matias said. "Bugs. I hate the bugs. Every planet has some bugs."

"Well, you guys are my best exterminators," Nero said, dialing up the bullshit.

Krait had to turn away to hide his sniggering. He faked coughing into his fist. No way he'd be going outside with any flesheaters. The idea of opening the door to let the hitmen out made his ass cheeks clench. He got where Nero was coming from, keeping the Xenos off the module for as long as possible, but once upon a time the zombies got into the comms hub because somebody opened the door. *Why make the same mistake again?* He rechecked the loaded shotgun leaning against his leg under the desk. It was a semi-auto with a drum magazine he'd swiped from the gun locker when the Silvas went to work on the vent. He liked it for close quarters combat. Krait was no marksman. But he didn't need to be with this weapon. *Rock 'n' roll.*

Mateo didn't like the vibe of the situation as soon as they stepped out from the comms hub module, but he didn't turn back, because that wasn't the way he or his brother operated. They went full throttle no matter what the mission was. He followed Matias's slip-sliding footprints, punching through the sandy soil that collected along the edge of the module's exterior shell. He couldn't detect any Xenos. Not yet. The string of homemade explosives dangled from his neck. Lemora had packed the shotgun shells, screws, and detonators inside old canteens. Matias wore another one that matched. Each bomb had a fuse wire noodling out the top, attached to a pull ring from a rations pop-top pretzel can.

"Jerk the ring and throw it," Lemora told them. "They're not precision devices, so I'm guessing you'll have five seconds before they go bang and eject those titanium screws."

"Got it, bomb lady," Matias said. "How'd you get to be so smart? They feed you pills?"

His brother was kidding around like he always did. It was his way to keep relaxed and wipe the cobwebs from inside his skull. Easy times or hard, he had a joke up his sleeve.

"I did all the things you didn't," Lemora said, giving it right back to him, which he loved.

Matias cackled. "You're all right for a doctor."

"I'm not that kind of doctor."

When Mateo heard the door make that sucking sound behind him, his mood changed. The others were sealed up behind ballistic shield materials, while he and his *mano* walked around with their asses hanging out, wearing armor that might deflect a bullet but wouldn't keep a Xeno from tearing off your arms and legs, slurping out your meat and juices like you were a craboid from the tank at a restaurant. Truth be told, if he was going to die, he wanted to go in a place like this, a wasted piece of dirt nobody cared about, but he'd go down fighting, causing pain to his enemies. It was the way of the warrior, as noble as it was ugly.

Matias jabbed four stiff fingers in the air: *I'm going to this side of the anchor.*

Mateo nodded.

They didn't need to talk. Matias told people they thought the same thoughts, as if they shared a brain: "Which means we only got one half a brain each. I don't know what we do with the other two halves. What do we do with them, Mateo?"

"We dream, bro," he'd say.

Matias would screw up his face the same way he did when he was a kid, biting on the inside of his cheek. "What're we dreaming about these days? I can't ever remember."

"Pretty guns, fast ships, and a beach where the laughing somebodies are lying in the sun."

"Laughing somebodies," Matias would say. "Sounds nice. When're we going there?"

"Soon," Mateo would say. He didn't know how seriously to take Matias, who always acted like he believed everything he said, like there was a beach – a real beach – out there somewhere. *He was a crazy dude, man, but he had a sweetness to him.* Nobody understood how a killer-for-hire clone could be like that, but his brother was a genuinely good person. A unique individual, despite how he came into this world – how they both did. They weren't products built in a factory. They were people, like everybody else. Matias would never hurt a soul, unless you paid him to do it. That was business, survival of the fittest, life in the jungle.

They didn't make this place, but they had to live in it.

Take this shit job right here – tossing bombs at monsters. Matias almost made it fun.

"The Xenos are one hundred meters out," Bak-Irp spoke into their helmet headsets.

"Copy that," Mateo said. Matias broke off, advancing to the next pole down the line.

"They're closing fast. The two groups are leapfrogging each other. I see the regular ones and a few of the fast, smart ones. I don't think they've spotted you. But they're acting cautious."

"The cautious ones are implanted," Lemora said into their helmets. "Be careful."

Be careful. Mateo had to laugh at that. Nothing about this setup was careful. And being careful out here in the shit was bad advice. It was the kind of thing somebody says when they're staying inside behind a door with a solid lock. He'd never been careful his whole life, Matias neither. Danger was their stock and trade. You gotta be tough. You gotta be quick. But leave being careful to the bosses. Let them worry. He peeked around the thick anchor post, as wide as a redwood tree he saw in a museum once. That tree had rings inside the trunk, one for every year it lived. It was a marvel to behold, those rusty circles telling a tale better than any book ever could.

Maybe they cut me open when I'm dead. They can count my rings, too.

"What'd you say?" Matias asked him. His voice was crackly, and each breath puffed.

"Nothing. I got sand in my throat is all." Which was nonsense, his suit was sealed tight.

"You got sand in your ass crack, bro. It's what makes you so damned mean."

Mateo chuckled. He couldn't see his brother's face, but he knew he was smiling.

When he turned back, he rested his hand on one of the homemade bombs. Just a little bit closer and they'd launch. They'd empty their magazines into the Xenos and hightail it home.

Then he saw it.

A shifting in the soil. Dry rivulets draining downhill like streams of water. Not out in front of the station where everybody was looking but from down underneath by the foundation. The berm of accumulated dirt mounded against the module's base was moving like it was alive. Islands of caked sand were pushed up and then they crumbled into pieces. Rocks spilled in tiny avalanches along the bottom edge of the module. Their passing footsteps didn't disturb anything. Anyway, it would've settled down by now if they had. Instead, the motion was increasing.

What the hell was that? An earthquake?

"Fifty meters," Bak-Irp said. "Forty. They're picking up speed. Prepare to throw."

Mateo froze. He didn't talk back because he was too shocked to form complete words.

The loose dirt fell away, revealing tall, dark shapes coming up out of the ground, like swimmers emerging from the sea, but they weren't dripping water, they were dripping sand.

Xenos.

"Thirty meters. Get those bombs in the air, boys," Bak-Irp said. "Twenty-five…"

The underground Xenos were a lot closer than that. Five meters… and closing. Before Mateo could do anything with his bomb or machine gun, they were on him. Two of the smart ones. They seized his upper arms, wrenching the limbs from the sockets with sickening *cracks.*

"Gahhh…" Mateo grunted. He screamed to warn his brother who was only a few steps away. But the bombs were going off in the distance. Matias couldn't hear him. He was attacking as ordered. Mateo tried to twist away from the Xenos, gritting his teeth and pushing away the terrible pain. But they had him good, their grips were so tight, like the rocks had grabbed him.

There were four Xenos who snuck up from behind them, who'd buried themselves and waited for this ambush. He and his bro practically stepped on them when they walked out the door. Mateo would've dropped to his knees in pain, except the two who had him by the arms held him upright, while a third cracked his faceplate with a tomahawk hand chop. The Xeno got up in his face and picked away a pizza slice shard of his faceplate, the air was gushing from his suit. Mateo couldn't breathe. His mouth hung open, gasping, and the Xeno shot the stinger out of its own mouth – a hooked claw twitching on the end of a muscle rope. The stinger smashed into Mateo's teeth, forcing its way into the back of his throat and twisting upward, digging…

He blacked out. When he came back it must've been a

few seconds later, but it felt longer. His head was like a fat balloon, and he was sitting slumped against the anchor pole and couldn't move. Paralyzed. He couldn't get any air into his lungs. There was no air out here.

The Xenos were gone, but he could hear them. And he could hear Matias shooting and screaming... and Mateo realized in those final moments that he didn't want to die in a place like this... it was too ugly and there wasn't anything noble about it... then he saw the beach and the laughing somebodies, and he knew it was going to be all right... pretty guns and fast ships... and LOOK! Sunny Matias was sitting at the water's edge telling a joke to a couple of sunbathers and he was pointing at Mateo and laughing, saying to look down at his chest which was ripped open and empty inside... *What's so funny?* Mateo said. Matias answered him with a big, stretchy grin.

Come closer, bro. We need to count your rings and see how old you are...

CHAPTER THIRTY
Six Fugitives Against the World

For a comms hub, it was awfully quiet. Shawna swished water in her mouth but couldn't get rid of the bitterness. They'd done what they could once they saw what was happening outside. Too little, too late.

Bak-Irp was yelling at everyone to get their helmets on and grab a gun. He flung the door open, unloading on the Xenos who were biting Matias. The hitman was dead. They knew that. It wasn't hard to figure out with the sand turning red and his spacesuit in shreds, Xenos picking him apart like a turtle turned on its back, and then they worked him out of his shell, morsel by morsel. The Thassian nicked one of the bombs, which was his plan, and everything blew, the remaining devices triggering off that first explosion. Xeno parts splattered on the viewport.

Too-ahka was outside in the thick of things blasting the flamethrower over the Xenos who were charging. They lit up, staggered, and fell; none of them were getting close to the alien. The creature swiveled around and torched Mateo who was dead by that time but had two Xenos hanging on him. That set off another round of detonations, and Shawna worried that the module might crack because the rumbling underneath them felt a lot worse than she'd expected.

But the structure held.

This was the result of Nero's bad idea. All of it. She couldn't fault him for ignoring his mistake. He lodged himself right there in the doorway, shoulder to shoulder with Bak-Irp, pumping bullets into zombies, crying out in frustration, talking to himself about how he messed it up, how he was going to kill every last Xeno, cursing out his sister, the Cybernetics Guild, the Coalition for putting them in this position by locking them up… he ran through a litany of enemies, people he didn't have in his gunsights, but the Xenos were a good substitute until the others arrived… when he stopped shooting there weren't any monsters left to kill. His gun barrel was smoking. It started melting, turning drippy orange, coughing metal embers, and then the end of it snapped off to the leftward side, so he'd have to find a new gun; he tossed the ruined weapon out the door and stalked away.

Krait got them sealed in. The air rushed, filling the muffled room. It made their ears pop.

"You can take your helmets off," the smuggler said. "We're back online."

Shawna realized that she hadn't moved from the long window. She'd stood transfixed. Never got a shot off. But she didn't need to, they had it covered without her. *Two dead. No more Matias and Mateo.* Shawna was reliving the deaths of her squadron; she'd been convicted of their murders, and the deaths weren't her fault any more than these two were, but she felt the responsibility for screwing up, not seeing something she should've, although she couldn't say what that was. In battle soldiers die, others live. It wasn't clear who got the worse deal.

Nero was kicking the furniture around. Talking to the ghosts of Matias and Mateo, he was swearing at them, telling them he was sorry, cursing the Xenos and his sister, and the gods.

Lemora came over to Shawna. Her bloodshot eyes were glassy and damp, but she wasn't stopping her analysis of their situation, she was pushing on, and Shawna appreciated it. The two women walked away to the far side of the module, Lemora leading her by the arm. "This was a premeditated attack," the scientist said in a hushed voice. "The Xenos who exhumed themselves from the sand also timed their ambush. That shows precision. And coordination with the other Xenos. These zombies didn't come up with that on their own. It was programmed by outsiders."

"The Cybernetics Guild," Shawna said.

"None other." Lemora quirked her lips and rested her hip on a filing cabinet.

"They're experimenting on the Xenos and modifying their programming in real time."

"But why?" Lemora asked. She clearly had an idea in mind that she wanted her to grasp.

Shawna shrugged, not having given it much thought since they first found the brainband. "It's what Nero said. They're breeding attack dogs."

"Again, I ask why," Lemora said. "Zoom out. What's the bigger picture? Their end goal is what exactly? Why take the risk of venturing out here, bagging and altering these highly dangerous creatures? How're they doing it? Getting in and out undetected, I mean. That's another huge exposure, because if the Coalition finds out, they'll pay for it. What's the upside?"

Shawna thought about the doctor's questions. Floating jigsaw pieces were fitting together. "They develop a new product to sell," she said. "The buyer would have to possess deep pockets to make it worthwhile. Some organization that can distribute weapons, put them to use."

"Does that sound like anyone we know?" Lemora asked. But she already had the answer.

"The Arms Guild," Shawna said. "Which means Neera." Shawna didn't know much about Nero's less famous sister, although she'd heard tell that the whole family was monstrous.

"Is it any coincidence then that she's one of the only people who knows we're here?"

"No way."

"No *freaking* way," Lemora said. "It wouldn't surprise me to find out that Nero's plan to escape to PK-L7 came from Neera. It's a setup. This place is a kill box, and we were lured here."

"Do you think he's figured it out?" Shawna jutted her chin toward the room where Nero was working through his anger. It sounded like he'd moved from beating up the furniture to pounding on the walls. She tried not to jump every time he connected.

"I don't think his ego would permit it, frankly," Lemora said.

"So, are we going to tell him?"

Lemora shook her head. "He'd lose his shit. Then he'd argue that we were paranoid, even though he's the most paranoid person I've ever met. No, he'll never be convinced. Unless..."

"Unless what?"

"He needs to see it for himself. To think he discovered the plot against us."

Shawna felt rage growing inside her. It was ridiculous that in order to survive they were required to subject themselves to the whims of Nero's fragile self-image. They had to pretend he was the smartest one among them, or he might react irrationally and get them all killed. It was so pathetic. And so very predictable. How many "great" men had she known in the military who were obsessed with the minutiae of their own reputation and rank; everyone around them walked on eggshells protecting them from criticism and real consequences. Frankly, it was exhausting.

"How do we do that?" she asked angrily. "Without dying in the meantime?"

Lemora clicked her tongue. She was drawing spiral patterns in the dust on top of the filing cabinet. "If this ambush we witnessed was Neera's work, as I'm sure it was, then she knows it failed by now. My guess is she's going to suddenly contact us out of the blue."

Krait leaned forward in his seat, clutching his earphones and concentrating. He licked his chapped lips as he adjusted the levels on the control panel, cleaning up the transmission he was hearing. It was riveting, whatever it was. He could hardly stay in his chair; his butt levitated.

"Hey, Nero!" Krait called out. "We must've wrangled a new sat link because I'm hearing voices, and it sounds like she's sitting next to me. I can almost smell her perfume."

Nero came rushing into the main room. "What're you talking about?"

"Neera. She wants to talk to you. She says she's coming to save our asses."

Nero snatched the headphones off him. He cupped the earpieces to his chest. "When?"

"Now," Krait said. "Just listen." He motioned for him to put on the headset.

Lemora exchanged glances with Shawna. "We need to be prepared. Don't you agree?"

Shawna nodded, watching as Nero talked to his sister. His mouth was going a mile a minute. Despite his high maintenance status, they needed Nero to perform. His contribution was vital to the escape. They'd have to bring Bak-Irp in on their plan. Krait and Too-ahka were wildcards. They were six fugitives against the world if everyone ended up on board.

"I'm with you all the way," Shawna said. For the first time she noticed the light on PK-L7 changing, getting dimmer. With the heavy cloud cover it was difficult to gauge the shift, if nighttime was still approaching or if this was the night – a midnight sun burning offstage – whether the light faded or not, one thing was certain. Things were getting darker on all sides.

CHAPTER THIRTY-ONE
The Empress Smighty

The wormhole opened like a sphincter in space. Neera sat in the command chair on the bridge of her ship thinking of the crude comments she could make, smiling to herself as she concluded that silence was the most intimidating posture for her to assume – she didn't need to talk trash to impress the boys, because every maggot on this ship was subservient to her. She terrified them, and that was thrilling. *Small and mighty*, the baron had called her when she was a girl. He'd given her a pet name that she hated at the time: *Smighty*. It didn't bother her now, she embraced it.

"Awaiting your orders, Your Imperial Highness," the Caridian said.

Yes, you are, she thought delightedly. *And wait, you shall, until I decide when to go.*

The Caridian wasn't piloting the ship. She had a skilled professional whose job it was to perform that task. The Caridian's role was merely ceremonial, a nod to his contribution to the effort. She gave him a seat on the bridge beside the actual pilot. *What an odd fellow Dr Kix was.* She didn't know what made him tick. Other than money, which was no surprise, since everyone had that motivation button built in at the factory. *Caridians look like walking locusts,* she thought. It wasn't a compliment. And this locust was bound to be as destructive to the galaxy as the ancient plague was to Egyptian crops trembling in the field. He'd become a symbol of death.

"Stretch out your hand over Egypt so that locusts swarm over the land and devour everything growing in the fields..."

Neera had looked up the biblical quote this morning. Soon she would be stretching out her hand over the Coalition lands and letting her Xenos eat them right down to the bone, unless they paid her ransom demands. She'd break the Coalition financially, and then she'd take them apart with violence, releasing her Xeno armies anyway, opening wormholes and dumping zombies on them like salt on chunks of raw meat. The mold would do the rest, changing non-humans into more fighters for her cause. The Augments would keep the new recruits in line. The Arms Guild would be unstoppable, and she would succeed where her father and brother had both failed. *Empress.* It had a nice ring to it. Too bad Nero wouldn't be alive to witness her dominion. She'd have loved to rub his face in her success and make him squirm, thinking about how she'd beaten him. *But you can't have everything.* She laughed. *Except for me. I can have it all. Neera Lupaster. The Empress Smighty.* She sat rigid in her command seat, eyes bright, tail wagging if she'd had one. She'd never been happier, though there was one detail to be ironed out. Nero.

"Let 'er rip, Dr Kix," she said.

The Caridian nodded solemnly as if he were launching an expedition in unknown worlds.

But they all knew exactly where they were going. The

Cybernetics Guild reps looked nervous, quaking and dyspeptic, sipping on their motion sickness tea. *PK-L7.* Arguably the worst place in the galaxy. Certainly, the most dangerous. A murder farm – they grew corpses there.

The wormhole loomed. It didn't look like much of anything to Neera. A whole lotta nothing was more accurate. Blacker than black, an empty, beatless heart, or a clean, clean tunnel.

As they flew into the void, she put on her mirrored shades. The last time she rode the space worm she dreamed about the strange colors for weeks, streaks and waterfalls flowing like blacklight rainbows; it made her queasy just thinking about them. She'd felt nauseated as if she were following a druggy headquest to other dimensions, out-of-body metaphysical shit, experiencing the skin-crawling heebie-jeebies without any of the euphoria or mind-blowing insights – she hated it. Consequently, she closed her eyes this time, but she didn't want them to see her not looking, especially the Cybernetics reps. *Those three geeks better be right about controlling the Xenos.* So far, they'd been a great disappointment to her, and she didn't take kindly to being disappointed. Sure, the Augments managed to kill a couple of well-armed convicts. But they didn't wipe out the crew, and her brother was still out there, probably more alert than ever. If he was on to her schemes, he'd make his move on PK-L7 after he had her ship. He probably suspected she was up to something by offering to help him, but he would just as certainly underestimate the scope of her strategy, given that he always assumed he was bigger and better at everything. But this time she had him beat. She was sure of it.

The ship began to move in a sort of swimmy fashion, which meant they were in the hole. Neera grabbed the armrests, her long, pointed fingernails digging into the foamy, black pads.

After the last screwup, Neera felt she had to be more hands-on. No more murder by proxy. She'd rounded up a rock-hard crew of her most loyal guards, mercenaries who'd served in the GDF Special Forces. Ex-Black Ops types who weren't shy about what team they played for. A dozen of them were hiding in the guts of the ship, waiting for her to announce, "Go-time."

If you wanted something done right, then you had to do it yourself.

Her plan was simple. They'd pop out of the wormhole, land on the mining station's runway, and open the air hatch for Nero and his jailhouse buddies. When Nero got close, the kill team would take them out. She wanted Nero's dead body. It was the only way she'd believe he was really gone. She'd played games for too long, hiring goons to assassinate Nero in XSecPen. Every attempt to kill him went sideways, and now he had that Thassian ex-bounty hunter watching his back. It should've been like shooting fish in a barrel. One goateed, smartassed fish.

Oh, well. She'd get the last laugh. Not only that, but she'd also enjoy the pleasure of seeing her brother finally get his due, kicking his corpse, and making sure he was forever in her rearview. The ship stopped the wavy, bouncy, unmoored business. It was back under control.

They had arrived.

She opened her eyes.

PK-L7 was as ugly as a busted toe. Who knew there'd be so much treasure buried inside such a dried-out hard turd of a planet? She took in the minefield sights: swarming drones and sentry guns. Her ship's cloaking was state-of-the-art; she wasn't worried about them. She might even leave the antique defenses running after she put down the Coalition. They'd protected the place well all these years, even if they hadn't been good enough to keep her out.

"Shall we initiate landing procedures, your Imperial Highness?" the pilot asked.

"My brother can see us, correct?"

"There's no mistaking a wormhole appearing in the sky," the Caridian said, chirping in.

"I concur," the pilot said.

"Then let's wait," Neera said. "I want him eager and racing into my welcoming arms."

"As you wish," the pilot said.

I do wish, she thought, with no small degree of satisfaction. *And my wishes all come true.*

CHAPTER THIRTY-TWO
A Long Walk

"Why's she just sitting there?" Nero said. He crawled up on the work counter, pushing aside computers and cables, plowing through a layer of dust that probably hadn't been touched by human hands for hundreds of years, so he could scoot up to the glass, pressing his face to it like a little boy searching the heavens for Santa Claus. Krait watched him the way a snake watches a mouse, and Lemora didn't like that. She knew she was smarter than Krait, and it helped that Krait thought he was the smartest person in every room he entered. It gave him a blind spot.

"Neera's probably getting the lay of the land," Krait said. "She doesn't want to walk into anything." Krait had that semi-auto shotgun with the drum underneath the desk. She saw him sneak it from the supply closet like nobody was paying attention. She'd found her own good fortune in that closet, a box of grenades, the kind that looked like shaving cream cans. She had the cans laid out on the table in front of her. A big gob of mold sat in a plastic container next to the bombs. She'd scooped it from where it dripped through a seam in the module by one of the doors they weren't using. The window in the door was covered in mold as if someone had hung a thick, wet, black blanket over it. The mold had a mildewy smell like a dirty shower. She collected enough for her purposes, dividing it into marble-sized balls with a spork from a drawer she'd rifled through earlier. She had to keep it away from Bak-Irp, but the rest of the team were immune. He'd been wearing his gas mask whenever he removed his helmet, but she'd seen him slipping it off now and again to breathe the module's scrubbed air.

"She's icing me," Nero said. "It's a taunt. She can't resist pulling a power play."

"I think you're paranoid," Krait said, hanging a little soft laugh on the end of his comment to take out the sting. "Neera's here. Where you asked her to be. It's a matter of time."

"Time for what?" Nero said sharply, because he was on edge.

"Until she makes the pickup and flies us out of here. We're practically home free."

"Bullshit. It's a provocation. I know her," Nero said. But he slid off the counter into a wheeled office chair. "Do you know my sister?" He narrowed his eyes at the smuggler, entertaining new treacheries, double-crosses springing up everywhere when he was like this. Lemora clenched up. They needed to stick together and work as a team against the Xenos and Neera. She wondered if Nero was starting to suspect Neera more now that her arrival was fast approaching. Pushing off with his boots, Nero shot in the chair across the floor, catching hold of Krait's arm. "I asked you a question. Do you know Neera?"

"I've never had the pleasure of making her acquaintance."

"Then leave her character analysis to me," Nero said. He spun off, turning in circles.

"Sure thing, boss," Krait said, making the *boss* sound like an insult.

Nero jumped up on his feet and came over to Lemora. "What're you two working on?"

Lemora had asked Shawna to help her top off the mold bombs. The lids were unscrewed, and Lemora dropped mold deposits into half the canisters. Shawna found a dried-out inkpad and added water to it; she was stamping the mold-containing grenades with blue thumbprints to tell them apart.

"Prepping," Lemora said. "The Xenos will attack again as soon as we leave the station."

"What's the mold for? They're already infected," Nero said.

"Who knows who's riding with Neera?" Lemora figured she'd play up Nero's lack of trust but keep it directed away from his sister. "There's a Caridian, you said. He gave her the wormhole tech. Well, Caridians can be infected. This'll give us something to threaten him with."

"Why would we need to threaten the Caridian?"

Lemora shrugged. "I hope we won't. The grenades are still grenades. We can use them on the Xenos, but this way we have options." Shawna tilted an open can toward her. She sporked a dollop of mold into it. Shawna then screwed the lid down. "I like having options. Don't you?"

Nero nodded, but he seemed like he wasn't entirely satisfied with her answer. "As long as they work on Xenos, I'm cool with it." He looked like he had more questions, but Bak-Irp cut in.

"Ship's coming down," the Thassian said. "They're kicking

up dust with their thrusters. We aren't going to be able to see shit. It'll be like walking in a sandstorm till it settles."

"I'm not waiting for the dust to settle," Nero said. "It'll cover us the same as the Xenos."

"I was afraid you'd say that," Bak-Irp said. "I'll remind you that we're two guns down."

Nero glared at him. Losing the Silvas hurt their chances of survival, hurt *his* chances. He didn't need reminding, and Lemora would've advised Bak-Irp not to say anything. Getting on the bad side of Nero was a deadly mistake, but Bak was a big boy who could take care of himself.

"How d'you want to do this, boss?" The Thassian was carrying a machine gun and a shotgun strapped to his back. He'd loaded up with as much extra ammo as he could carry.

Nero snapped back to the matters at hand. He said, "You and Fuzzy take the point together. Him with the flamethrower, you keep us on track to Neera's ship. Krait and I will be behind you—"

"I don't like him where I can't see him," Bak-Irp said.

"Too bad."

"I resent that, Bak," Krait said. "I'm part of this team whether you like it or not."

"Well, I don't like it."

"Shut the hell up," Nero said. "Both of you. Bak, I'm behind you with Krait. I've got his ass covered, and I've got you covered. The ladies will have the grenades and come out last."

Lemora sliced a canvas hammock into strips. She and Shawna wore the strips in "X" patterns across their armored bodies. The grenades clipped to the strips where they rattled like tree ornaments tossed out with the trash after the winter solstice holidays. They were noisy but easy to access.

Lemora kept her fingers crossed that the explosives weren't unstable after all the time in storage. The fuses looked fine, but you could never tell. She didn't want to blow herself to smithereens. You don't fight battles with the weapons you want but the weapons you have.

"Toss those bombs far ahead of us. I don't want to get fragged," Krait said.

"Don't worry, honey." Lemora leaned in close. "If I want to frag you, you won't see it."

"But I'll feel it, right?"

"Not for long."

Bak-Irp was impatient to get things going. Waiting was fraying his nerves, making him jumpy.

"They landed." Krait pressed the headset to his ears, battling the roaring thrusters outside.

"How close? Sounds like they're putting down right on top of us," Bak-Irp said.

"Close is good," Nero said. "I don't want a long walk."

The dust masked everything in a yellow-orange fog. Bits of gritty sand ticked at the viewport glass like hailstones. The air boiled with mini blooms and dust devils whirling about.

"Can't see shit," Bak-Irp complained.

"They want us to come out," Krait shouted. "They said, '*Now*.' We should go now."

"What?" Nero said. He pointed to his ear inside the helmet, indicating he couldn't hear.

"They're waiting for us. The air lock is open. Ramp deployed. They said to run for it."

Bak-Irp unsealed the module's doors. The jetwash from Neera's thrusters raged. Whoever was piloting that ship was gunning them, stirring up debris. Clouds of loose soil swirled inside. It felt like they were standing at the back of a troop transport, ready to parachute blindly into the murk. Bak-Irp didn't like it one bit, but he wasn't giving the orders. He started stepping down. Until Nero snagged his elbow, hauling him backward.

"Hold up," he said. He turned around to address Krait. "Tell them to meet us halfway. I want to see my sister before I go anywhere. Say that I want a visual of Neera or the deal's off."

Krait relayed the message. Then he was shaking his head, pursing his lips. "They said, 'No way. Come now or forget it. She won't take that risk.' What should I tell them, Nero?"

"If I don't see Neera in the flesh, I'm not budging. Let them fly away. I want Neera."

Krait repeated what Nero said into his mic. He clutched his headset, twisting the knobs. "It's dead. I've got silence," he said. Yanking off the headset, he tossed it down in disgust. "You blew it." Krait stomped off into the far reaches of the module, toting his shotgun.

Nero didn't respond. He stood braced in the doorway, feet apart. The dust was already building up on the module's floor behind him, a carpet of sharp silicates that sparkled in the harsh fluorescence of the overhead lamps. "C'mon… c'mon… show your face…"

Bak-Irp said, "I don't think she's coming." He withdrew, grabbing the handle to seal them in again. He put his head down as he swept the threshold clear with the edge of his foot.

"There!" Nero pointed into the obscurity.

Bak-Irp jerked his head up, squinting, trying to see what the arms dealer saw. The ship thrusters quieted to a low, chest-vibrating hum. The churning particles thinned. A yellow-orange wall of airborne debris became a series of veils, peeling away. Standing amid the turmoil was a figure wearing royal purple armor, with a submachine gun slung over one shoulder, resting jauntily on its hip. The figure stuck its arm out toward them, lifting its hand higher and higher.

"She's calling us out," Bak-Irp said. He didn't like the situation. It felt funky, off-kilter.

Nero barked with harsh laughter. "No, she isn't. Neera's giving us the finger."

"What do we do?" Bak-Irp braced for the worst. His job was to follow Nero's orders and try to keep the man alive. Sometimes it was hard to do both at the same time.

"Why, we go to meet her, my Thassian friend." Nero ducked inside. "Fuzzy, you ready?"

The one-of-a-kind alien sparked the flamethrower and bounded out the doorway. Bak-Irp went next. Nero landed at his side. One by one, they hit the sand, passing the bodies of their two fallen comrades and the dead Xenos littering the ground, as the ochre dust began to bury them.

CHAPTER THIRTY-THREE
Everyone is Your Enemy

This is so stupid, Shawna thought. She had her eyes glued to Nero's sister, but her peripheral vision was working overtime, trying to spot zombies, or Neera's henchmen, if Lemora was right about the two guilds – Arms and Cybernetics – joining forces to mass produce brainjacked Xenos and eliminate Nero along the way. It sounded so greedy and underhanded that she had no trouble believing it. Her opinion regarding fairness and large institutions had taken a nosedive since her arrest and trial, not to mention her incarceration. She couldn't bring herself to trust faceless organizations and was never one for believing in conspiracy theories before the day that changed her life forever. Afterward, she knew with certainty that somebody was out there who had it in for her; they'd seized control of her fighter and used it to murder her friends, then left her holding the smoking gun. So, some conspiracies did exist. Knowing that didn't make it any easier to deal with her predicament. It didn't explain the motive. Her mind reeled, turning over the details, sifting for clues around the awful event. *Why would anybody do that to her?*

She was feeling a little lightheaded inside her suit, nothing outside the range of normal; armored spacesuits were hot and confining, add a dollop of stress and a degree of vigorous exercise and a person might get dizzy. It didn't help that the air was full of floating debris, erasing hard lines, melting the sky and ground together.

As she did every day of her life, she had to stuff the topic of her wrongful conviction down deep inside, because if she let herself run with the possibilities, the who, why, and how of the con job that got her put away for life, well, following along the various strands, she might never return to the land of sane people. Instead, she'd be lost in the wilderness of her head, alone.

The dust kicking up around them reminded her of the mountain fog that floated up in the misty mornings back home. She barely remembered anything from her childhood. But the fog – she always liked the fog, how it felt like good magic. This chalky amber haze wasn't good though, it was suggestive of corruption, flying granular bits worn down and as infectious as rusty blades. Somewhere in it was the source of the nightmare, hovering like an evil presence – the xenium – and the mold.

The convicts trudged over open ground. Now and again the stark middle distance would clarify into view, she'd scan it quickly for signs of activity, then snap back to the threat in front of her: Neera, posing in her gaudy armor. Her face glowed like a pale moon, and Shawna realized she was wearing face paint. The female Lupaster had huge sapphire eyes like a cartoon character who'd come to life. She bore a resemblance to her twin – the same high cheekbones and aura of arrogance. What a family that must've been to grow up in, a nest of gigavipers, oozing poison from their pores, always on the hunt, fangs out to the world, and each other.

"Miss me?" Nero asked his twin.

"I wouldn't if my aim was better," she said without a smile. "You ready to ride?"

"Born ready." He started for her.

"Stop right there." Neera raised the barrel of her SMG, leveling it at him. Here came the smile: dazzling white teeth in a white face, framed by her full, white lips – a grinning apparition.

Nero stopped and threw up his arms in mock surprise. "Whoa! What have we here?"

She was out of reach of Too-ahka's flamethrower, but Bak-Irp had her in his sights. If she elected to shoot her brother, the Thassian would cut her down. *Was this a murder-suicide pact?* Shawna unclipped a grenade, hooking her thumb into the safety pin ring. A quick flip and she'd be ready to frag the baron's daughter. *Where was Neera's backup? What was she trying to pull?*

"You didn't think I was really going to take you home with me, did you?" she said.

"If your kin won't take you back home, where will they take you?"

"To the graveyard?"

A hot wind blew. Not coming from the ship's thrusters, but a harsh desert gust that raced across the treeless PK-L7 landscape, scouring the rocks, rasping the sharp corners off boulders – a current of sour-looking, punchy air that felt purposeful and mean, like it wanted to shove you around and hurt you bad. Shawna had to widen her stance to keep from being knocked over. The blast wiped the scene clear like a spritz of glass cleaner on a filthy window. She picked up more information than her attention could handle at one time. To her left – more than a dozen humanoid figures were spaced out on the hardpan between Neera and her revving ship. To Shawna's right – vague traces of movement, maybe nothing but a trick of the eye backdropped by a quirky, unfamiliar horizon – but the movement vibed like a bad omen, flowing along the ground as if a flash flood of turbulent water surged toward them, roiling… it might've been a mirage.

A second gust dirtied her view again.

"Where's the Caridian?" Nero said. "Better yet, where are the Cybernetics reps? I know they're here, Neera. You think you can screw me over. Dust me and take control, right?"

Neera shrugged, acting unperturbed. "Why not?"

So, Nero wasn't oblivious to his sister's machinations. He'd put together the same pieces that Lemora had, only he needed to see it to believe it – family turning on family, and why would that surprise a man who'd killed his own father? Maybe it wasn't a surprise but confirmation of a personal hypothesis he poked at idly in the cold, ashy oven of his heart: everyone is your enemy. Her heart sank – here she was, stuck in the middle of a bloody family feud on a zombie infested planet, with no way out that didn't depend on the people who were causing all the problems.

"Then we go down together," Nero said. "If that's your call, I'm ready. Let's do it."

"Cool."

Neera dove for the dirt, hitting the ground, splaying out flat.

Bak-Irp held his fire, alert, watchful. "Her boys are coming now," the bodyguard said.

Mercenaries in jet black body armor coalesced through the shifting dust veils; like reapers from the underworld they marched, but instead of scythes they wielded automatic rifles. Nero drew his pistol and took aim at his sister clinging to a shallow dip in the soil. It wasn't enough to hide her from his bullet. Shawna hadn't signed up for a suicide mission. She debated with herself about retreating to the comms hub, but she'd never make it. And it was better to die face-to-face in a hail of gunfire, than to take a volley of slugs in your back as you ran from the fight.

"What're they doing here?" one of the mercs called out. He pivoted his rifle from the escapees to a dark wave cresting to Shawna's right side. "I thought they were under control."

"Xenos!" Krait yelled. "There must be hundreds! Frag 'em!"

Gunfire erupted. Cracks and whumps of differing caliber pummeled her eardrums.

But it wasn't mercs shooting at her team, or her team shooting at the mercs. All the guns were pointed at the Xenos who came at them, rushing out of the dust, a horde of them, hundreds like Krait had said, and they'd snuck up stealthily, creeping around with their snouts in sand and grit and powdery soil that made up the surface layer of PK-L7. Xenos descended from miners who ate rocks and breathed rock particles and lived on that stuff for generations. That movement Shawna thought she'd seen before? Yeah, that was them. They were the flood.

Oh shit, she thought. *Oh shit, oh shit…*

Lemora lobbed a grenade and had a second in the air before Shawna got her first off.

BOOM!

Damn, that was a short fuse.

BOOM!

The explosions were louder than the guns, but the guns never stopped. Mercs and cons were pumping bullet after bullet into the army of Xenos who seemed to appear out of nowhere.

They must've come up from underground, Shawna thought. This ground must be like an anthill or a piece of Swiss cheese, riddled with tunnels, and the Xenos – no guessing how many there were – probably lived down there, spent most of their time snuffling in the dark, digging, and who might speculate what monsters did in their downtime? But they knew their way around. They had a sense of their location and how it corresponded to the planet above, and when they wanted to, when they chose to, they turned their claws upward and lifted the lid off their world.

"Fall back," Shawna shouted.

Krait passed her in a full run. Bak-Irp was walking backward, taking deliberate steps, firing from the hip. Nero delivered pistol headshots at the nearest Xenos, but he quickly holstered that weapon and opened up with his fully automatic machine gun. The Xenos in the front line toppled, and the others behind them stepped on them as if they wanted to catch bullets, too. And catch them they did. The mercs were pros who didn't hesitate, playing the percentages when it came to dispensing lead souvenirs: every Xeno who showed its face got a prize, and if it didn't kill them, it disabled them, knocking out their legs, slowing the advancement of the mob.

There was no time for negotiation with Neera's attack force. But the fighters all understood that they needed to cooperate – at least for now – or none of them were going to live. Shawna stood next to a tall merc, an African woman with a Nigerian flag tattooed on the side of her neck.

"Give me some of those," the merc said in a muffled voice, opening her hand.

She was talking about the grenades hanging off Shawna's homemade bandolier. The ex-pilot unclipped two canisters, passing them to the woman who hurled them high and far into the rising tide of Xenos. The devices exploded, sending alien body parts airborne. Shawna cut one of her bomb straps – it held the cans with no thumbprints and no mold – and handed it over. The merc nodded, shooting her automatic rifle one-handed and throwing bombs with her other arm.

Shawna dropped to one knee and shouldered her weapon. Picking targets wasn't a problem, because the field was target rich. Although several fast and limber Xenos were leaping sideways now that they understood where the danger was, choosing to avoid getting shot, not retreating but flowing to the outer edges, rushing wide around the group of soldiers-for-hire and former prisoners – others bulled straight on, absorbing ammo before dropping into lifeless heaps.

"They're trying to get behind us," the merc said. "The fast ones. Look at them go." Not taking any chances, she left her position, heading off to guard their flank and taking the rest of the printless grenades with her.

As soon as she was gone, Bak-Irp fell in beside Shawna, breathing hard.

"Can we go back to the module?" Shawna asked. Bak was taller and had better eyesight.

"No way. They're crawling all over it."

"Where to then?"

The Thassian slammed another magazine into his weapon. He fired off a burst. "I don't know. Where's Nero?"

Shawna swept her gaze across the battleground chaos, but the man wasn't there. She wasn't at the point of panicking, not yet, but she could see it from where she was.

Bak-Irp repeated his question. "Where the hell is Nero?"

CHAPTER THIRTY-FOUR
The Crystal Men

Nero was chasing his sister. He'd glimpsed her popping up off the ground and scrambling away from the Xeno attack, and he pursued her. She wasn't going to get away. No matter what happened he was determined that she wouldn't win this competition. She would never be the head of the Arms Guild, not if he was alive and out of prison. They'd both die first. He'd make sure of it.

That cheesy grape suit of armor made her easy to spot. He had to give her credit for her scheme, bringing together the Caridian with his wormhole tech and the Cybernetics geeks who were massaging the Xenos' brains, rendering them compliant or controlling them or whatever it was they were doing – that was a bold stroke of genius. He'd be sort of proud, if she wasn't using the deal to screw him out of his rightful position at the head of the family empire. He'd earned it! *But query me this, sister Neera, if the Cybernetgeeks are doing such a bang-up job, then why are you running from the Xenos?* He chugged after her. Suddenly she was gone. Vanished.

But how–

Nero found himself falling. Not far. He'd stepped into one

of those Xeno potholes that pocked the runway. His crater made a ninety degree turn about two meters down, essentially putting him into a Nero-sized hole. Now, there was no way he wanted to explore where the tunnel below his knees went after changing direction. But it was a decent place to stand for the time being, out of the fray, allowing him a chance to catch his breath and think, damn it, *think*.

If he could somehow get the Caridian and the Cybernetics engineers away from Neera long enough to make a counteroffer, to explain what skills and vision he brought to the table, then he was sure they would conclude that he'd be a superior partner. Not Neera. *I mean, c'mon.*

"Turn them off!" a voice screamed.

He feared at first that there was somebody coming up from inside the passage at the bottom of his cavity, but nobody was. Although the voice – and other voices, too – were being amplified by the acoustics of the tunnel. He figured out what was going on: there was another pothole, like his but farther down the line, and he could hear what the occupants inside it were discussing. The occupants were of great interest to him. The screaming voice unmistakably belonged to Neera. She was taking the Cybernetgeeks to task. Castigating them for the debacle happening above ground, the mighty Xeno screw-up. It had ruined her plans to assassinate Nero, and it imperiled her kill squad as well as the geeks. Her party had pooped itself.

"Shut them down!" she said. "Can't you even do that? They want to kill, like, all of us."

"We're trying, Your Imperial Highness. This awful dust is interfering with our instruments, which are delicate and highly susceptible to environmental fluctuations," one of the geeks said nasally. They all sounded alike in his experience. That was one of the many reasons he'd never gotten very far with them. They were impossibly flaky and had the most fragile constitutions. *The Crystal Men*, his father called them. They looked pretty but broke easily, and so did their inventions. Nothing ever worked as they promised it would. Forever tinkering, they had their excuses. *Excuses! That's what they make better than anything else*, his father would say with a loud guffaw. He'd kidnapped a few to steal corporate secrets, and they all died before the torture got into full swing. The baron viewed them as a waste of time. And so had he. Until now.

"Hand me that controller, so I can smash your head with it," Neera said.

"Imperial Highness, please… no…"

Imperial Highness, was it? Nero had to laugh at that. Same old Neera. She never changed. Boss of bosses, who if she didn't get her way, would take the toys, break them over your head, and then run crying to the nanny bots claiming she was the injured party in need of pity. He wondered if he might sneak through the tunnel and shoot her with his pistol. Then he could have a private confab with the geeks, although the geeks would be too terrorized to forge new alliances. Nero decided to stay put for the moment and listen. He crouched lower into his hole, inclining toward the void to hear better. The fighting had died down – probably not the best word to use – and the worst of the skirmish had moved away from his rocky gap. Things quieted.

"Look at the display, Your Imperial Majesty. The Augments are retreating. We've successfully directed a group of them to the station to prevent your brother and his friends from returning there. The tech is working magnificently. But there are a few wrinkles still–"

"Wrinkles!" Her exasperation was evident.

Nero heard the slap of metal on metal. *How the engineer's ears must be ringing! Ha!*

"Who is up there still attacking my guards? Who? Am I imagining them?"

"No, no, you are not," an engineer said. "If you can spare a bit more time, you'll see–"

"It's the young ones," another engineer said, cutting off the honker doing all the talking.

"What did you say?" Neera asked. "Speak up, you. Who are 'the young ones' exactly?"

The interrupter said, "Your Imperial Majesty, the Xenos have bred, naturally. Only the toughest of the young survive their juvenile years. These youths who are entering adulthood are difficult to control, not only for their elders but for our Augments. They act out rebelliously."

"Teenagers?" Neera said. "The aliens who are trying to murder us are Xeno teens. Is that what you're telling me?"

"Correct," the engineer said.

The bark of Neera's frantic hyena laughter was alarming. Spending so much time away, Nero had missed hearing her. Come to think of it, as adults his sister had never laughed with him. It was sad what happened to some families, how they drifted apart, becoming strangers.

Enough of this shit.

He vaulted out of his hidey hole. The Xenos were still out there fighting with the mercs and his team. The whole gang had worked their way back toward Neera's ship. The speed cruiser had a coating sprayed on it, silver and gold matte. Classy. He recalled the Arms Guild R&D scientists developing it in the lab, an anti-tracking layer; it rendered whatever you slathered it on invisible, not to the naked eye but to forms of tech surveillance. They must've progressed to the experimental phase while he was away. Maybe they were selling it now. It looked dynamite. Expensive. The sleek ship stood out like a wedge of precious metal, unpolished and raw. He wondered for a sec what xenium looked like when they chunked it out of PK-L7. Did it shine?

"Surprise," he said, looming over the rim of Neera's foxhole. Apparently, she'd left her SMG when she took off. Anyway, she didn't have it on her. The Cybernetgeeks were unarmed, too. And there was another dude crammed in there with them. He hadn't said anything before, and he wasn't talking now. He raised his hands like this was a stickup. Funny-looking guy even for an alien – a Very Grumpy Grasshopper. His eyes were far apart; Nero could've planted his fist between them without blocking the guy's vision whatsoever. He had a vertical slit mouth and dreary grayscale skin. *Ick.* "You must be the Caridian. Mr Wormhole Whisperer," Nero said.

"Don't kill me," the Caridian said, barely audibly, unable to maintain eye contact.

"Oh, I'm not going to kill you. Him on the other hand…" Nero picked the shakiest member of the Cybernetics trio and shot him in the face. The bullet hole in his forehead made quite an impression on the others. Nero waggled his pistol at them, ordering them to vacate.

"What do you want?" Neera asked, trying to sound unfazed, but failing miserably.

That was how Nero liked to start a conversation, with people asking for his demands.

"We're going to take a little jog back to your ship. Just like we'd planned, sweet sister. I'm willing to call this a bump in the road." The battleground looked like all battlegrounds: organized chaos. Bodies running, bodies dying. Blood and sand swirled; a cacophony of screams lifted up like a terrible song. His team had scattered. Too-ahka was out there toasting Xenos – bless his little oddball heart. Bak-Irp and Shawna were nowhere to be found. That didn't mean they were dead, only missing. He spotted Lemora and waved to catch her attention. Then he happened to glance at the sky. The wormhole squatted above them, dilated, and softly pulsating.

CHAPTER THIRTY-FIVE
Pointy-Snouted, Silvery-Golden Dragon

It was a mistake to count the Xenos out. Lemora knew that. The multiple species that made up the Xeno population had proved themselves resilient. They were the model of tough survivalists. Little was known about their origins. They weren't from here. They'd come for the work just like everyone else. The mining company kept their dealings with Xenos secret. No contracts existed in the Galactic Historical Archive office, if there ever were written contracts. Many alien groups distrusted written agreements, having had no history of them in their worlds or signing contracts only to watch them be broken by the other parties, often human. The infected Xenos could be considered a separate and unique class of beings. Obviously, they were not homogeneous. Time and the cybernetic alterations had recreated them yet again.

Individually, she felt sorry for them. This existence of theirs wasn't living, you couldn't call it that. But in congregate, as a swarm of berserk and insatiable killing machines, she wanted them destroyed. If not destroyed, then perhaps the best thing was to abandon them as the Coalition had done – isolated and walled-off permanently from the rest of life in Terran space. She'd read about the workers and the hunters, and she'd seen both subgroups up close since they arrived. The Cybernetics engineers implanted the hunters' brains with devices that tapped their sensory organs and input programming to control, or at least influence, their behavior. In the scant reports she digested back in her cell at XSecPen, she came across references to tanks – a stouter, immensely powerful, and defensive subgroup – but none of them had shown up yet, so perhaps they'd died out. Rarer still were the legendary spoiler abominations, hulking brutes, said to be nearly damage-proof, who were reputedly the source of the mold – Lemora doubted they were real. More likely, they were a mythological representation of the worst attributes of this mysterious, terrifyingly transformative plague that haunted PK-L7, a physical embodiment of the unknown cause behind the outbreak and the ongoing dangers lurking in this hostile place.

And yet...

Nero and Neera rejoined the combined merc and escapee forces who were holding off the onslaught from the Xenos in the short term. They'd formed a staggered defensive line, a half-circle that faced the Xenos as it steadily backed its way toward the waiting ship. A third of the mercs were dead, torn apart and eaten before their eyes. No one in this impromptu cadre was a stranger to death. They fed it and then dodged past it – their whole lives had been a slow dance with death. But no soldier, fighter pilot, bomb maker, arms dealer, or cybernetic vivisectionist would claim they didn't harbor a fear of being eaten alive. It was the credo of all life forms throughout space: don't let them eat you. Fear of devourment was as primal as it was energizing.

Lemora's heart was pounding, her whole head ached from the noise, tension, and pressure squeezing in constantly. She'd saved a handful of grenades, all with thumbprints, though she'd tossed a few of them into the Xenos. The mold had no effect, she'd have been surprised if it did. These things lived in the presence of mold. They touched it; they probably ate it if they still consumed rocks as they did in their pre-infected states. Mold particles no doubt permeated the air on PK-L7, although airborne exposure had never been proven. The dose was probably too low to spark a physiological change. Shrapnel still ripped their flesh, thankfully.

She felt shaky from the adrenaline, wrung out and weak-kneed. A numbness crept over her body, nerves tingling, bones rattling, and her mind detached itself and floated somewhere above her like a tethered helium balloon. She was watching herself fighting, as if her avatar were in the battle, and she wasn't ever going to die. Not really. Yet she felt petrified at the same time. Absolutely convinced she *would* die, as if she were already dead, her cards dealt, and it was a bad hand she could do nothing with, except throw them in the center of the table and call it a day.

"Lemora! Lemora, get over here! I need you." Nero beckoned. His voice in her helmet sounded like it was underwater, and far, far away. But he was right there, a few meters at most, hustling toward Neera's ship with three others who didn't look like fighters. *Nero needed her.*

Neera recognized Lemora and nodded. Her face was blank. Sweat ran through the white makeup, leaving trails like clown tears. She was moving stiffly. Had she been injured? No. As Lemora got closer, she spotted the pistol Nero held pressed against his sister's back. The others – two humans and a Caridian – appeared as if a Carfaxian vampire drained them of their blood.

"What are we doing?" Lemora asked him.

"My sister is going to accompany us on board her ship. Aren't you, dear?" Nero nudged her with the gun.

"Whatever." Neera stumbled, and Nero caught her with his free hand. He stuck the gun barrel in her armpit, twisting. Neera's face contorted in pain. "Quit it. I'm doing what you said."

"Just checking."

They walked up to the front of the ship. The ramp leading into the airlock chamber was deployed, so the ship resembled a pointy-snouted, silvery-golden dragon with its mouth hanging open, slack-jawed. Inside, Lemora spotted a second sealed hatch at the rear of the airlock.

"Everybody's going, right?" Lemora asked him. "We're all leaving here like you said?"

"As long as they're quick about it. A promise is a promise, and I gave them my word."

Lemora thumbed the comms button on her wrist, broadcasting to the whole team. She could see them out there, figures fighting in the dust, only a football pitch away. "It's boogie time, my darlings. Drop what you're doing and come aboard. We're expecting you."

Bak-Irp responded with a growl. "I drop what I'm doing, my ass is getting overrun. Got that?" The rat-a-tat-tat of his weapon punctuated the last sentence. "This is hairy. You hear me?"

"Loud and clear, big fella," Nero said. "But the bus is departing. I can't park here."

"Hold that ship," Shawna said. "We're coming."

The ramp was narrow, no wider than a two-person rover. The airlock looked like the inside of a commercial autoclave and was as large inside as a jumbo fuel-hauler truck. It was basically a long steel tube with slippery curved sides and little room to stand comfortably. The hatch at the back was round; only one person at a time would fit.

"You three wait here with Dr Pick," Nero said. The Caridian and the other two non-combatants shuffled off. "Engineer!" Nero poked his pistol at one of the men who was holding a small remote controller. "Work out the kinks on your implants, or you'll end up with an extra drain hole like your compadre we left back in the pit, yeah? Feel my meaning?"

The man swallowed dryly, his bulging Adam's apple pumping as if he were choking.

"I do, Your Imperial… Your Majestic… ah, Supreme Leader…?"

Nero nodded and turned to follow his sister up to the hatch.

"Cybernetics engineer?" Lemora inquired of the man.

"I am, yes…" He was trembling; his body quaked, shivered, bucked involuntarily.

"And you can control the Xenos with that device?"

"Some of them, I can. The young adults are proving to be uniquely uncooperative."

Lemora smiled, remembering. "Oh, I don't know how unique that is. Teenagers," she observed. "They know everything. And listen to no one. I was much the same at their age. A wild child." She took the engineer gently by the arm and steered him toward the lip of the ramp. "You do your best. Help my friends and your armed escorts to return safely. I have faith in you."

The man thumbed buttons and toggles. Lemora detected no effects on the Xenos. A foursome of hunters seized a merc whose gun had jammed. They pulled him like taffy, and he separated, spraying streams of red droplets high into the air. A jet of flames covered the four Xenos. They split apart, each running in a different direction, but none could outrun the fire.

The fire sputtered and shrank down to a trickle. Too-ahka's last fuel canister was empty. The alien used the depleted flamethrower as a club, battering the head of a worker who thought it wise to rush the stumpy, furry creature now that it had lost the power to burn. As the worker staggered, momentarily stunned at the pummeling it received, Too-ahka leaped and tore its throat out then drank the hot, spouting liquid before it soaked into the thirsty, hardpacked soil.

"Too-ahka, come with me. We must go now." Shawna was calling for the feeding to end.

To Lemora's astonishment the alien left its feeding and joined the pilot, running for the ship's ramp. They hit the treads and piled into the airlock. "Where's Bak-Irp? I'm not leaving him," Lemora said.

"There!" Shawna pointed to the Thassian who was trapped against the ground with a Xeno on his back, cranking his arm between his shoulder blades in a hammerlock. The pilot raised her gun. Slowly blowing out her air, she took aim and fired. The Xeno's head exploded.

Without a moment's hesitation, Bak-Irp was up and pumping his legs, sprinting to them.

Nero was screaming at his sister, who was hesitating at the

control panel. She was spitting words at him, and he wasn't happy. "OPEN UP THE DAMNED DOORS!" He shoved his pistol against the back of her helmet. Her posture signified defiant refusal. She was literally digging in her heels and striking out at him blindly. "ONE LAST CHANCE, NEERA, DO IT!"

"Nero! Don't!" Lemora screamed. And she ran to stop him from making a mistake. If he killed Neera in a fit of anger, they'd never get inside the ship. Or off this planet.

But she was too late.

He pulled the trigger.

CHAPTER THIRTY-SIX
Damage Radius

Nothing happened. *What the hell? Oh, shitballs.* He was out of ammunition. Nero bashed Neera with the pistol grip. But she was wearing an armored helmet. It didn't knock her out, it made her angry. She dropped to the floor like an incensed cat and scissored her legs through his, wrapping up his ankles and tripping him. Dumped on his ass in that narrow end of the airlock tube, he had trouble swinging his big gun around. He was tangled up in himself, hands sliding on the slick floor. Lemora was diving in to save him. She grabbed him under the arms and dragged him backward, avoiding Neera's steel-toed kicks. Then Neera was up on her feet, punching at a keypad next to the hatch. The circular door curved away into a slot in the wall; it looked like a waning moon, and about halfway through the cycle she had room to squirt through to the other side, where she spun around and heel-thumped an emergency switch.

The hatchway closed with a steely, clunking noise, then came a pressurized sigh.

Neera's disembodied voice screeched through a speaker. "Ha! Screw you, brother!"

He was standing, shrugging off Lemora who tried to restrain him. He ran to the hatchway and braced a hand on either side; his head hung low as he said, "We can still hammer out a deal. Talk to me, Neera, let's calculate a way where we both benefit. Nobody has to be the loser here."

"You tried to shoot me in the head!"

"Is that what this is about? You're mad at me?" He pictured her eyes rolling, hard. Red-faced with rage, she'd be grinding her teeth like when they were kids, fighting in the baron's sky mansion. Nero said, "Grow up, all right? Since I got arrested, you've been paying assassins to punch my ticket. We're natural born killers. That's who we are. It doesn't have to interfere with our negotiations." He took a deep breath. *Don't lose your temper. If she's talking, there's hope.* "Hey, sis, c'mon. Open sesame. I've got your Caridian pal and the Cybernetics crew. It's a party."

Nothing. The silent treatment.

Well, fine. He could wait, too. He had the wormhole guy and the Xeno mind control dipshits on his side of the hatch, and she needed them. She had to strike a bargain, didn't she?

The vibration came to him through his feet. It was mechanical, greased gears turning.

"The ramp," Lemora said. "She's retracting it." Like a metallic tongue the ridged walkway withdrew into a slot, and at the same time, the airlock began to shut, the dragon's jaws clamping down slowly. From outside, a keening whine picked up.

"They're powering the thrusters." Shawna emptied her machine gun into the trim belly of a Xeno who contorted, flexing its supple muscles before it backflipped off the edge of the ramp and crashed to the ground in its death throes. "The ship's getting ready to take off. Do we stay or do we jump?"

The ramp stuck out like a pirate's plank, a few meters off the ground, where it continued to retract, being swallowed steadily into the ship. Soon they'd be sealed in the airlock, and Neera could blast into the atmosphere, where she'd dump them like so much garbage.

Nero couldn't believe it. He was stunned, absolutely stunned.

"I... I don't... arrrgghhh..." he screamed at Neera locked in her flying fortress. "YOU ASSHOLE! I HATE YOU!" He started shooting uselessly at the hatch. He knew he was wasting bullets, but he didn't care. The ricocheting slugs sparked off the metal and pinged around the airlock's shiny interior. Any one of them might hit him. But they didn't. He took that as a sign.

The attacking Xenos kept charging, hoisting themselves up on the last few meters of ramp, scrambling over the lip of the airlock, thrashing with outstretched claws, their bites snapping loud and fast: a chittering, stomach-turning noise. They flung thick strings of drool when they wagged their angry heads. A human scuffled among them, beating them with the butt of a shotgun, not one of the mercs, but a man wearing scratched, dirty white armor. It was Krait.

He pinned Nero with a homicidal glare and jabbed a finger at him, shaking with fury. "You were leaving me." Krait swept his accusatory digit around the chamber. "All of you. Backstabbers! Murderers! You were going to let me die."

"Not me, buster," Nero said. "It's Neera. I'm the one attempting to stop her. Be logical."

"I am logical." Krait swung his shotgun like a bat, knocking a young Xeno unconscious. He shoved the zombie off the ramp. The falling body knocked into two other Xenos, aggravating them. When the airlock finally closed, Nero made a quick count. The Xenos outnumbered them two to one. A few of the mercs had made it inside. An unfortunate latecomer found himself trapped between the two closing halves of the airlock which crunched him, splintering his black armor. Then it chopped him in two. The color drained from his face, and a pair of Xenos quickly emptied the upper portion of his suit, pulling out the soft parts, chomping on bones, cracking them with their teeth to suck out the marrow. The dead merc's mouth was still moving.

The Caridian sank, horrified, into a puddle. The two Cybernetics reps wrapped themselves around each other in a heap. They'd finished taking turns with the controller; since the Xenos in the airlock hadn't been implanted, the device had no influence over their attitudes or actions.

"Get against the hatch door. As far back as you can. NOW!" Lemora shouted.

Nero listened, as he almost always did, to his top advisor. Shawna and Bak-Irp crowded on top of him. Fuzzy was right there, too, its dish-like face incapable of human expression, yet Nero had the distinct feeling that the creature was sizing him up as if he were a menu item.

He might've said something, if there had been more time. Like, *What the hell, Fuzzy?*

But Lemora pitched a grenade at the other end of the airlock tube where the Xenos were flailing about, thrashing their long sinewy limbs, their chests puffed out – a dominance display.

The Caridian and the Cybernetics reps were too frozen in terror to move. They stared.

Too bad for them.

The grenade exploded. *CRAAACCKKK!!!*

Fragments of shrapnel shredded the closest Xenos. The blast blew a hole in the airlock, and when the smoke sucked out of the hole, Nero saw dirt and rocks – a way out. Although the Caridian and the engineers were spared the worst of the impact, they were still well inside the damage radius. Both reps were dead. Tiny shards of metal perforated their armor, then their bodies. The Caridian was bleeding but alive, and conscious, although barely. Blood gushed from his ears. His head was leaky. He was sitting there, blinking, with the dead reps rearranged on his lap.

"OUT. OUT NOW." Shawna dove for the blast hole. Too-ahka beat her to it, stuffing itself through the gap – *wumpft!* Then Shawna went. Lemora, Krait, and Nero followed.

The Xenos and the mercs were all dead or dying. None of them was going to be a problem. As he was butt-scooting to freedom, Nero turned to Bak-Irp. "Take the Caridian."

The Thassian snagged the shaky scientist, tossing him over his shoulder.

As the ship began to lift off, the escapees dropped outside, one after another. They ran for the station through a field of scattered young Xenos who had never seen a flying ship so close before. The zombies stared up in awe at the spectacle. Yet Nero suspected their real thoughts.

Kill, kill, kill. Eat, eat, eat. Kill, kill, kill, eat, eat…

CHAPTER THIRTY-SEVEN
Get Angry

"Will it fly? I don't know, probably. The landing struts are totally shot. The generator might have cracked, but I don't know that for sure. At least she never exploded. If you're asking me about the risks, I'm saying they outweigh the chance that everything will work perfectly." Shawna poured water onto a tee shirt she found folded on a shelf in the storeroom. It bore the mining company's logo – a pick and shovel crossed over a shining nugget – and the words emblazoned on the chest read: BETTER LIVING BEGINS UNDERGROUND in glittery letters.

"I don't need perfect. And I'm not worried about landing," Nero said. "Not yet."

Shawna shrugged. She'd given him her honest assessment, which was what he asked for. She wiped the grime off her face with the shirt. Nero started pacing the length of the comms hub. The team had fought their way back through the zombies. Fortunately, most of them had scattered. Lemora suggested that it was because the implanted Xenos had lost their Cybernetics controllers. Neera's rising ship scared off the rest. Neera hadn't gone away. Her ship hovered a few meters above her original landing spot on the runway, kicking up dust clouds. Nero said that proved how much she needed the Caridian; she wouldn't leave without him. Shawna rolled the shirt, tucking it around her neck to cool down. It felt luxurious. She sensed Nero's eyes on her.

"But it's not impossible," he said, staring. "The *Andronicus* might fly again."

"Maybe I can get her in the air. The wormhole is right there. So, I guess it's possible."

"Because the only alternative I see–" Nero didn't get to finish. Lemora cut in.

"Is that we steal Neera's ship." Lemora shook her head. "Which will never work."

"We make a play for her ship, then she's bound to take off. Leaving us in the dust, shaking our heads and feeling inadequate," Shawna said, adding to the bombmaker's argument.

"And she closes the wormhole on her way out the door," Lemora said. "BAM!"

"Not without him, she won't." Nero tipped his head toward the Caridian who was looking better than he had in the airlock. Shawna had checked his injuries; none were life-threatening. He was deaf in one ear, and his head was ringing, but he could talk. His brains weren't scrambled. "Can she use the wormhole without you being there to supervise?" Nero said to their hostage.

"Possibly." The Caridian's voice was a low whisper. "Although I don't think she would try it. Her pilots and scientists have the scientific background but limited experience. She likes for me to be there. She's superstitious. And she hates traveling through the wormhole."

"Hates it, why?" Lemora said.

"The motion nauseates her. But it's more than that. She doesn't trust it to do the job."

"See?" Nero was excited, working himself up to a big decision. "Why else would she still be here? Her ship is damaged, right? Her slick death squad is dead. Believe me, she's scared." He fell back onto the office couch; dust puffed out of the limp cushions. Krait was lying on his back on the same couch with his knees drawn up, head tipped back. He hadn't spoken to anyone since they got back to the module. The Xenos were out there keeping a safe distance back, out of gunshot range. The zombies seemed to be suffering from battle lag, or they were cooking up something, but Shawna doubted that. Nero said now that the Cybernetics reps were out of the picture, and the controller wasn't in use, the implanted Xenos were in standby mode. They were confused, not having thoughts pumped into their heads. It caught them off guard. Nobody was issuing orders or bossing them around; they must be feeling adrift. The young Xenos wouldn't hold back for long. They'd be coming, all of them, sooner rather than later. This was the eye of the storm. It wasn't going to last. That was what Nero was saying, and Shawna had to agree.

Krait lifted his head. He looked tired and irritated. Dark circles ringed his eyes like coffee cup stains. "There's a bigger reason Neera can't leave." He talked to them as if they were stupid.

"Yeah? What's that?" Nero said.

"She wants to know that you're dead. If you make a run at her ship, she gets another shot at you. If you try this crazy idea that you're proposing... taking off in the *Andronicus*, she shoots you out of the sky. Either way, she has the absolute proof she needs. She's waiting to see what you'll do next. We're more vulnerable than she is. Maybe she gets lucky, and the Xenos break into the hub and eat us. What she won't do is leave before she knows how Nero dies." Krait dropped his head back and closed his eyes.

As much as she hated Krait, Shawna had to admit that he saw things they overlooked.

Nero walked over to the viewport. The panoramic vision of PK-L7 resembled a hallucinatory painting depicting hell. Mutilated bodies were strewn across an arid plain. Shawna imagined him as the ruler of the underworld, surveying his kingdom of the damned. Did he like what he saw? The sky had cleared. Yellow light smeared with burned orange streaks. Morning, it felt like morning. The two spaceships sat on the runway less than a hundred meters apart, starkly representing the decision that they had to make: Neera's ship or the *Andronicus*. Take your pick.

Shawna had been considering a third way. If only she could make a call to the Coalition, then she'd lead them here. The Galactic Forces would have the opportunity to capture Neera and her brother. Shawna wasn't naïve. She didn't expect them to commute her sentence and set her free. They'd never do that unless there was new evidence clearing her of her crimes. But maybe she could negotiate a transfer out of HT, away from XSecPen, someplace where she'd be able to work on her appeal in peace, receive visitors, spend time outside, breathing air that wasn't canned, enjoy a view of the starry sky and hear frogs croaking – small stuff that mattered. But how was she going to do it? First, she needed to be alone. Second, she had to figure out how to send the call. Nothing was ever simple. It wasn't realistic either, given the current obstacles. Which meant there really were only two choices…

"Nero, I've been thinking about what you said, and I've decided that I'm ready. Put me in the cockpit of the *Andronicus*, and I'll get her flying," she said. "It won't be easy, but I'll do it."

Nero's face lit up. He ran over, and for a second she was afraid he was going to hug her.

"That's winner talk," he said. "You're inspiring me." Then he hugged her tightly.

"Krait's correct," Lemora said. "Neera will try blasting the Tri-T. We need to hit her beforehand. It doesn't need to be fatal, but something that'll tie her up. Dump so many problems in her lap that we can get away." She toyed idly with the belt of leftover thumbprint grenades.

The Caridian noticed her staring in his direction.

"What?" he said. He cocked his head like he had water in his ears from swimming.

"I said, 'Does Neera have many nonhumans on board her ship?'"

The Caridian considered the question, calculating an estimate in his head. "Roughly a third of the crew, I'd say. Why? Is that important?" He blinked, switching his gaze from Lemora to Nero and back.

She told him why it was important.

"Oh, I see." He made a steeple of his fingers. "You're going to infect them. Change them into those things." He pressed the tip of the steeple to his chin. "That might actually work."

Shawna watched Bak-Irp who was standing, scanning the

horizon with his binocs. He must've been a hell of a bounty hunter. The guy never quit. He always had his game face on and didn't let distractions bother him. She wouldn't have wanted him chasing after her. Dude was persistent.

"If I ask you something, you promise you won't get angry?" she said.

"I'm already angry. Go on, ask."

"How did Nero manage to put together his escape plan? Why did he know they were going to be moving us?" The subject had bugged her since she saw the mold bomb blow above their heads. The hush-hush transfer played perfectly into Nero's escape plan. *Very convenient.*

"I was in the dark mostly. But I've been thinking about it, too. Nero complained to me that there had to be a snitch in HT. The prison bosses were tipped off about too many things. Well, what if Nero was the snitch? He feeds them details about an upcoming breakout. They make sure the transfer to XSecPen2 is so secret that there can't be an escape plan. Except the transfer *is* the escape plan." It sounded right to Shawna. The pieces fit. "He's a sneaky mofo."

"Not as bad as Krait," she said.

"Nobody's as bad as Krait. That man's a coward who doesn't like to dirty his hands."

Shawna jerked back from the window – something out there was gliding up like a ghost. She glanced over her shoulder and saw Krait. It was his image she'd seen reflected in the glass.

"I hear you two mention my name?" he asked, smirking.

"Not me," Bak-Irp said.

Shawna shook her head.

"Liars." Krait sneered at them. "I appreciate that. Deception is always more fun than the bald truth. I prefer complex lies. A network of them is ideal. You can catch things in them. Like ships." Krait was sucking on the end of a drinking straw he'd pilfered from a canteen juice pouch. The juice was powdered. When he reconstituted it with water it looked like diluted blood. He took a sip and spit it back out on the floor. They all watched him do it. He said, "Tastes awful."

Shawna could feel that he wanted to tell them something. Call it a confession. But it wasn't that he felt guilty. To the contrary, he was proud of what he'd done, this was bragging.

"I made my money in piracy, you know that. I hijacked cargo ships using my computer. Remote control. I'd sync up with the ship's navigation controls. Once I plugged in, it was like I was playing online games. It was too easy, so I got bored. But work's work, right? If it was all fun, they wouldn't have to pay you, or in this case I paid myself, but it's the same principle. Anyway, I had to create challenges for myself to keep things interesting. Like, can I steal two ships in one day? One time I used this huge tanker-hauler to ram all the other nearby ships around this major dockport floating city. Playing demolition derby." Krait stopped, laughed, but the laughter was fake, part of this put-on show, or whatever it was he was presently engaged in.

"Wherever this is going, I've had enough," Bak-Irp said.

"No, let him finish," Shawna said. "I want to hear this."

"Thank you, Lieutenant Colonel Bright," Krait said. "Have I got your correct rank?"

"Yes."

"Awesome." Krait rolled the straw from one side of his mouth to the other, then he took it out of his mouth and inspected the end, which was chewed flat, wet, full of bitemarks. "You flew fighters, didn't you?" Like a snake, his eyes never blinked.

"I did," she said. Her guts were flopping over. She felt like she might be sick.

"That's funny," he said. "So did I. Not regularly – there was no money in it. But for shits and giggles, I tried it. I was, like, a million miles away, and I had no real reason for doing it other than I wanted to see if I could. I knew they'd never catch me, that I was the real pilot that day."

Shawna didn't say anything. She felt dizzy and gripped the edge of the counter.

"Hey, you feeling all right?" Bak-Irp went to steady her, but she waved him off.

"Oh, man, I had a real blast that day," Krait said. "I don't need to tell you, do I?"

Shawna clenched her teeth. She wanted to shoot him then and there. But if she did, there would never be a way to clear her name. Krait knew it, too. Cruelty was his turn-on. A psychopathic sadist – nothing was real to him except his own desires, living in his fantasy world that he controlled. He told her what he'd done so he could rub her face in it. Getting inside people's heads and injecting them with poisons – that's how he got his jollies, watching others writhe around in pain, like insects he was pulling apart for his own amusement. It was his way of having fun. People, fighter ships, dead pilots – all were toys to him. She had to find a way to record his confession. If he died before that happened, she'd never be exonerated. He'd win.

"Looks like they're feeling brave again." Krait nodded to the window, chewing his straw.

The Xenos were assembling; gnarly silhouettes filled the horizon, a forest of zombies.

But all the monsters weren't outside.

They were as close as the person standing beside you.

CHAPTER THIRTY-EIGHT
Fireworks

Lemora said, "You don't get a weapon. We have to make it look like you're our hostage. We're trading you for a ride out." The Caridian wasn't stupid. He had to know he *was* a hostage, and now they were using him as bait. As a rule, bait was not something you wanted to be. The survival odds for bait were startlingly abysmal.

"I understand," he said.

"We're not going to tie your hands or anything," Nero said.

"I appreciate that."

The team decided that the best way forward was to split up. Nobody was thrilled with the idea, but it would have to suffice. Nero and Lemora would take the Caridian, whose name was Kix, and walk out to Neera's ship brandishing a white flag. Nero sacrificed his tube sock for the purpose of serving as the flag; it was gritty gray by this time, but Neera would get the idea. Once they got her to open the hatch, they'd unleash a mold bomb. It had worked on the *Andronicus*. It should work here. Before her crew realized what was happening, the aliens would be turning.

Bak-Irp, Too-ahka, Shawna, and Krait would stay back at the module waiting for them to return, then the team, plus Kix, would haul ass for the *Andronicus*, and fly up to the wormhole.

Easy-peasy.

"Bak, what're they doing now?" Nero asked.

"Still standing there," the Thassian said. "Each one uglier than the last, down the line."

He was monitoring the Xenos gathered in the distance. They had no clue what the zombies were up to, but Nero said his hypothesis was they were waiting for the god voice they'd been hearing, which was the Cybernetics engineers, and if god didn't answer soon, they were going to charge the station in the old-fashioned style of their forebearers – a frenzy attack.

"As long as they hang back until we're finished with my sister," Nero said.

"Fingers crossed," Lemora said.

"Let's get it on," Nero said.

Bak-Irp opened the door and out they went, the Caridian leading the way with Nero behind him, a shotgun nestled against Kix's spine. Lemora had two mold bombs in a fanny pack clipped to the back of her armor suit. They gave Kix the white flag tied to a plastic broomstick.

"Keep waving that thing," Nero said.

"What if she still has a sniper on board?" Kix was whipping the flag back and forth.

"Then we're going to die today. All three of us. Think happy thoughts instead, buddy."

That put a stop to the talking.

Nero was surprised how simple it was to convince Neera

to let them in the airlock. He experienced a rare feeling of hesitation when the ramp slammed down on the dusty soil, then he realized what it was that was bothering him: self-doubt. Screw that. He shoved the Caridian forward, partly to make a good show of things and partly because he wanted to shove somebody, anybody. They trudged up the ramp, straight to the hatch. Neera was already bleating at them through the speaker.

"Stop right there," she said.

Kix halted, and Nero kicked his heels until the guy shuffled ahead a few more steps.

"I said, 'Stop!'"

"Chill," Nero said. "Here's the deal." Then he explained the deal, she gets the Caridian if she takes them out of here, he'll collect his share of the baron's inheritance and go, she'll never need to worry about him again, he was sick of this bickering and power grabbing, blah, blah, blah… "Whaddaya say, sis? Shall we call a truce and shake hands? Let bygones be bygones."

She must've been more desperate than he suspected. Or more confident. He never found out which it was. The hatchway door started rotating sideways into its slot in the hull, and as soon as the gap grew large enough, Lemora pulled the grenade pins, rolling them inside. One to the left, one right. He did catch a last glimpse of Neera eyeing the canisters turning over and over. She had another SMG pointed at him, but she was waiting for the Caridian to get out of the way, and that didn't happen, because Nero snagged Kix's collar and jerked him up like a shield.

"Run, boys, run!" Lemora cried out.

They booked it out of the airlock, diving off the ramp,

tumbling in the dust like three tumbleweeds. Nero had just risen to his feet when the pair of explosives detonated. He felt them in his chest. Big, bass-toned, dull thumps that jarred his bones. He saw the Caridian duck, as if Neera was throwing champagne glasses at their fleeing figures. The poor sucker had to be kicking himself, he was having a lousy day, losing his meal ticket and his hearing, and who knew what might be coming at them next. Nero almost felt sorry for him. But he had his own worries.

The ship's thrusters slammed into high gear, stirring up a humongous cloud of debris. Heavier rocks took flight and whizzed around them. Blinded, the trio threw themselves flat on the ground. The land was shaking as Neera's ship lifted off. Through a hole in the whirl of disturbed particles, the three observers watched the ship ascending, its airlock hanging open, hampering the aerodynamics of the vehicle, which strained as it was buffeted by dangerous crosscurrents. It grew smaller and smaller. The airlock closed, and it seemed as though their plot to sabotage the flight had failed.

The trajectory of the ship approached the wormhole, veering starboard but still on course to reach the space-time bending portal, until in a final lurch it missed its target, swirling out of control, careening wildly, spinning end over end, breaking apart, a starburst smoking over the horizon. The Xenos stared up as the doomed ship passed overhead. Lemora felt a wave of relief.

"Neera always loved fireworks displays," Nero said, without a twitch. "Now she is one."

He knew he sounded cold. But coldness was what he felt inside, a glacial cleaving, the same as when the baron came crashing down to reality. He took no pleasure in it. Not really.

It was only business.
And Nero was a businessman.

CHAPTER THIRTY-NINE
Sole Survivor

It was after they witnessed Nero, Lemora, and the Caridian
die out there on the runway that Krait decided what he
would do. He had to be the sole survivor. The wormhole
was of no use if they had no way to reach it, and now that
goal seemed but a pipe dream. Neera's ship disintegrated,
crumbling into bright chunks of superheated metal; the
pretty trails etched the atmosphere as if a giant cat's paw
ripped the yellow cushion of the sky and tufts of white foam
erupted from the tears. The three on the ground had to be
dead. Had to.

As soon as the sky show ended, the Xenos charged, walking
at first, then gaining speed, finally breaking into an all-out
run, their screams piercing the module shell like missiles.
It was chilling, and final. The wave of them crashed over
the place where Nero and the other two had been standing
seconds earlier. It was as if the wave had swept them away or
the earth had swallowed them. After the Xenos passed, the
land lay barren, lifeless – a table of trampled, claw-scraped
rock unworthy of a second glance. No people, that's for sure.

The Xenos were coming for the module now. Watching them made Krait's heart pound.

Bak-Irp opened the door and dragged the couch across the lower half of the entry. He knelt and laid his machine gun over the back of the couch, taking aim, sending short bursts of bullets into the innumerable monsters rushing at them. What was he hoping to accomplish?

I'd rather live as a coward, than die a hero, Krait thought. Survival was the only victory that counted. Survivors wrote the history. There would be other battles, other teams of players. First, he had to get out of this jam. He went over to the comms panel, reset the long-range distress beacon, and switched it on. A red light flashed continuously. The Coalition would come now. When they arrived, they would find only one person left alive. Krait had some things to do.

Shawna and Too-ahka busied themselves. She took up the triple-bladed saw and began cutting away the same air vent the Silva brothers had repaired. The vent was a possible escape route. It led throughout the station complex, and now it was more likely a way for the last team members to crawl out than for Xenos to drop in. Too-ahka pried apart the hub doors that led into one hallway they'd yet to explore. Krait pretended to work on another set of doors, but he already had them open. And he had a secret advantage he hadn't shared with the others: a map.

He'd come across it in the station's stored files, along with a lot of useless info like background on the alien miner species, and a roster of names of the people who worked at the station. A quick download added the map to his suit's memory, and now he could call up the schematics on his visor. The doors he'd chosen led to a hallway that branched off several times but eventually would deliver him to an underground bunker where the xenium was stored until it could be transported off-planet, a vault to keep thieves from getting ideas about stealing the xenium. If there was one place built to last and hide until the cavalry arrived, that would be it.

He had extra oxygen, water, and his old light machine gun. All he needed to live. But he needed to make sure he was alone. That was going to take some finesse. Now that Shawna knew he was the person who framed her for crimes she didn't commit, the woman surely wanted him to pay. The look on her face was worth it – the way she turned pale, and how her legs trembled. But she wouldn't kill him, not here and now. She needed his testimony to free herself. Good luck with that. The Thassian was a bigger problem. He'd kill Krait without any hesitation.

He brought the bounty hunter extra ammo boxes, stacking them beside the couch, making a production out of lugging them from the storeroom, huffing and puffing so the big guy noticed.

"Here you go, Bak. I thought you could use these for later."

The Thassian didn't reply. He kept shooting through the doorway at the zombies, concentrating like Krait wasn't even there talking to him, the ungrateful jerk.

A knife inserted just so into the big man's power pack would shut down his life support. He'd be strangling for breath.

Krait couldn't risk it. If he missed, or if the Thassian moved too quickly, that would be the end. *Finito, Hans.* Krait had to be patient and let the Xenos help him solve his problems. Like many fortuitous opportunities in life, it would be a matter of proper timing. Life was a dance.

"Krait, give me a hand with this," Shawna said, calling to him over the buzz of the saw.

Ordering him around as if he worked for her, how typical. "What do you need?" He was careful not to get too close, so she could carve him like a goose. *Did she think he was an idiot?*

A roughly rectangular section of metal suddenly dropped out of the bottom of the air vent as she pulled the spinning blade away. It rang against the floor with a warpy, thunderous clang.

"Never mind," she said.

"Hey, good job. I'm going back to working on jimmying these doors. I almost had them, but Bak needed more ammo. Call me if you want any help." He pointed with a screwdriver. "I'm right over there, holler if you need me."

Shawna didn't say anything.

Fine. She'd be out of his life soon. She and the Thassian were as good as dead. Krait smiled to himself, rechecking the map in his visor, as he made a sham of fiddling with the door.

Bak-Irp tried not to think, not about the payment his family was never going to see if Nero was truly dead, not about how they were going to find a way to reach the *Andronicus*, and certainly not about how outnumbered they were against the Xeno force. No, sir, he was focused on shoot and reload. Shoot, reload. He pretended the Xeno heads were gray boulders and he was cracking them open with his bullets to see what treasures might lay within.

POP-POP-POP-POP-POP-POP.

He had the couch wedged into the doorway, and he was using it as a shooting bench. Too-ahka joined him for a while.

The little alien shot pretty good, not as good as he did, but with those long, spindly fingers, holding the gun seemed unnatural. Not much about Too-ahka looked natural, or at least familiar; truth be told, the creature was unsettling to be around even when it was on your side of the fight. Out of the corner of his eye, Bak-Irp saw Too-ahka's mouth hanging down, its teeth like a fistful of syringes, and drooling from one corner of its rubbery lips, as if the alien were hungry and daydreaming about a banquet. Hell, maybe that's what the Xenos looked like through Too-ahka's eyes – underneath all those Xeno claws and teeth, the flat, cloudy eyeballs, and covered as they were with nodules and circular orifices that resembled suckers of some kind – apparently this Too-ahkean feast made the furball's mouth water.

Shawna called Too-ahka away, and they started talking. Half the conversation was non-verbal, so Bak-Irp was only hearing what Shawna had to contribute. She was sending the alien up into the air vents.

"Scout it," she said. "Come back and show us a way out. We're depending on you."

The lithe, faster Xenos arrived at the module. They scrabbled up the curved building, scratching their talons into the viewport as they climbed above, jumping up and down, and ripping at the roof. A few of them hurled sharp rocks against the glass. The cacophony of the attack frayed his nerves, but Bak-Irp told himself it was a storm, that's all, and it would pass.

Shawna replaced Too-ahka at his side, firing a second machine gun. The upper half of a hunter dropped into view, right in front of them, hanging down from the top of the module and reaching inside with its muscular arms, groping, hands snatching at the barrel of Shawna's weapon. She blasted it in the neck. A spray of blood showered them, drenching the couch, too.

"Damnit! Get out of my house!" Bak-Irp shot the Xeno again, purely out of aggravation.

The bullet-riddled body plummeted.

He needed to reload again and grabbed one of the ammo boxes Krait had left.

The box rattled. "You see this? This shit is empty. Where is that fool? I'm gonna stomp him." Without ammo, they weren't going to last long. He was furious with Krait. The coward might as well be fighting for the enemy. Bak suspected that Krait had hatched some plan for his own slimy self-preservation. He'd love to foil that plan himself, but first things first – the ex-bounty hunter jumped up, setting aside his gun to hammer the incoming Xenos with his fists.

Shawna hit the door's control panel, shutting the doors. But the couch, and too many zombies, were clogging the space. She fired at the aliens who lashed out at her. They seized hold of the couch, yanked it into the doorway, smashing it to pieces, and throwing the scraps behind them, outside. Bak was fighting hand to hand with a pair of workers, when a huge, clawed hand reached through the logjam of Xenos, and clamped onto Bak-Irp's helmet, ripping it off. Then a second hand seized his head, covering most of his face, the tips of the claws digging into his jaw.

"Eeaarghhh!" Bak-Irp screamed, pounding at the Xeno's fat wrist to no avail.

Its grip tightened.

Shawna fired the rest of her magazine into the gigantic Xeno's forearm, shredding the flesh and punching holes in the muscle, but the damage didn't appear to faze the beast. It pushed aside its brethren and stuck its face into the module, a writhing mass of tentacles.

Bak-Irp had trouble breathing. The air rushed out of his suit around his face as he gasped. He was blacking out, coming to, blacking out again, as the creature shook him.

"Krait!" Shawna shouted. "Help us! We need you!"

But no one came.

Shawna didn't know what kind of Xeno it was that took Bak-Irp. Larger than the rest, thicker and bulkier, with a gnarled body that reminded her of the trunks of ancient oak trees back home in Appalachia, a mass of tentacles writhed around its face, more than the others had; its head was twice the size of theirs. It roared into Bak-Irp's face, coating him with flecks of gray spittle.

But Shawna was out of bullets. She still had a few grenades on her bandolier, but there was no way she was going to blow them and turn Bak into a zombie. She'd never do that.

"Go…" Bak-Irp said weakly, waving her away. Blood ran from the deep claw marks gouged on either side of his pale, hairless head. The chunky Xeno slathered its tentacles over the Thassian's exposed skin, licking, tasting him. Bak-Irp's eyes were lidded, with little slivers of amber showing because some Thassians had amber eyes the color of wild honey like Kentucky panthers did. And Shawna's heart squeezed thinking about what was happening to him, and thoughts of home and that day when her squad mates died for nothing, no reason… Krait.

Shawna didn't want to watch another friend die. She couldn't take much more grief in this lifetime, but she couldn't abandon him either, despite his urging, so she ran to the supply closet for another gun. They'd loaded all the weapons, leaning them against the wall for quick access. She chose a shotgun. Not to kill the Xeno. But to put Bak-Irp out of his misery.

Only it was too late for that. As she emerged from the storeroom and racked a shell into the chamber, the tank-like Xeno shouldered through the doors, bulling its way fully inside the module. It lifted Bak-Irp as if he were a ragdoll, and he wasn't screaming anymore. Then the hulking intruder tucked the Thassian under its arm and twisted his head sharply, all the way around. The sound of cracking bones made Shawna feel like throwing up. Instead, she pumped shell after shell into the Xeno's head. Its skull must've been as thick as a Tri-T's nosecone. Buckshot peppered its scalp and sheared several of the tentacles from around its mouth, but it didn't slow the beast down. Shawna felt like a stray cat who'd pissed off the biggest, meanest dog in the neighborhood. Slinging the shotgun on her back, she ran for the air vent, leaping, grabbing hold of the edges and hoisting herself into the hole she'd cut.

At least the hulking Xeno won't be able to fit in here, she thought.

On hands and knees, she crawled. Too-ahka's footprints left tracks in the dust for her to follow. Behind her, the brawny Xeno smashed its fists into the vent, heavy blows that crumpled the space inside the air shaft as if it were a candy wrapper.

Krait had cut and run. That was no surprise. Bak-Irp was dead. The chances that Nero, Lemora, and the Caridian had survived outside as the Xeno horde passed over them were slim.

She wondered how Too-ahka was faring. Amid the bloodshed, the alien's unwholesome killing and feeding practices seemed weirdly less bizarre. She'd never fully grasp the other creature's behavior, but she tried not to judge it too harshly. Whether or not Too-ahka came back for her, she hoped it had made it somewhere safe. All she had left was the furry oddball.

And myself, she thought, *I have myself,* hoping that was enough to pull her through.

CHAPTER FORTY
Hard to Kill

Click-click-click. The alien called Too-ahka didn't need light to see, and it was comfortable exploring in the dark. More than comfortable, it sought the dark, hunted there, made it its home, a place of security. It knew nothing of fear. On a purely intellectual level, fear denoted a nervous response to an anticipated loss. Too-ahka had lost everything before its first memories. It knew nothing of family, friends, or others of its kind. It had never had a real home. It experienced pain on a neural level but without any emotional component. I am like a robot, it thought, in many respects. People, if they knew my mind, would think of me as cold. I wonder if I am cold? *The alien scouted the air vent in search of a better place for the team to go.* That has been my whole existence. *Seeking a place where I can live better than before. A distant cry of pain. Too-ahka turned its head, listening, since it recognized the voice as belonging to the Thassian. The Thassian was dying. Shawna's voice was absent. She was still alive. Too-ahka sensed that and continued its search. It pushed out vent screens with its feet and clicked its clicks into the rooms. Scanning. Many, many rooms. All dark and empty, except for the dead, old and dry husks, bones and bones and more bones. The Xenos were a terrible foe. Hard to kill. But tasty, nonetheless. Good to drink. Bitter juices full of bottled rage, the infection imparted a flavor Too-ahka had never experienced before. Sandy, mildly sulfuric, but with a light effervescence, a smokiness, and a lingering tang, not at all unpleasant. Too-ahka sniffed.* Mold. *It had reached a fork in the vent. One way was very, very moldy. The air was thick with the boggy scent of it. Too-ahka chose the other way. The mold was not good to eat. Edible, yes. But not tasty. This other way smelled, too. It smelled of Xenos, the living dead, it smelled of food. Neither way would be good for Shawna, but perhaps if Too-ahka might kill – and eat – the Xenos first, then it could show her the way to this place. She did not like to see Too-ahka eating and drinking. It knew that now and would take care not to offend her. She was a good partner, a teammate, as the people called it.* What a strange thing it had been for Too-ahka to work with others. I might try it again. *Too-ahka lifted out a screen and dropped into a dark, dark room. Not dark for Too-ahka though. All along the floor they were sleeping in rows. Xenos with scars on their heads. The ones with the implants in their brains. They gathered here and slept together, and Too-ahka stepped carefully over them, stopping, sniffing, thinking these were far too many to fight at once. Numbers were hard to defeat, a matter of mathematics and not skill. Fighting was hard labor, as was scouting the air vent, and Too-ahka's stomach growled. Eyes opened. The room began to move everywhere at once, squirming, flexing, stretching. Awakened, the Xenos stirred, eyes aglow, instantly ignited with rage. Too-ahka found itself surrounded by them.* They see me, too. *And then they attacked.*

CHAPTER FORTY-ONE
JA

Krait located the bunker. Without the map it would have been next to impossible. This station was, for all its modular functionality, a bit of a labyrinth. The bunker lay at the bottom of an elevator shaft. The elevator wasn't working because the electricity wasn't on. But luckily, there was a maintenance ladder attached to the wall plunging down the shaft. Krait wasn't fond of heights, so he kept his eyes forward, staring at the wall; his helmet light shone a bright orb there. The orb descended. At the bottom of the shaft the elevator doors were closed, but he found the manual key hanging on a hook beside the doors, and he unlocked them.

His biggest worry was opening the vault. He possessed no safecracking skills, and with the power out to the station, well, he anticipated problems breaking in. But all his worries were for nothing. The vault's enormous circular door was open! He could see it as soon as he left the elevator shaft. Stepping forward, his foot sank into unseen slime as thick as rice pudding.

"Gah! This mold is ridiculous."

Krait lifted his boot to shake off the goop, but it was useless. He shone his headlamp on the floor. The mold was everywhere! *What a nightmare.* Well, this excursion appeared to be a complete waste of time. He couldn't possibly stay here. Krait was about to leave the way he'd come when he noticed something heaped inside the vault, where the xenium was kept. He'd never put his eyes on xenium before, and he was curious. Was this the stuff dreams were made of? A fuel source that people died, and killed, for. He had to see it. Perhaps he'd take a souvenir.

A lucky nugget to carry in his pocket.

He waded through the slop and entered the vault. *Just a quick peek,* he told himself. He cast his orb around the chamber. *It's like a tomb down here,* he thought. *Or a flooded basement.*

They must've left behind quite a haul of precious material. His light wandered over a small gray mountain of what he presumed to be raw xenium piled at the back of the crypt, its slopes dripping in glistening streaks of mold that sparkled under his light. *This dull, wrinkly, lumpy heap was what the fuss was all about? This was xenium?* If someone had told him he was looking at the dregs of mining, the effluvium, he would've believed them. Worse than its lusterless, unimpressive appearance, the xenium had things growing on it. Disgusting, awful things he couldn't put a name to – long, greasy, black tufts of what looked almost like fur, and little hornlike protrusions of various sizes poked up from the motherlode. Between that and the pools of mold, he'd had enough. *No, thank you, I'll stick to piracy. Some jobs are too dirty...*

He laughed out loud. "What a mess."

Krait was turning to leave when the pile sat up and looked at him. An array of eyes like red blisters on a rotten gray melon. At first, he thought, *jewels,* then *giant spider.* It was neither.

A later report from the Coalition investigators concluded that Hans Krait had the very bad misfortune of walking smack dab into the lair of a Juggernaut Abomination, an exceedingly rare variety of Xeno of which little is known and even less can be proven. No Juggernaut Abomination has ever been visually documented. In the case of Krait's encounter, a short audio snippet was later discovered when the remnants of his armor were retrieved by a Galactic Forces Recon unit who entered the xenium vault on PK-L7. It seemed that acting in a panic, Krait accidentally switched on his suit's voice recorder. The following is a transcript of that recording:

Krait: Oh god no.
[A squelching sound. Thought possibly to be the JA rising from its resting place.]
Krait: I mean you no harm. Sorry to disturb your... slumber... I'll go now.
[A roar. Initially suspected to be an explosion, later analysis suggests it might be the JA vocalizing toward the subject {H.K.}. Following the vocal outburst, a great gushing of liquid.]
Krait: (in a muffled voice) PLEASE, PLEASE, PLEASENODON'TPLEASE...
Krait's voice cuts off at this point after a significant

amount of shrieking, which may be A) the subject screaming, B) his armor being crushed, or C) the JA emitting a high-pitched cry [of delight???]. Interpretation by GF audio experts suggests it may be a combination of all three.

CHAPTER FORTY-TWO
Prelude to an Escape Plan

Nero had managed to pull their fat out of the fryer yet again. That's what he was claiming when they emerged from the Xeno tunnels inside the station's cluttered mess hall. Lemora wasn't going to argue. She'd thought they were doomed as soon as the Xenos charged, but Nero directed them to a pothole in the runway that looked as if it might fit no more than a single person. Once they sank to the bottom of the hole, there was a tunnel made by the Xenos for the Xenos, and therefore sizable enough to accommodate them. They didn't even need to hunch over, which made running easier. Above them the zombies stampeded, shaking the soil down like dirt rain from a seismic event. Lemora was sure a few of the Xenos would chase after them, and she'd die underground like a rat in the mouth of a scaly reptile. That didn't happen.

Perhaps it was a primitive herd mentality that saved them. The Xenos, who not long ago were being remotely controlled by the Cybernetics Guild's programming, latched onto the mob's collective will and followed whatever the majority decided to do. And the majority wanted to storm the station, specifically the comms hub module. That was where they were headed when Nero, Lemora, and Kix dived into the cavity to save their skins.

"A-ha," Nero said. "We're in the kitchen, and I, for one, am starving. Who's hungry?"

Lemora didn't bother to tell him that if there was any food in the cupboards, it wouldn't be edible. She knew he was only joking. He did it to cope with difficulties. And if Shawna and the others had perished, the difficulties were only beginning. None of them knew how to fly. Whatever equipment Krait had restored in the comms hub would never survive a second assault. And Krait, he was probably dead, too. So, no way to call out for help to his lieutenants in the Arms Guild. And none of them could work a wormhole without Dr Kix. Kix sat slumped in a chair, resting his head on a long institutional dining table, like the ones they had at XSecPen, and he was sobbing.

"Buck up. Things could be worse," Nero said, taking hold of his arm.

But the Caridian remained inconsolable.

Lemora pulled up a chair and joined him. Nero wandered away, to peer out of a smudgy porthole in the middle of the mess hall door. He slid up to it slowly, flicking his eyes into the dark, cluttered hallway on the other side.

"How's it looking?" Lemora asked.

"Good. No signs of activity, Xeno or otherwise. Furniture's got us blocked in. But I was hoping to rest a spell and catch our breath. The chow hall is as good a place as any to do that."

Lemora glanced around at the dust-filled salad bar, the soda dispensers, and rusty ice cream machines. The opposite side of the room catered to non-Xeno aliens. There was a

Thassian scorching stone and various Fushnallan live tanks, containing the remnants of artificial coral reefs, sea-farmed plants, and acidic chemical soups that were popular with several species of aliens. Lemora tried to imagine the miners sitting at these tables, eating and talking, kidding one another the way hard laborers always do – she pictured them on the night before the first Xeno attack, when the worst thing they thought might happen to them was a cave-in, being trapped in a mine, as the headlamp batteries on their suits dimmed and the oxygen sputtered.

What they didn't know was how bad it was going to get, how hell was coming up from underground to pay them a visit. Their lives would be forever changed. Most of them wouldn't live through the next day. She could almost hear the knocks of the first infected breaking in–

"What is that?" Nero said.

Exhausted, she tried to clear away the cobwebs in her head. "What's what?"

"That knocking." He stepped away from the porthole, ears cocked, turning his head.

Lemora listened. *Had it been more than the sound of her daydreams? Yes!* "I hear it, too."

"Yeah, but where's it coming from?"

The Caridian lifted his head. He pointed to the air vent at the end of the room. "There."

The three of them ran to the vent. It followed along the ceiling in the center of the module until it turned ninety degrees over the salad bar. Dust sifted through the vent screen like beige snow.

"Get me out of here," a voice said.

Lemora saw eyes peering through the vent – Shawna's eyes.

The pilot banged at the screen. "Out, out... c'mon. My legs are cramped, and I feel like the walls are closing in on me."

"Hold on," Nero said. "The corner of the screen is bent. Let me pry it loose." Lemora and Kix helped him drag a table up to the salad bar. Nero leaped on top of it. He picked at the screen with his gloved fingers, and the vent cover fell away, clattering on the floor. "Take my hand."

Shawna jumped down. She swiveled on her butt and skidded into a waiting chair.

Nero had his head in the air vent. He switched his lamp on, looking both ways. Then he climbed down and sat at the table with the others. Shawna was staring at her boots, blank-faced.

"Where are the others?" he asked.

"Bak-Irp's dead. Krait abandoned us. Too-ahka was scouting the vent ahead of me, but I lost the tracks in the darkness. I was crawling through here when I heard your voices. I thought I must be hallucinating. We watched the Xenos overrun your position. I thought you were dead."

"Nothing can kill Nero," Nero said. "I'm bulletproof and never lose. Well, I haven't yet."

"You're insufferable," Shawna said.

"Insufferably charming."

"I should've stayed quiet and kept crawling."

"It's great to see you too, Highflyer. Now can we get out of here?"

They stared at him. Only Lemora knew for sure that he was serious. People died around Nero; they had all his life. What he did was he moved on. People betrayed him, too, like Krait, and he expected as much, in these cases he never forgot the transgression. Lemora valued Bak-Irp's skills, and she was sad to hear he was out of the game. Even more than that, she worried about Krait still being alive. He could become another threat to them. Nero was catching a second wind, the thrill of victory rising in his blood; she could see it in his cheeks, a pink blush. The good news was that Shawna was with them again. Lemora trusted her to do her job well.

"You still want to try for the *Andronicus*?" Shawna asked Nero.

"Duh. Yeah, I do. The plan worked, y'all. Neera's out of the picture. The Xenos aren't even lurking by the ships, I'll wager. They're here, looking for us. We're going back out there."

"The tunnels?" Lemora said, knowing already what his intentions were.

"You bet," he said. "That'll deposit us a few meters from the Deathcan. Then it's boom and zoom. Everything's golden. Kix here will walk us through the wormhole business. Heck, we get back to the Arms Guild, old Kixy will vouch for me and help get the Cybernetics weirdos to reopen talks about the Xeno master plan my sister was cooking up. It's a damn good plan. I only wish I'd thought of it. But I'm driving the bus now, and I see no reason to throw out a perfectly fine scheme to take over Terran space and wipe out those Coalition bastards once and for all. It's showtime, folks." Nero was wired. She'd seen him like this before. Like a gambler who thought his luck had turned and he was untouchable, every throw of the dice would be a winner. Golden.

Lemora noticed Shawna had a grenade in her hands. She was flicking at the pin.

"Where'd you get that?" she asked her. The pilot was nothing if not resourceful.

"I kept a few from before." Shawna hooked her thumb into the bandolier belt tied around her waist. Four mold bomb canisters dangled from the belt, minus the one she had in her hand.

"Whoa!" Nero said, looking at the bombs. "Were you going to use those in the air vent?" He pantomimed throwing the grenade and blowing himself up. "Kind of close quarters, no?"

"I had them in case they caught me. I don't want to be eaten," she said, matter-of-factly.

"None of us do, Highflyer," he said, his mood turning serious suddenly.

Shawna gave the pin a final flick and clipped it back on her belt.

Lemora held out her hand, palm up. "You'd better give me those. I'm the demolitions expert." Shawna had an independent streak in her, and Lemora knew she didn't agree with Nero's ambitions. There was no telling who'd she'd blow up if the situation deteriorated. The plain truth was that if there were explosives, Lemora wanted them in her possession. She was greedy like that. But she bore no animosity toward Shawna whatsoever, she admired her resilience.

"OK." Shawna untied the belt, passed it to Lemora. Then to Nero she said, "Let's fly."

Nero high-fived her.

CHAPTER FORTY-THREE
Escape: Take Two

The tunnel was quiet, and Nero became aware of the sound of his boots scuffling along the carved-out floor, his own breathing, and the distant racket of the Xenos above, tearing apart what remained of the station. The quicker they got out of dodge the better. He was convinced his plan was solid, but you never knew what you didn't know until it popped up and bit you in the ass. His headlamp beam glowed noticeably weaker, shrunken, burning low like a fire going out. He only had so much fuel left in his tank, literally and figuratively, and the others were the same. Everything had to work. Oxygen, ammo, life supports, and fuel on the *Andronicus* – there were a million things that might go wrong. But as the team leader he had to keep a smile on his face. Eyes on the prize. If doubts crept in, they'd turn corrosive, and people would quit. He never quit.

"Here we go," he said, looking up at the spill of lemony light pouring into the pothole. "The Deathcan is about thirty meters to our right." He pivoted around for a last look at the team, or what was left of them. Loyal Lemora, the brains behind his own brilliance. Shawna, the hotshot flyer. And Kix. The Caridian was a jumble of nerves, eyes darting, face twitching – Nero hoped the guy could hold it together, because he needed him with his head in the game, focused. He wished he had another gunner in his arsenal, Bak-Irp or one of the Silvas; he'd even have settled for Fuzzy, but you fight with the army you have, not the one you wished for. "We ready?"

He could count on the women to keep their shit together. The Caridian was a wildcard.

"I'm good," Lemora said, smiling at him with a glint of adventure in her dark eyes.

Shawna simply nodded.

The Caridian… leaned against the side of the tunnel and shivered.

"Hey," Nero said. "Hey, it's a short jog out to the ship. We climb on. We fly away."

Kix nodded, unconvinced, it appeared. Nero couldn't blame him, really, because things were going to be more complicated than he'd stated, but the basics were essentially the same. Nero stepped aside to make room for Shawna, who they'd decided should go first, straight to the cockpit. He and Lemora would head down to the armory, get fresh weapons, re-up on ammo. They'd need them if it took a while before takeoff, if the Xenos noticed them and came a-calling.

Nero boosted Shawna up out of the pothole. She didn't hesitate. He heard her boots running, the *poc-poc-poc* crunch heading off in the direction of the ship. Next came Lemora. He had to help the Caridian out, too. He had no confidence that if he left him to go last, the guy wouldn't freeze and curl up in a ball like a dead bug. So, Nero was the last one out of the hole.

He looked right at the ship. Saw Shawna sprinting up the dune to the Tri-T's door. That was the good news. The bad news was that a few Xenos had spotted them. Stragglers, he guessed, not in a hurry to rush the module complex like the others. Skinny, apathetic-looking suckers, they were literally lounging on the wing of the ship, sprawled there catching the rays, sunning themselves like lizards on rocks. When they picked up their heads, they were alert, instantly energized. He watched one kick another awake. A posse of them gathered there, about a dozen.

"Shit," he said under his breath. He fired off a burst over their gray, bulbous heads. They were all what Lemora told him were called workers, or descendants of workers; they looked feral and mean. His shots caused them to stand up and step to the edge of the wing. They struck poses, screaming, throwing back their shoulders and tightening their muscles, veins bulging in the necks that he could see even at this distance. *Dumbshits*, he thought. *If you're trying to intimidate me, you picked the wrong guy. I'm Nero Lupaster IV, ruler of all I survey! Take that!*

He rattled off another long burst of bullets. He hit one of the posers. The zombie tumbled over, somersaulting like a diver leaping off a cliff, but instead of landing with a splash in the sea, he plopped in the sand like a sky turd. "Hell yeah!" Nero pumped his fist.

The Caridian was running without using his arms, which he had wrapped around him, giving himself a hug.

"Pick up the pace, Kix."

Nero passed him and gave the back of his helmet a whack. That got the guy going again.

The Xeno posse exited the wing and formed a circle

around Lemora. She was taunting them, kicking dust, shooting at their feet, and mocking their roars. When they moved in on her, she juked into a space between two of them, causing them to stumble and fall. Laughing, she ran for the tail section of the ship. Maddened, they flung themselves at her in fast pursuit.

She's luring them away.

If there was a better number two leader in Terran space, Nero wanted to know who it was. He'd put Lemora up against the best of them. When they got back to Guild headquarters, he was going to give her a big, fat bonus, and he was putting her in charge of the Xeno invasion. Forget xenium. The most valuable commodity on the market was loyalty. He'd pay top dollar.

Nero dashed up the dune, surprised to find Kix right behind him. Maybe it was the sight of the Xenos that had slowed the wormhole-ologist down. Nero flung the door open and rushed the Caridian inside.

"Go left. Into the cockpit. Help Shawna. Do whatever she tells you to do."

Kix disappeared into the shadows.

"Time's up, Lem. This bus is leaving," he said into his suit mic.

He stood in the entrance, machine gun resting on his hip, waiting to welcome her aboard.

"Give me a sec." Her reply crackled with static. He couldn't see where she'd gone.

Where were the Xenos?

She must've taken the skinny lizards on a run around the outside of the ship. He leaned out of the doorway looking toward the nosecone. Nothing.

"Lem, where are you?" The tiniest tickle of concern brushed his brain.

She didn't respond. He turned up the volume on his speaker, listening for her voice. Then he saw her looping around the tail section. *Doubling them back, that's smart. Why was she running so slowly? Was she that gassed?*

"We're not so young anymore, Lem. Not like the old days."

But she wasn't talking. As she got closer, he saw she was limping, dragging one leg through the dust, her ankle turned to the side. *Bad wheel*, he thought. *That's gonna swell up.* But she was going to make it. They always made it – Nero and Lem, a pair of legendary survivors.

But she wasn't looking so good. Slow, she looked slow. And pain etched her face.

Nero started out down the dune to go get her. He'd haul her up here one way or another.

"No!" she shouted. Both of her arms shot up in the air, signaling him. "It's over, darling."

Her words froze him. *Over? What's she talking about?*

Then Xenos rounded the tail, and they didn't bother to run. They stalked her. Flicking their tongues and striding confidently through the dust. Within seconds they were on top of her.

Nero didn't know what to do. He wasn't prepared to lose his only friend. But if he fired, he might hit her. He'd never forgive himself for doing that. But the Xenos weren't playing; their claws had a hold of her now. Lemora tossed something to him. A grenade with the pin in.

"Something to remember me by," her voice sizzled in his ear. "Time to cash out."

He didn't understand. *Cash out?* What was she talking

about? Giving up? Nero never gave up. And he didn't lose. The *Andronicus* came back to life. Her engines whirred, the thrusters were screaming, louder and louder. He had to get Lemora. He couldn't leave her. She was acting so foolish, thinking he'd go back home without his favorite advisor, his only friend.

Nero fired into the ground around the pile of Xenos. He was at the bottom of the dune when her belt of grenades exploded. Xeno body parts flew into the air. A red mist rose, and the wind took it and ripped it away like a magician pulling the tablecloth in a trick, leaving the candlesticks and crystal goblets undisturbed. Except when the smoke cleared, nothing was there – just an empty crater in the dirt.

Nero turned and walked back up the hill. He'd never felt like this before. A hole opened inside him, so deep that the only thing that would ever fill it would be a cold, palpable darkness.

He shut the door.

CHAPTER FORTY-FOUR
Purple

"What took you so long?" Shawna asked. Nero dropped into the co-pilot's seat without a word. "The generator is intact. Systems are glitchy but online. We're ready for takeoff. I heard an explosion after I fired up. I'm afraid it might be the auxiliary engine. Where's Lemora?"

"She's dead."

Shawna wasn't sure that she'd heard him correctly. *Lemora, dead?* First Bak-Irp dies, then Too-ahka goes missing inside the labyrinthine air vents, never to be heard from again... and now this. It was too much.

"What are you talking about? How?"

"Blew herself up. To save me and the Caridian."

Shawna was staring hard at the side of his face, but he wasn't prepared to meet her eyes. Defeated, she thought. For the very first time she was seeing another side of Nero, vulnerable and human. His color was ashen, and he was sniffing loudly, wetly, choking back his emotions.

"I'm sorry," she said.

"Yeah, I am, too."

•••

The *Andronicus* performed above and beyond, though a large part of that was probably because of the skill of the pilot. The ride was bumpy until they got high enough out of the winds. The one working screen showed the wormhole pulsating, a blacker than black darkness that might hypnotize you if you let it. It seemed to be looking at you. Nero felt another pair of eyes on him, and he glanced over his shoulder to spot the Caridian sitting in the corner as if he'd been sent there by his teacher for misbehaving. He'd almost forgotten about him. Almost. Although it was one of the toughest things he'd ever done, Nero hoisted himself out of his seat. He felt like lead, like artificial gravity was working extra hard on him, and he was swimming through thick, clear fog.

"Kix, you come with me."

"Where?"

"To the armory in the belly of this ship. We need to check on things. I want a new gun."

"Oh, all right." The Caridian sounded like he didn't believe him but was too scared to protest. He got out of his seat as if he'd been glued to it.

"When do we reach the wormhole?" Nero said to Shawna.

"We're nearly there. Most of my screens are down, but the gauges I have are reading adequately. It won't be the smoothest flight. But at least it's a short one." She tried smiling.

He couldn't do it either.

"Kix and I will be quick." Nero lifted the floor hatch and pointed. "Get down there."

Kix did as he was ordered.

Nero climbed down and nudged Kix ahead. "Keep going. It's not far." He could tell the Caridian was worried, thinking Nero was blaming him for Lemora's death, or holding a grudge because he'd worked with Neera and the Cybernetics Guild. Nero did nothing to dispel his fears. After they passed through the avionics bay, they entered the cargo hold. Shawna had the life support system going again, but Nero hadn't bothered to take off his helmet. *Never know if I might need it again*, he thought. *Can't predict anything that happens to you on PK-L7.*

"You got a light on your suit?" he said.

"What?"

"A headlamp. Mine's about dead." Nero waited for him to find his button. "That's good. Aim it deeper into the hold. See that big, boxy thing in the middle. That's where we're going."

They walked into the armory.

"Sit down," Nero said, pointing to the bench by the spacesuits. There were a half-dozen suits still hanging there like deflated people. The bench was for putting your boots on. Nero sat.

He showed him the mold bomb. Told him what it was.

"Take your helmet off."

"Why?" Kix said, his voice quavering.

"Don't make me say it again."

Kix removed his helmet.

"Now." Nero rested his hand on Kix's knee. "You're going to do me a favor. When we get home, we're calling on the Cybernetics Guild, and you're telling them how Neera screwed up, but I saved your butt. I'm the one they can trust. Then you can have whatever deal you made with my sister. I'll honor that. But… listen to this part carefully, if you flake out on me, any time between now and then, I'm going to turn you. You'll be a Xenos zombie. No money, and you want to eat everybody all day and all night. That's not a hard choice, Kix. Promise me, OK?"

"I promise."

"There you go." Nero put the grenade where Kix didn't have to look at it. "Now help me find a new gun. I don't want my old one. It has bad memories attached. And I'm starting over."

Kix got up from the bench and went over to the array of weapons. "I don't know guns."

"Sure, buddy, that's fine." Nero noticed a cabinet open that he didn't remember looking inside the last time he'd been here with Lemora. *Lemora.* "What's in that one, Kixy?" Nero chose a new combat pistol, a speed loader, and an SMG, not as fancy as his sister's but sick, a real badass piece of hardware, compact, and nasty to behold. He hefted it, then tested the bolt.

"Oh, my. You'd better look in here," Kix said. "It isn't weapons."

"What is it, then?"

"They look like eggs. Metal eggs. And the label on the top says POD #1 and POD #2."

Nero hurried over to join Kix. "I'll be damned. They're escape pods. You know, I bet our pal Shawna knows about these. If they're standard on a Tri-T, she does. But she forgot to mention them when we were hijacking this rust bucket last time. That's awfully sneaky of her, don't you think?"

Kix didn't answer him. Nero backed up a step and looked around the side of the cabinet.

The Xeno had its hand over Kix's mouth. That was why he wasn't answering. Or maybe it was because the point of the Xeno's claw had slashed through his vocal cords. A curtain of Caridian blood washed down the front of Kix's armor suit, staining his chest. What a clever Xeno it was, creeping up on them while they were chatting away. The Xenos were smarter than he gave them credit for. The shadows moved. Kix had his helmet off, sitting on the bench shining toward the escape pods, so the Xeno was half in shadows, looking spooky as shit.

"You got your gang with you, I see." Nero picked out two more Xenos from the semidarkness. They were hunters, probably modified by the Cybernetics brainbands. He wasn't going to stick around to find out. Without breaking eye contact, he pressed the button to open the escape pod. Pods were pretty basic equipment. They had to be because people don't practice with them, and the only time you ever used them was probably going to be the first and last time you did.

The egglike capsule hissed at him. It was open now: an ergonomic seat, not much else.

Nero backed his way inside and quickly slammed the inner plate to seal and launch it.

He felt suddenly weightless. Falling and falling. He worked his arms into the straps and removed his helmet. *Holy shit. That was a close one. Too close. Adios, Shawna,* he thought. *I'd rather see ya than be ya.* But he couldn't see anything past the inside of the pod, all snug and foamy, dyed orange like a real Earth egg yolk. The distress beacon was an auto function of the pod. He didn't have to do anything. It blinked. The ovoid chamber began to fill with blue hypersleep solution. He'd done hypersleep before and never liked it. The worst part was when the liquid got up to your mouth and nose. You had to force yourself to breathe it in, and despite it being perfectly safe, you felt like you were drowning. Then you went nighty-night. *Ah, Lem, we were so close. I hope the Coalition doesn't find me. But if it's them, I'll deal. I always deal. And usually, I win. Not always, Lem, but most of the time...*

The warm blue liquid spilled into the neck of his armor,

soaking his jumpsuit. It felt weird. He blew his final breaths of air, trying not to get too worked up about the drowning part that came next. As the solution reached his chin, he detected something might be wrong. He chalked it up to nerves. He'd had too much adrenaline lately, it wrung him out like a dirty rag.

Then he saw the spindly fingers in his peripheral vision. They were coming around on both sides at once. The liquid sloshed as something of size shifted behind his seat. *Huh.* There must be more room back there than he thought. Reddish fur. He couldn't see it yet, but he felt it brushing the side of his head, the back of his ears. He couldn't see the red eyes either, but he knew who it was squished in here tucked up like a spider under the seat, hiding right behind him.

"Fuzzy? That you, bud?"

Too-ahka grabbed his face and bit his neck. The fur tickled for a second.

Just a second.

Then he was screaming until the screaming turned to bubbles and blue became purple.

CHAPTER FORTY-FIVE
Snarls

Shawna watched the escape pod jettisoning off inside the wormhole. "No, no, no…" The *Andronicus* was flying inside the wormhole, too. Both vessels would pass through eventually. She didn't have to do too much once she guided the ship inside the portal. Dr Kix hadn't come back, so she was short on details. *How stable was the wormhole? Would it kick the ship out at the same place Neera's ship went in?* She guessed her questions wouldn't get answered now. Kix was most likely dead. Nero had murdered him, and then he'd taken his chances in the escape pod. There'd been a lot of noise and commotion coming up from inside the hatchway. She didn't think Kix would put up a fuss or try to fight off Nero. But something was making noise. Slamming doors. Banging around. Obviously, they'd discovered the pods in the armory. She was still hearing things, knocks and footfalls, after the pod dropped. Which meant Nero left Kix alive…?

Shawna didn't regret not taking the escape pod during the initial hijacking. What good would it have done her? No. She'd decided it was better to work her way into Nero's team. Now she was stuck on the ship, and Nero was ditching her.

Why would he do that? It made no sense. She was cooperating, and despite the pod being a safety feature, it provided less control than staying on the *Andronicus*–

A loud rattling. And… snarls.

Kix didn't snarl.

Shawna engaged the autopilot, set a course to maintain current headings. She had to go back there and see what was up. Because now she was convinced there were Xenos aboard in the cargo hold. She still had her spacesuit on. *Check the oxygen levels.* Not great. But she saw no other way to do this. With the flat of her hand, she pushed all the life support sliders down to zero. Xenos might be able to breathe PK-L7 atmosphere, but they couldn't breathe in a vacuum. She'd suffocate them. She slipped the barrel of her machine gun through the handles of the floor hatch, acting like a bolt to keep it secured, and she waited for the Xenos in the hold to die. The Tri-T wasn't in great shape, leaking like a sieve; her roll, pitch and yaw were touchy, threatening to lose control and stability. The wormhole helped, because the ship didn't have to attempt maneuvers that required precision. The wormhole carried it along like flotsam in an ocean current. She looked at her screen, her clock.

Alarms started going off as soon as the ship emerged from the wormhole. The *Andronicus* bucked, shuddering like she wanted to come apart at the seams. Shawna switched everything off that wasn't necessary. Powering down. Conserving energy.

The cockpit lights flickered out.

Floating. A castaway adrift in the biggest void of all – space.

"I've got no damn choice," she said, finally.

Shawna admitted to herself that the *Andronicus* was dying.

At any moment she could snap in two, or end up like Neera's ship, a streak of smoky, burning lights like dying embers.

She rechecked her screen, observed a sector of space she didn't recognize. Her navigation was down for the count. Comms down. Life supports off. It was now or never. She removed her gun barrel from the hatch handles, checked her mag to find it was empty. She tossed the gun aside. Unarmed, she lifted the lid, and climbed down into the avionics bay. This was the quietest the ship had been since she was force-marched aboard from XSecPen. Silent but not peaceful.

She found the Xenos in the cargo hold just as she suspected. They weren't interested in her, because they were too busy choking to death. There were four of them. All hunter types. Three zombies were sitting on the floor of the armory. The fourth was lying on its back. *All of them are still alive. But not for long.* She felt their anger, their desire to hurt her. Four pairs of eyes tracked her as she made her way to the second escape pod. She stayed out of arm's reach. There was no sign of Dr Kix or Nero. Although she assumed Nero was the one to take the first pod. Maybe he wasn't a total asshole, he'd left a pod for her when he might've cast it off empty.

As if she were watching someone else, Shawna opened the second pod's hatch, climbed into the seat, clipped her straps, sealed the door, and initiated the launch. A strong physical pull told her the pod had ejected successfully. *I feel so strange,* she thought. Somewhere past pain, past sadness and worry, a comfortable numbness wrapped around her as tangible as the pod's inner foam. Blue hypersleep solution rose past her waist. It looked like mouthwash, and that made her think of bedtime. *I just want to go to sleep,* she thought. *I deserve a nice, long nap.*

She removed her helmet and closed her eyes. The liquid filled her suit, touched her lips, and she sucked it inside her lungs. She felt a spasm, a desire to cough as a hard lump formed like a fist in her chest, under her sternum; her body reflexively tried to push the solution back out, and in that fraction of a moment her mind flashed on an outside view of the escape pod from far away, from the *Andronicus*, seeing the egg floating, undiscovered in the void, endlessly adrift.

Shawna opened her eyes, felt the warm blue fluid lubricating her eyeballs.

The pod's distress beacon signal light flashed at her. She counted the flashes.

One, two, three...

The Silvas, Bak-Irp, Lemora... they were all gone... Too-ahka, maybe it was dead, too, or stuck out there alone as it had always been... Nero escapes. He wins again. And what about her?

Shawna wasn't ready to die. *I want to live!*

That was her last thought before she went to sleep.

CHAPTER FORTY-SIX
Demeter

Shawna woke from troubled dreams with a start. She bolted up in bed, clutching her chest, scanning the room for Xenos. She was alone. Measuring out her breaths, she gradually took in details about the room. It was white. Clean. Not a tidy clean but a sterile clean. No decorations except for a mundane print of pastel seashells.

OK, it was a medical suite, too big to be a cubicle in a sick bay; perhaps it was a private room in a floating hospital. She had a tube leading to a needle in her arm, electrodes stuck to her abdomen and head. They'd washed her, but her hair was still greasy, full of PK-L7 grit. She hadn't been here for too long or they would've shampooed her hair. Throwing back the white sheets, she discovered she was wearing a patient gown. Her legs were bruised, the marks turning yellow, purple, and green like butterflies she tried to catch in the fields back home in the mountain holler. She was healing, but not yet fully healed. Her mouth was dry and had a terrible taste in it like sour paste, and she was as thirsty as she'd ever been. There was a pitcher and cup on a wheeled tray beside the beside.

She poured herself water and drank, careful not to gulp

too quickly. Her stomach was queasy, but after a short while it settled.

Remember, Shawna. Remember...

The escape pod. Nero had already launched after they made it into the wormhole. They were the only two to escape the planet alive. Was this Nero's ship? Was she at the Arms Guild?

Wincing, Shawna pulled the needle from her arm. She got out of bed, and the blood inside her body sloshed around giving her an awful head rush and an instant headache. A cold sweat broke out on her forehead, as she braced her arms on the bed to steady herself. She was about to attempt her first real steps when the door whisked open, and a startled woman entered.

"My goodness! You're awake! And on your feet, I see." The woman smiled at her, but she was clearly concerned and doing her best to keep Shawna calm.

"Where am I? What is this place?" Shawna said. Her own voice sounded odd, raspy.

"You're aboard the *Demeter*. My name is Shanti, and I'm your nurse. You're safe here."

"Safe?"

The woman had kind, sympathetic eyes. Her manner was calm and unrushed.

"We picked you up," she said. "You were in an emergency escape pod. You're lucky we found you. Few ships venture this way." The nurse made no attempt to get closer. She clasped her hands in front of herself, as if she wanted to offer more help but was holding back until she was given permission. She used a perfume or lotion that smelled faintly of roses in bloom.

"When did you find me?"

"Three days ago." The nurse's gaze shifted to the water on the tray. "I see you took a drink. That's good. How did it go down? That hypersleep solution leaves a bad taste in the mouth, no? I'm sure the doctor will be happy you're up and about. Captain Broome as well. Shall I call them? Do you feel up to it?"

"Yes... I have questions."

"I'm sure you do."

The doctor was a Thassian woman. Seeing her gave Shawna pangs of grief, a flashback of Bak-Irp in his final moments – the thickset Xeno twisting him, cracking his neck bones...

Captain Broome was also a woman, a fellow American with a no-nonsense New England manner; she exuded competence. Steely-eyed, with gray streaks in her dark brown hair, she was slim and tall, and light on her feet. A curved scar encircled her left eye socket, an old wound.

After an informal debriefing, where Shawna told them little about herself and how she came to be in the pod, claiming her memories were fuzzy, the captain offered to take her on a tour of the *Demeter*. "If you're able to walk with no trouble," she said.

"I can walk."

"Very well, then. Let's start in the docking area. I have a surprise to show you."

The two of them walked together. The doctor kept one step behind them. Shawna's legs were rubbery, but the longer she walked the stronger she felt. She tried to pay attention to what the captain was telling her. Her mind was racing with questions and answers she wasn't ready to say aloud.

"We're a Coalition transport vessel. Fully loaded with homestead modules and terraforming equipment…"

Farmers. Whole families of them according to the captain, their destination was a moon Shawna had never heard of. They were heading there to plant fields and grow food crops, to build communities. There was no mention of PK-L7 and the Xeno hordes. The captain paused before a long, commercial-sized door marked: HANGAR. "Here's your surprise," Broome said.

She pressed her palm flat on a reader panel, and the door lifted.

Shawna felt her stomach drop. She was stunned, speechless.

"We managed to find your vessel!" Broome strode into the brilliantly lit hangar. She turned back. "Aren't you coming? I know this must be a shock. We found the *Andronicus* soon after we picked you up." The captain led Shawna up to the heavily damaged ship.

"Did you locate the other escape pod?"

Broome looked away and thinned her lips. "Sadly, no."

The shock of her survival hit Shawna hard. Confused, she didn't know how to process it. She felt grateful and guilty but also numbed by the horrors she'd passed through to get here.

"What about aboard the *Andronicus*? What did you do with the bodies?" Shawna thought about the Thassian doctor. The captain had said that two thirds of the farmers were non-human. If they were exposed to the mold… but Shawna wasn't ready to tell them the whole story yet. They probably wouldn't believe her if she did.

"Bodies?" Broome looked at the doctor, cocking an eyebrow, silently inquiring if Shawna was mentally fit. "There were no bodies. We did find some blood and bullet holes. I was planning to ask you about those. What were you doing on this ship? What was the mission?"

"I… I can't remember." Shawna saw the *Andronicus* door hanging open. "Can I go onto the ship? It might jar things loose. Help me to remember." She had to see the dead Xenos. *How could they miss them?* They were in the armory. Maybe the armory hadn't been investigated yet.

"By all means," Broome said.

They toured the ship from cockpit to tail. Shawna detected that Broome was sharp-minded; her plan all along had been to get Shawna to talk about what happened, the tour was designed to take her here, to show her the abundance of evidence, and ask her to fill in the blanks. "This was a hell of a firefight. Are you telling me that you can't remember it?"

"I remember that there's an armory one deck down. It's where I launched the pod. I want to go there and see it." Broome swept her arm in the direction of the cockpit, the floor hatch.

"We've gone over this ship thoroughly, Shawna. Why don't you tell me what you're looking for?"

"I'll know it when I see it." Shawna raced through the avionics bay. She was practically running by the time she reached the armory. Standing inside it, her heart sank. No Xenos. She sat on the bench by the spacesuit lockers, head in her hands. It made no sense. The Xenos had to be here. They were almost dead when she passed by them. How could they have gotten out…?

"Level with me, Lieutenant Colonel Bright," Broome said. "We ran your DNA. You may not know who you are, but I do. You're a war hero. And an escaped prisoner. What happened out there? Where are the others? If you tell me the truth, I'll do what I can to help."

Shawna wasn't listening. She had her own questions she wanted answered.

"You haven't removed anything from this ship?" she said. "You're sure of it?"

"Not a thing," Broome said. The captain shifted, moving off to the side. Shawna twisted so she could look the captain in the face, officer to officer. That's when she saw it. The missing piece of the puzzle. The spacesuits. When she left the *Andronicus* there were spacesuits still hanging in the lockers, helmets in the cubbies. If the Xenos had managed to put them on…

"The spacesuits," Shawna said.

"What about the spacesuits?"

"They're gone. Every last one of them."

ABOUT THE AUTHOR

S A SIDOR is the author of four dark crime thrillers and more recently two splendid supernatural-pulp adventures, *Fury From the Tomb* and *The Beast of Nightfall Lodge*. He lives near Chicago with his family.

sasidor.com // twitter.com/SA_Sidor

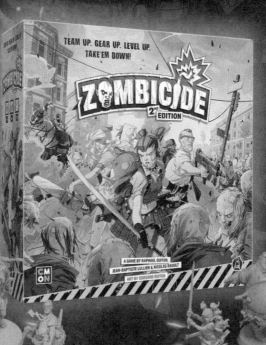